According to Aggie™

created by Mary Richards Beaumont,
Dan Nordskog & Genevieve Kote

Published by American Girl Publishing

This book is a work of fiction. Names, characters, places, and incidents
are either the product of the author's imagination or are used fictitiously, and
any resemblance to actual persons, living or dead, business establishments,
events, or locales is entirely coincidental and not intended by American Girl.

17 18 19 20 21 22 23 24 QP 10 9 8 7 6 5 4 3 2 1

Writing and Editing: Mary Richards Beaumont
Art Direction and Design: Dan Nordskog
Illustrations: Genevieve Kote
Production: Jeannette Bailey, Caryl Boyer, Cynthia Stiles, Kristi Tabrizi

Library of Congress Cataloging-in-Publication Data
Names: Beaumont, Mary Richards, 1974- author. | Kote, Genevieve, illustrator.
Title: According to Aggie / created by Mary Richards Beaumont, Dan Nordskog,
art direction and design, & Genevieve Kote, illustrations.
Description: Middleton, WI : American Girl, [2017] | Summary: When best friends Aggie
and Fiona drift apart in fifth grade, Aggie grows to understand that fading friendships
are normal, and she makes a new friend who shares more of her interests.
Identifiers: LCCN 2016042044 (print) | LCCN 2016053537 (ebook) |
ISBN 9781683370109 (pbk. : alk. paper) | ISBN 9781683370277 (ebook)
Subjects: LCSH: Graphic novels. | CYAC: Graphic novels. | Friendship—Fiction.
Classification: LCC PZ7.7.B399 Ac 2017 (print) | LCC PZ7.7.B399 (ebook) | DDC 741.5/973—dc23
LC record available at https://lccn.loc.gov/2016042044

? americangirl.com/service

For anyone who has ever
been a friend,
or lost one,
or found one

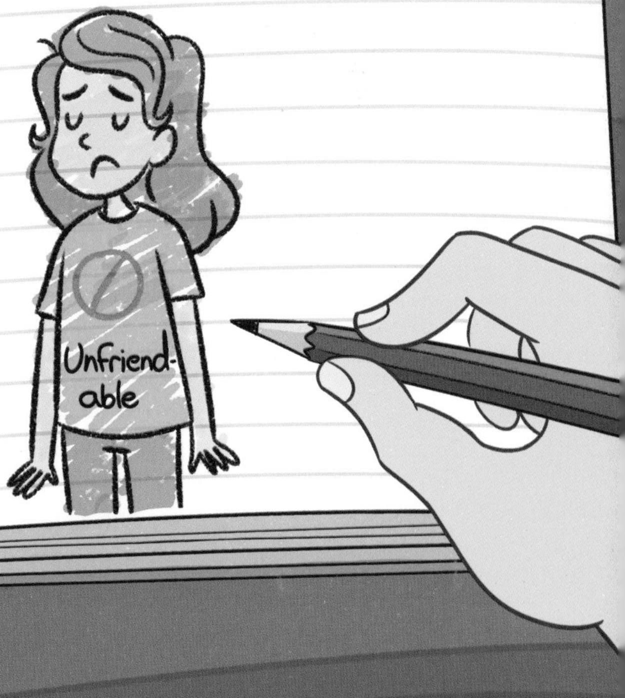
Unfriend-
able

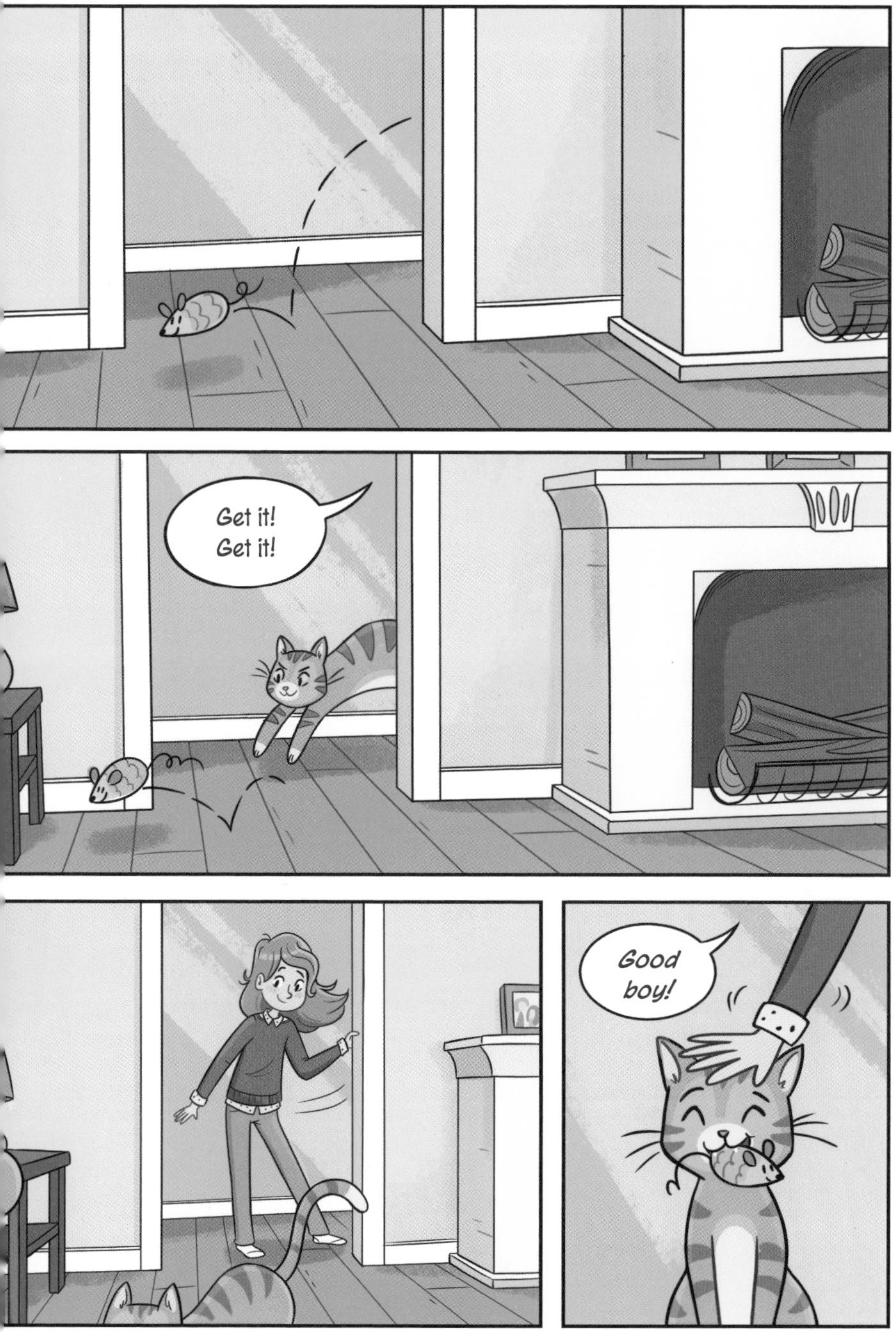
Get it! Get it!
Good boy!

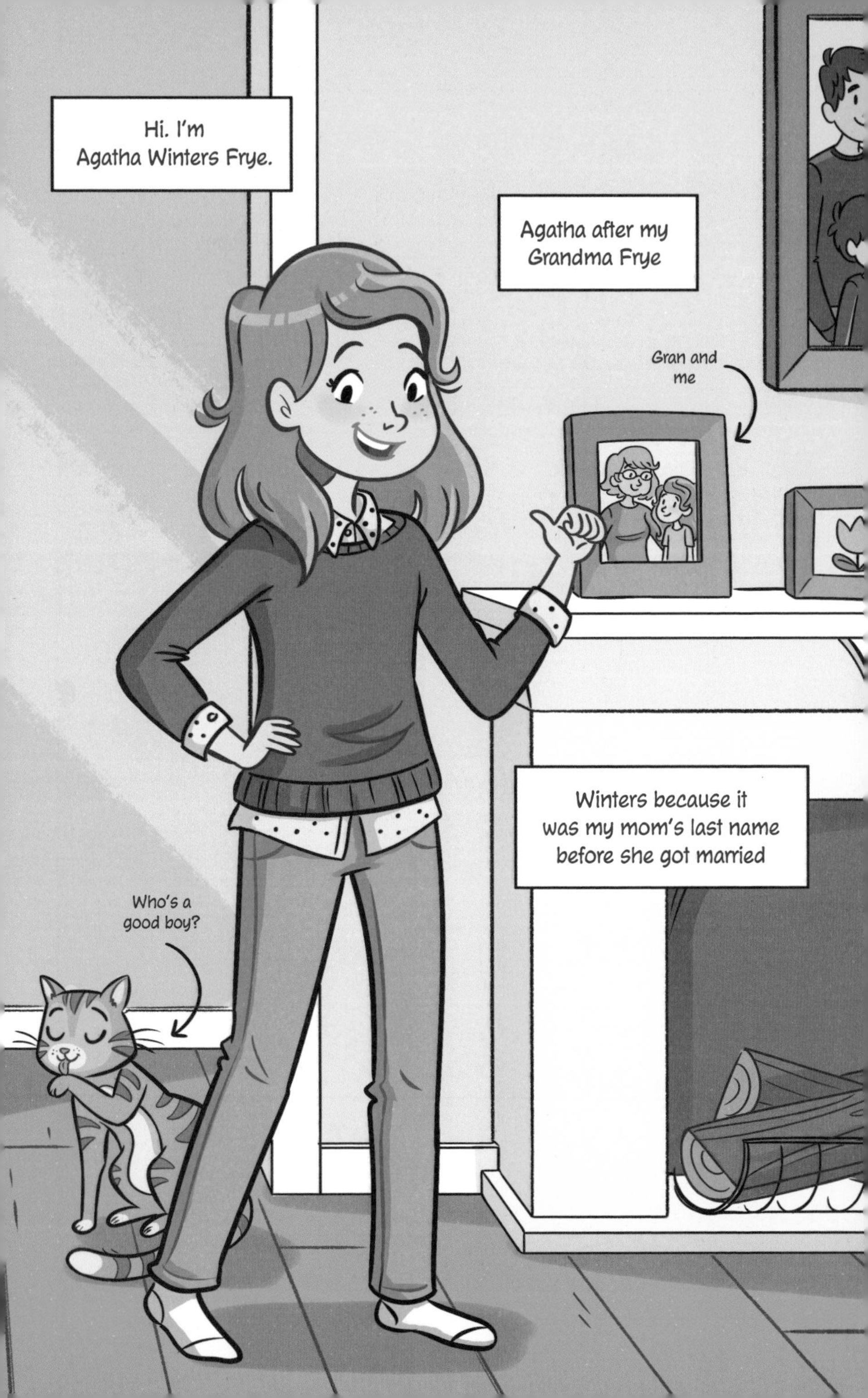
Hi. I'm
Agatha Winters Frye.
Agatha after my
Grandma Frye
Gran and
me
Winters because it
was my mom's last name
before she got married
Who's a
good boy?

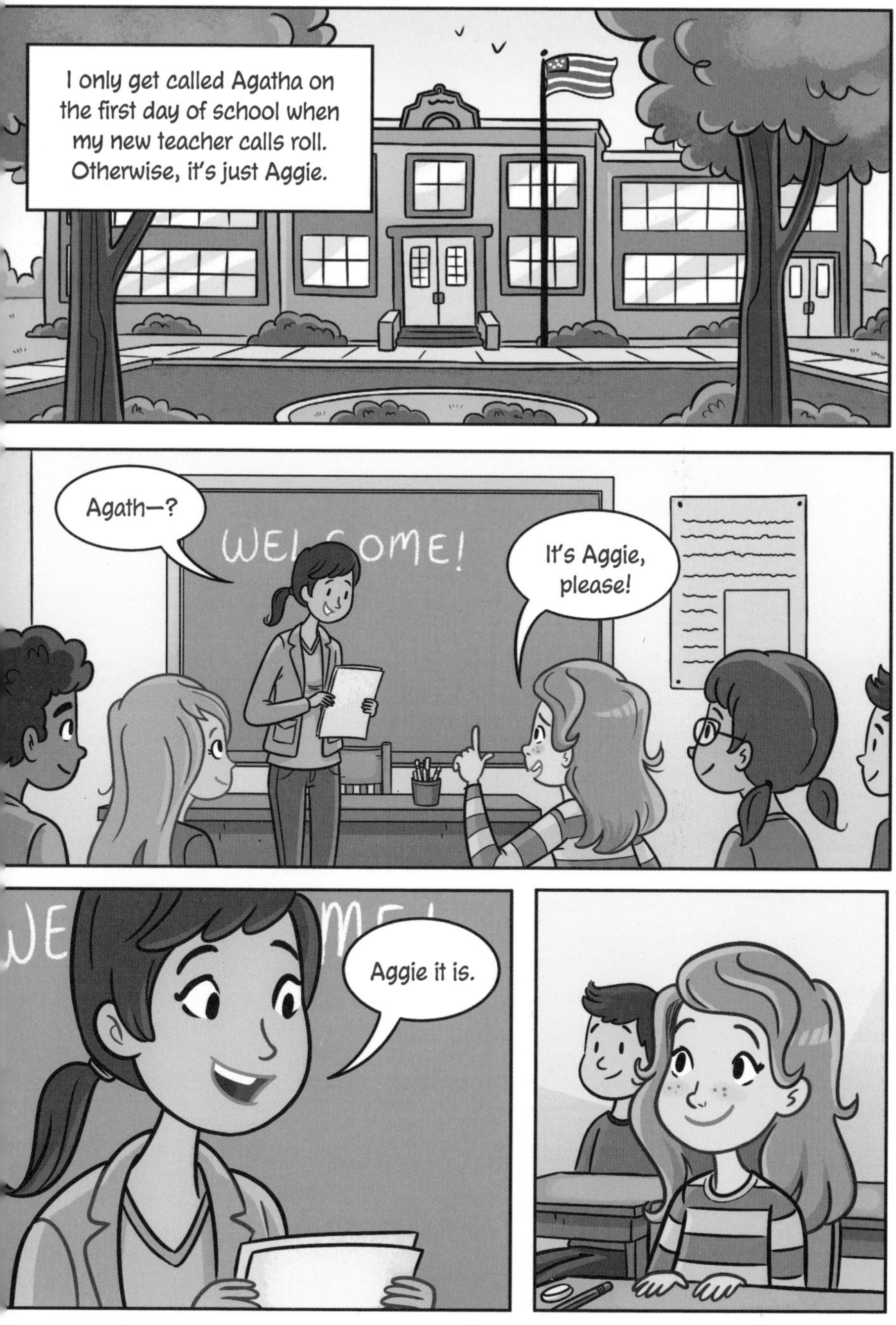
I only get called Agatha on the first day of school when my new teacher calls roll. Otherwise, it's just Aggie.
Agath—?
WELCOME!
It's Aggie, please!
Aggie it is.

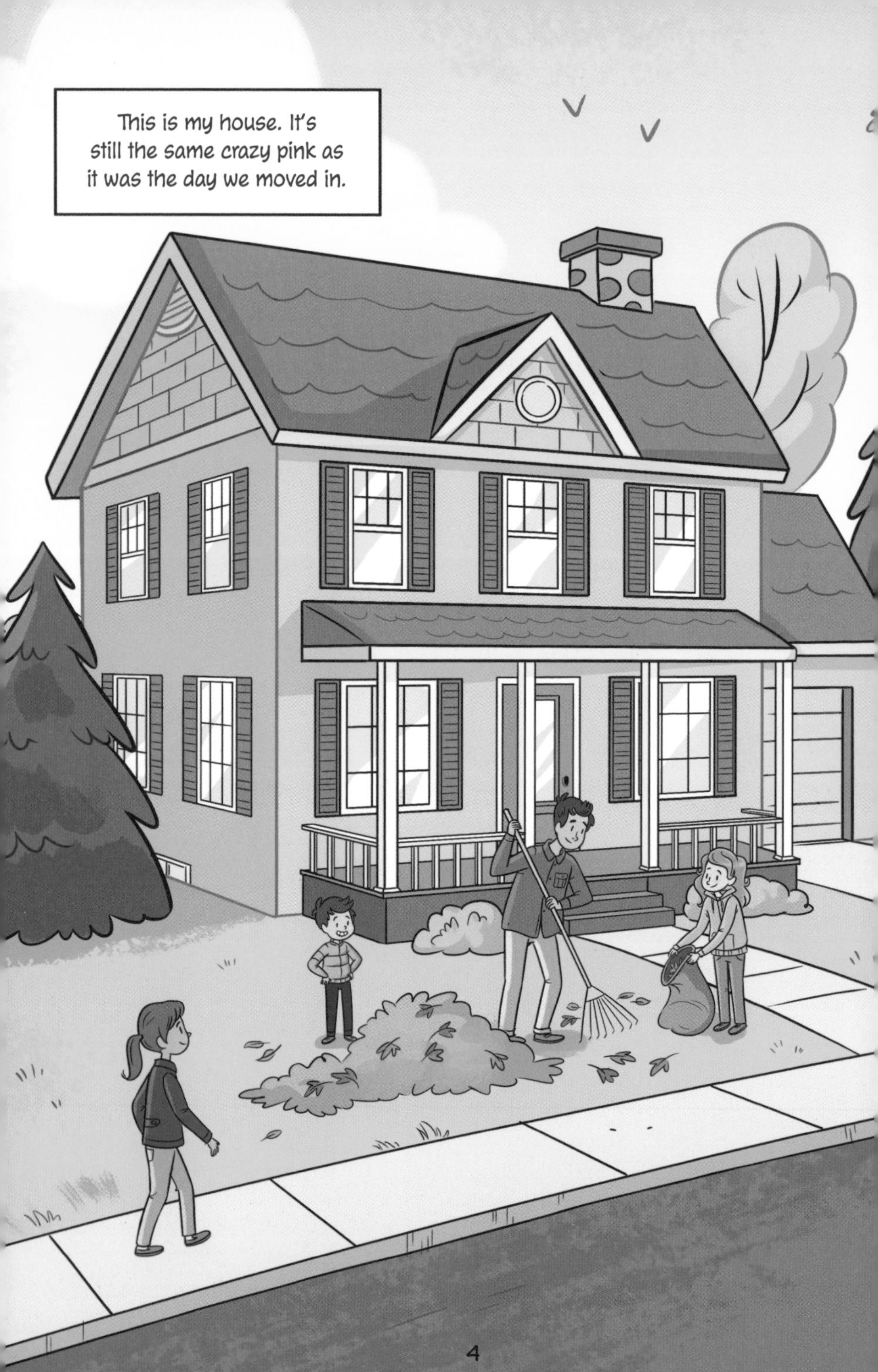
This is my house. It's still the same crazy pink as it was the day we moved in.

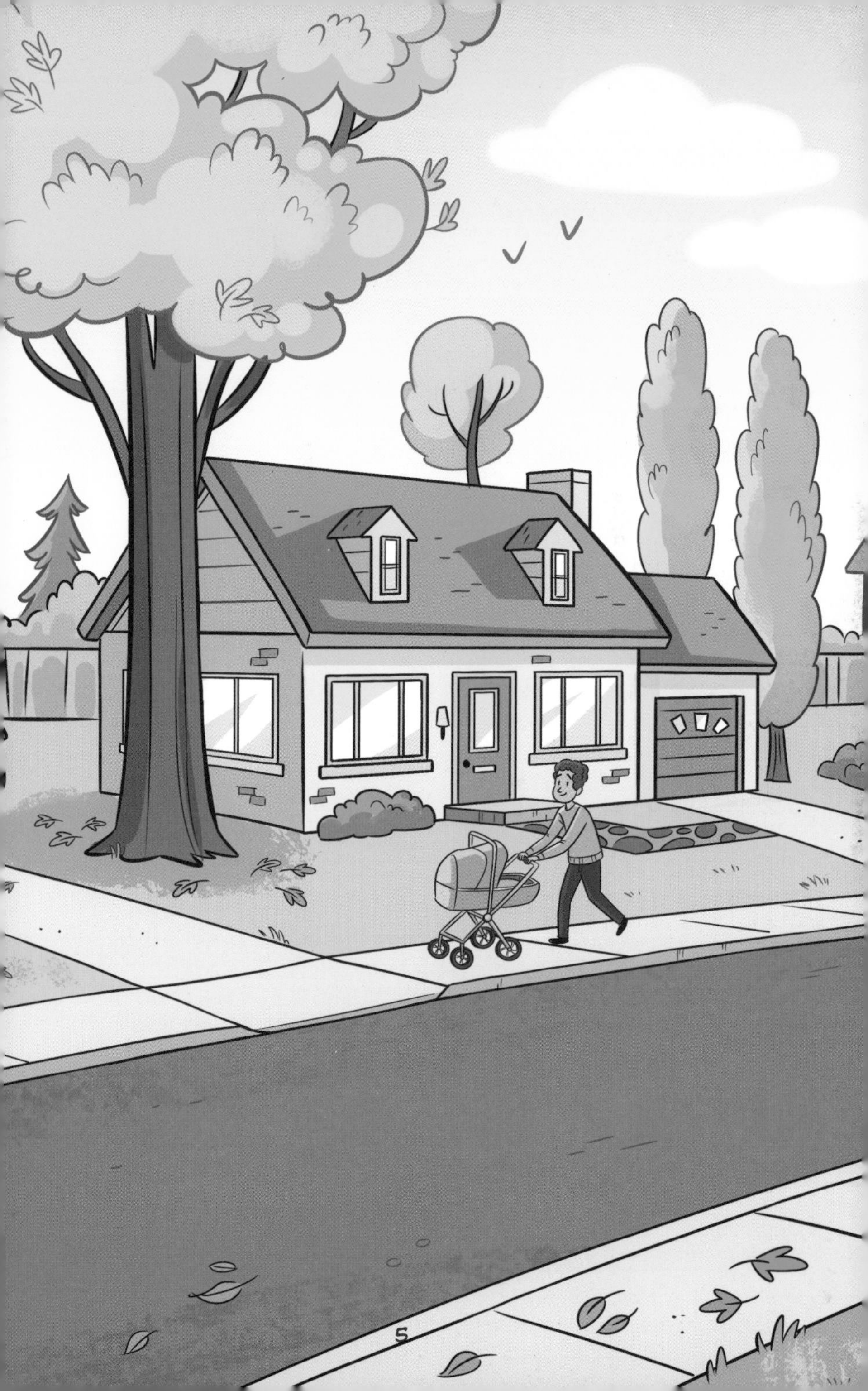

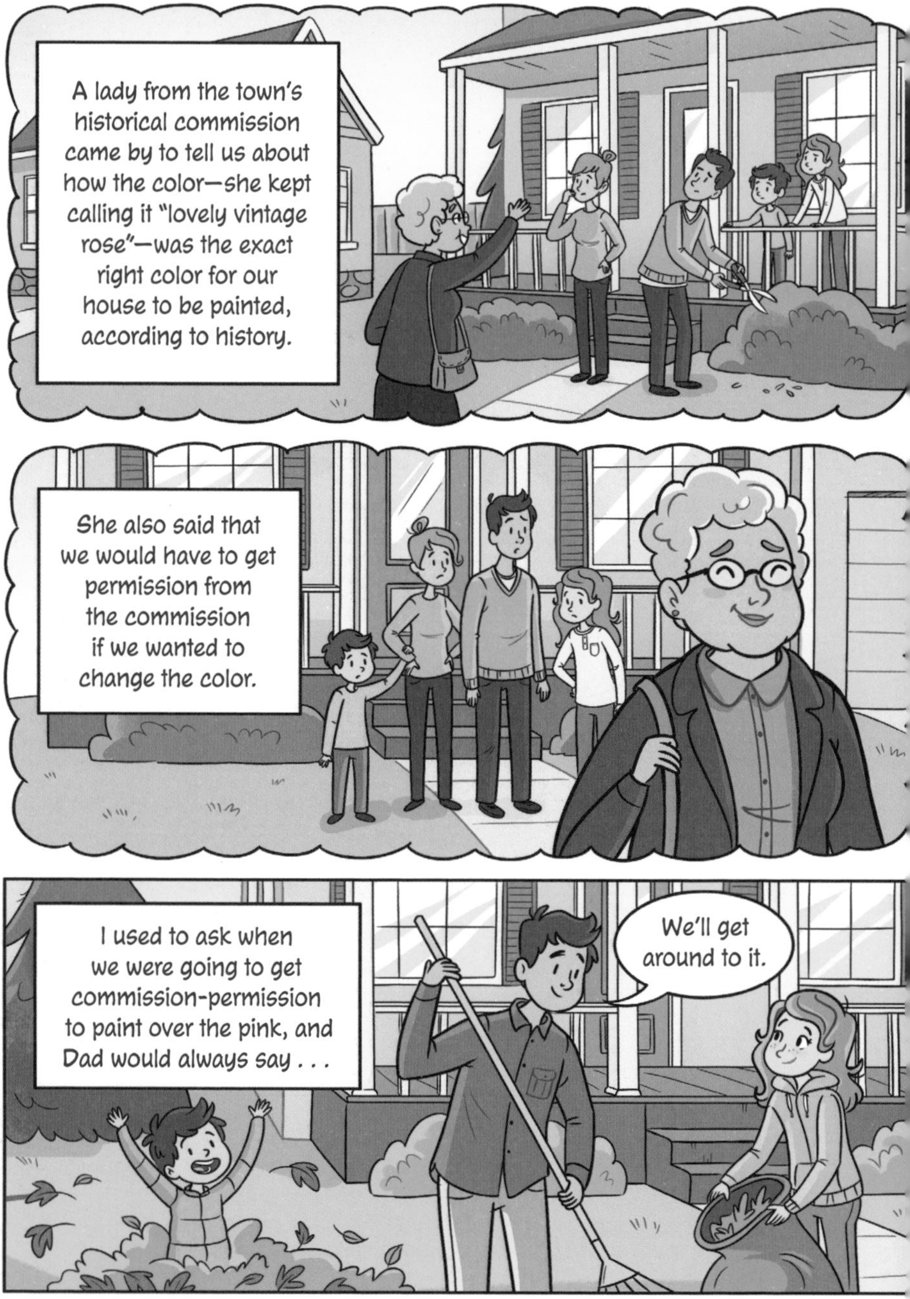
A lady from the town's historical commission came by to tell us about how the color—she kept calling it "lovely vintage rose"—was the exact right color for our house to be painted, according to history.
She also said that we would have to get permission from the commission if we wanted to change the color.
I used to ask when we were going to get commission-permission to paint over the pink, and Dad would always say . . .
We'll get around to it.

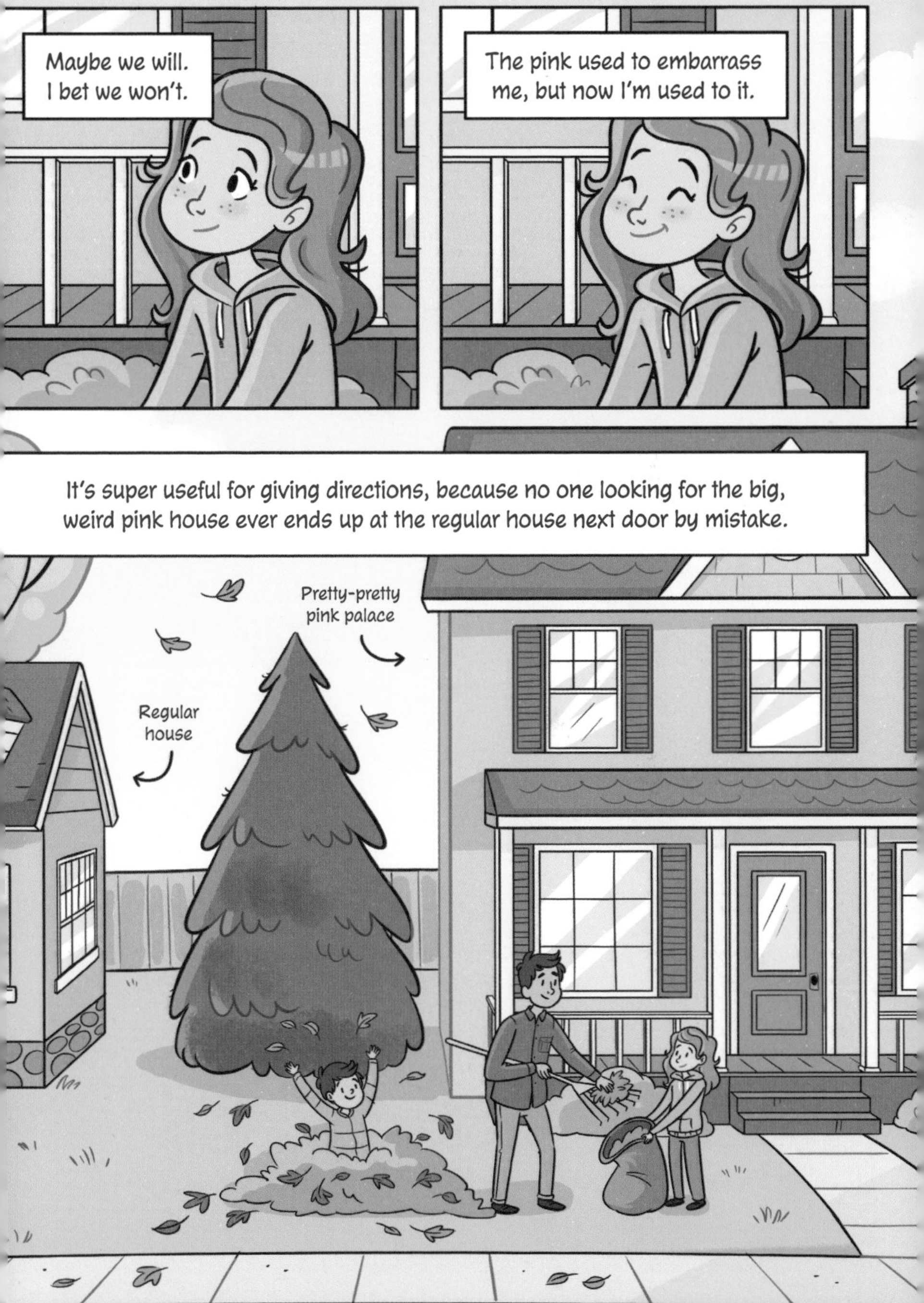
Maybe we will.
I bet we won't.
The pink used to embarrass me, but now I'm used to it.
It's super useful for giving directions, because no one looking for the big, weird pink house ever ends up at the regular house next door by mistake.
Pretty-pretty pink palace
Regular house

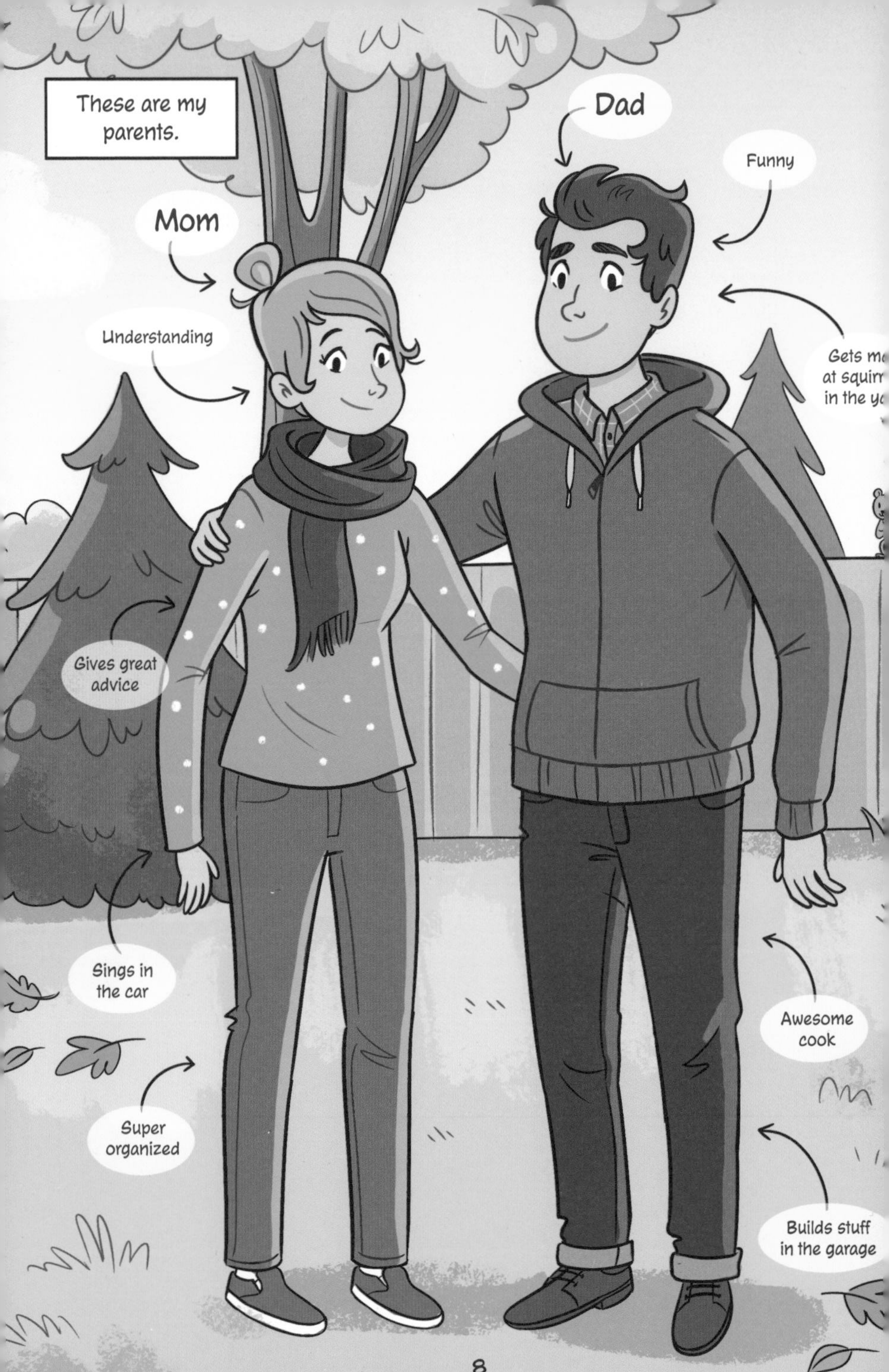
These are my parents.
Mom
Understanding
Gives great advice
Sings in the car
Super organized
Dad
Funny
Awesome cook
Builds stuff in the garage

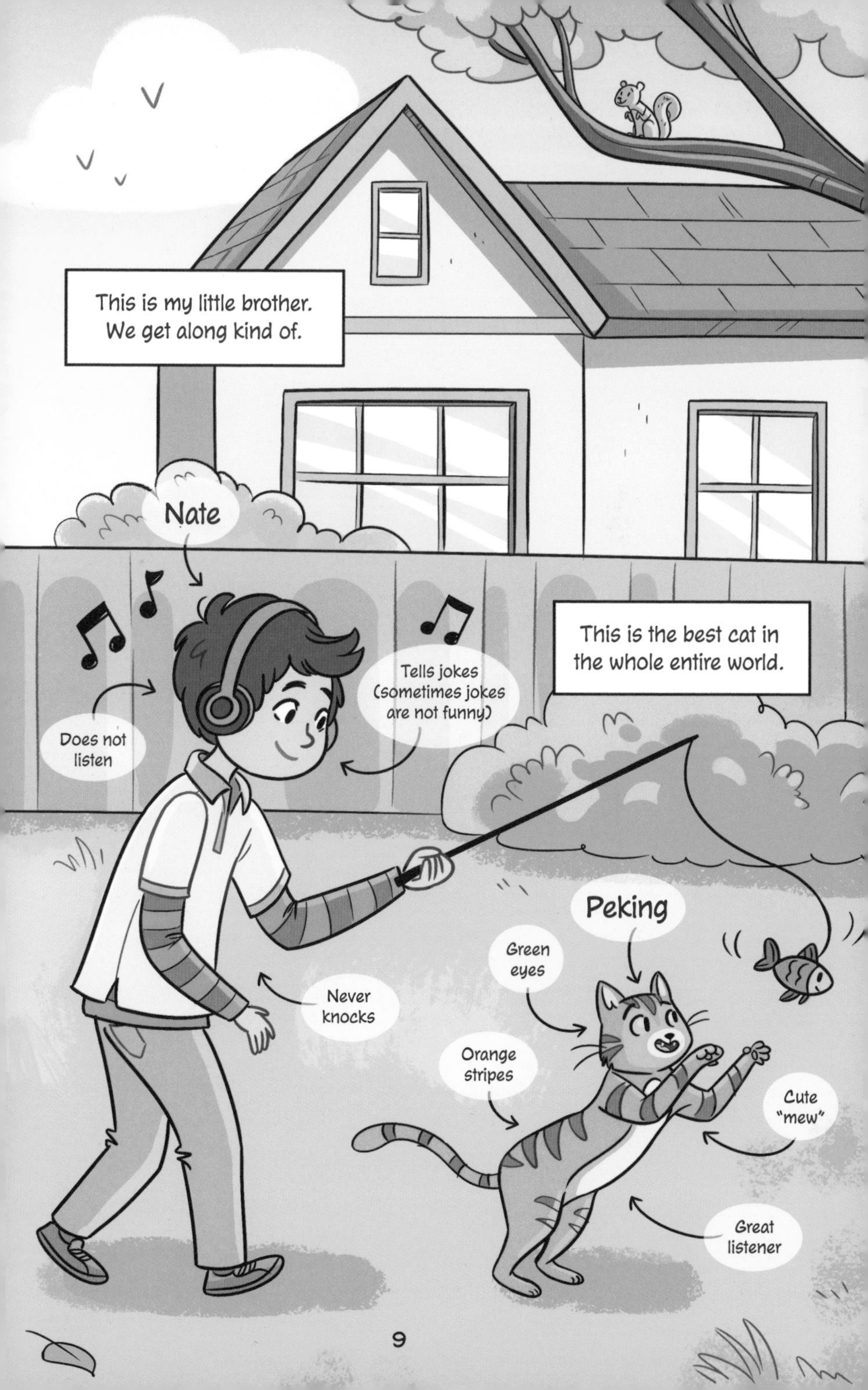
This is my little brother. We get along kind of.
Nate
Does not listen
Tells jokes (sometimes jokes are not funny)
Never knocks
This is the best cat in the whole entire world.
Peking
Green eyes
Orange stripes
Cute "mew"
Great listener

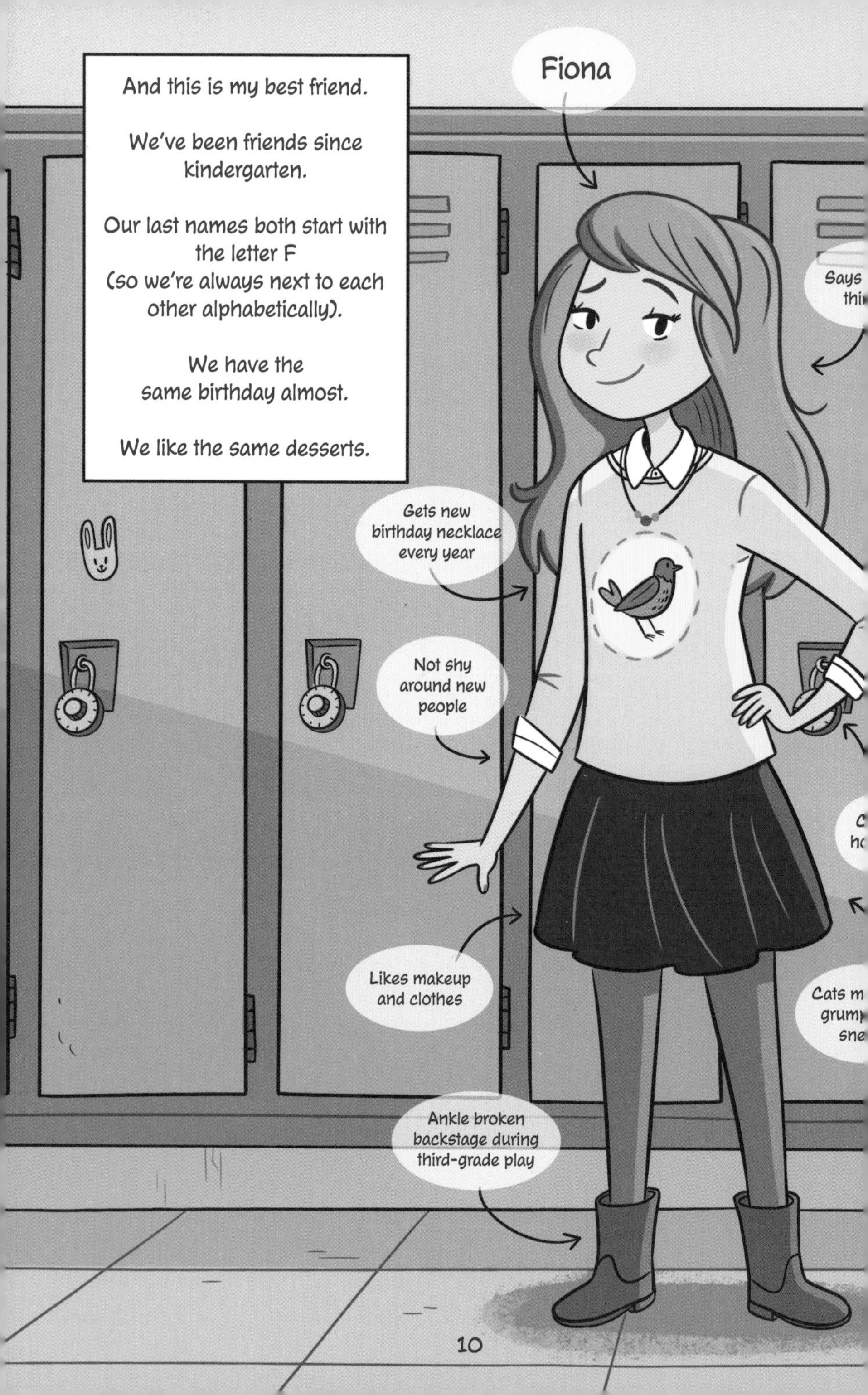

And this is my best friend.
We've been friends since kindergarten.
Our last names both start with the letter F (so we're always next to each other alphabetically).
We have the same birthday almost.
We like the same desserts.
Fiona
Gets new birthday necklace every year
Not shy around new people
Likes makeup and clothes
Ankle broken backstage during third-grade play

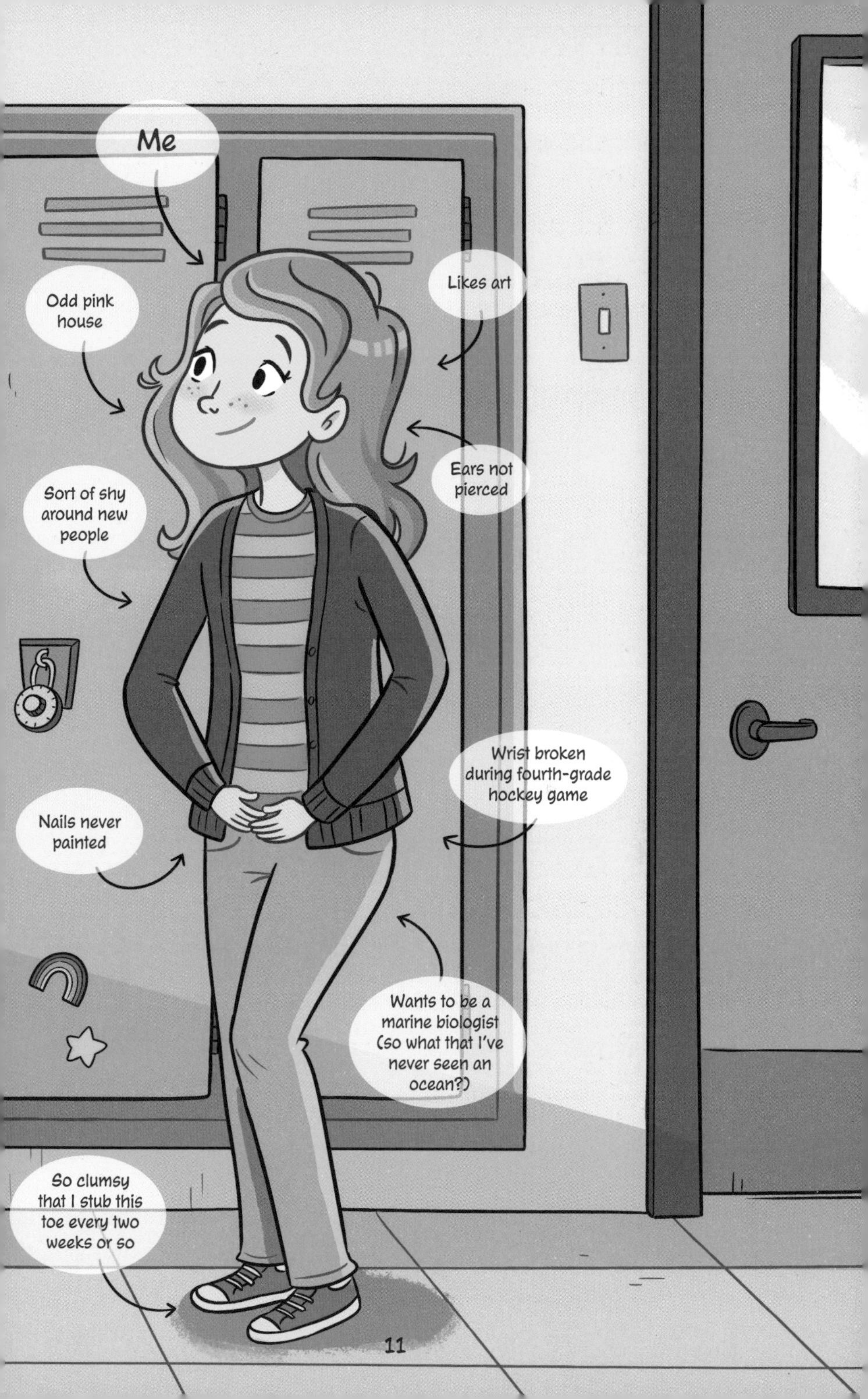
Me
Odd pink house
Likes art
Ears not pierced
Sort of shy around new people
Wrist broken during fourth-grade hockey game
Nails never painted
Wants to be a marine biologist (so what that I've never seen an ocean?)
So clumsy that I stub this toe every two weeks or so

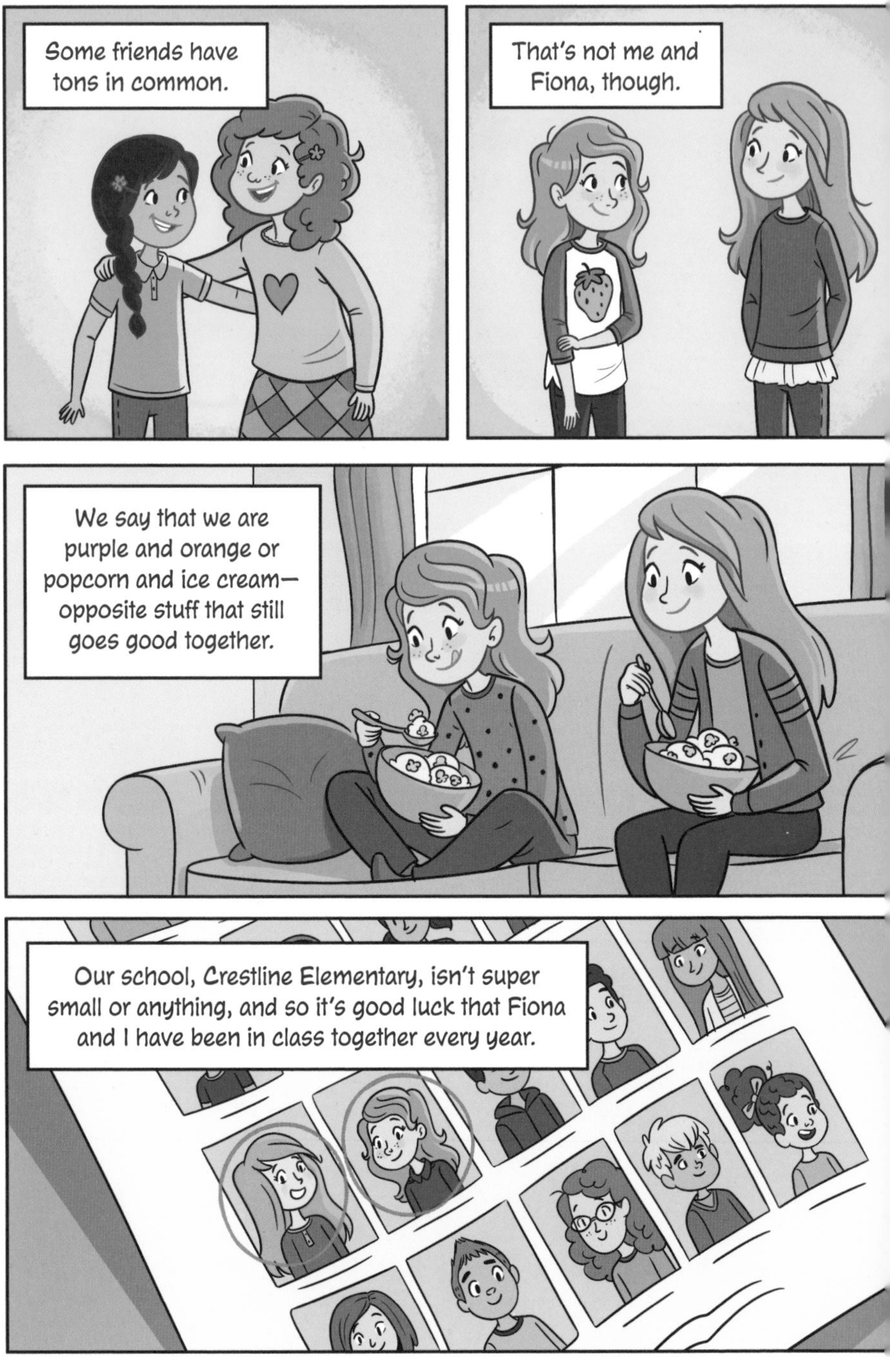
Some friends have tons in common.
That's not me and Fiona, though.
We say that we are purple and orange or popcorn and ice cream—opposite stuff that still goes good together.
Our school, Crestline Elementary, isn't super small or anything, and so it's good luck that Fiona and I have been in class together every year.

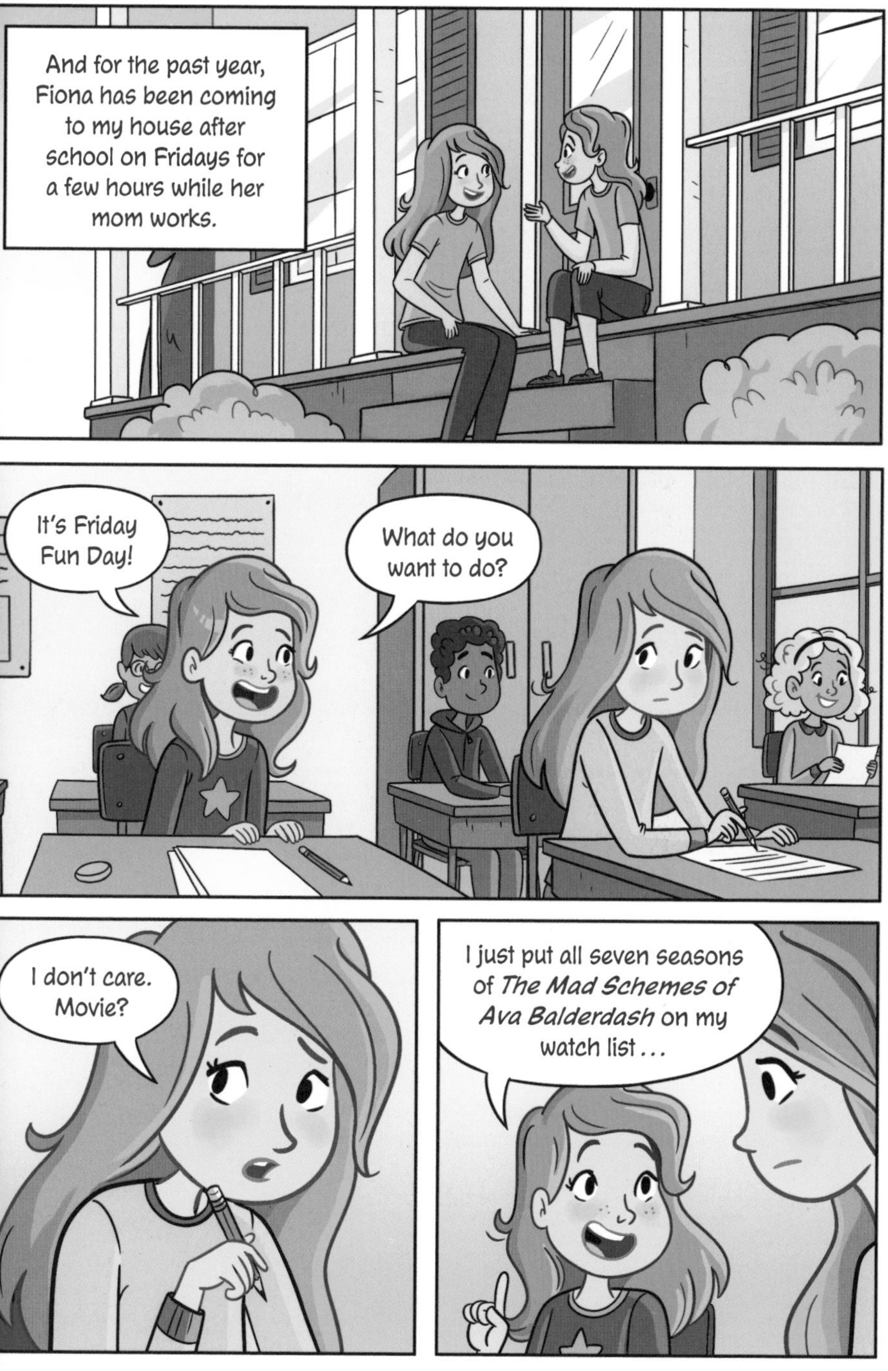

And for the past year, Fiona has been coming to my house after school on Fridays for a few hours while her mom works.
It's Friday Fun Day!
What do you want to do?
I don't care. Movie?
I just put all seven seasons of *The Mad Schemes of Ava Balderdash* on my watch list . . .

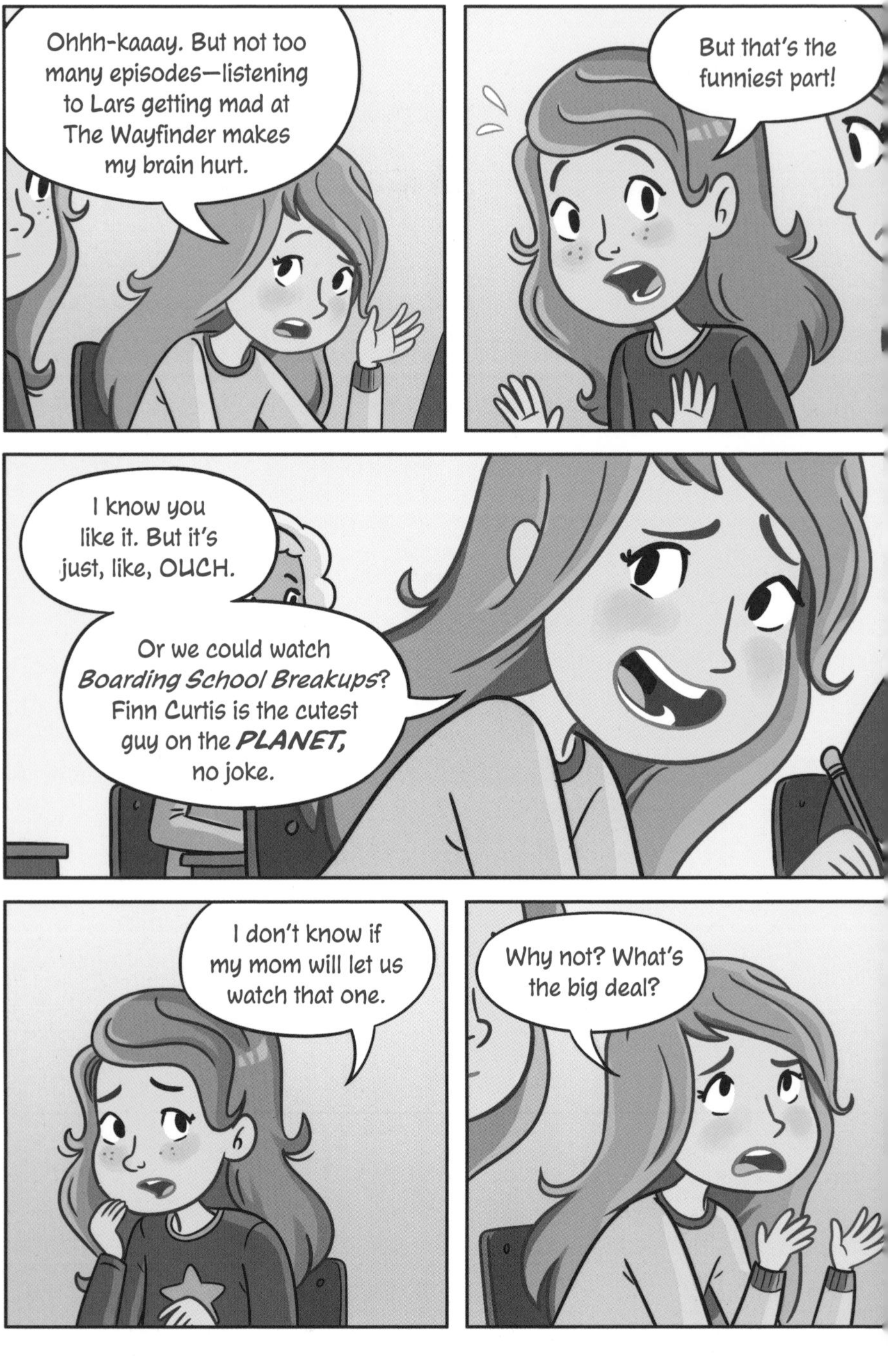
Ohhh-kaaay. But not too many episodes—listening to Lars getting mad at The Wayfinder makes my brain hurt.
But that's the funniest part!
I know you like it. But it's just, like, OUCH.
Or we could watch *Boarding School Breakups*? Finn Curtis is the cutest guy on the ***PLANET,*** no joke.
I don't know if my mom will let us watch that one.
Why not? What's the big deal?

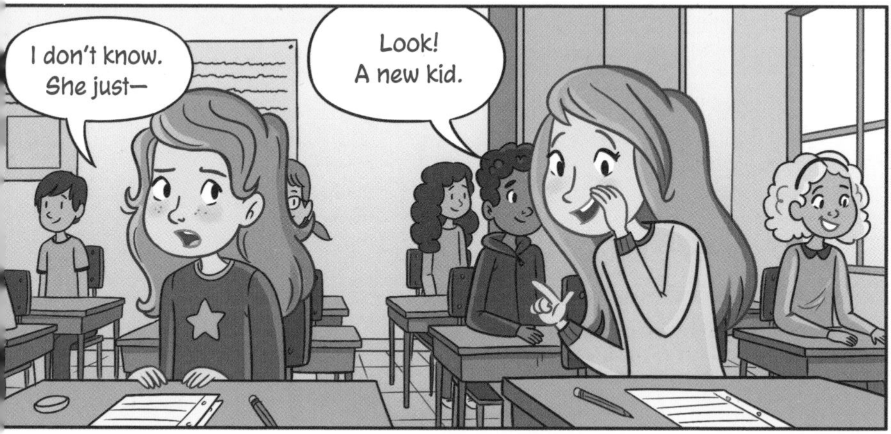
I don't know. She just—
Look! A new kid.

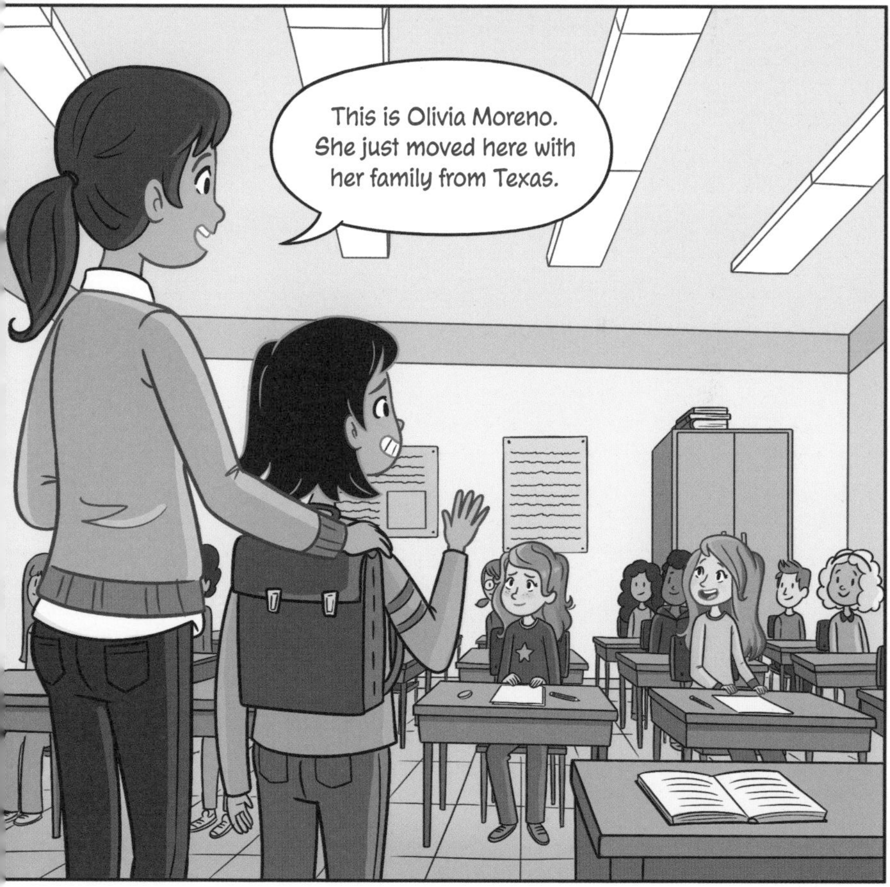
This is Olivia Moreno. She just moved here with her family from Texas.

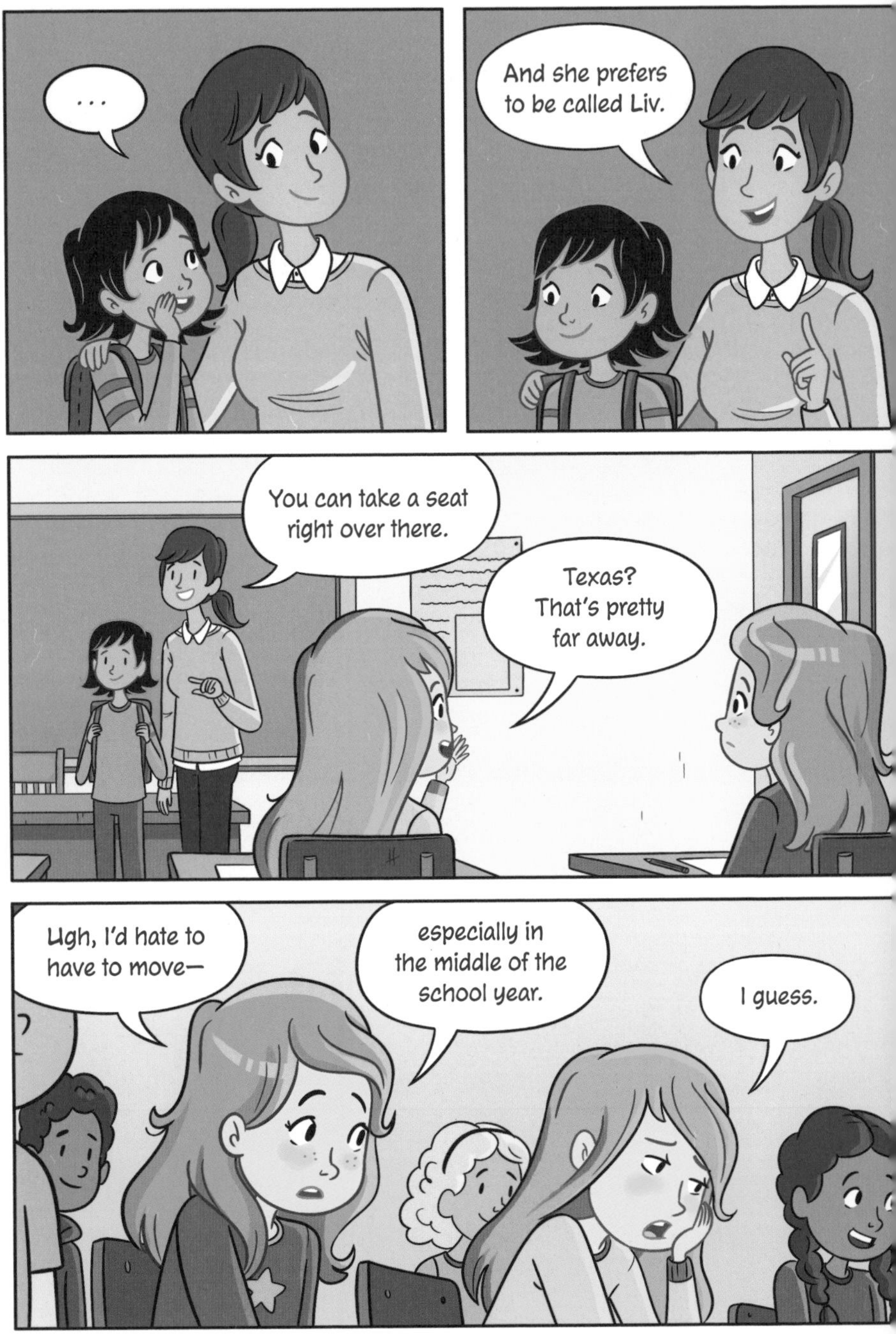

...
And she prefers to be called Liv.
You can take a seat right over there.
Texas? That's pretty far away.
Ugh, I'd hate to have to move—
especially in the middle of the school year.
I guess.

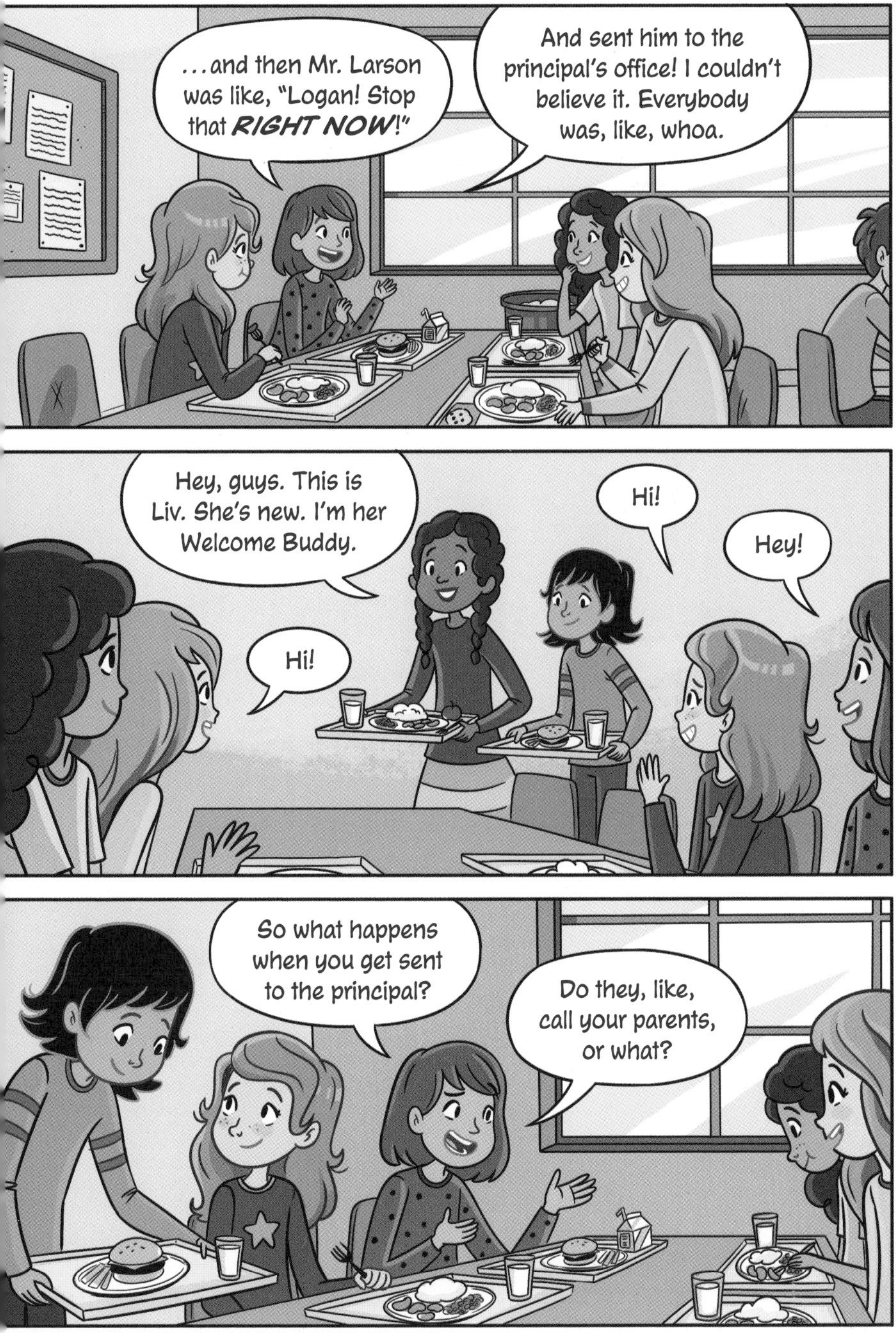
...and then Mr. Larson was like, "Logan! Stop that RIGHT NOW!"
And sent him to the principal's office! I couldn't believe it. Everybody was, like, whoa.
Hey, guys. This is Liv. She's new. I'm her Welcome Buddy.
Hi!
Hi!
Hey!
So what happens when you get sent to the principal?
Do they, like, call your parents, or what?

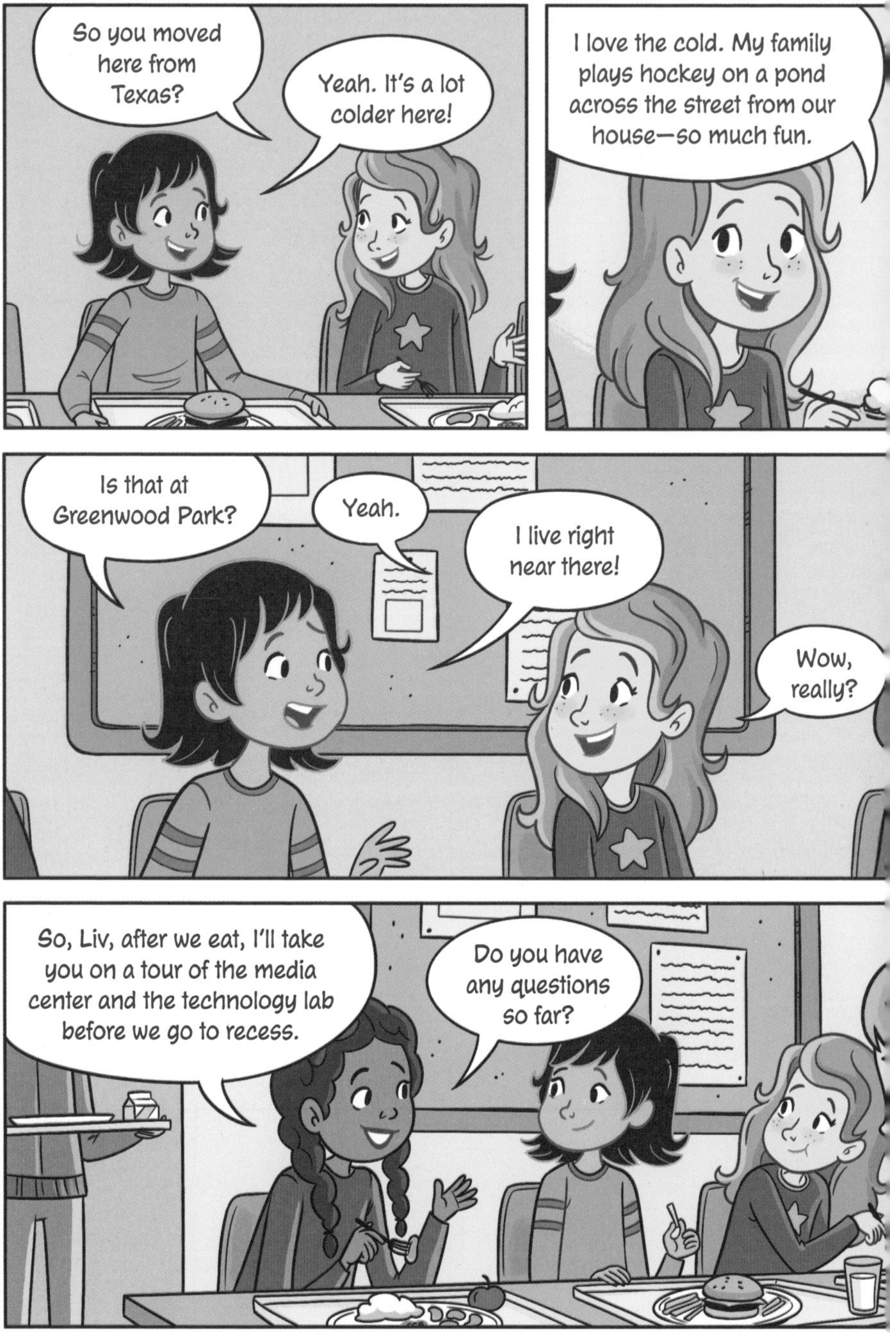
So you moved here from Texas?
Yeah. It's a lot colder here!
I love the cold. My family plays hockey on a pond across the street from our house—so much fun.
Is that at Greenwood Park?
Yeah.
I live right near there!
Wow, really?
So, Liv, after we eat, I'll take you on a tour of the media center and the technology lab before we go to recess.
Do you have any questions so far?

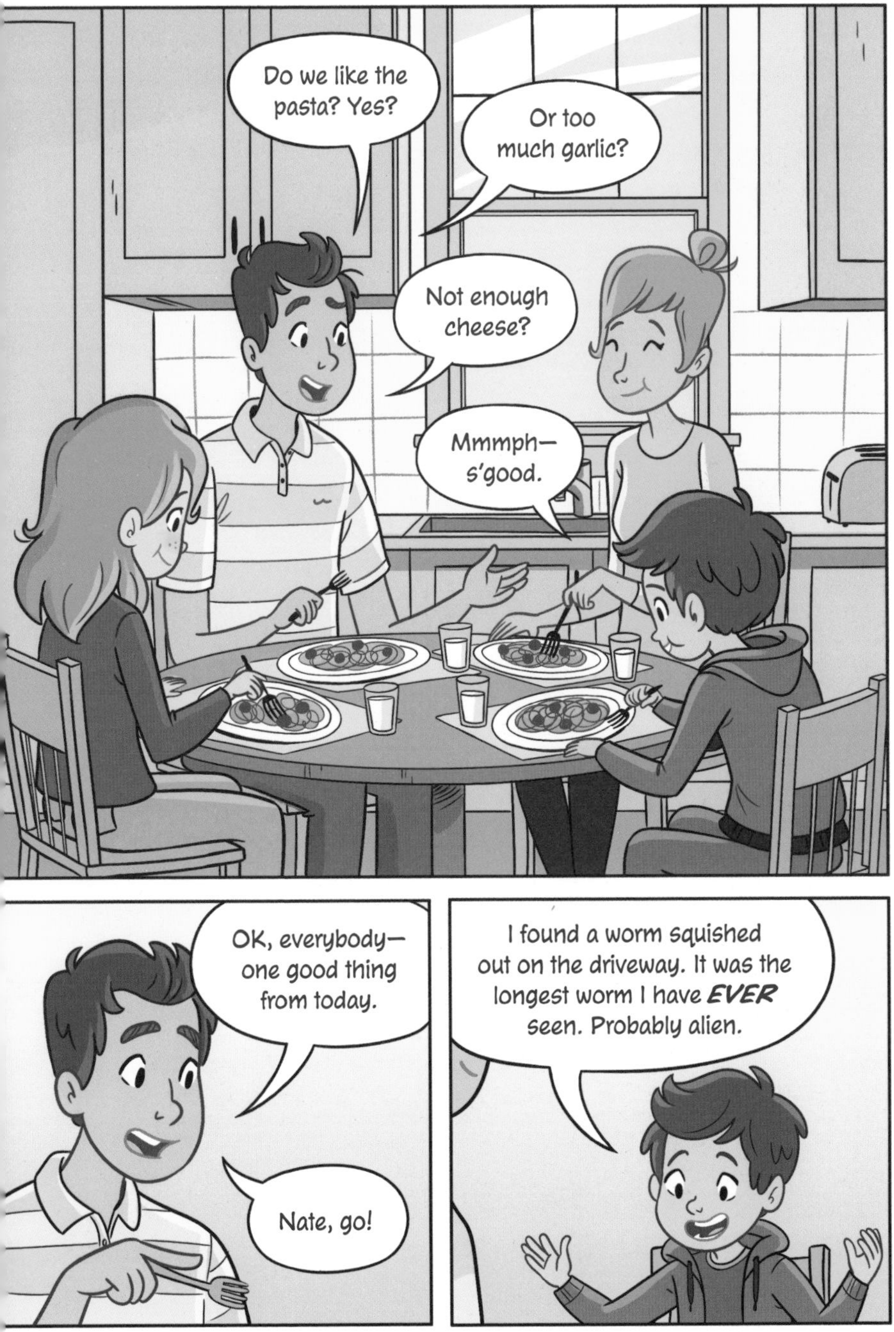
Do we like the pasta? Yes?
Or too much garlic?
Not enough cheese?
Mmmph— s'good.
OK, everybody— one good thing from today.
Nate, go!
I found a worm squished out on the driveway. It was the longest worm I have ***EVER*** seen. Probably alien.

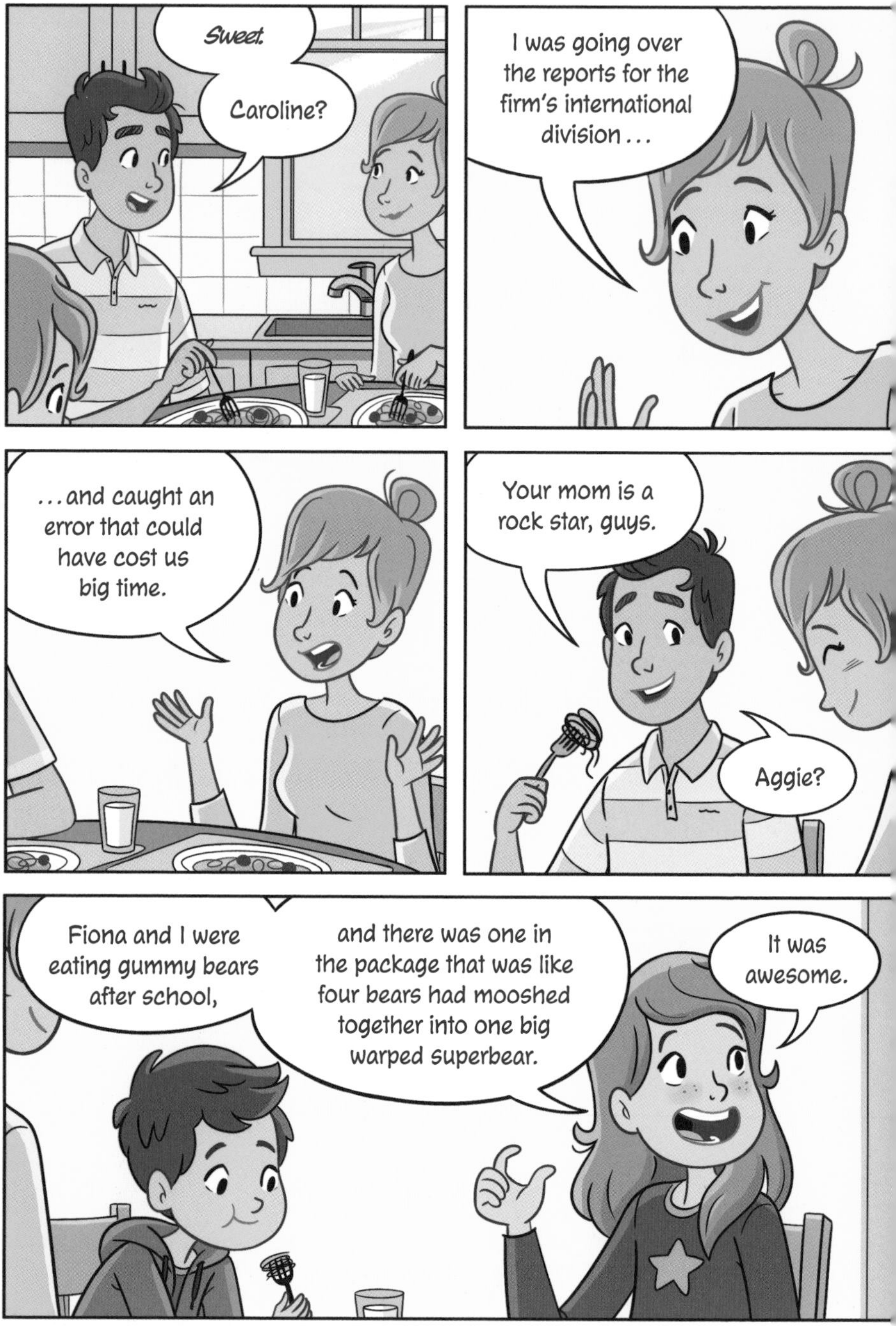
Sweet.
Caroline?
I was going over the reports for the firm's international division . . .
. . . and caught an error that could have cost us big time.
Your mom is a rock star, guys.
Aggie?
Fiona and I were eating gummy bears after school,
and there was one in the package that was like four bears had mooshed together into one big warped superbear.
It was awesome.

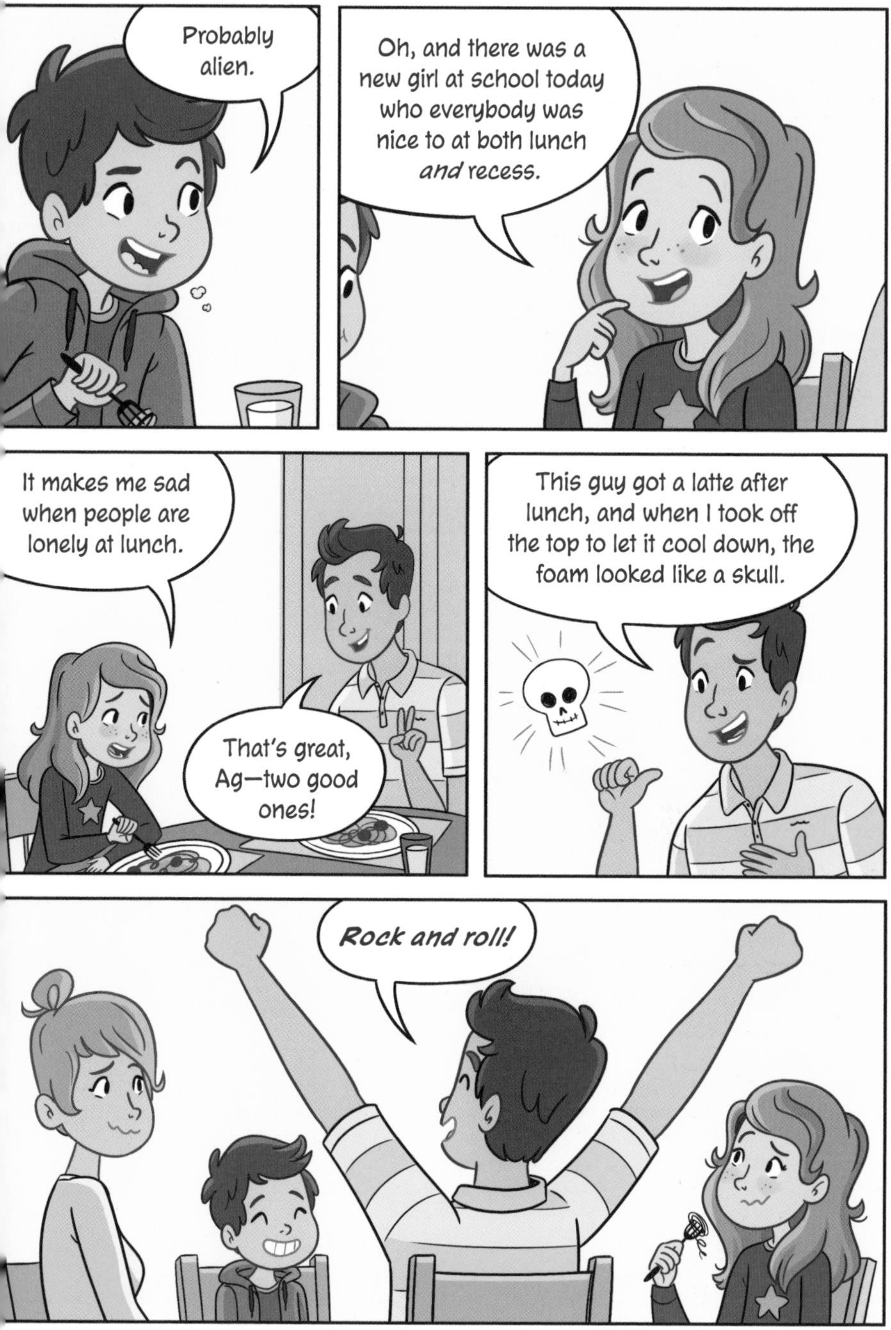
Probably alien.
Oh, and there was a new girl at school today who everybody was nice to at both lunch *and* recess.
It makes me sad when people are lonely at lunch.
That's great, Ag—two good ones!
This guy got a latte after lunch, and when I took off the top to let it cool down, the foam looked like a skull.
Rock and roll!

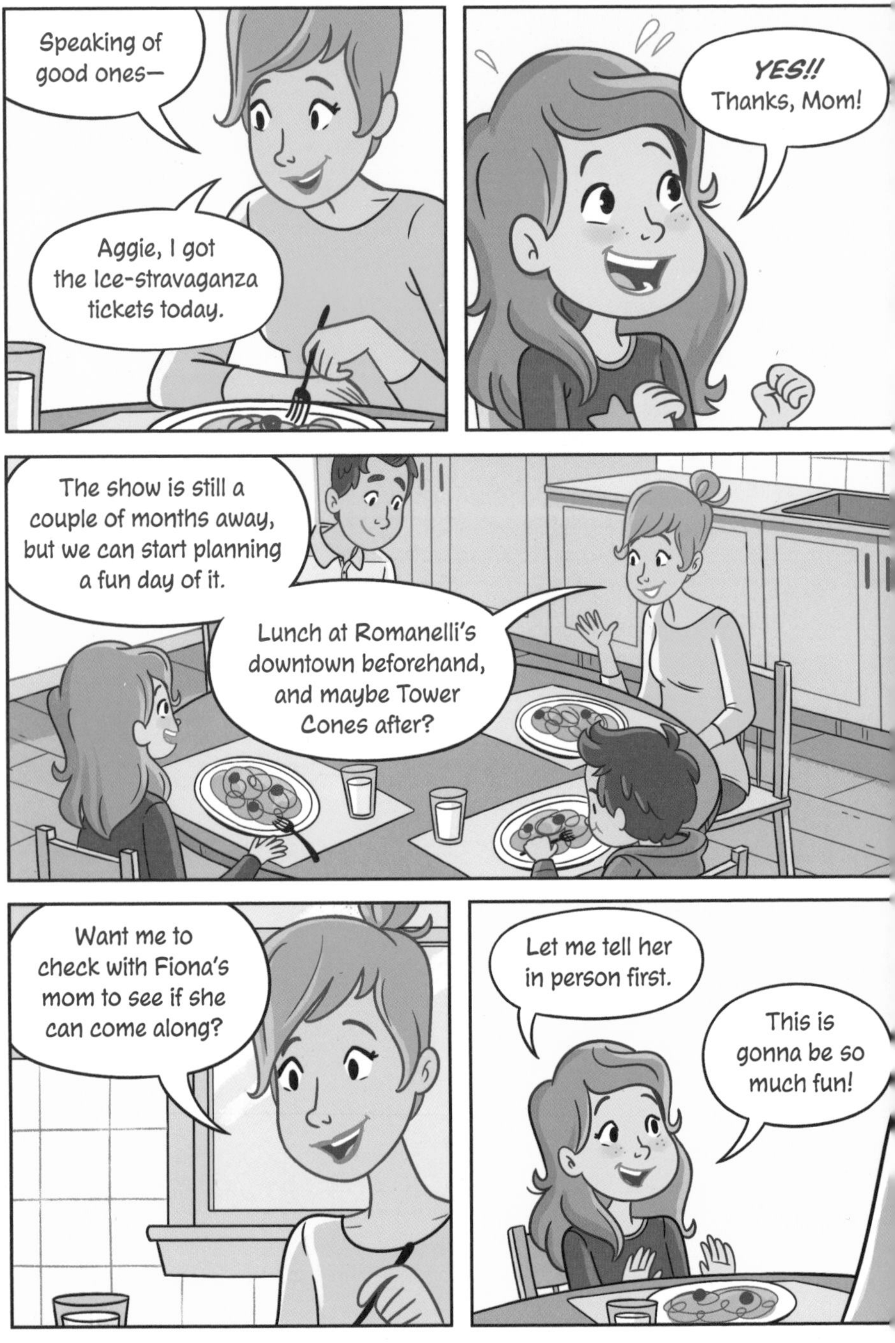
Speaking of good ones—
Aggie, I got the Ice-stravaganza tickets today.
YES!! Thanks, Mom!
The show is still a couple of months away, but we can start planning a fun day of it.
Lunch at Romanelli's downtown beforehand, and maybe Tower Cones after?
Want me to check with Fiona's mom to see if she can come along?
Let me tell her in person first.
This is gonna be so much fun!

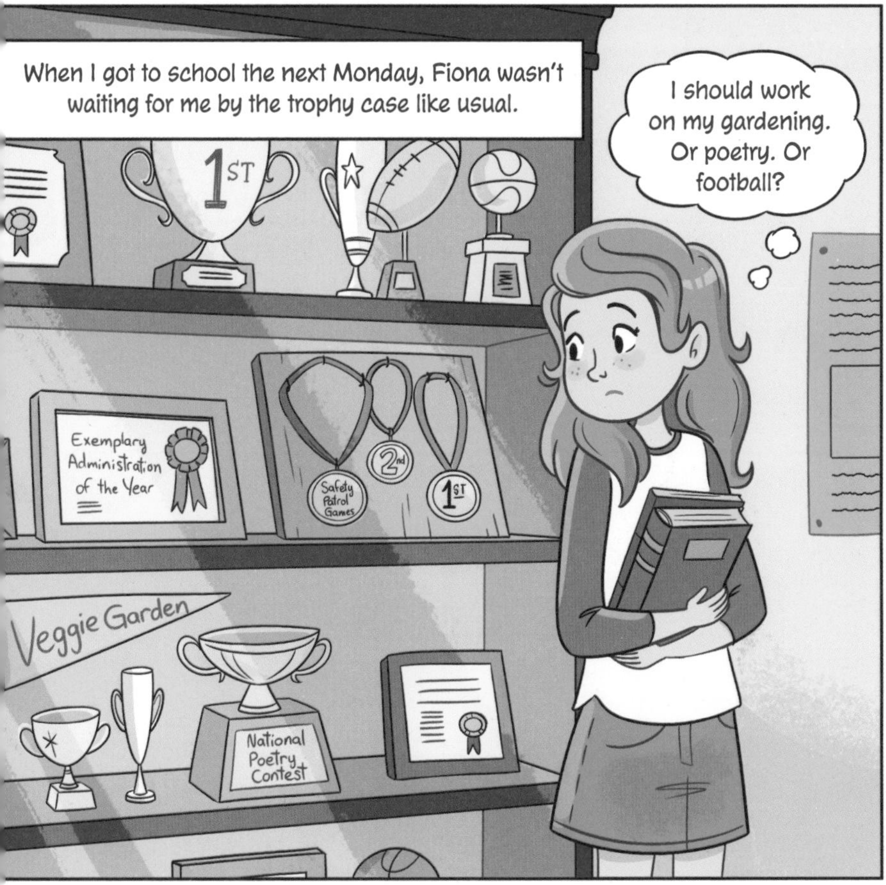
When I got to school the next Monday, Fiona wasn't waiting for me by the trophy case like usual.
I should work on my gardening. Or poetry. Or football?
1ST
Exemplary Administration of the Year
2nd
Safety Patrol Games
1ST
Veggie Garden
National Poetry Contest

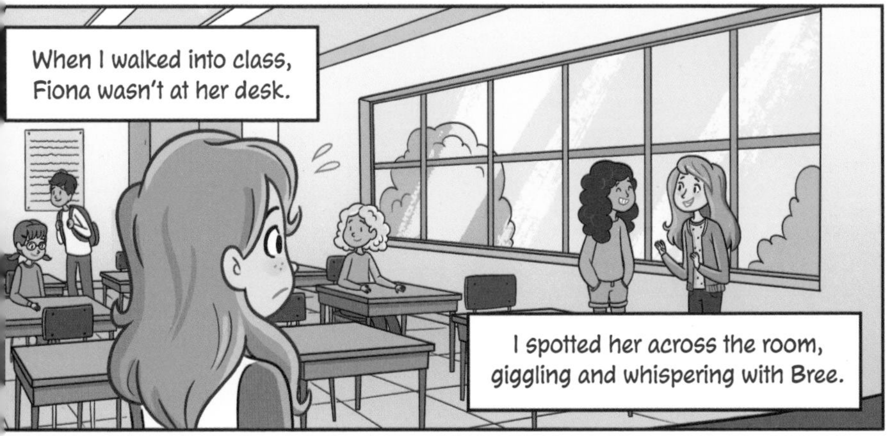
When I walked into class, Fiona wasn't at her desk.
I spotted her across the room, giggling and whispering with Bree.

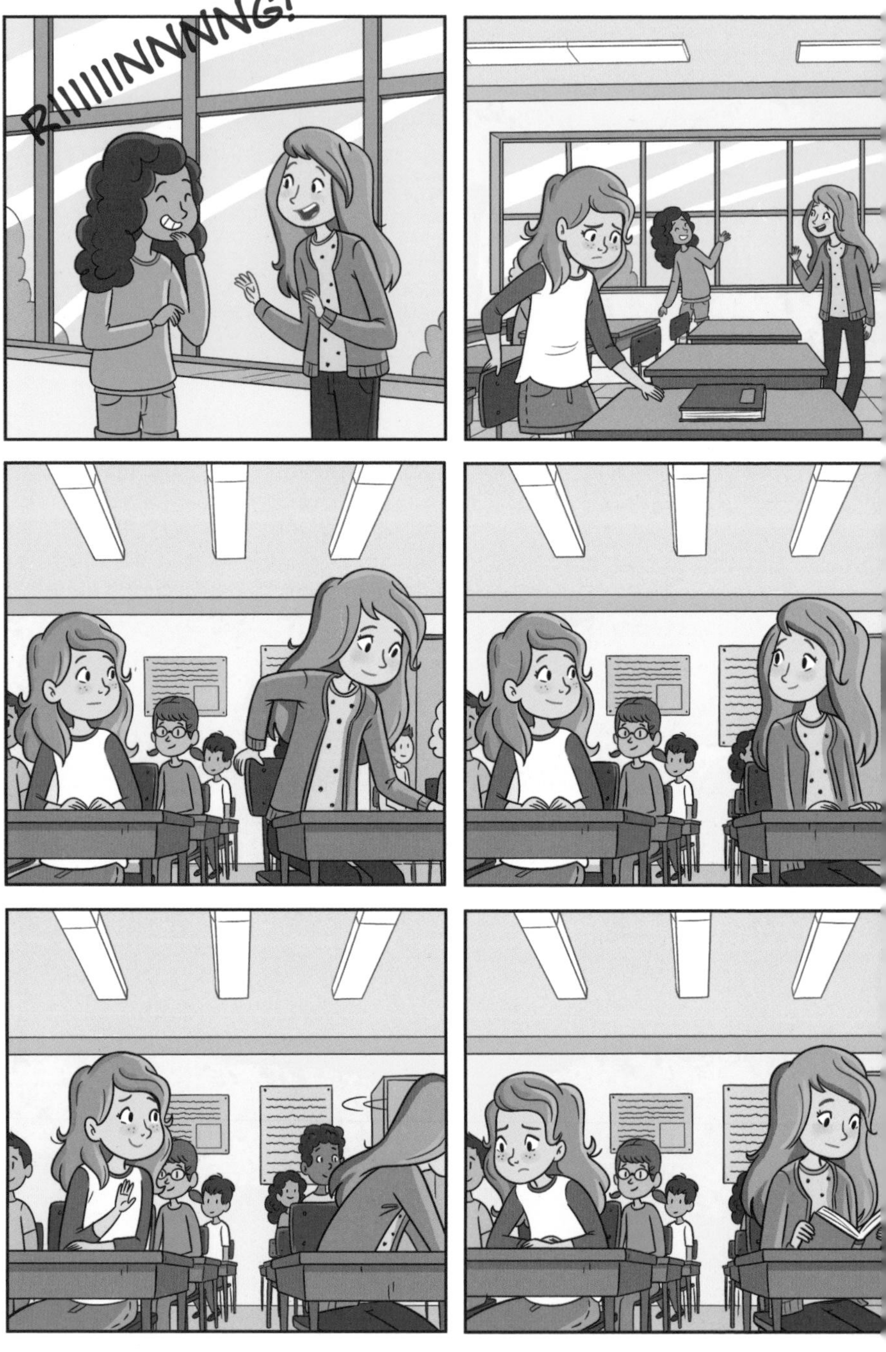
RIIIIINNNNNG!

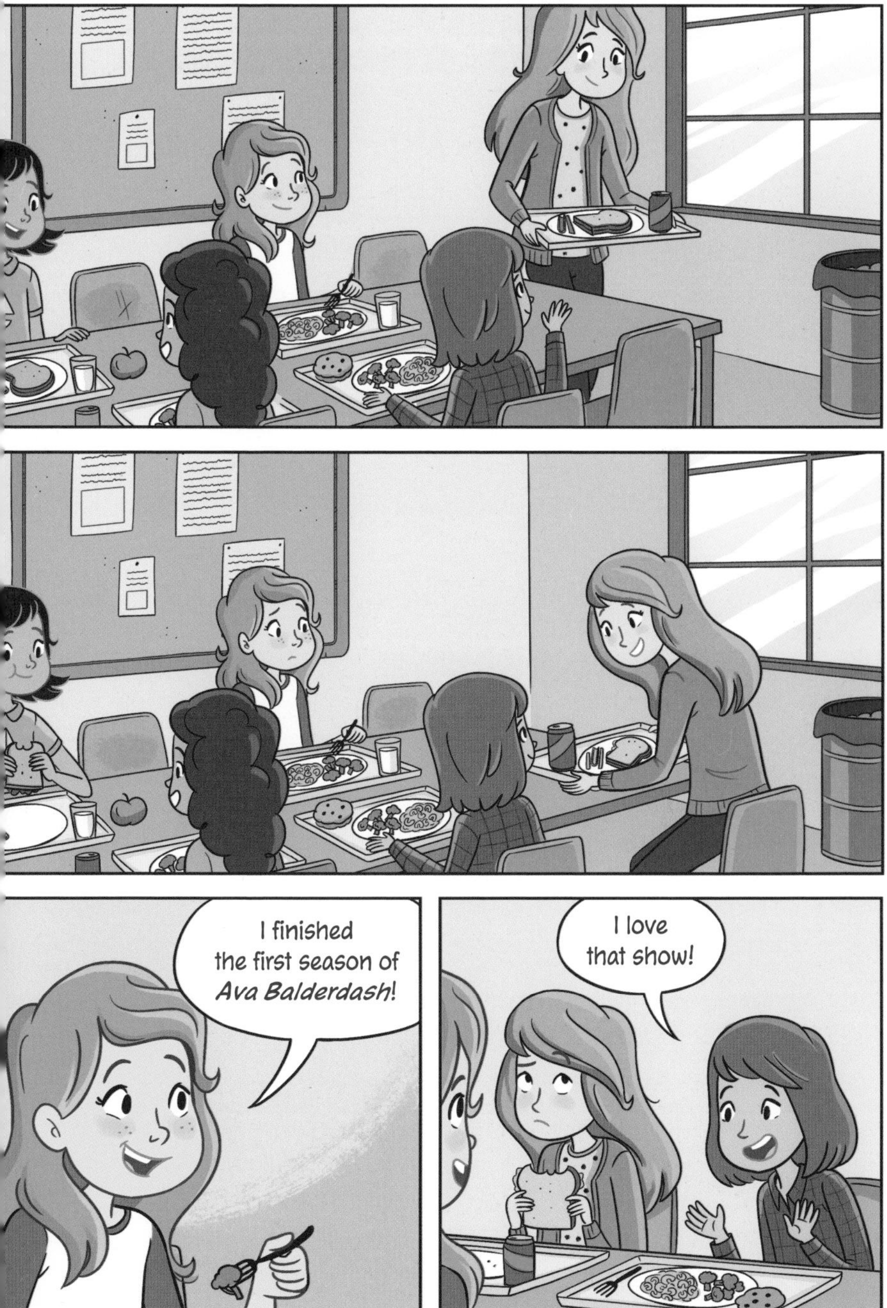
I finished the first season of *Ava Balderdash*!
I love that show!

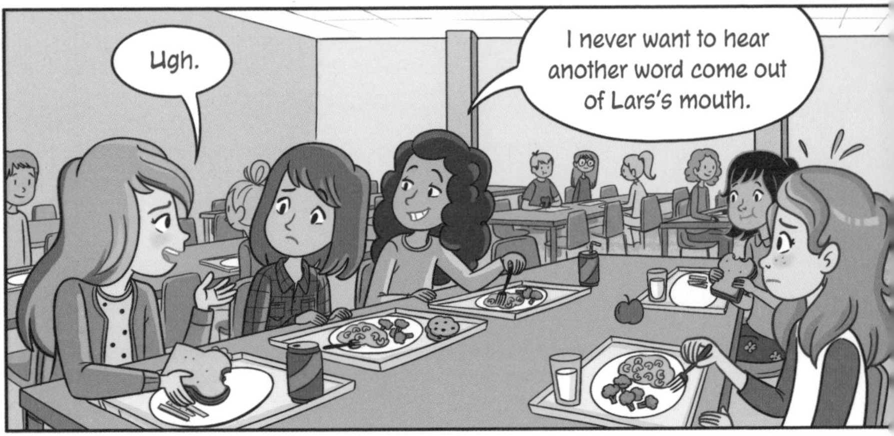
Ugh.
I never want to hear another word come out of Lars's mouth.

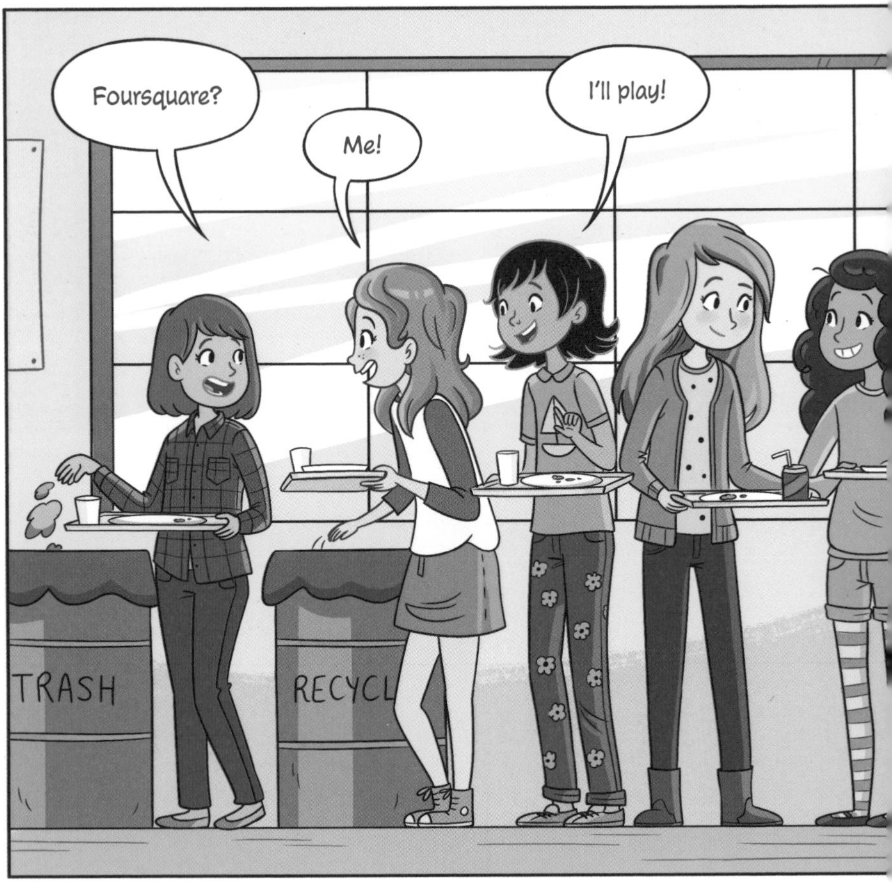
Foursquare?
Me!
I'll play!
TRASH
RECYCL

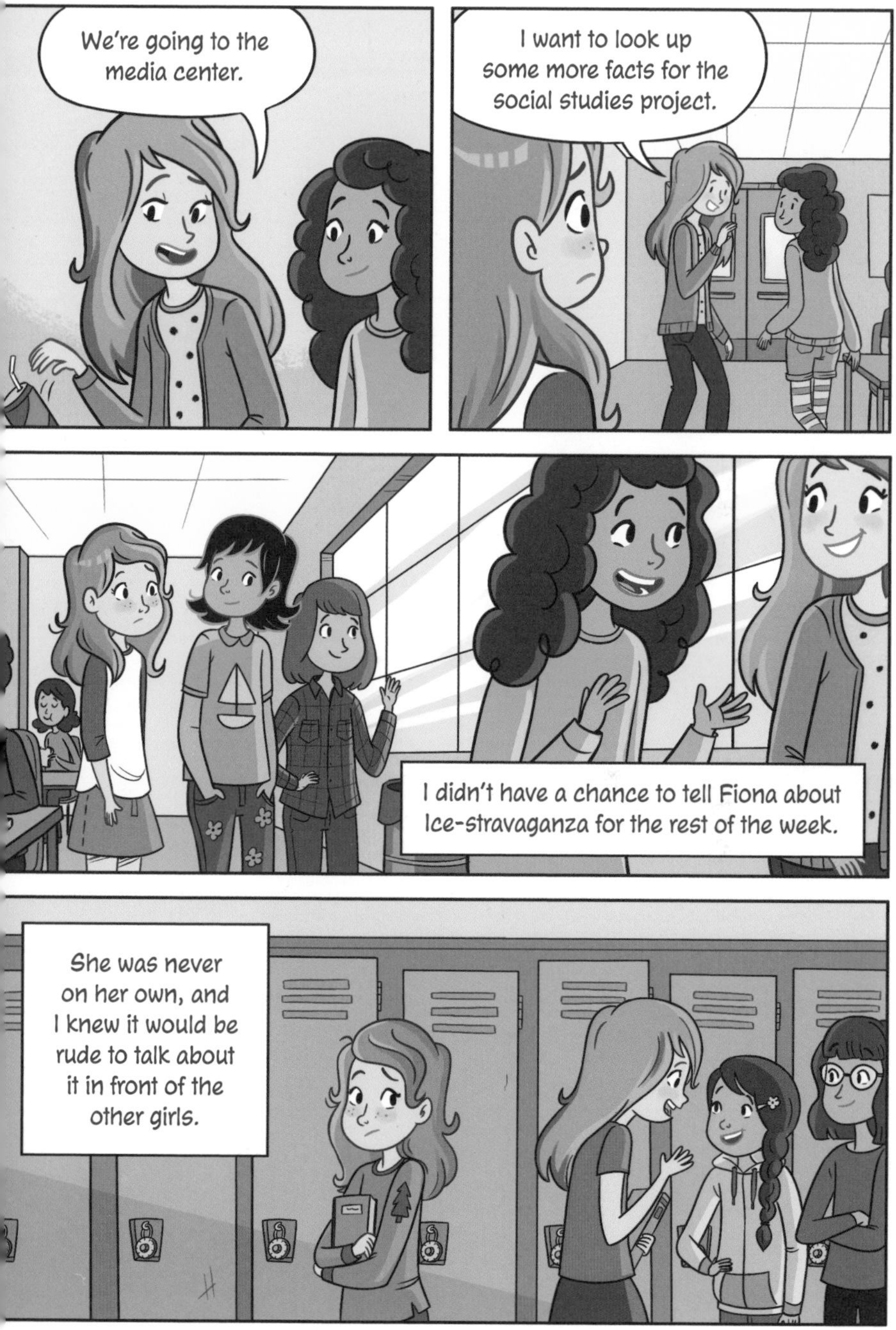
We're going to the media center.
I want to look up some more facts for the social studies project.
I didn't have a chance to tell Fiona about Ice-stravaganza for the rest of the week.
She was never on her own, and I knew it would be rude to talk about it in front of the other girls.

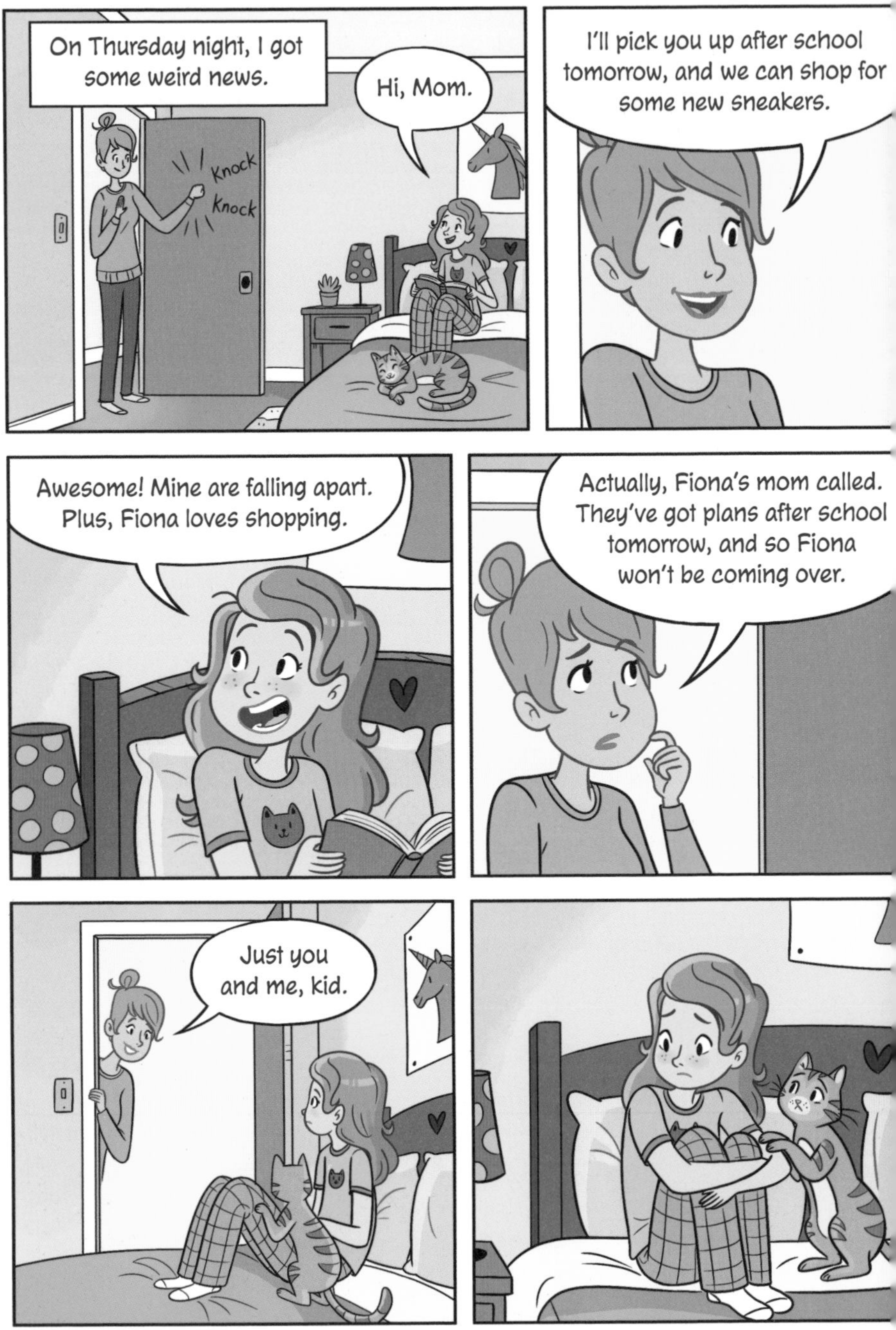
On Thursday night, I got some weird news.
Knock
Knock
Hi, Mom.
I'll pick you up after school tomorrow, and we can shop for some new sneakers.
Awesome! Mine are falling apart. Plus, Fiona loves shopping.
Actually, Fiona's mom called. They've got plans after school tomorrow, and so Fiona won't be coming over.
Just you and me, kid.

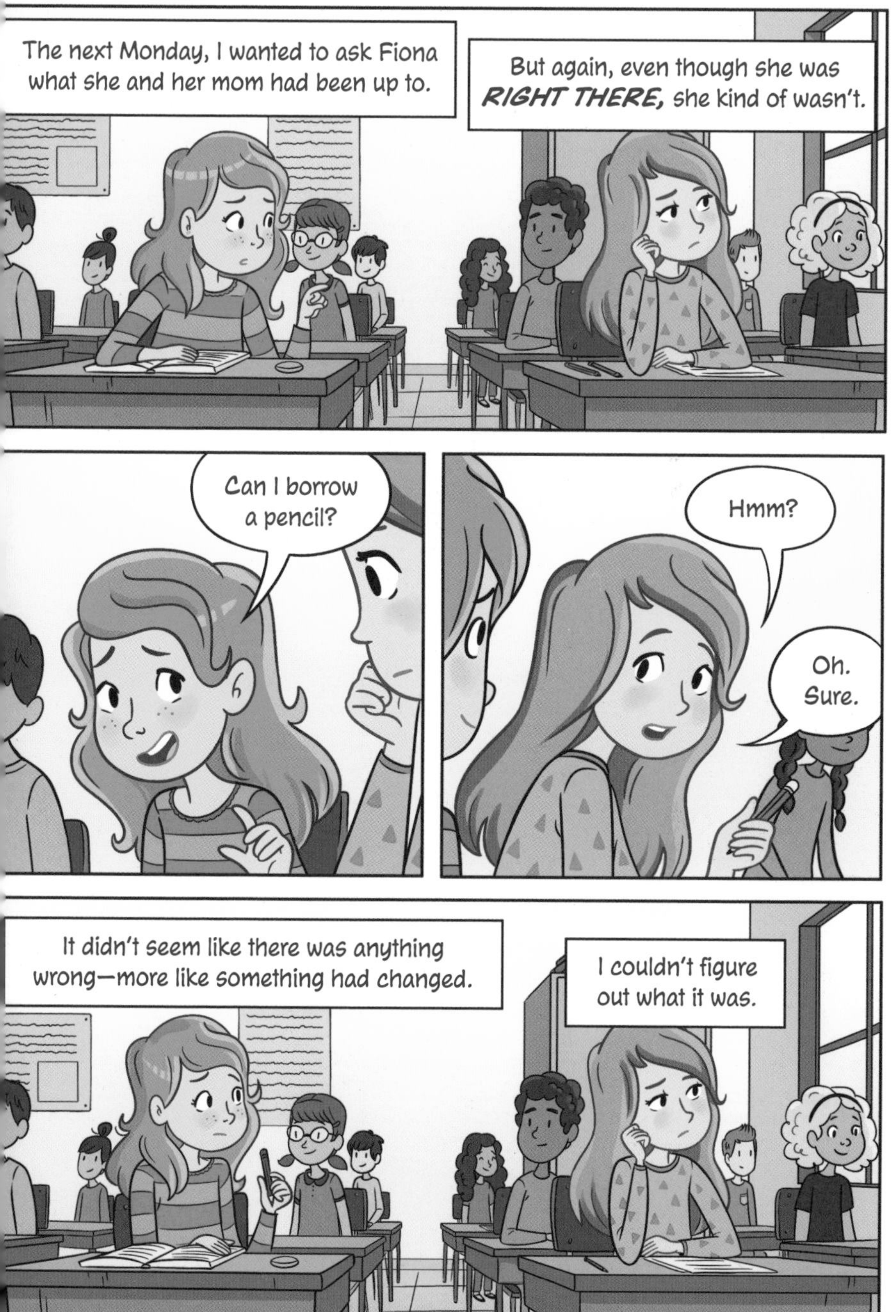
The next Monday, I wanted to ask Fiona what she and her mom had been up to.
But again, even though she was ***RIGHT THERE,*** she kind of wasn't.
Can I borrow a pencil?
Hmm?
Oh. Sure.
It didn't seem like there was anything wrong—more like something had changed.
I couldn't figure out what it was.

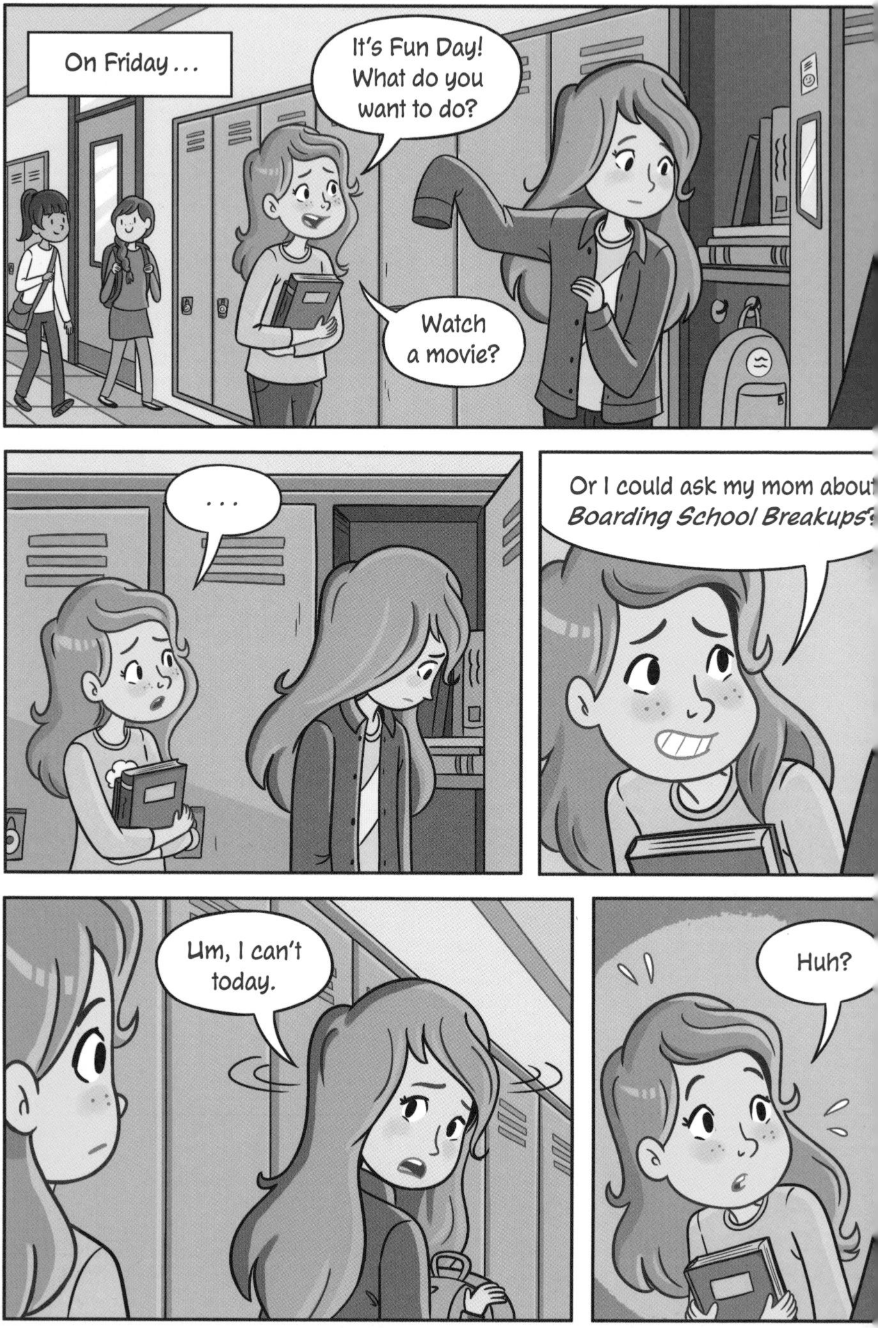
On Friday . . .
It's Fun Day! What do you want to do?
Watch a movie?
. . .
Or I could ask my mom about *Boarding School Breakups*?
Um, I can't today.
Huh?

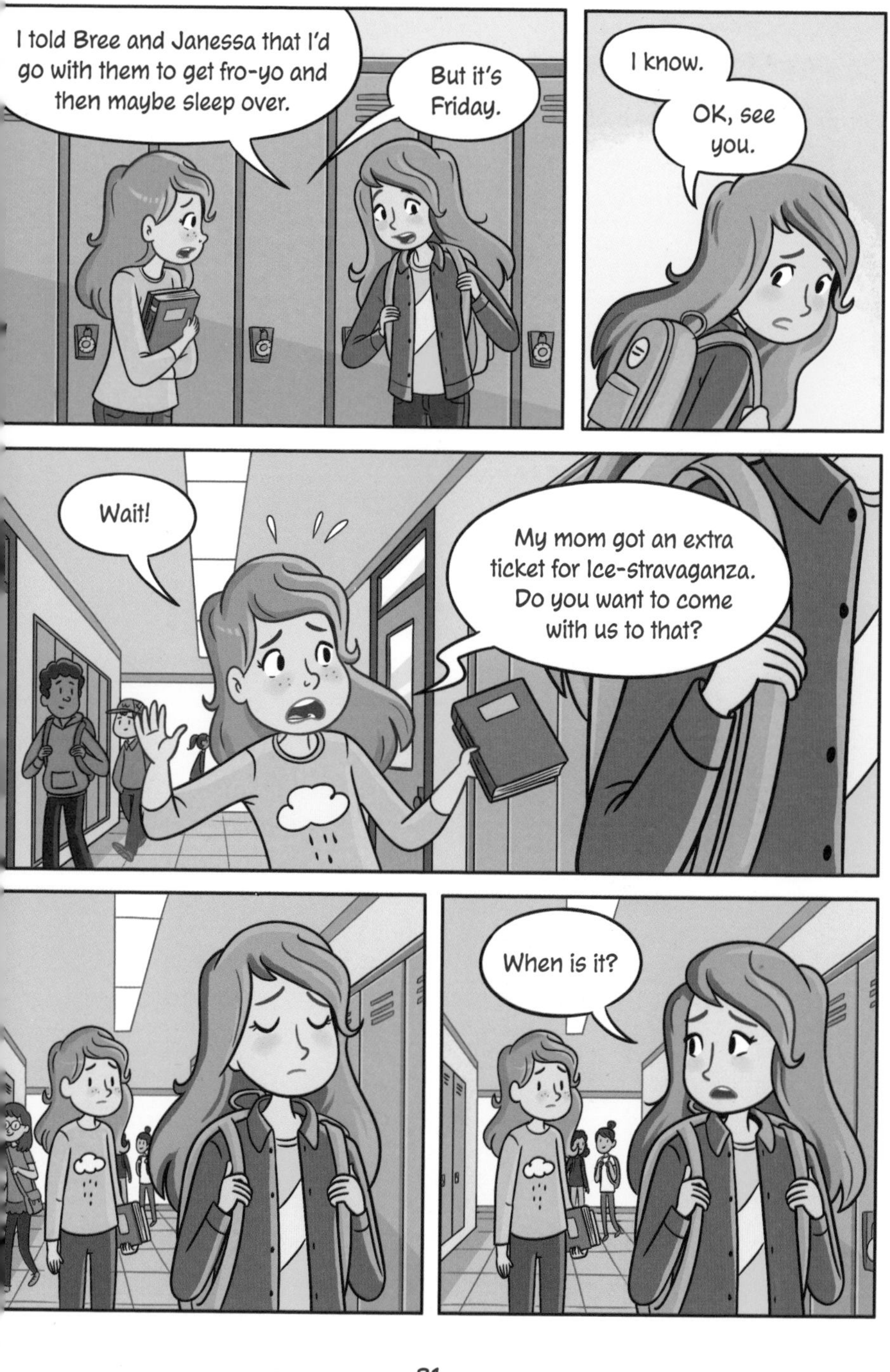
I told Bree and Janessa that I'd go with them to get fro-yo and then maybe sleep over.
But it's Friday.
I know.
OK, see you.
Wait!
My mom got an extra ticket for Ice-stravaganza. Do you want to come with us to that?
When is it?

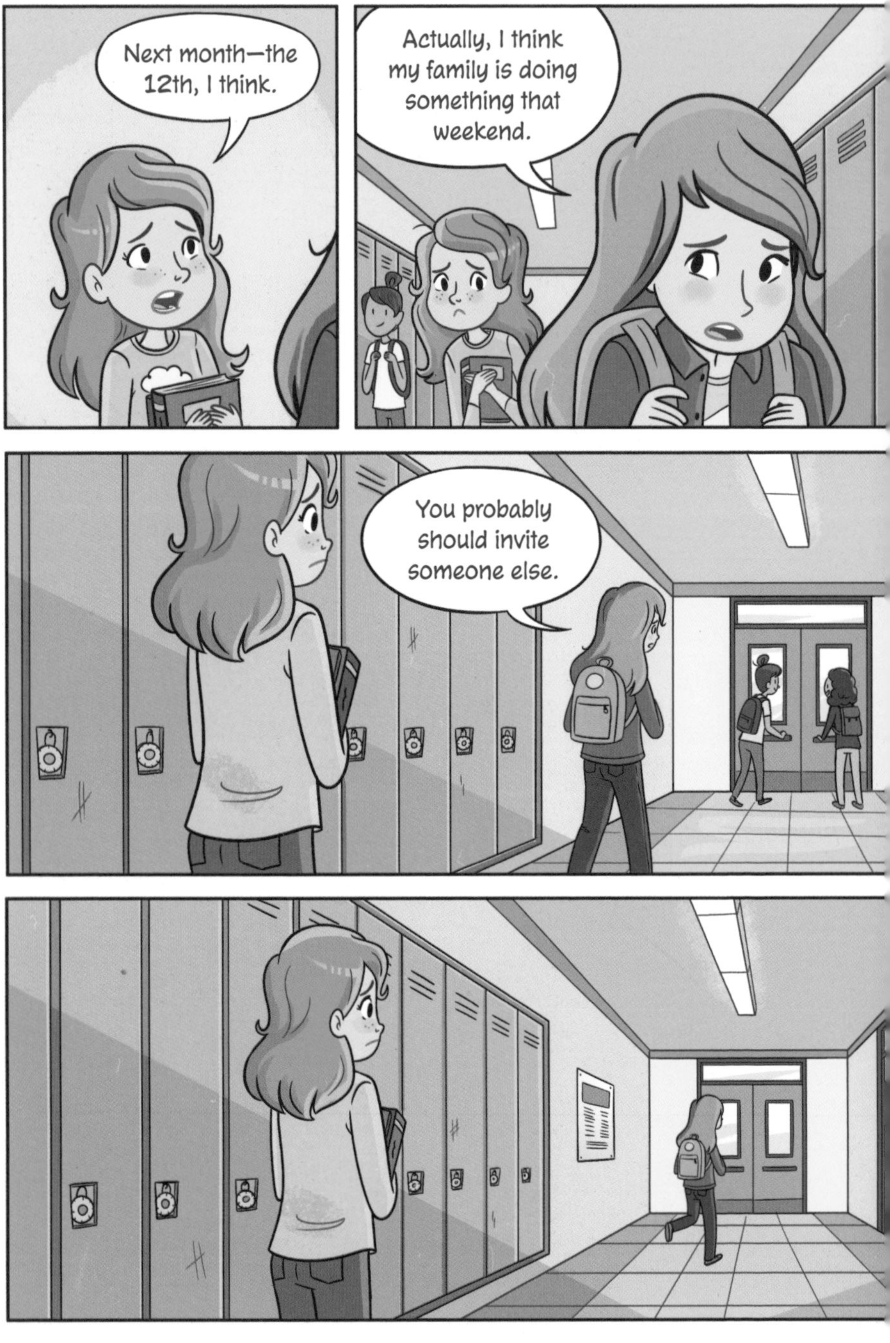
Next month—the 12th, I think.
Actually, I think my family is doing something that weekend.
You probably should invite someone else.

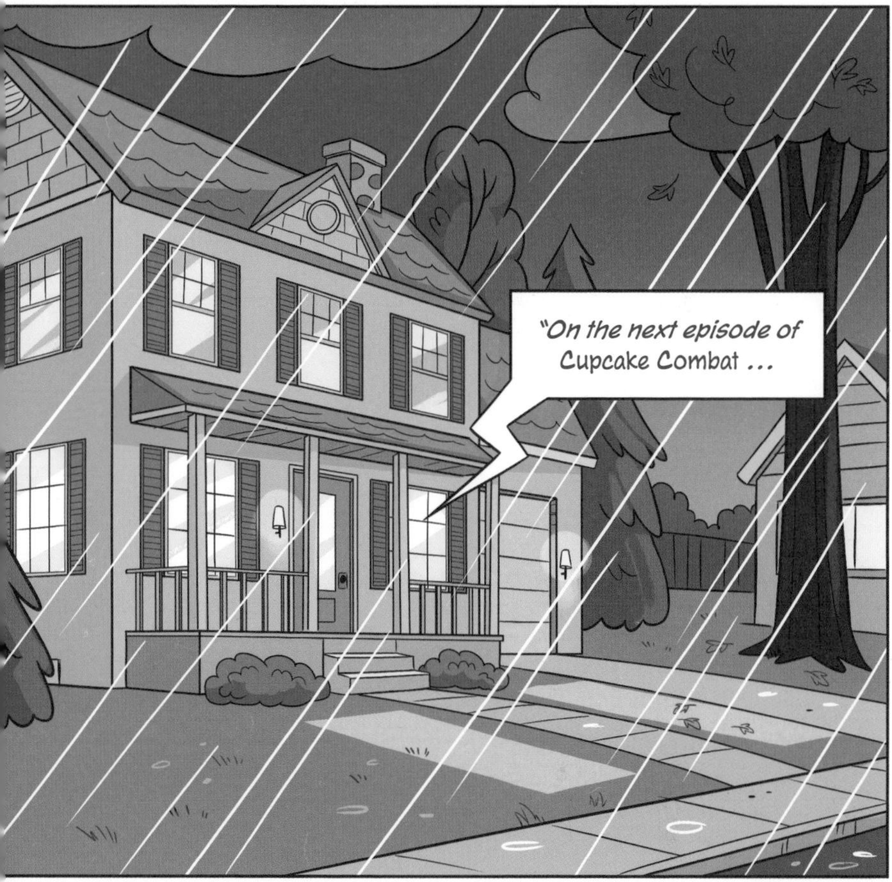
"On the next episode of Cupcake Combat . . .

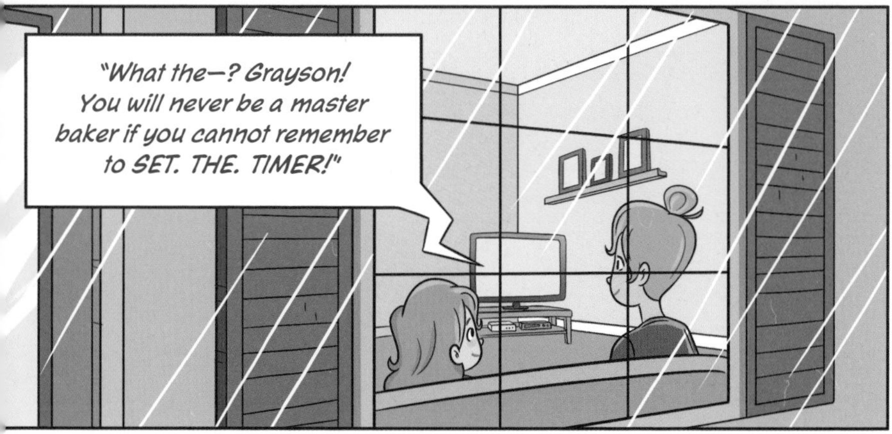
"What the—? Grayson! You will never be a master baker if you cannot remember to SET. THE. TIMER!"

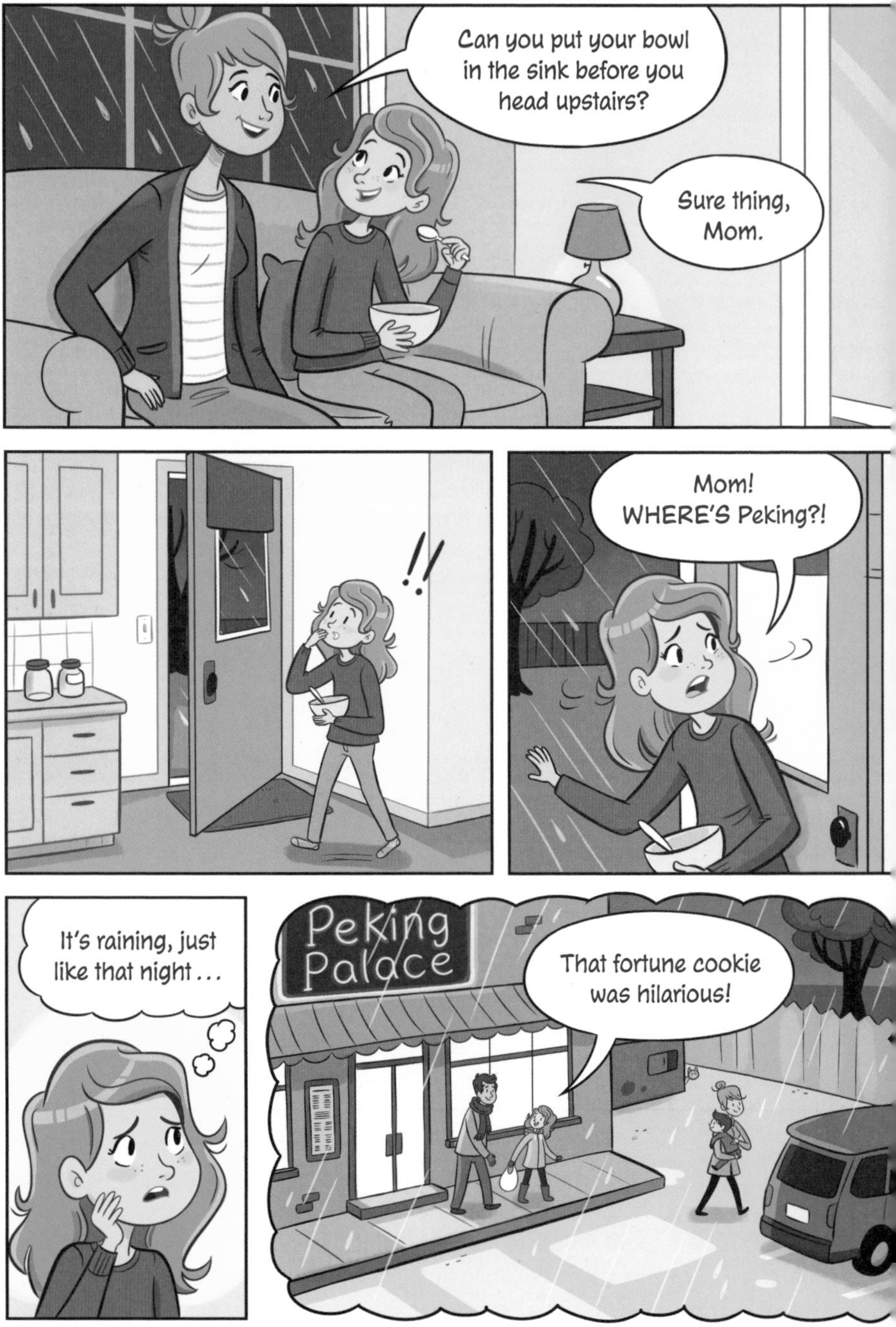

Can you put your bowl in the sink before you head upstairs?
Sure thing, Mom.
!!
Mom! WHERE'S Peking?!
It's raining, just like that night . . .
Peking Palace
That fortune cookie was hilarious!

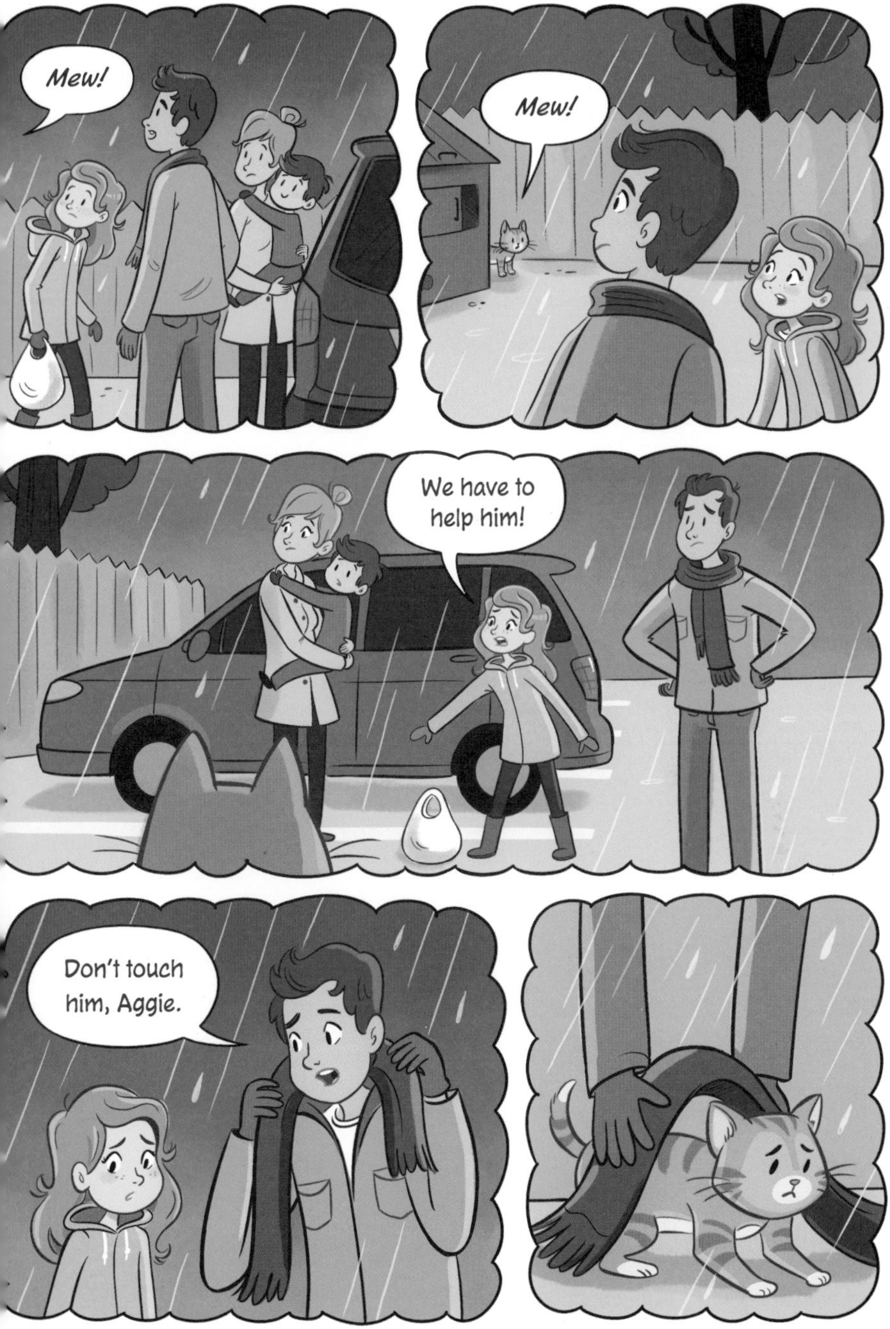
Mew!
Mew!
We have to help him!
Don't touch him, Aggie.

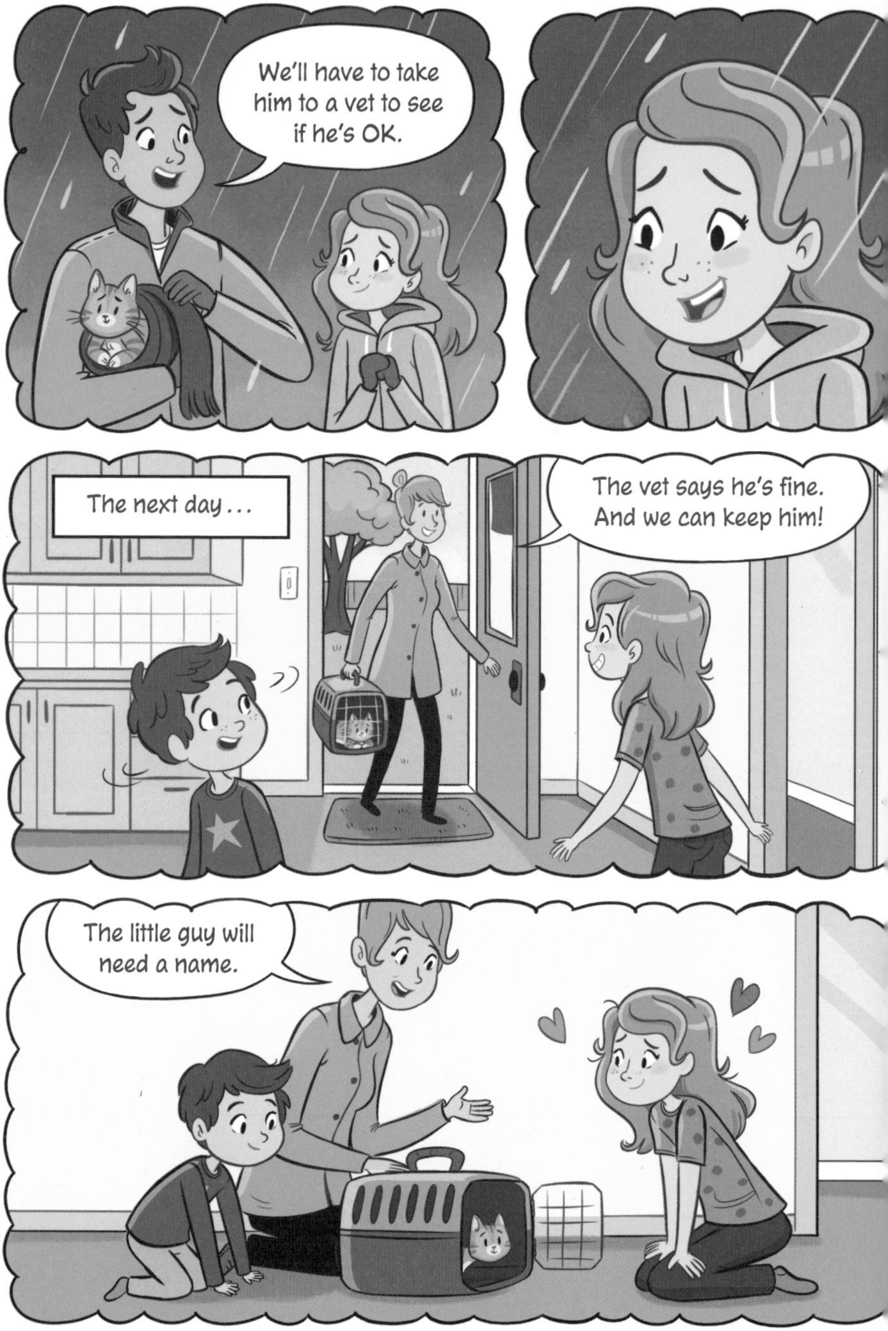
We'll have to take him to a vet to see if he's OK.
The next day . . .
The vet says he's fine. And we can keep him!
The little guy will need a name.

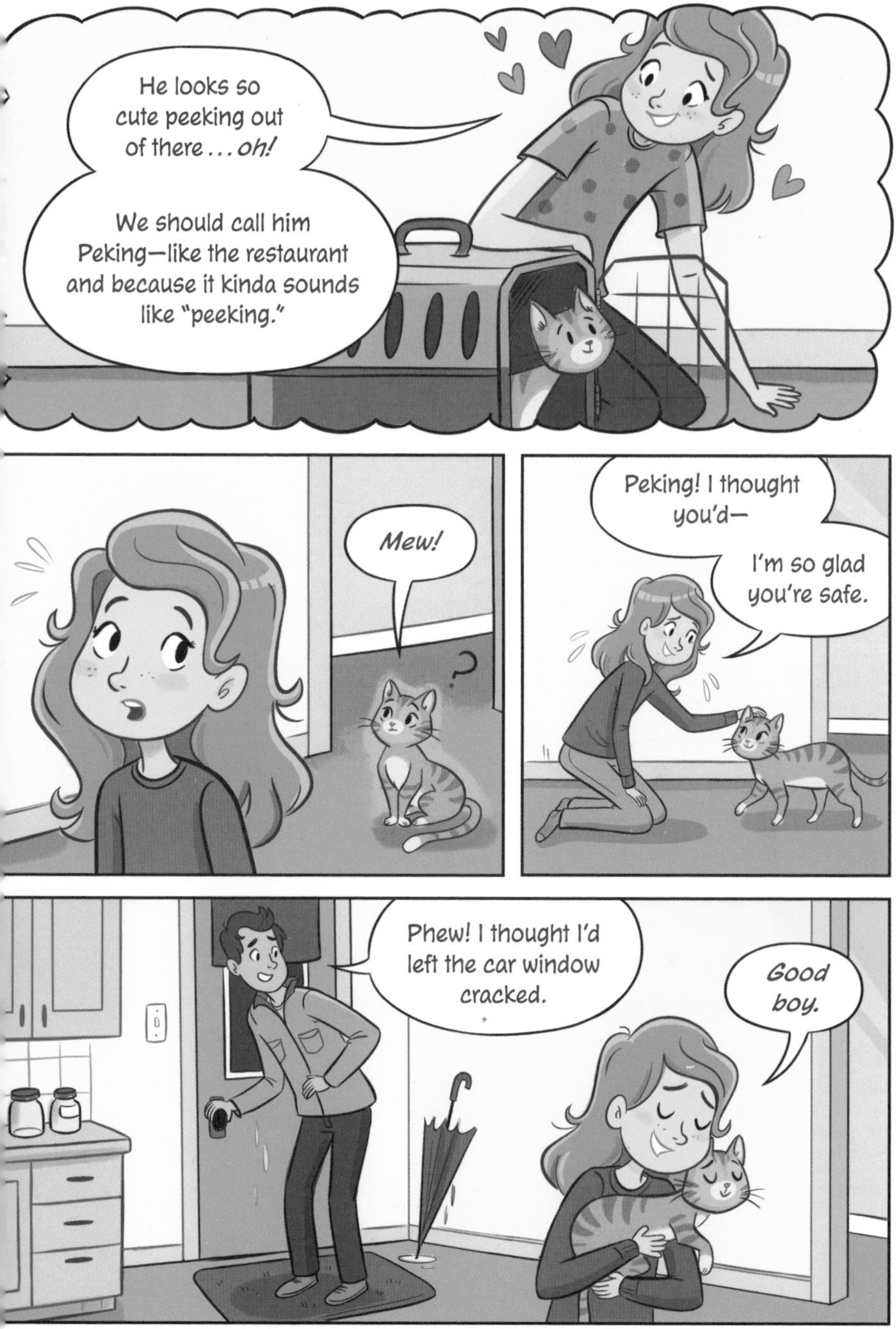
He looks so cute peeking out of there . . . *oh!*
We should call him Peking—like the restaurant and because it kinda sounds like "peeking."
Mew!
Peking! I thought you'd—
I'm so glad you're safe.
Phew! I thought I'd left the car window cracked.
Good boy.

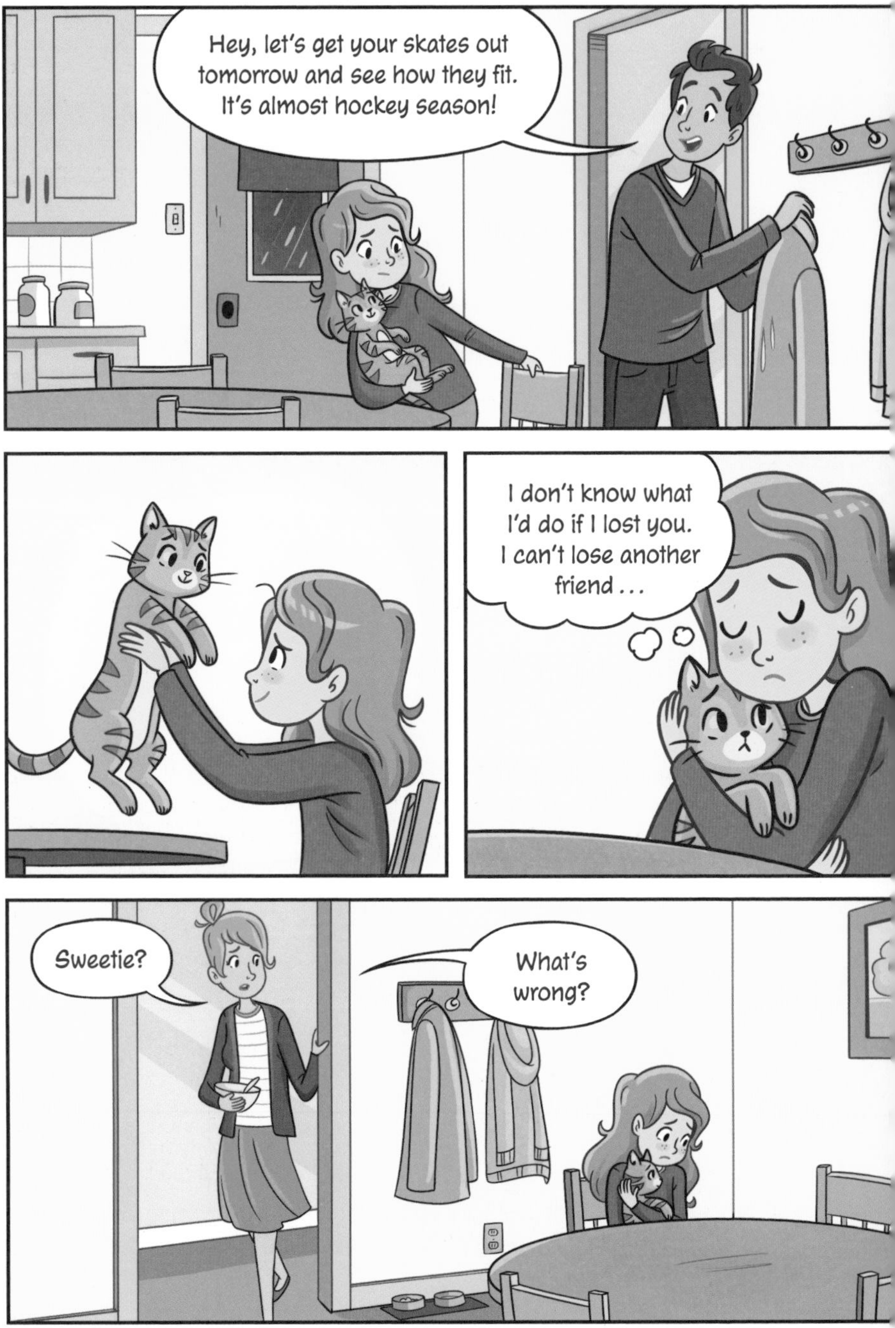
Hey, let's get your skates out tomorrow and see how they fit. It's almost hockey season!
I don't know what I'd do if I lost you. I can't lose another friend . . .
Sweetie?
What's wrong?

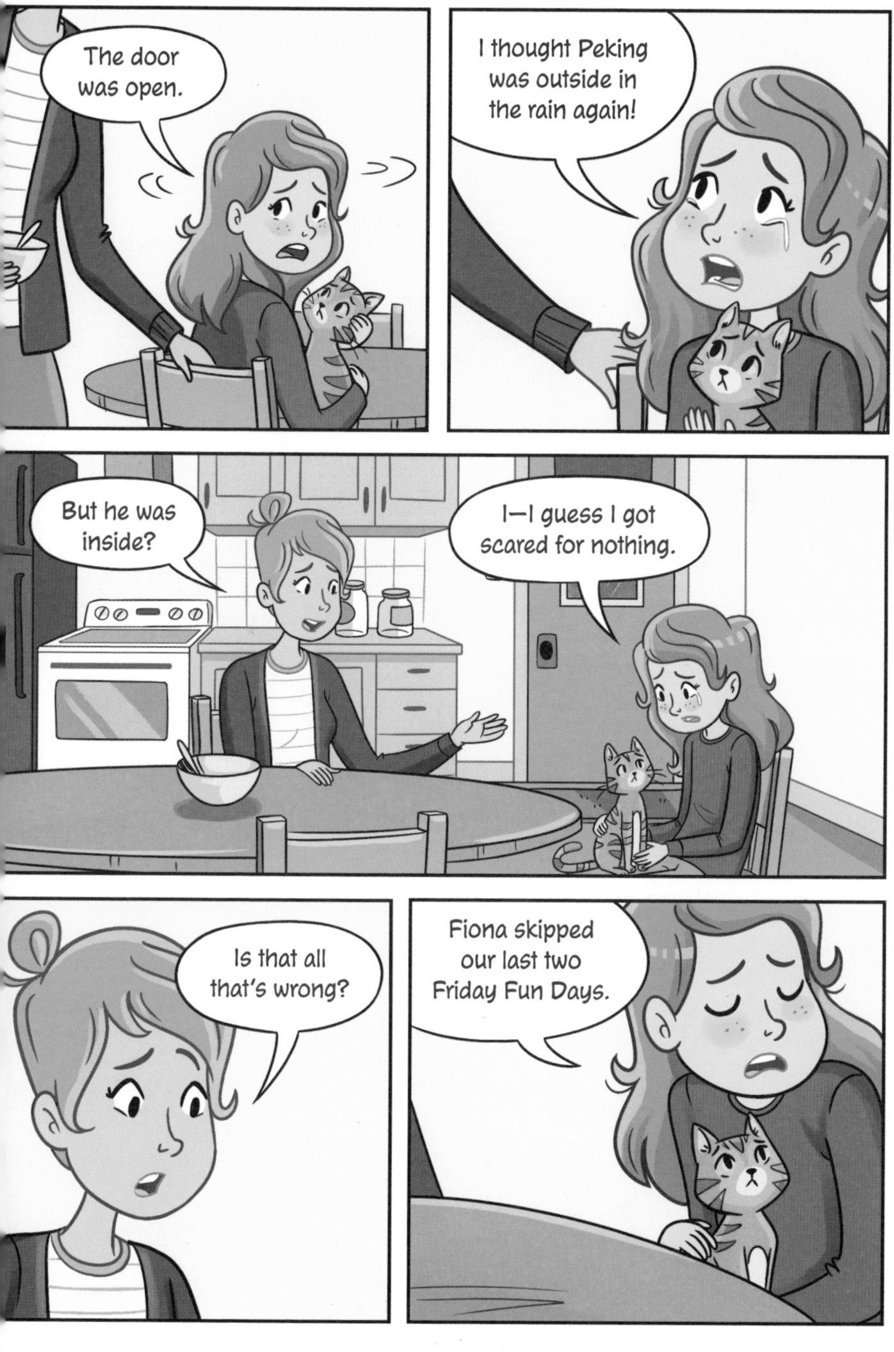
The door was open.
I thought Peking was outside in the rain again!
But he was inside?
I—I guess I got scared for nothing.
Is that all that's wrong?
Fiona skipped our last two Friday Fun Days.

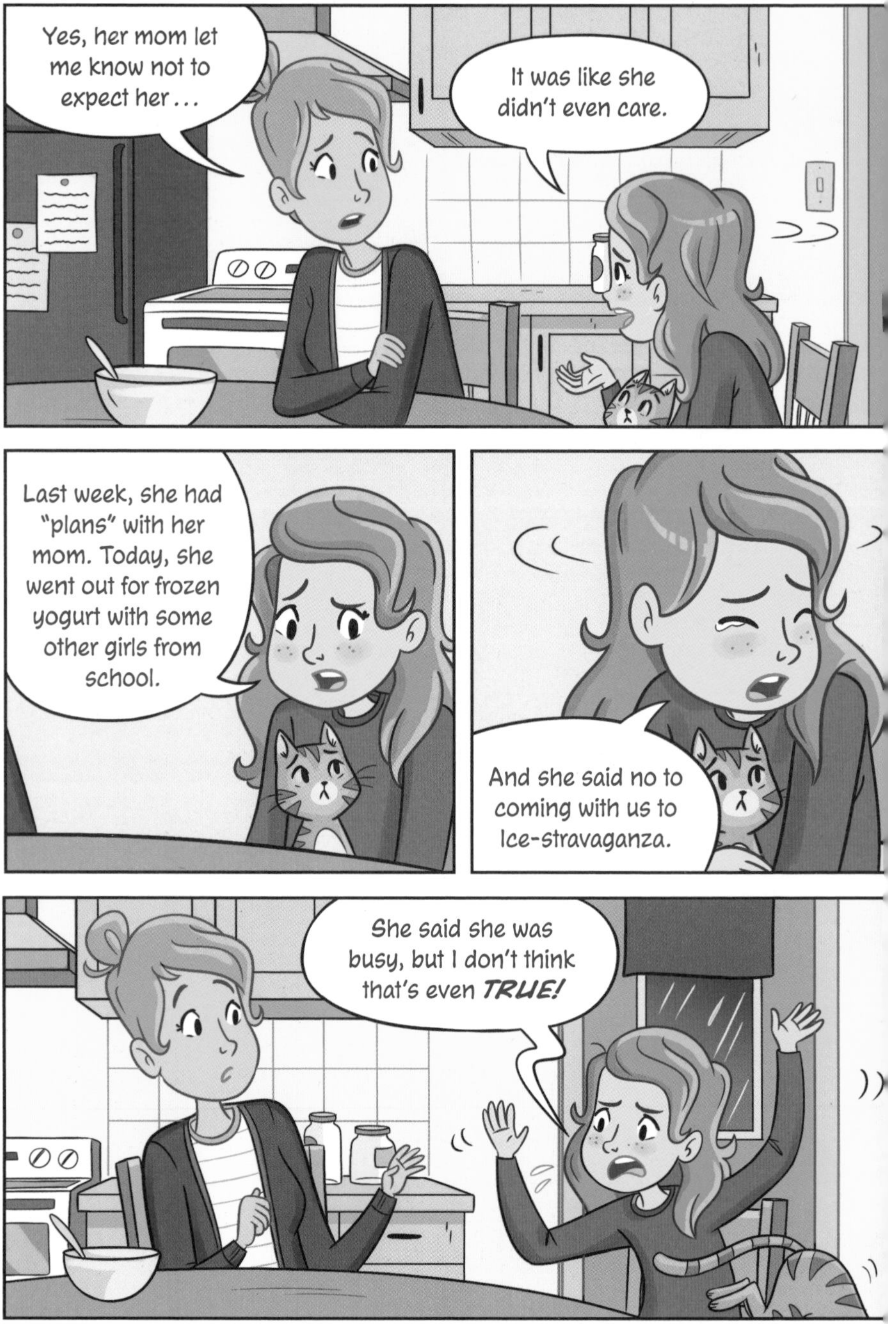
Yes, her mom let me know not to expect her...
It was like she didn't even care.
Last week, she had "plans" with her mom. Today, she went out for frozen yogurt with some other girls from school.
And she said no to coming with us to Ice-stravaganza.
She said she was busy, but I don't think that's even ***TRUE!***

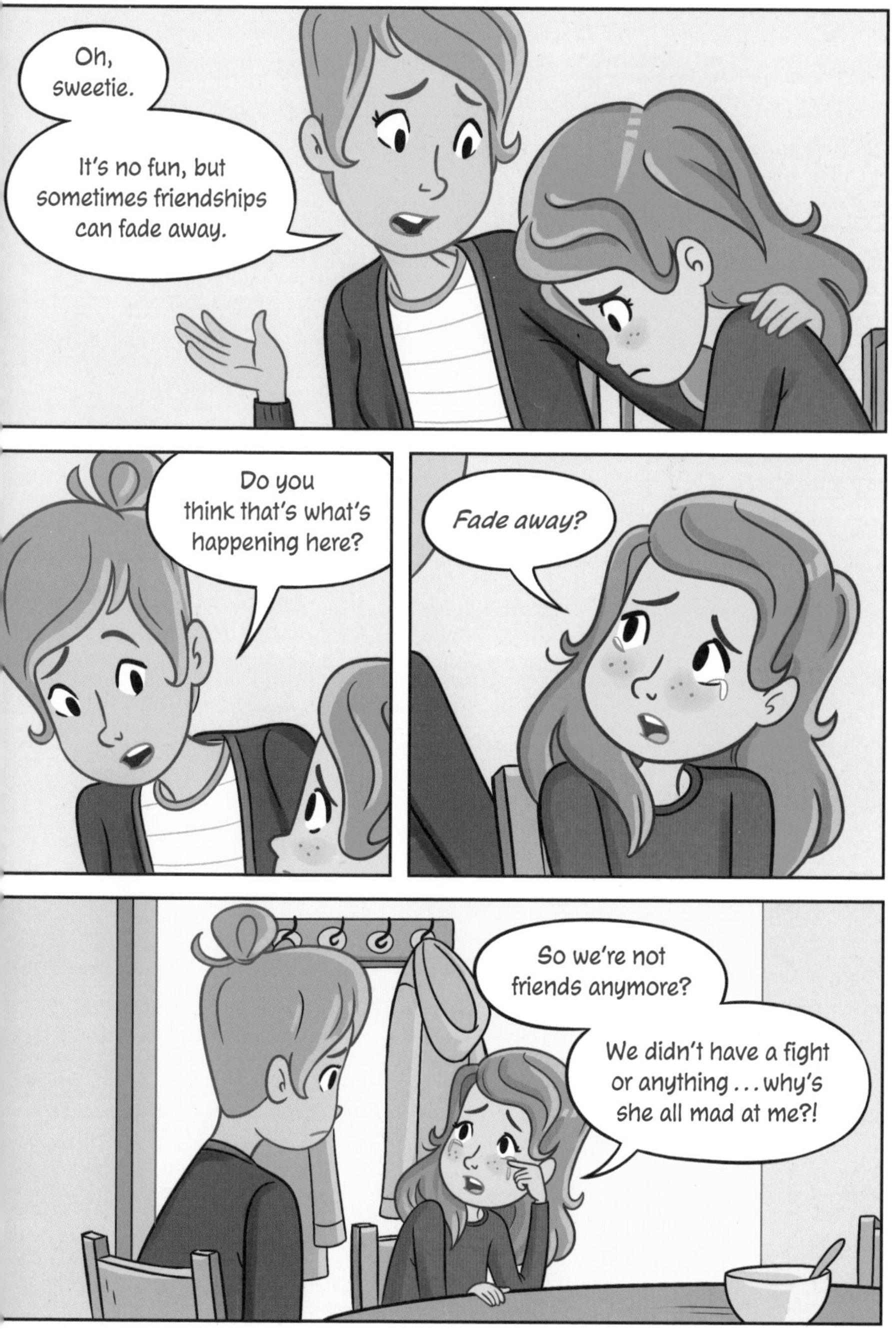
Oh, sweetie.
It's no fun, but sometimes friendships can fade away.
Do you think that's what's happening here?
Fade away?
So we're not friends anymore?
We didn't have a fight or anything . . . why's she all mad at me?!

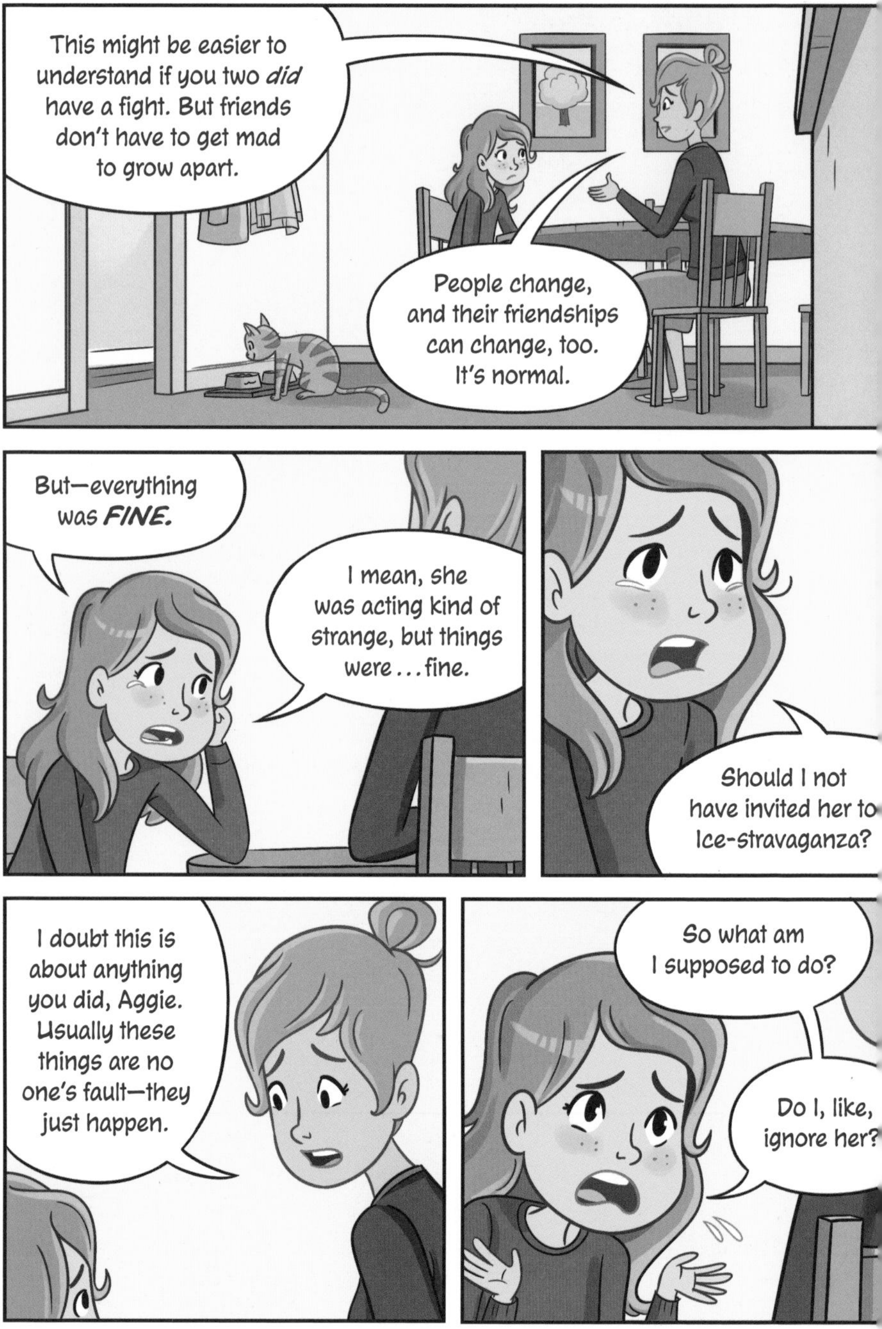
This might be easier to understand if you two *did* have a fight. But friends don't have to get mad to grow apart.
People change, and their friendships can change, too. It's normal.
But—everything was ***FINE.***
I mean, she was acting kind of strange, but things were . . . fine.
Should I not have invited her to Ice-stravaganza?
I doubt this is about anything you did, Aggie. Usually these things are no one's fault—they just happen.
So what am I supposed to do?
Do I, like, ignore her?

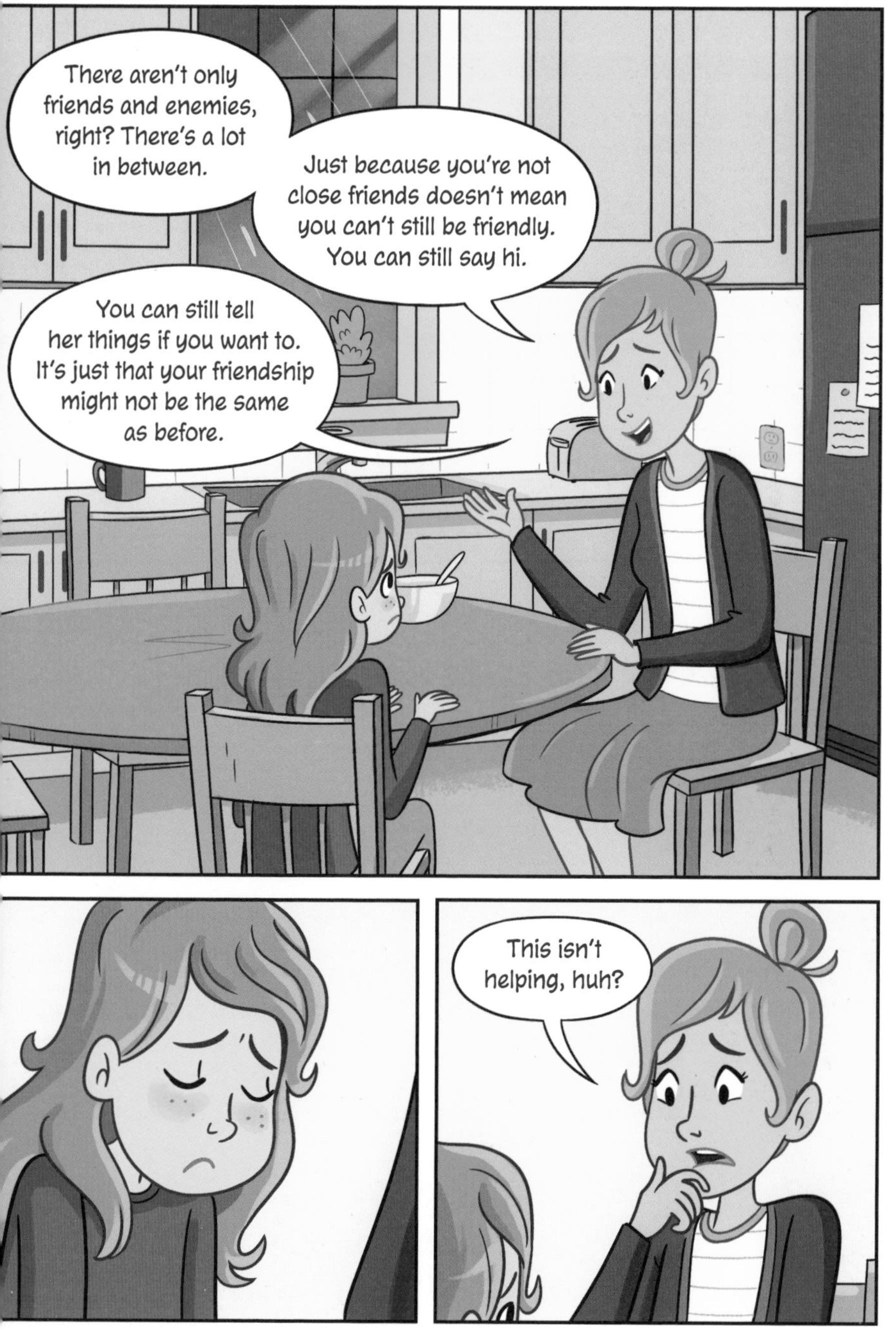
There aren't only friends and enemies, right? There's a lot in between.
Just because you're not close friends doesn't mean you can't still be friendly. You can still say hi.
You can still tell her things if you want to. It's just that your friendship might not be the same as before.
This isn't helping, huh?

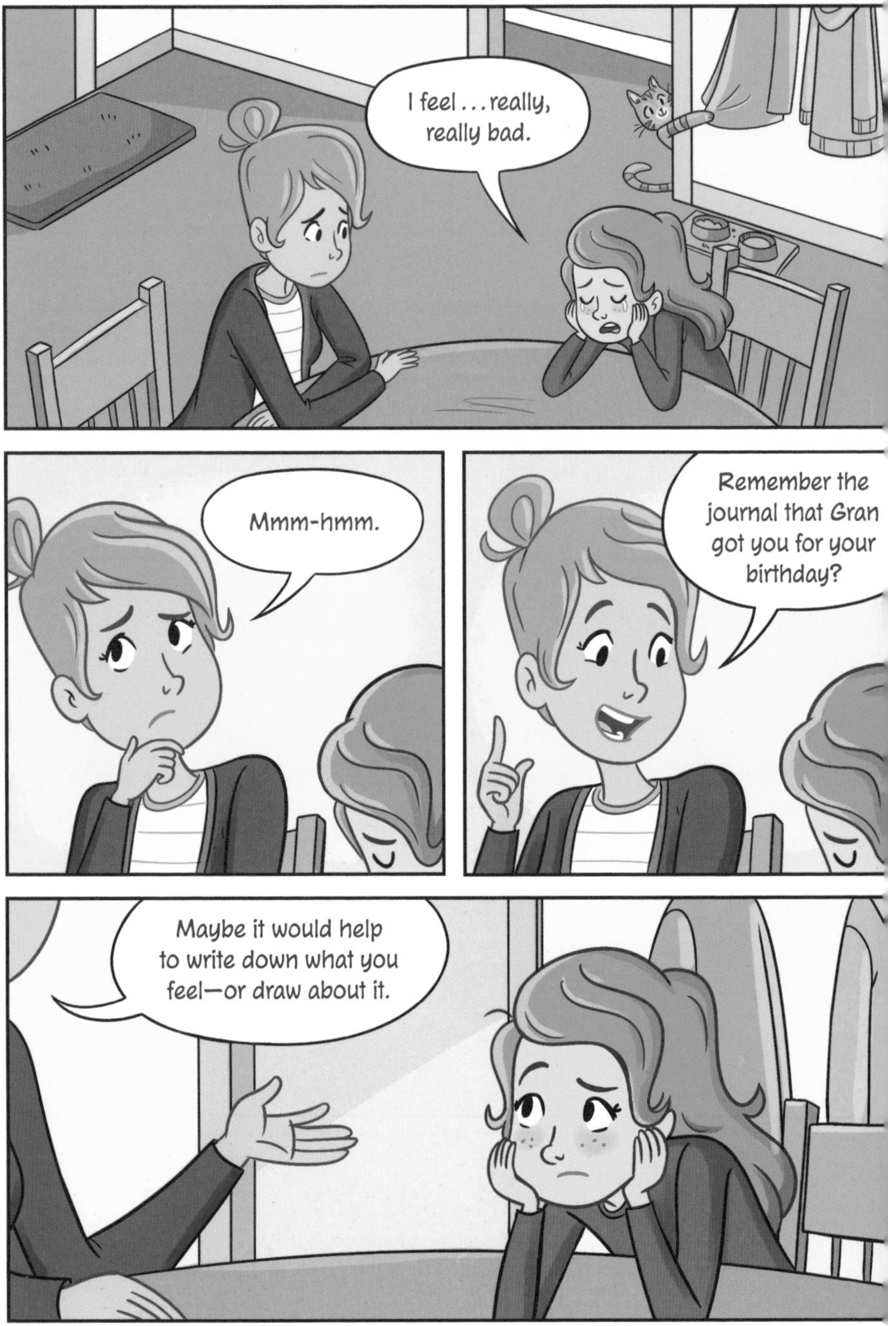
I feel . . . really, really bad.
Mmm-hmm.
Remember the journal that Gran got you for your birthday?
Maybe it would help to write down what you feel—or draw about it.

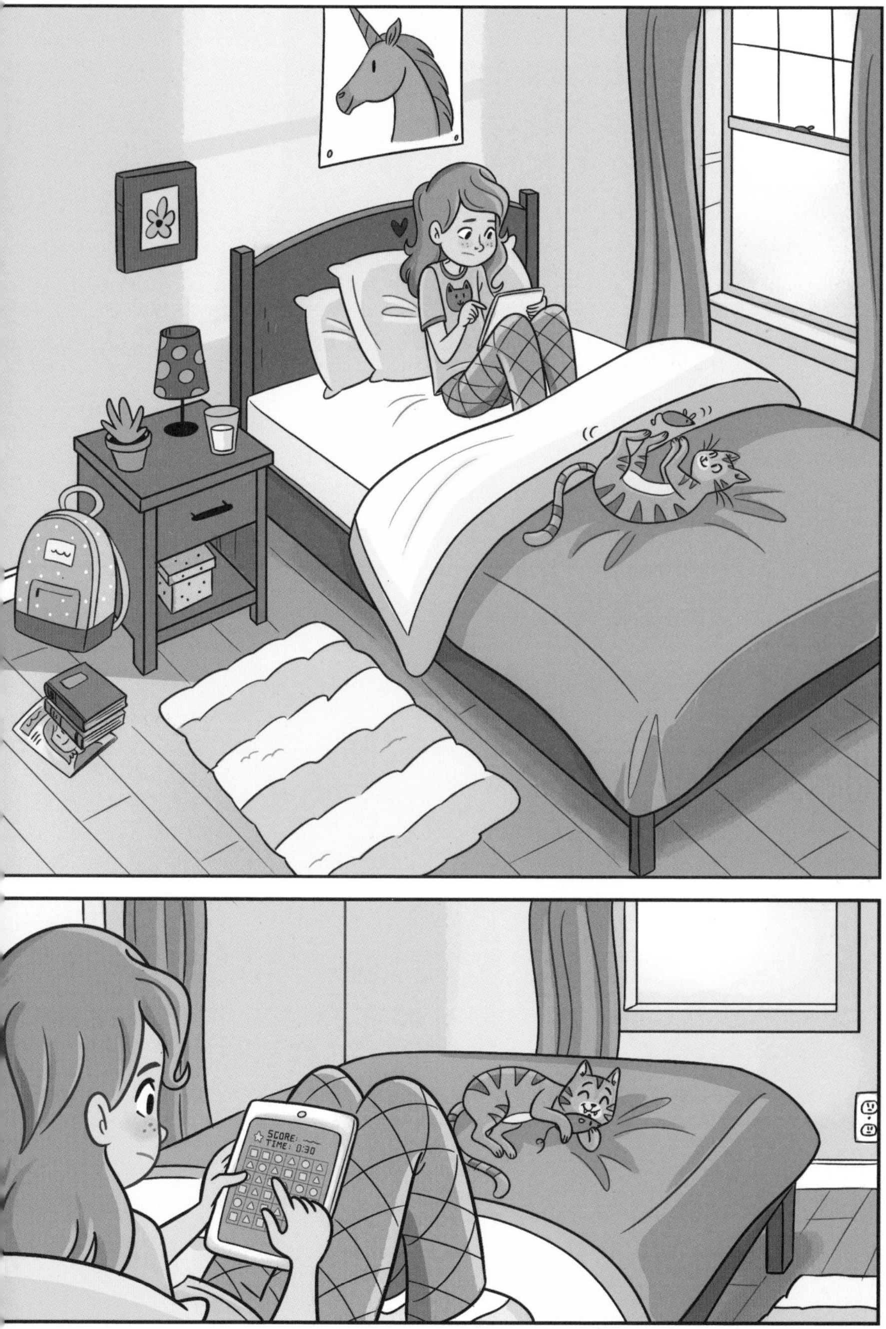
SCORE:
TIME: 0:30

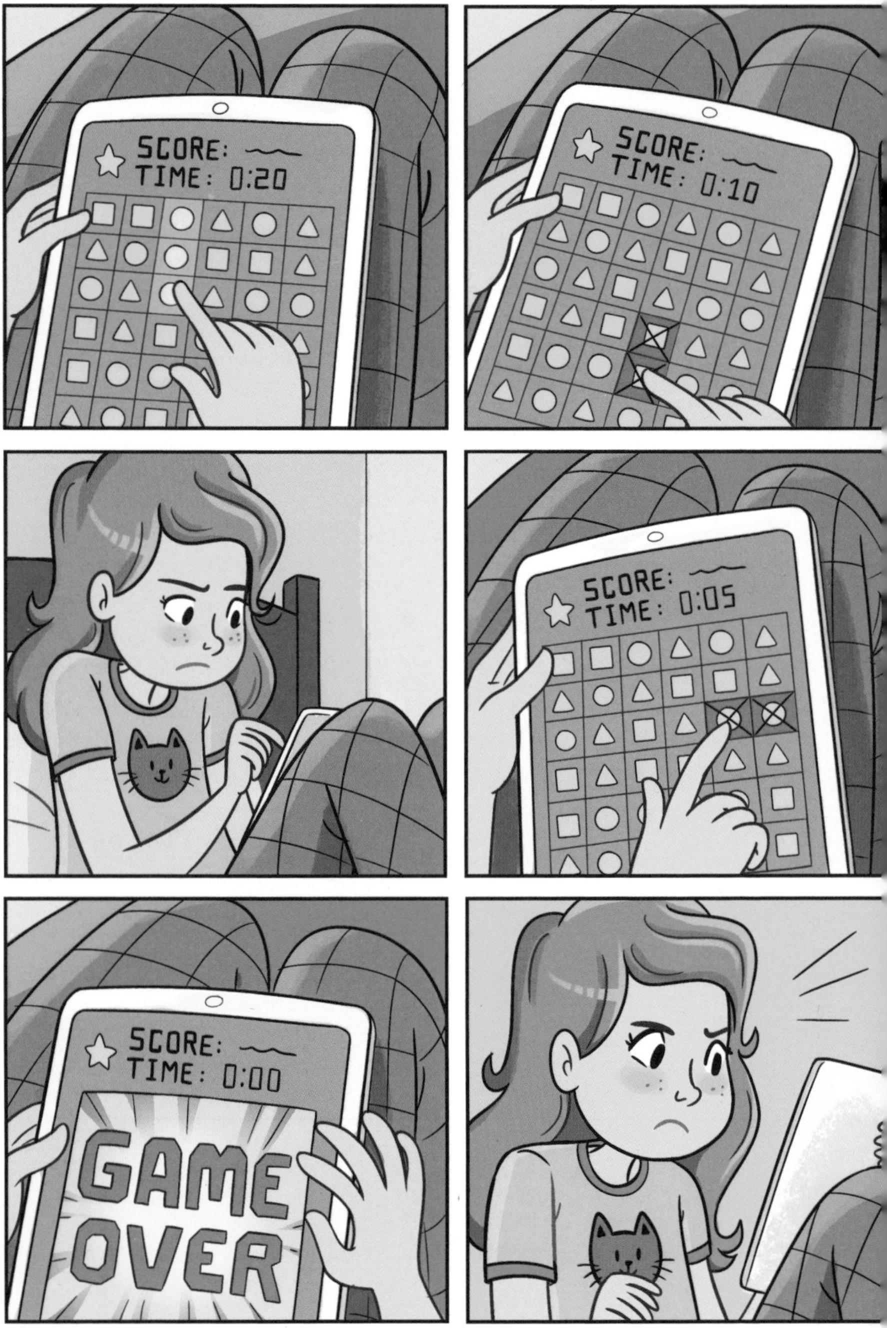
SCORE:
TIME: 0:20
SCORE:
TIME: 0:10
SCORE:
TIME: 0:05
SCORE:
TIME: 0:00
GAME OVER

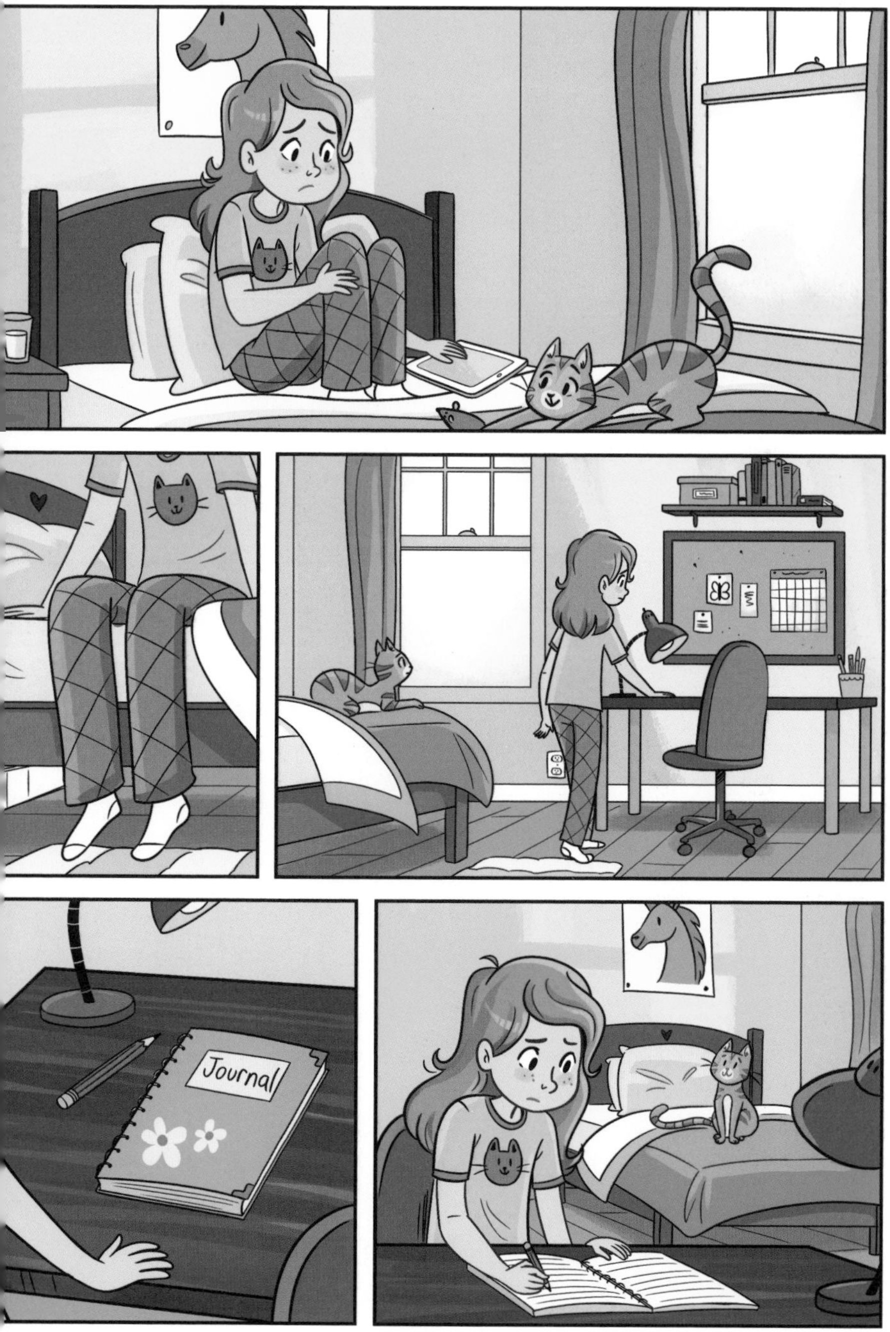
Journal

According to Aggie

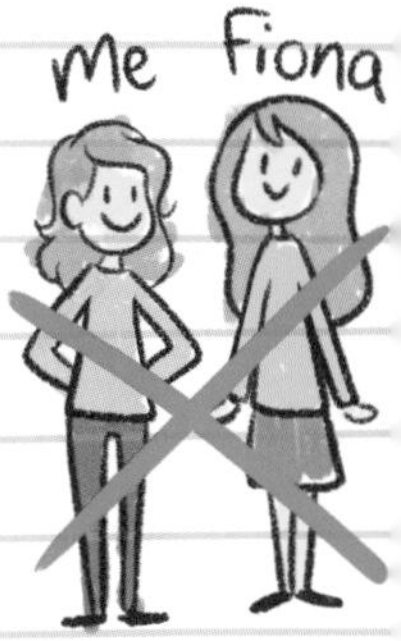
Me
Fiona

So I guess Fiona and I aren't ~~freinds~~ friends anymore. How can that be true? We have been friends forever. Maybe she doesn't like me anymore.

Mom says that people change and it makes friendships change but I haven't changed that much. Have I? Did Fiona change? Is this all my fault?

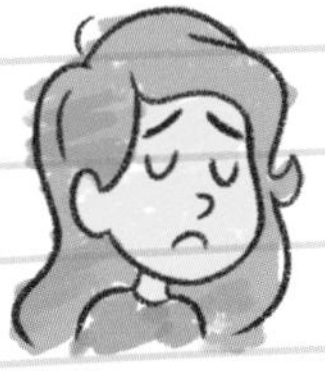

How I feel:

- Sad
- Mad, kind of
- Like I made a mistake in front of a bunc of people (embarased) (sp?)
- Like everyone will know she doesn't war to be my friend anymore
- Like no one else will want to be my fr
- Alone ...

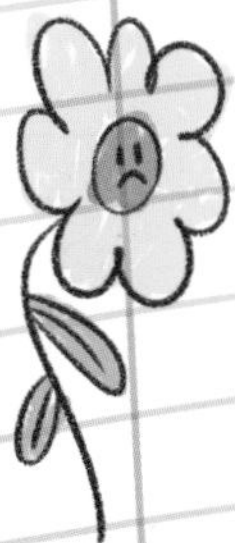

Maybe I can remind her of why we're friends.

Things Fiona and I ♡ LOVE ♡

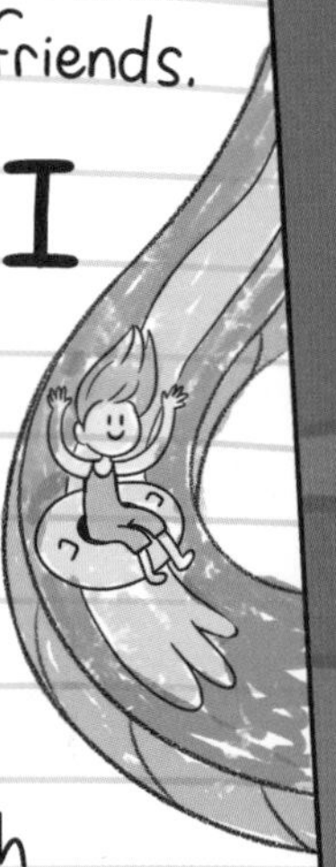

- Big slides at the water park

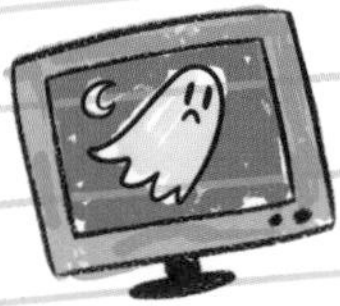

- Movies that make us scared but also make us laugh so we don't get nightmares

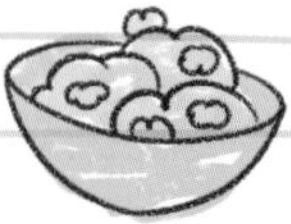

- Putting salty popcorn on vanilla ice cream – yum

- Watching animal videos online

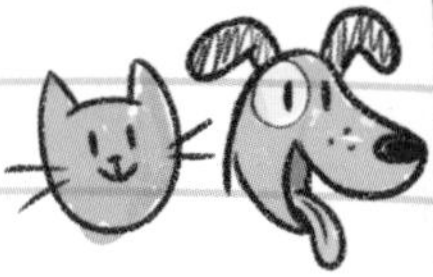

Is it strange that this list isn't longer?
I'll think of more.

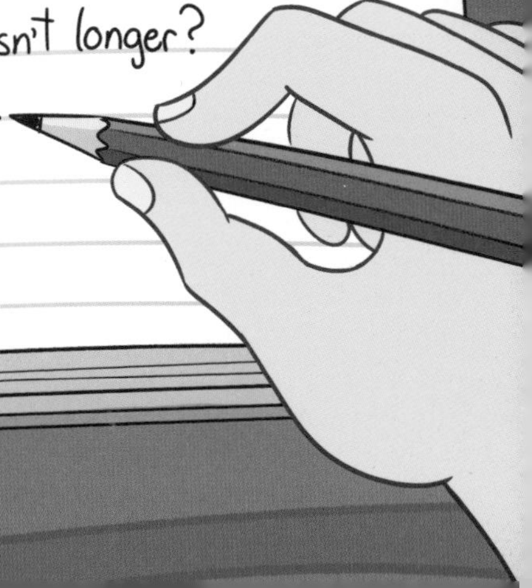

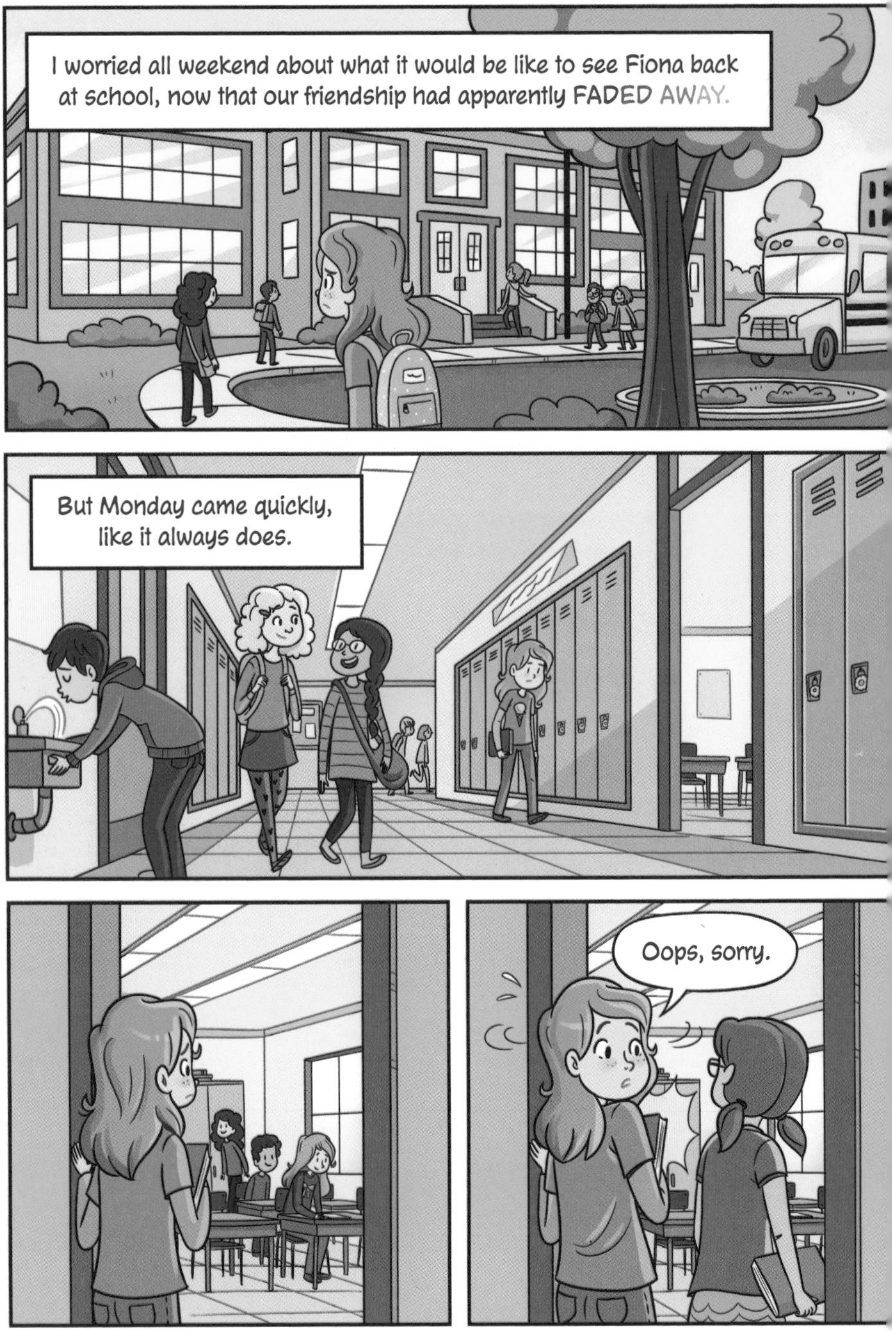
I worried all weekend about what it would be like to see Fiona back at school, now that our friendship had apparently FADED AWAY.
But Monday came quickly, like it always does.
Oops, sorry.

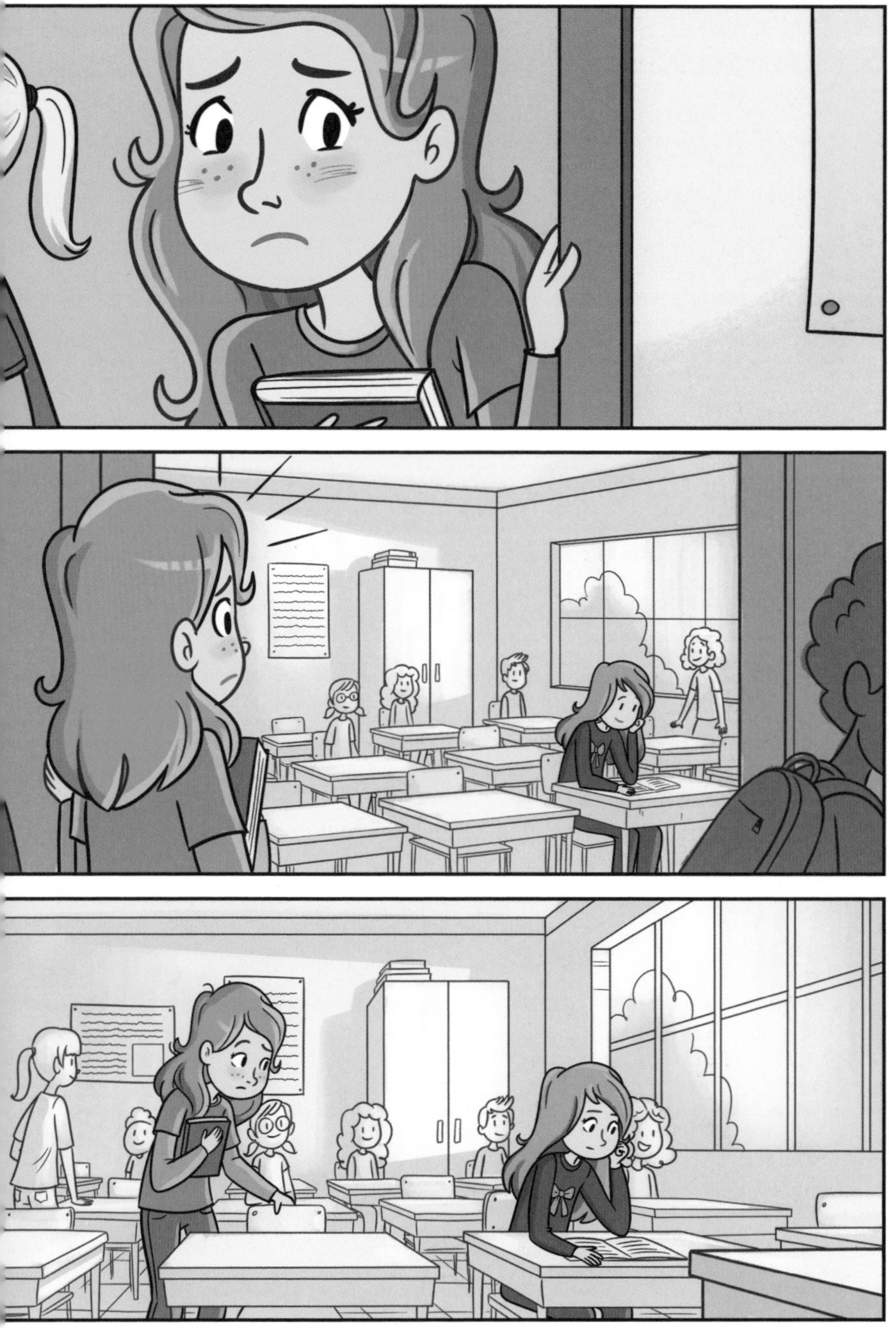

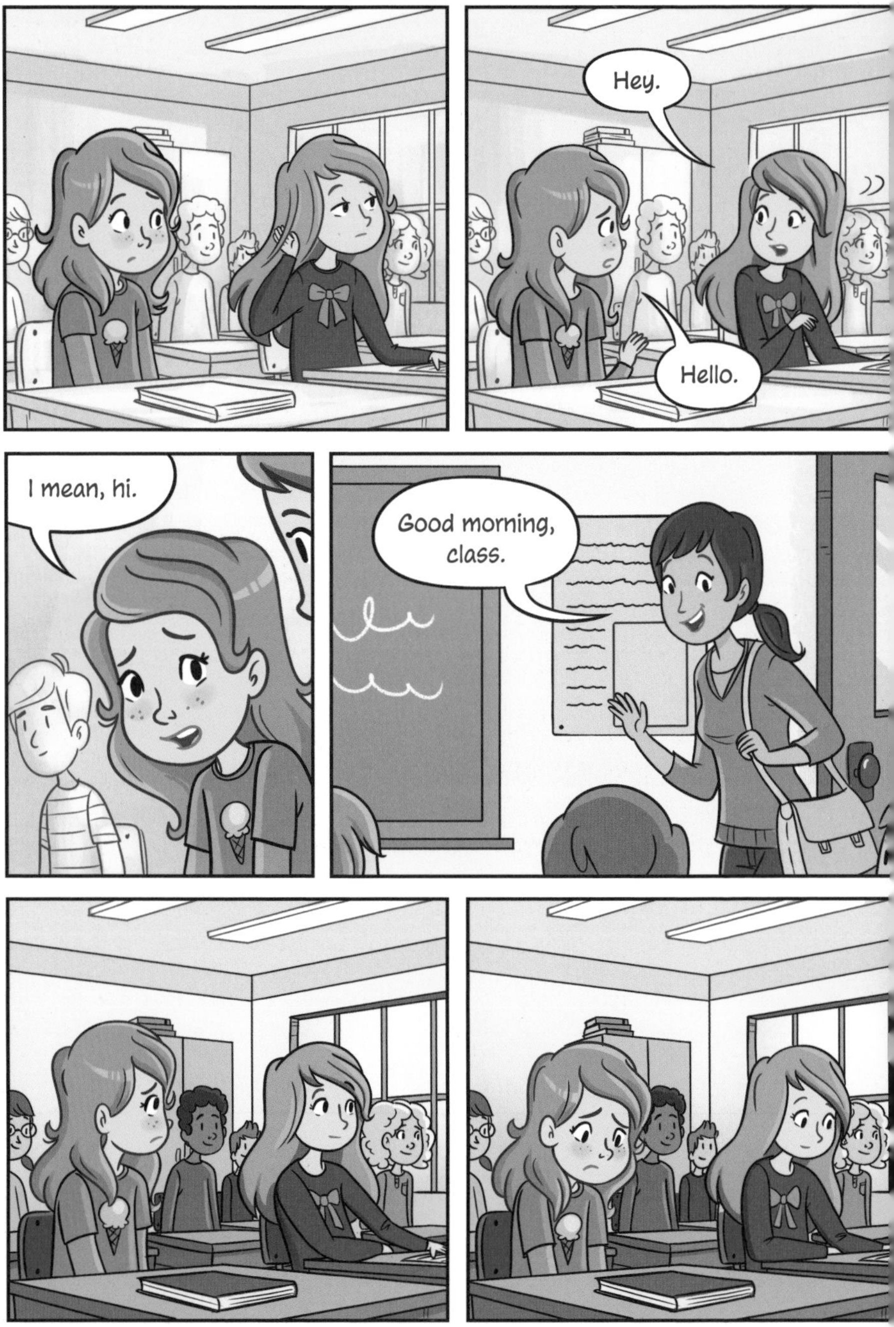
Hey.
Hello.
I mean, hi.
Good morning, class.

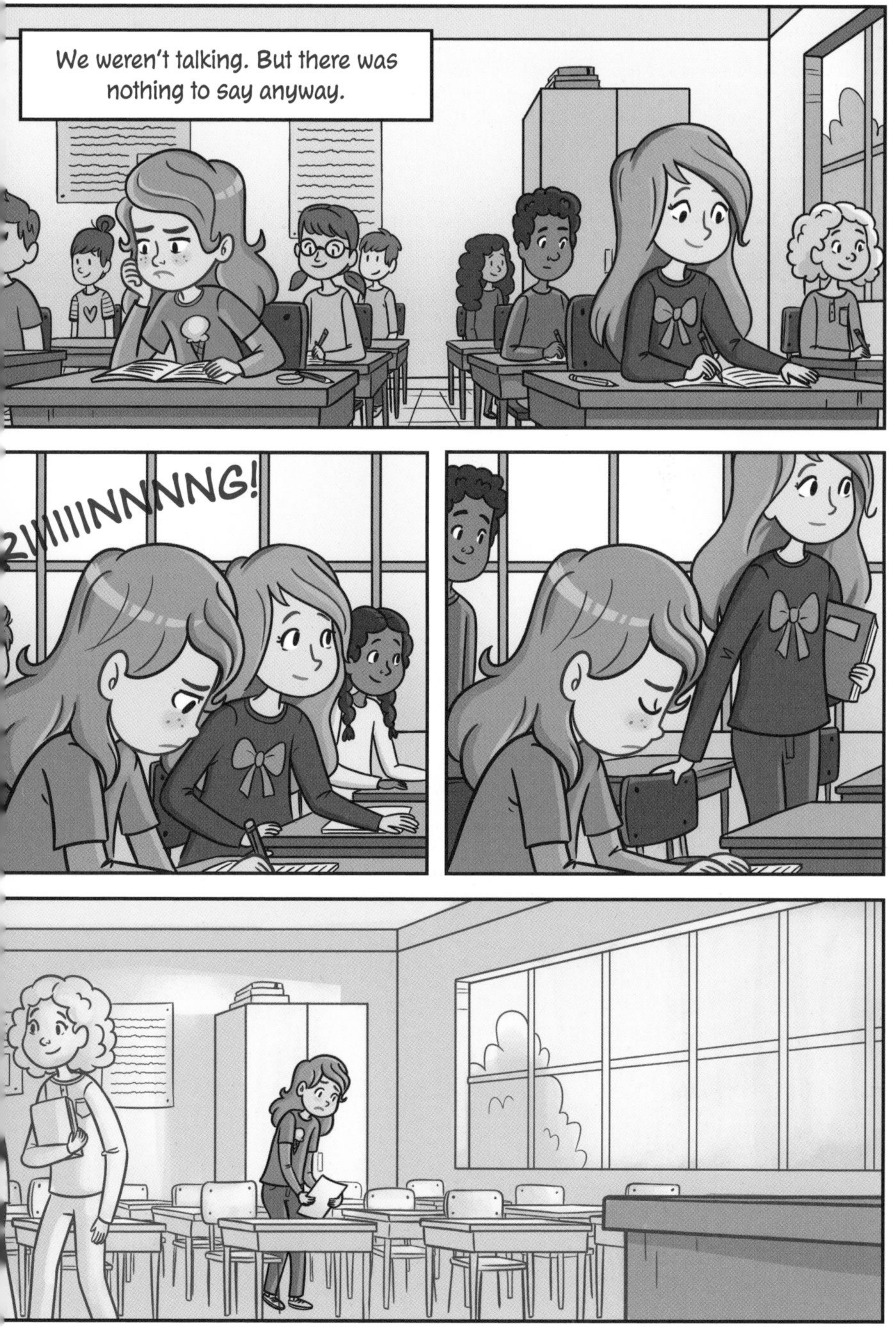
We weren't talking. But there was nothing to say anyway.
RIIIINNNNG!

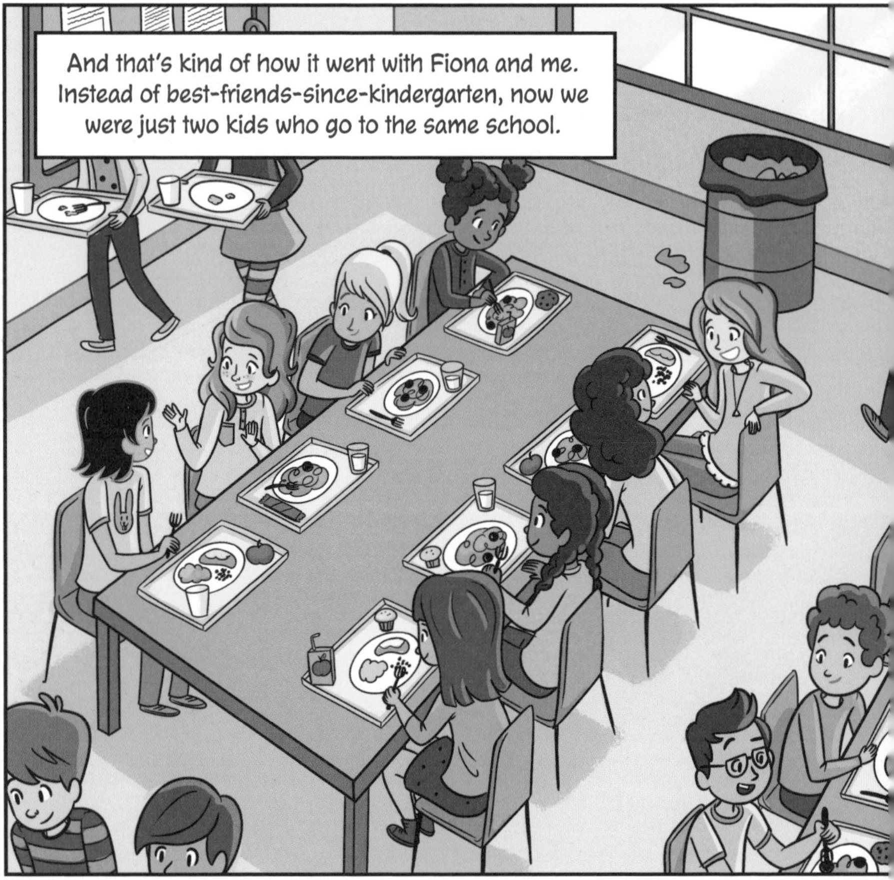
And that's kind of how it went with Fiona and me. Instead of best-friends-since-kindergarten, now we were just two kids who go to the same school.

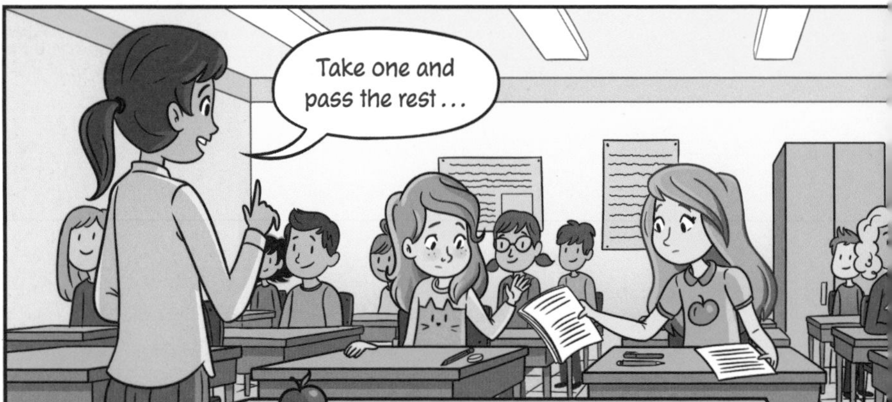
Take one and pass the rest . . .

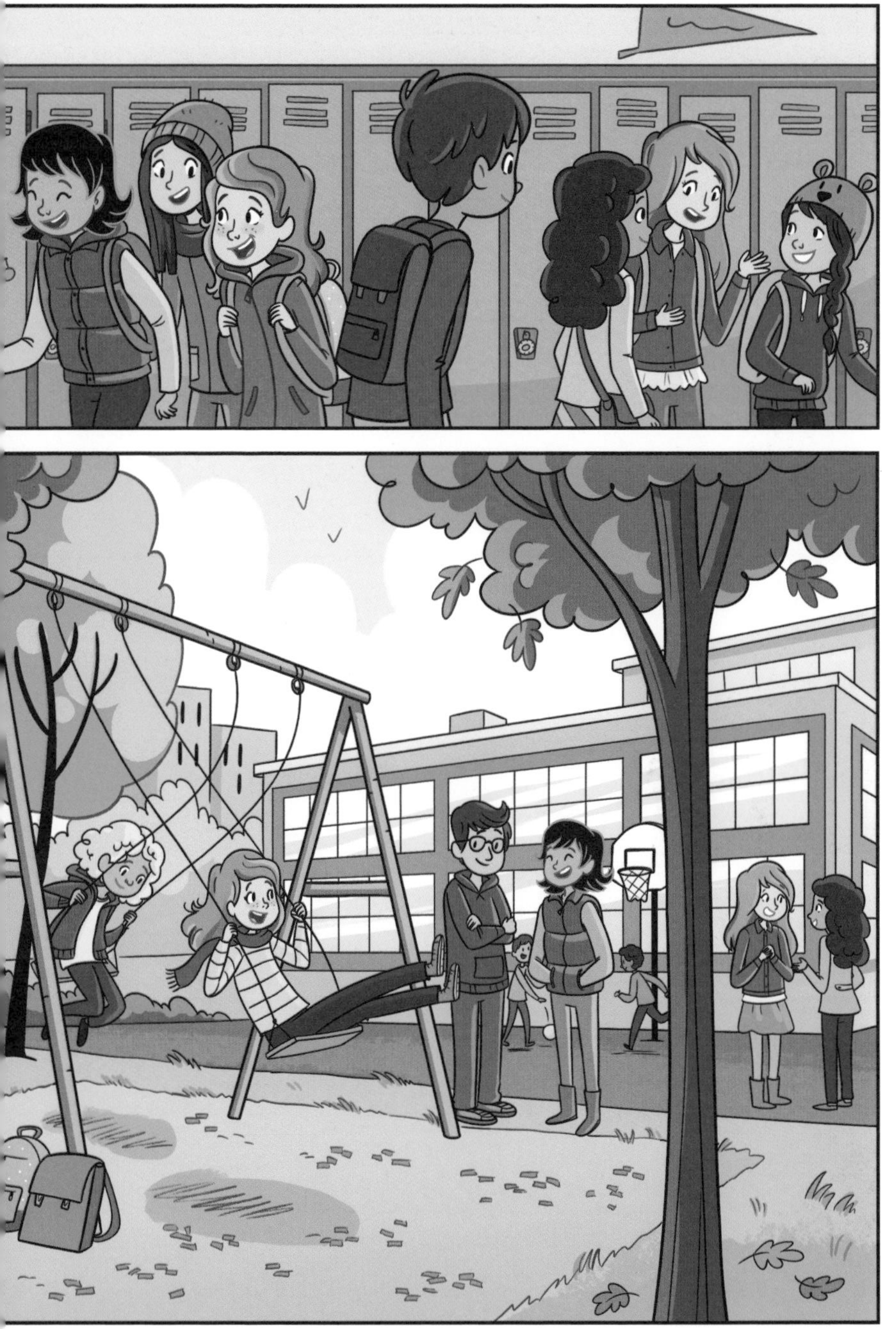

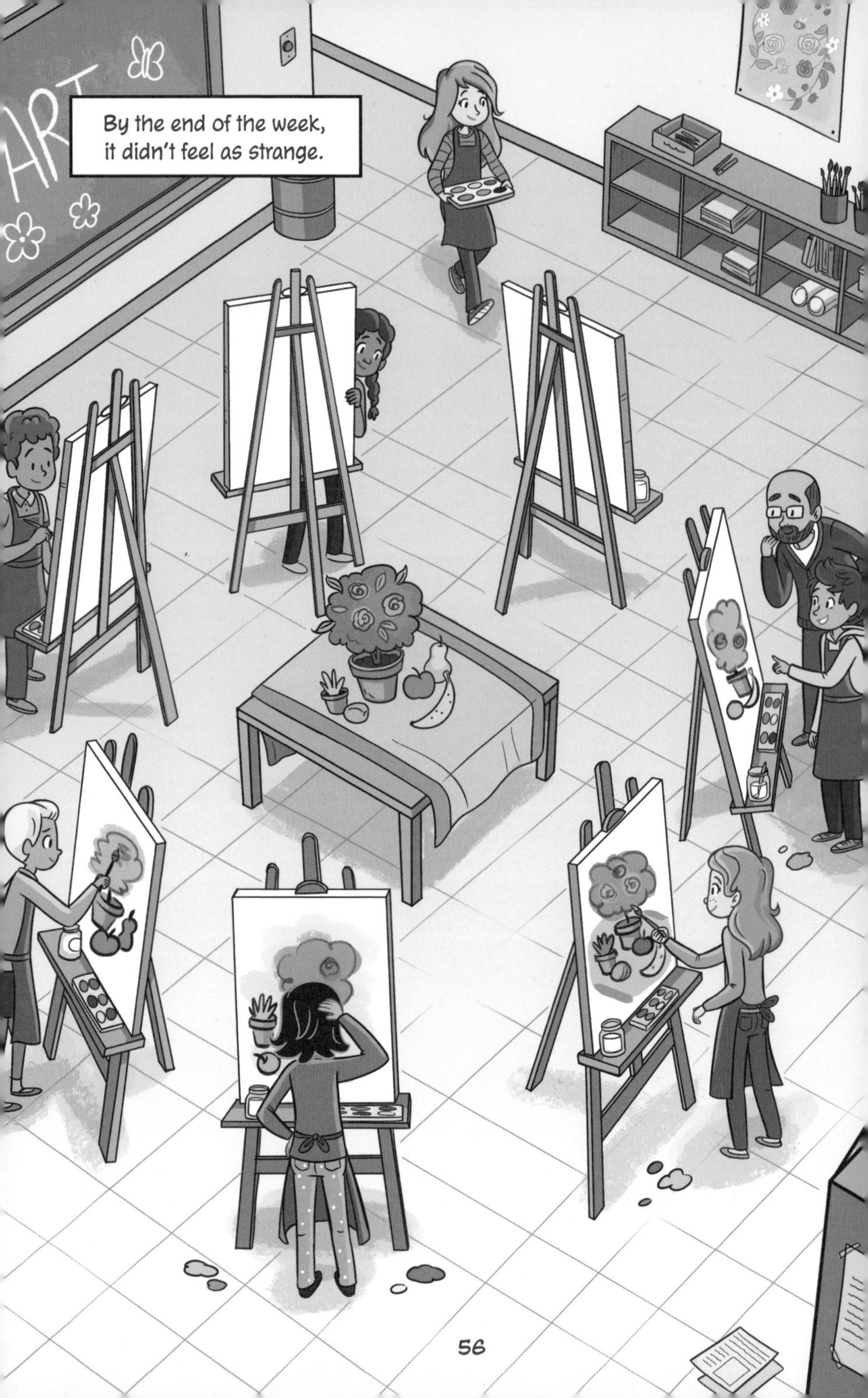
ART
By the end of the week, it didn't feel as strange.

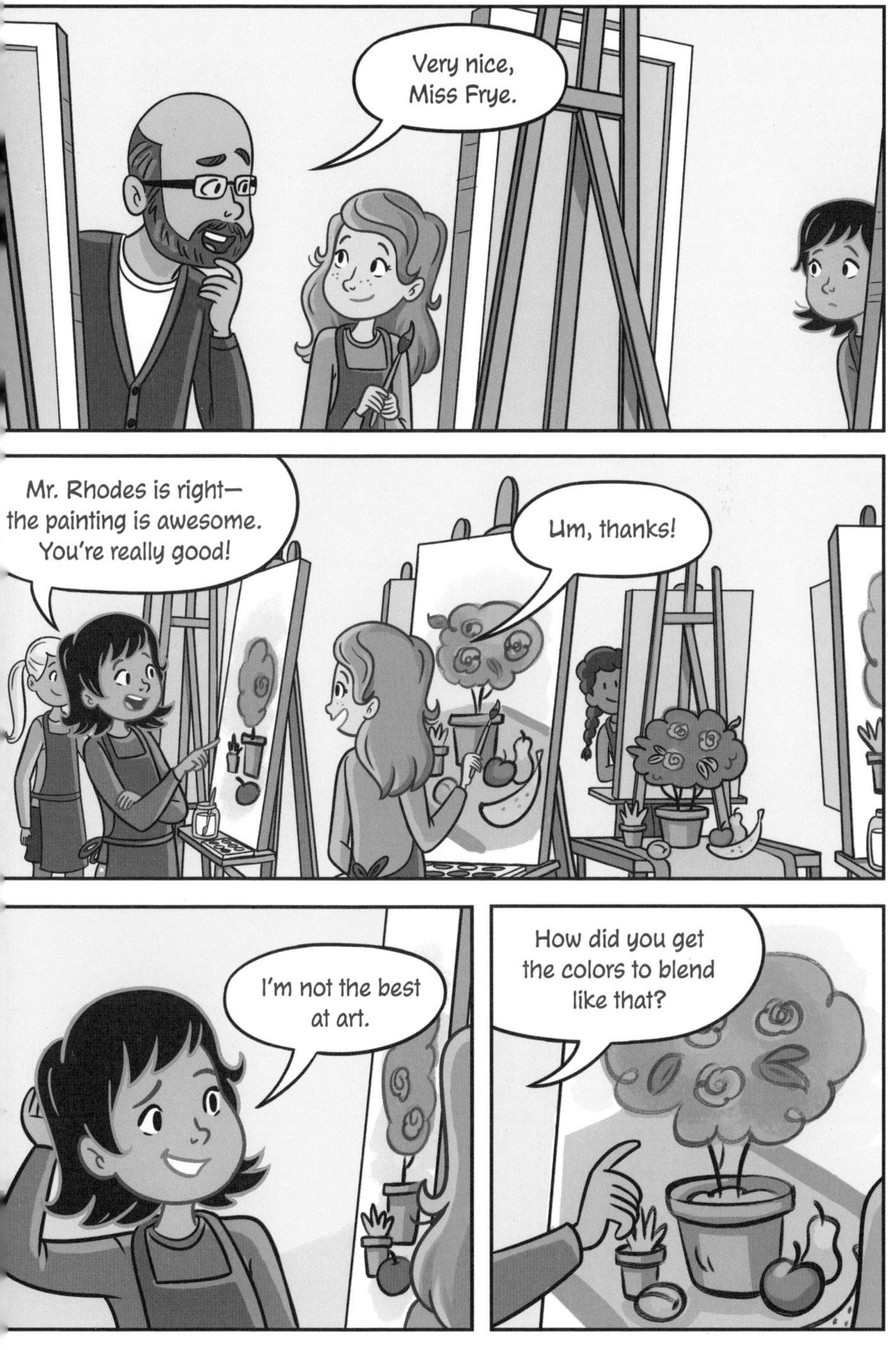
Very nice, Miss Frye.
Mr. Rhodes is right—the painting is awesome. You're really good!
Um, thanks!
I'm not the best at art.
How did you get the colors to blend like that?

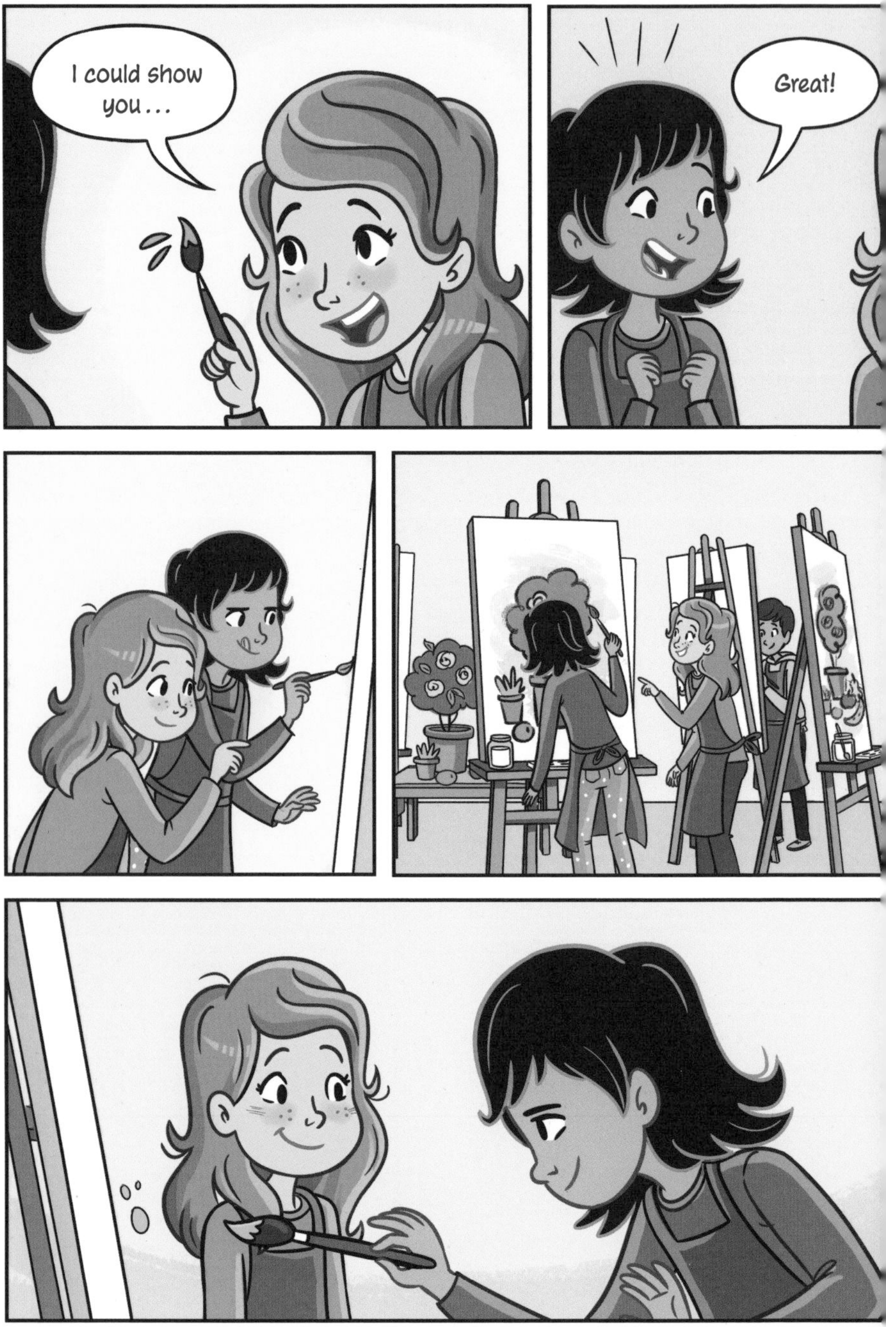
I could show you...
Great!

Today is the fourth Friday in a row that Fiona hasn't come over.

It's kinda strange. She's been over pretty much every Friday since her mom started her makeup business two years ago.

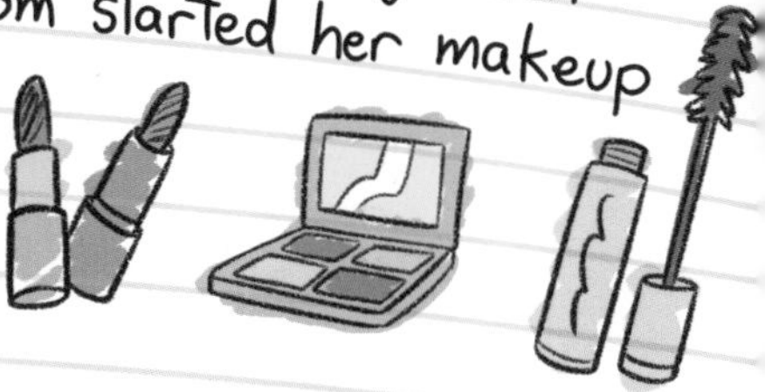

It's also kinda... nice?

I don't mean that to be mean. Having her over was fun. But now if I want to not do anything after school but lay on my bed with my head hanging off the side and look at all the junk stuffed underneath, I can do that without anyone being like,

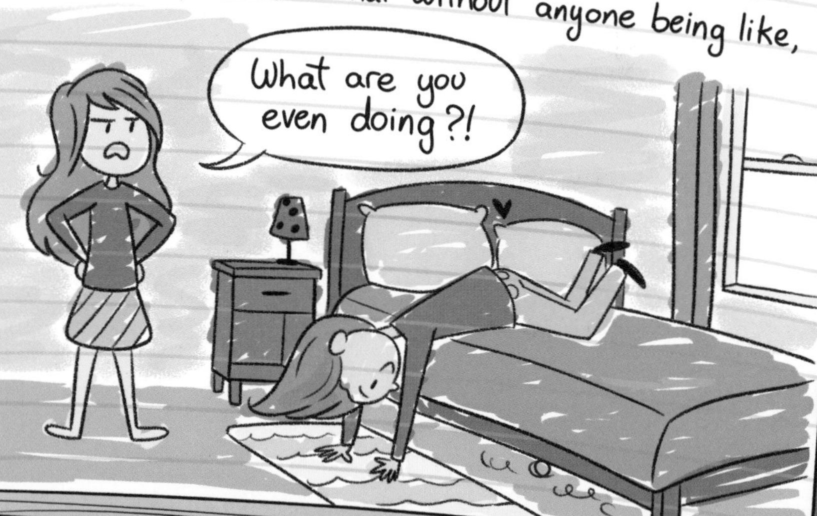
What are you even doing?!

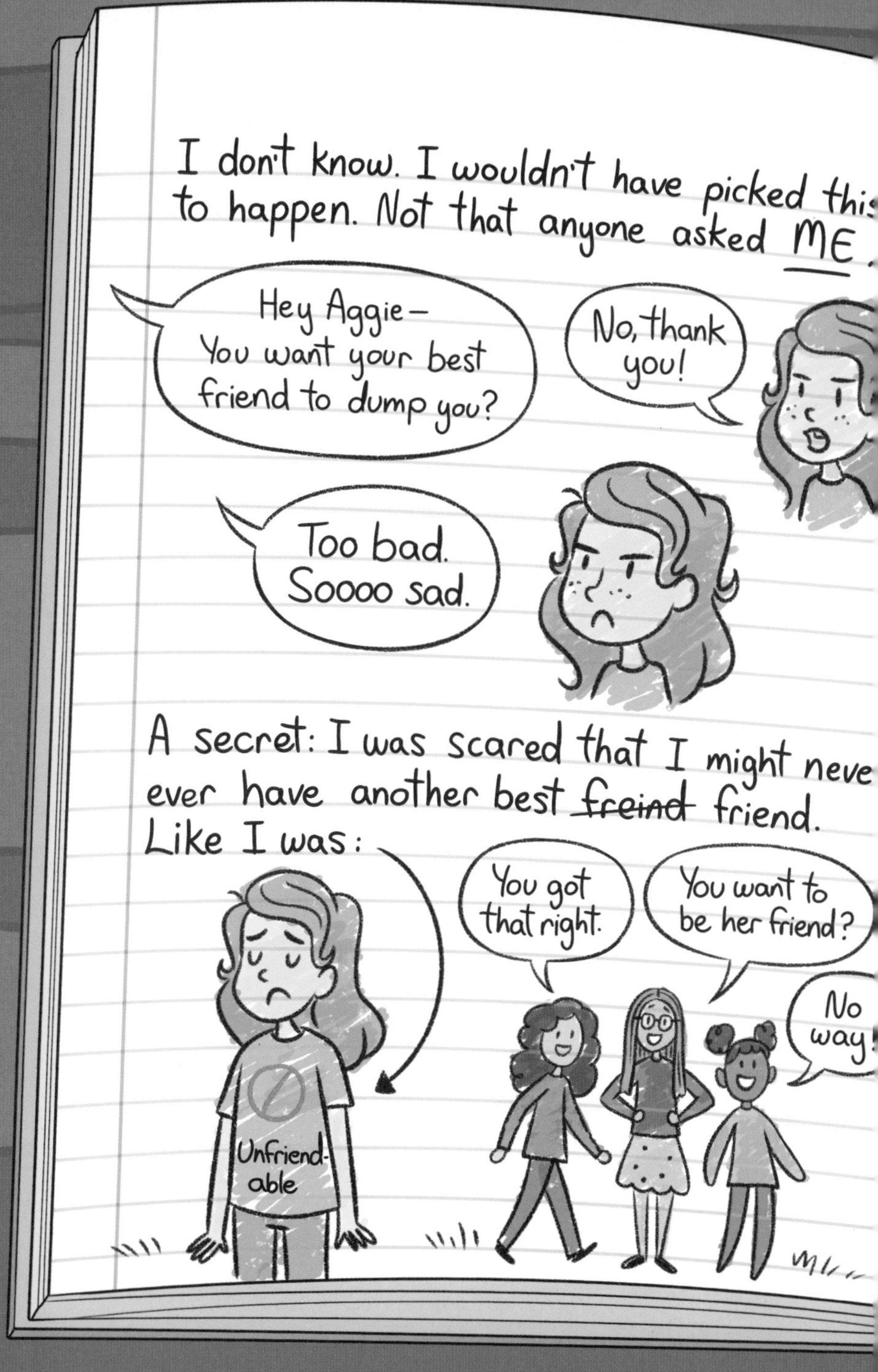
I don't know. I wouldn't have picked thi
to happen. Not that anyone asked ME.
Hey Aggie— You want your best friend to dump you?
No, thank you!
Too bad. Soooo sad.
A secret: I was scared that I might neve
ever have another best ~~freind~~ friend.
Like I was:
Unfriend-able
You got that right.
You want to be her friend?
No way!

I still feel unfriendable sometimes. Like everyone knows that Fiona and I aren't friends anymore and it's because of ME.

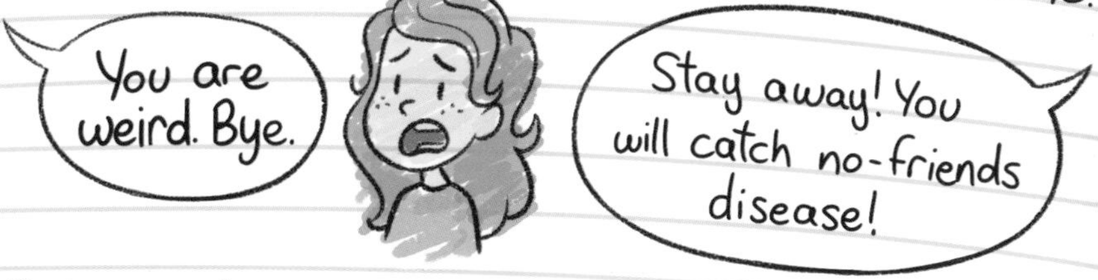
You are weird. Bye.
Stay away! You will catch no-friends disease!

But I don't actually think that there's anything wrong with me. I can still have friends, right?

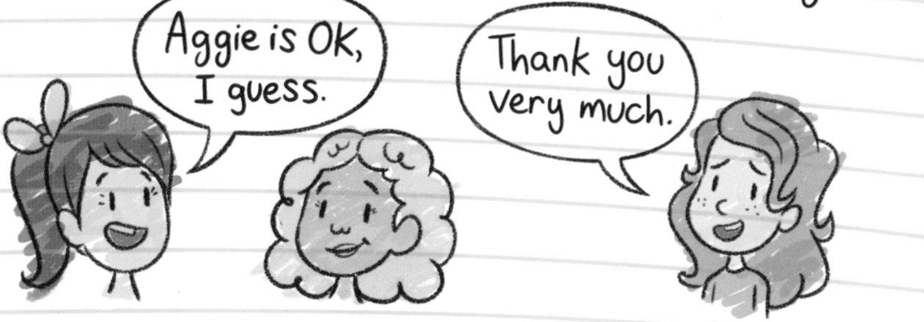
Aggie is OK, I guess.
Thank you very much.

Dad always says that if you want to stop worrying, you should just DO something.

So I'm gonna go see if we can bake some cookies. Because COOKiEEES

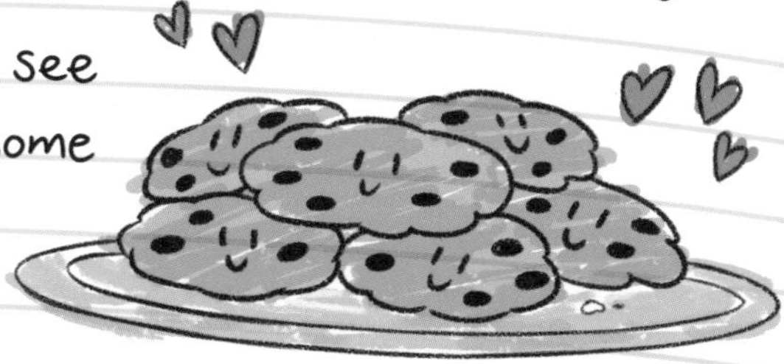

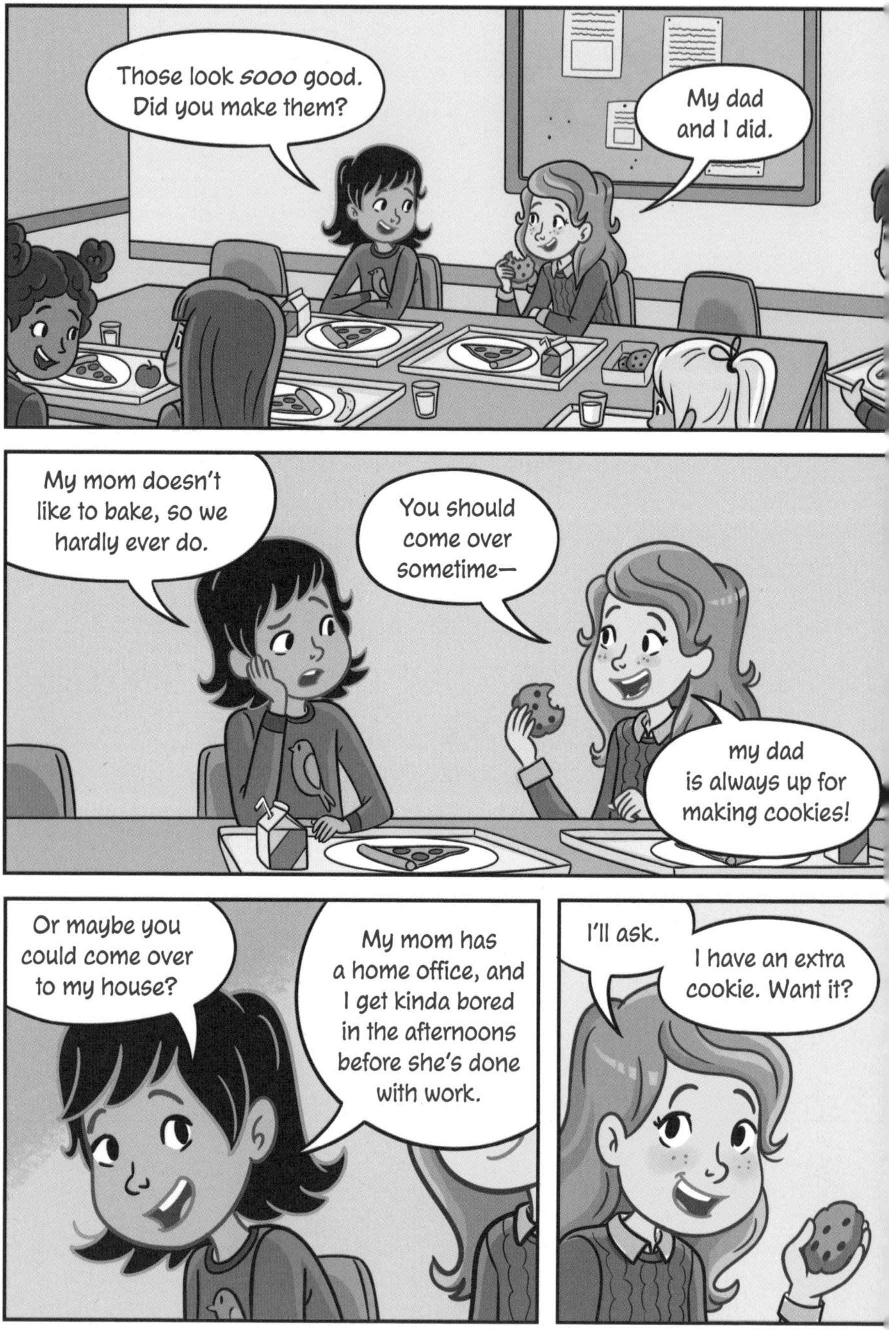
Those look *sooo* good. Did you make them?
My dad and I did.
My mom doesn't like to bake, so we hardly ever do.
You should come over sometime—
my dad is always up for making cookies!
Or maybe you could come over to my house?
My mom has a home office, and I get kinda bored in the afternoons before she's done with work.
I'll ask.
I have an extra cookie. Want it?

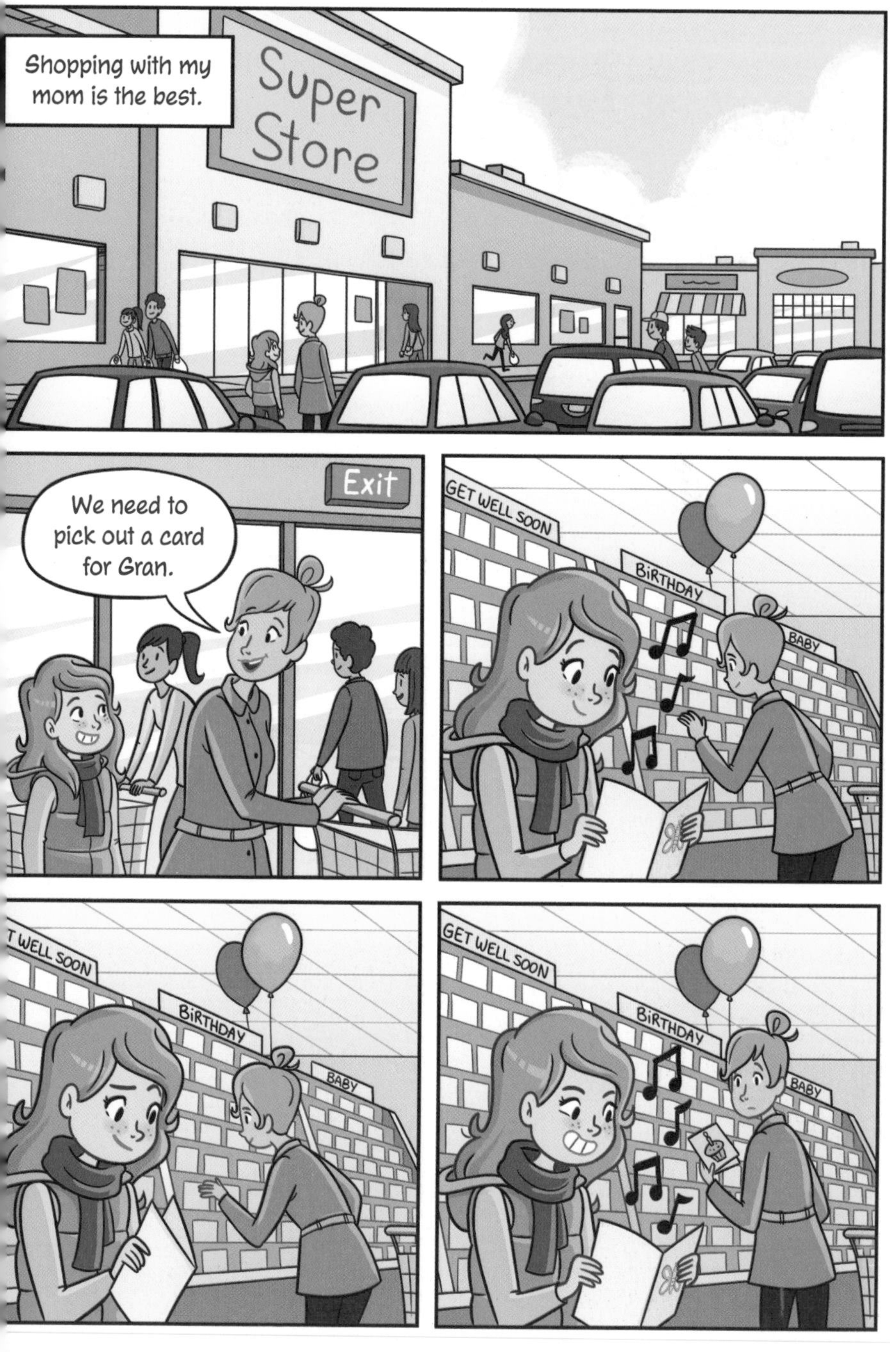

Shopping with my mom is the best.
Super Store
Exit
We need to pick out a card for Gran.
GET WELL SOON
BIRTHDAY
BABY
T WELL SOON
BIRTHDAY
BABY
GET WELL SOON
BIRTHDAY
BABY

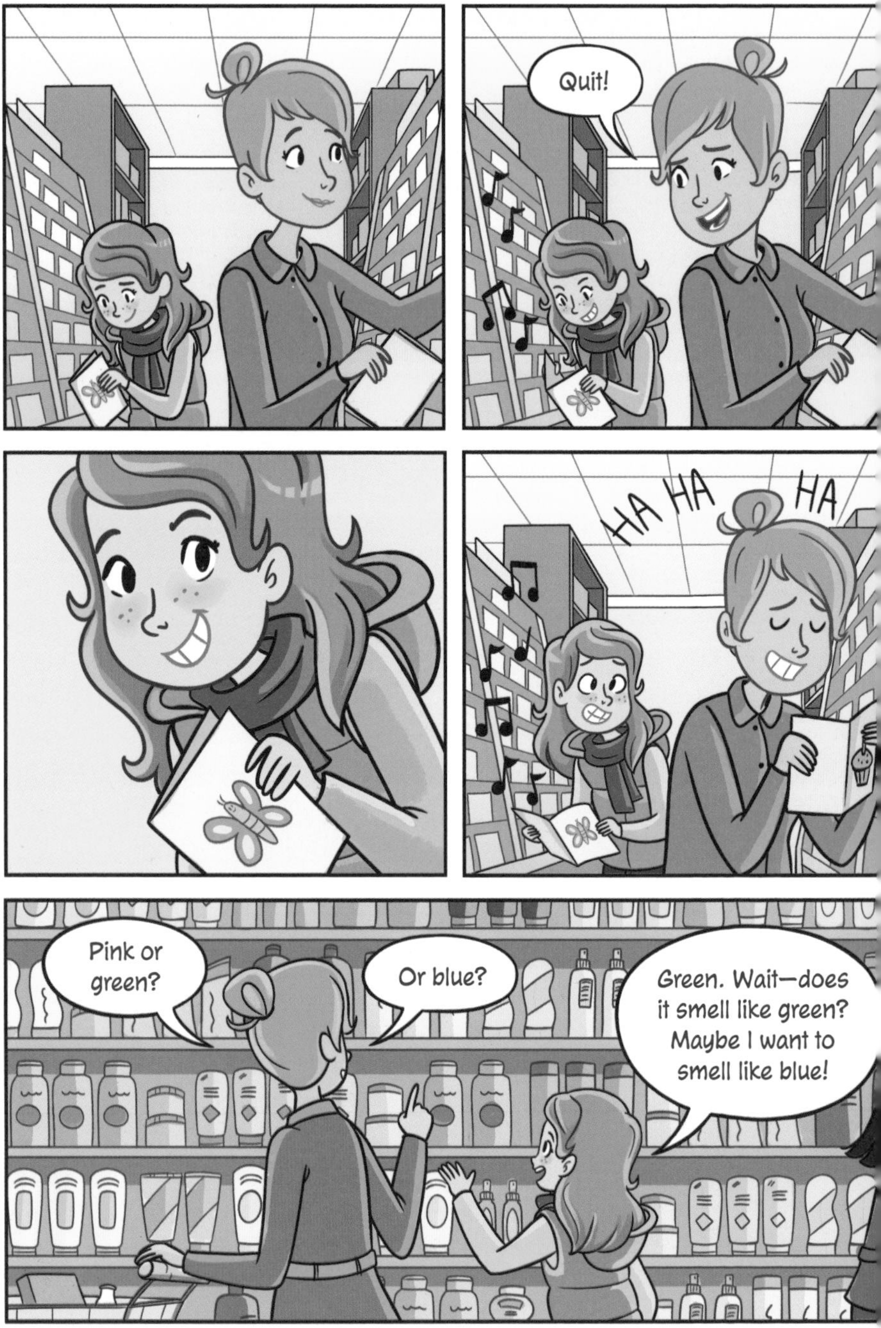
Quit!
HA HA
HA
Pink or green?
Or blue?
Green. Wait—does it smell like green? Maybe I want to smell like blue!

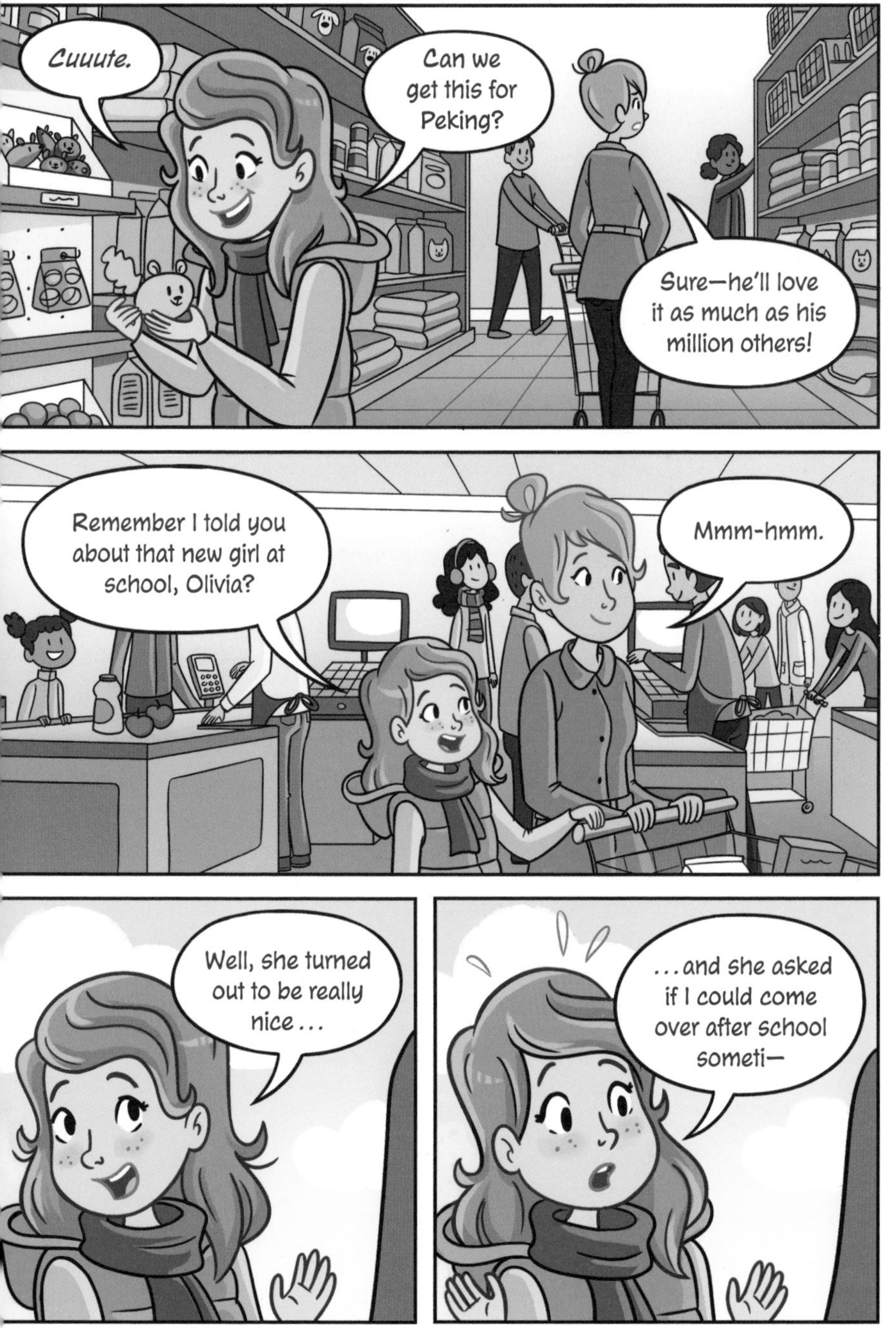
Cuuute.
Can we get this for Peking?
Sure—he'll love it as much as his million others!
Remember I told you about that new girl at school, Olivia?
Mmm-hmm.
Well, she turned out to be really nice...
...and she asked if I could come over after school someti—

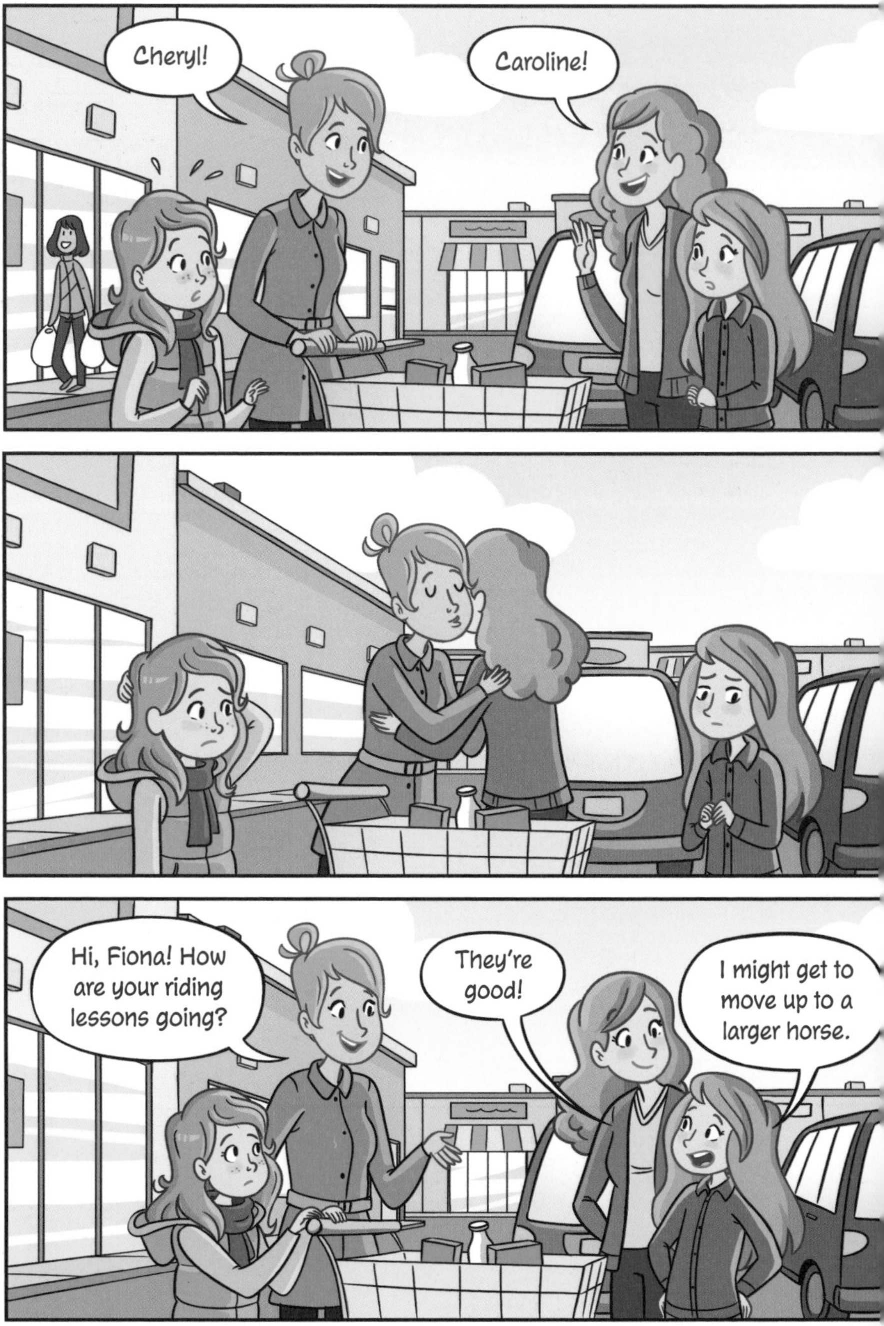
Cheryl!
Caroline!
Hi, Fiona! How are your riding lessons going?
They're good!
I might get to move up to a larger horse.

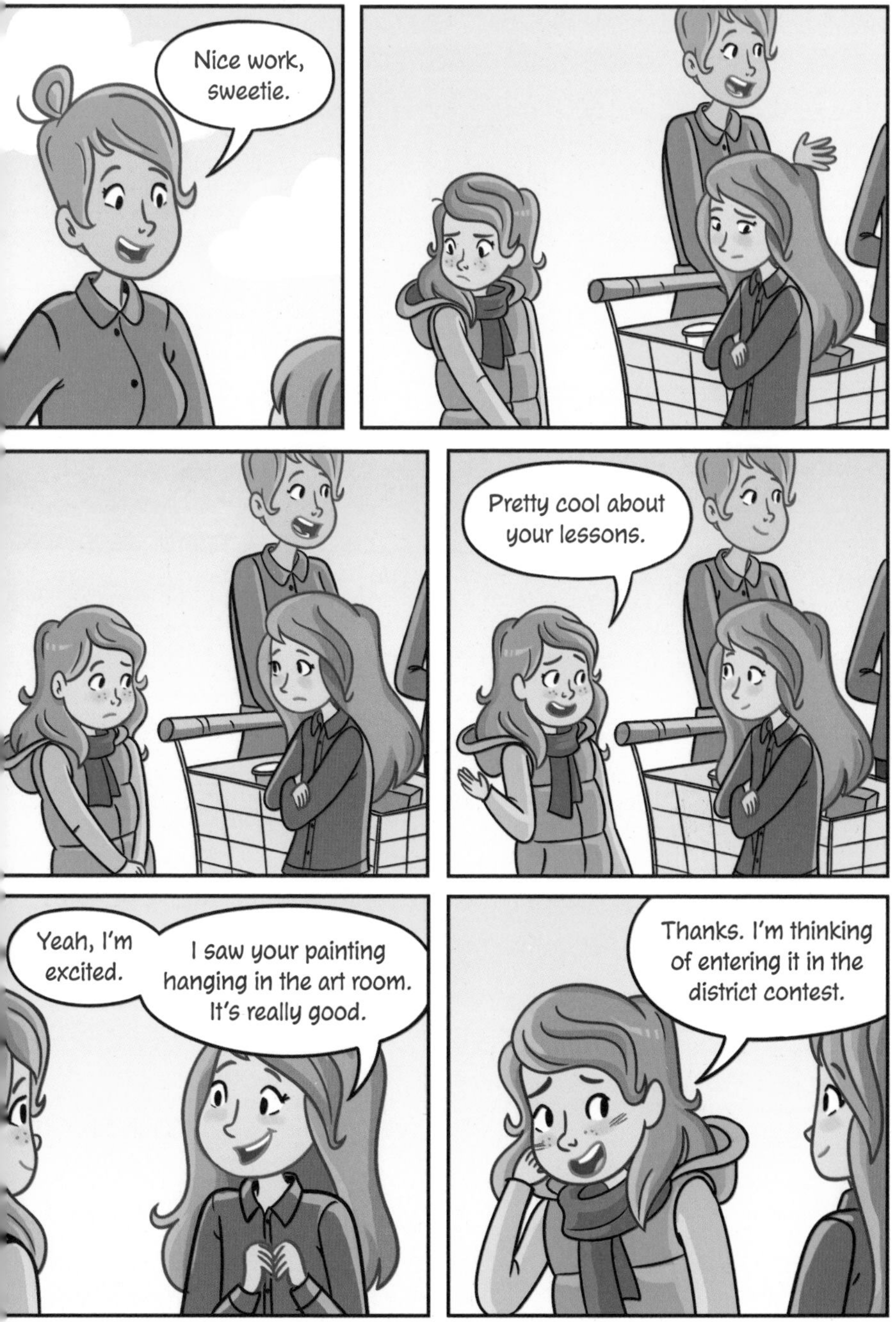

Nice work, sweetie.
Pretty cool about your lessons.
Yeah, I'm excited.
I saw your painting hanging in the art room. It's really good.
Thanks. I'm thinking of entering it in the district contest.

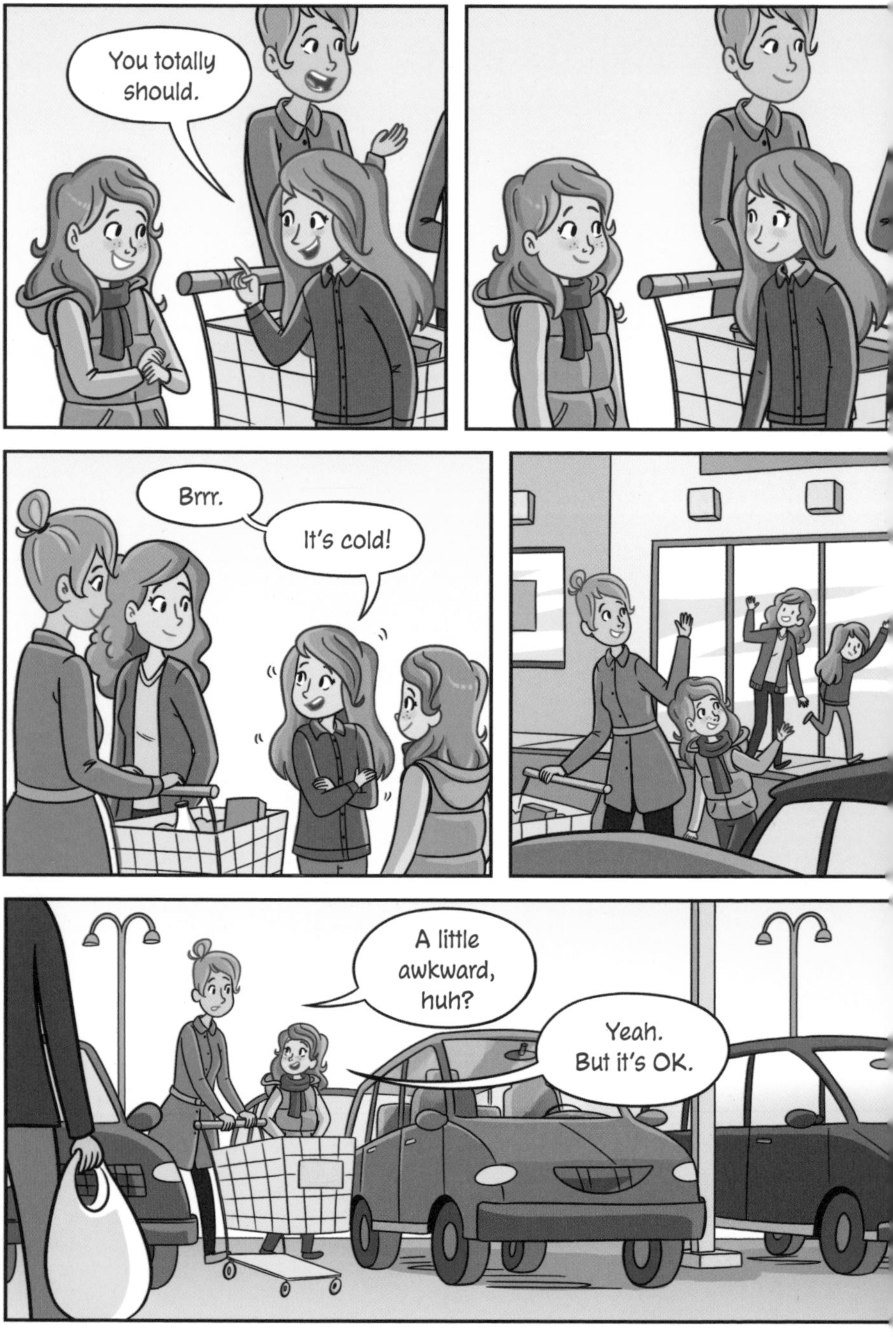
You totally should.
Brrr.
It's cold!
A little awkward, huh?
Yeah. But it's OK.

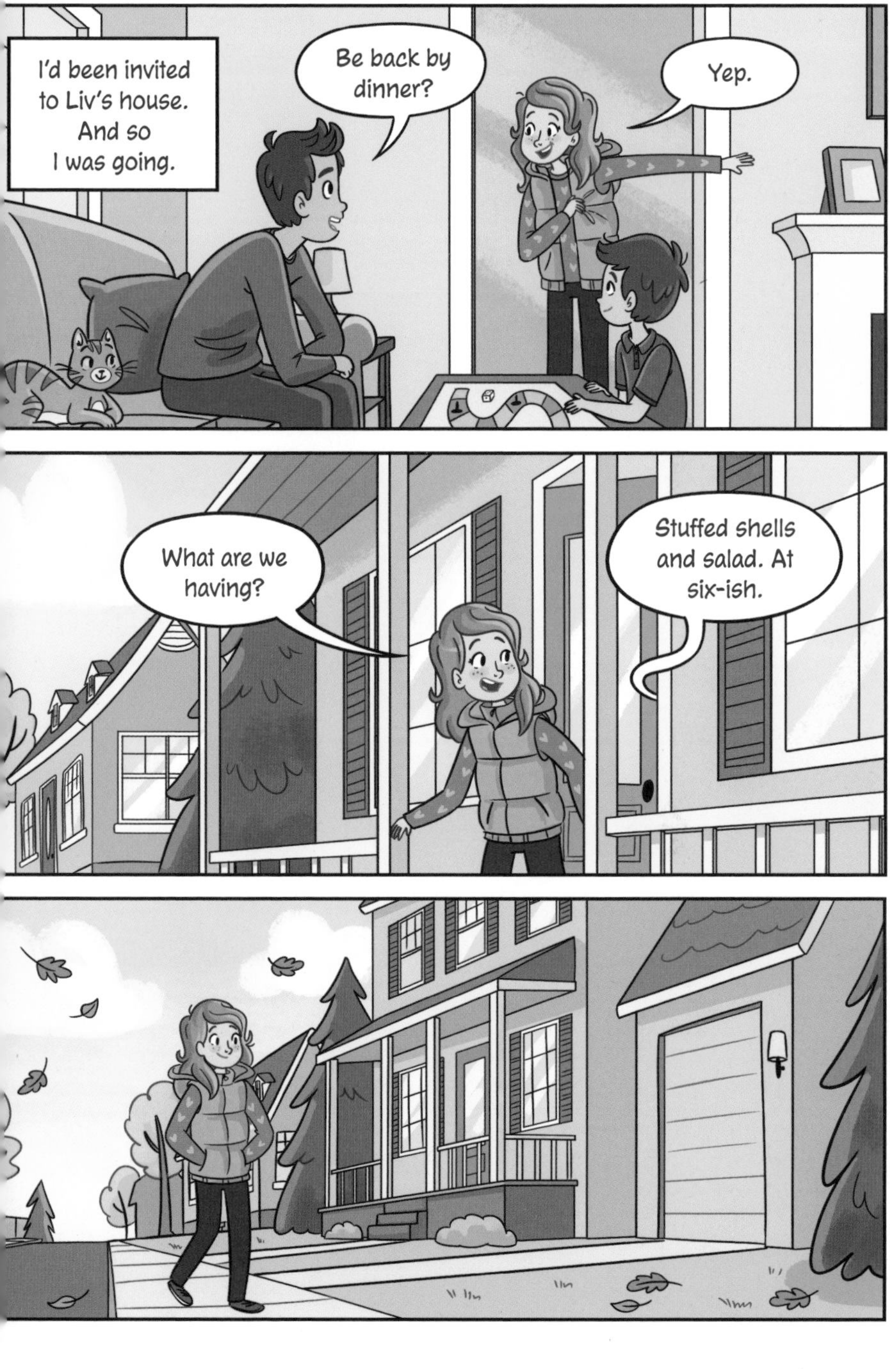
I'd been invited
to Liv's house.
And so
I was going.
Be back by dinner?
Yep.
What are we having?
Stuffed shells and salad. At six-ish.

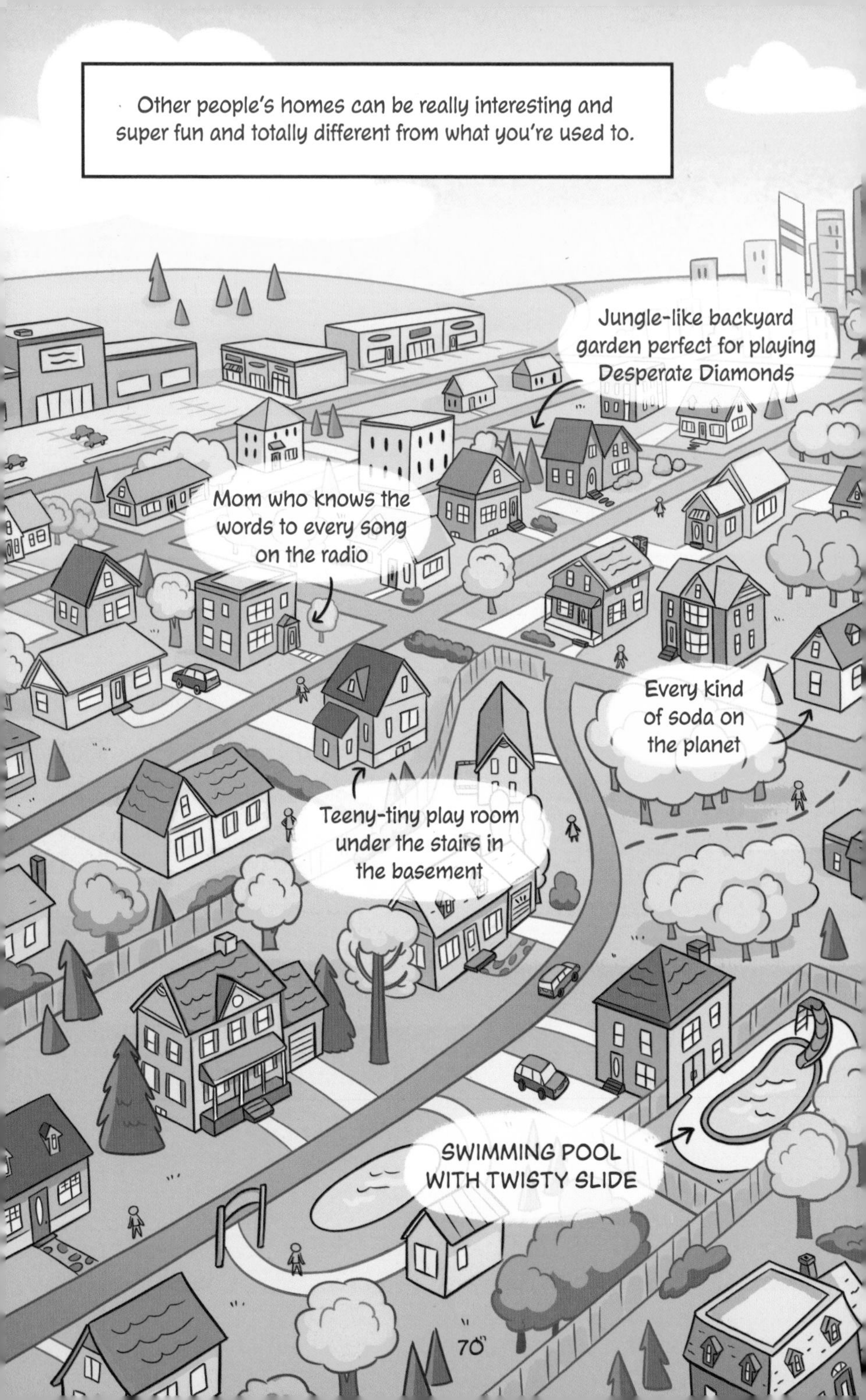
Other people's homes can be really interesting and super fun and totally different from what you're used to.
Jungle-like backyard garden perfect for playing Desperate Diamonds
Mom who knows the words to every song on the radio
Every kind of soda on the planet
Teeny-tiny play room under the stairs in the basement
SWIMMING POOL WITH TWISTY SLIDE

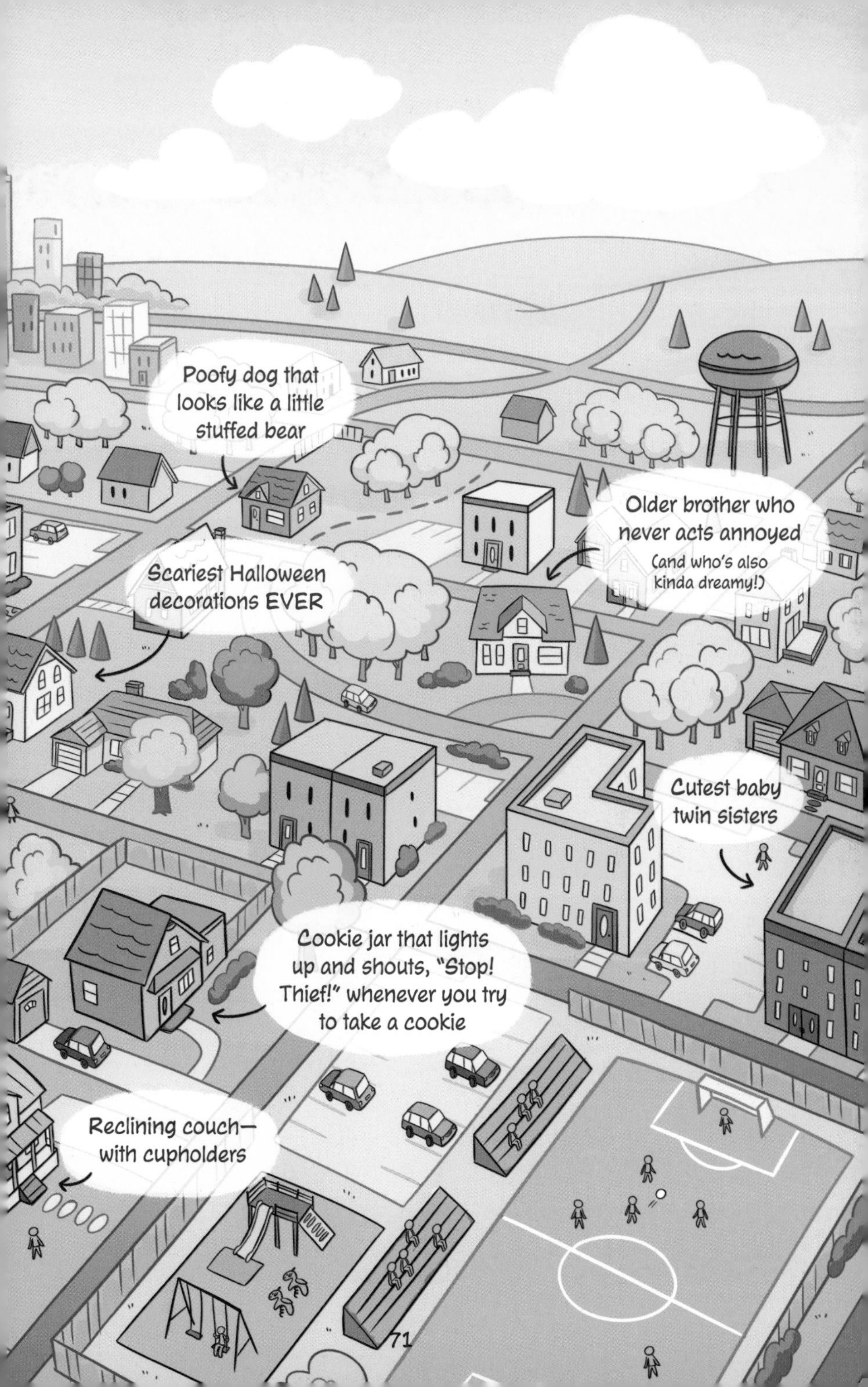
Poofy dog that looks like a little stuffed bear
Older brother who never acts annoyed
(and who's also kinda dreamy!)
Scariest Halloween decorations EVER
Cutest baby twin sisters
Cookie jar that lights up and shouts, "Stop! Thief!" whenever you try to take a cookie
Reclining couch—with cupholders

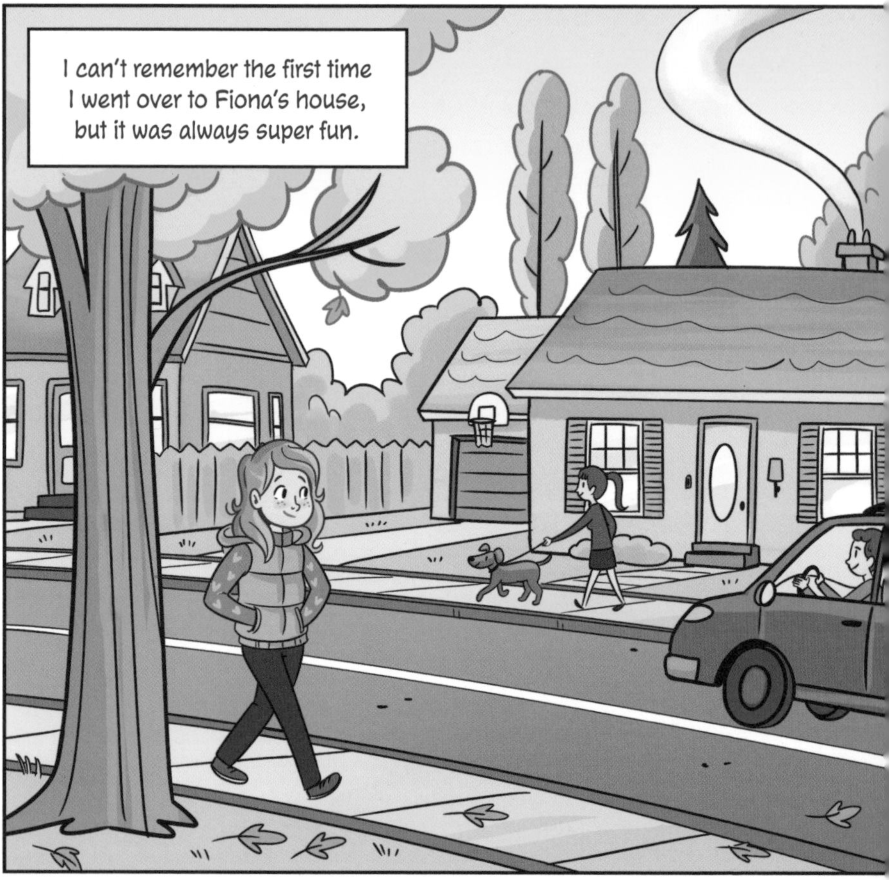
I can't remember the first time I went over to Fiona's house, but it was always super fun.

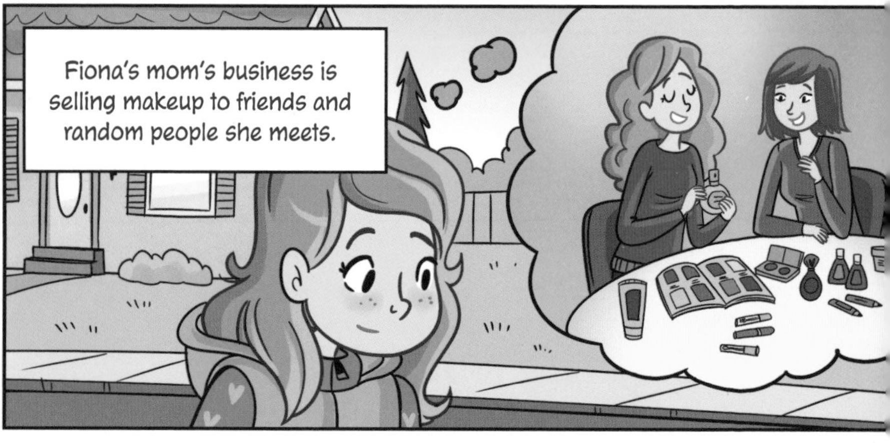
Fiona's mom's business is selling makeup to friends and random people she meets.

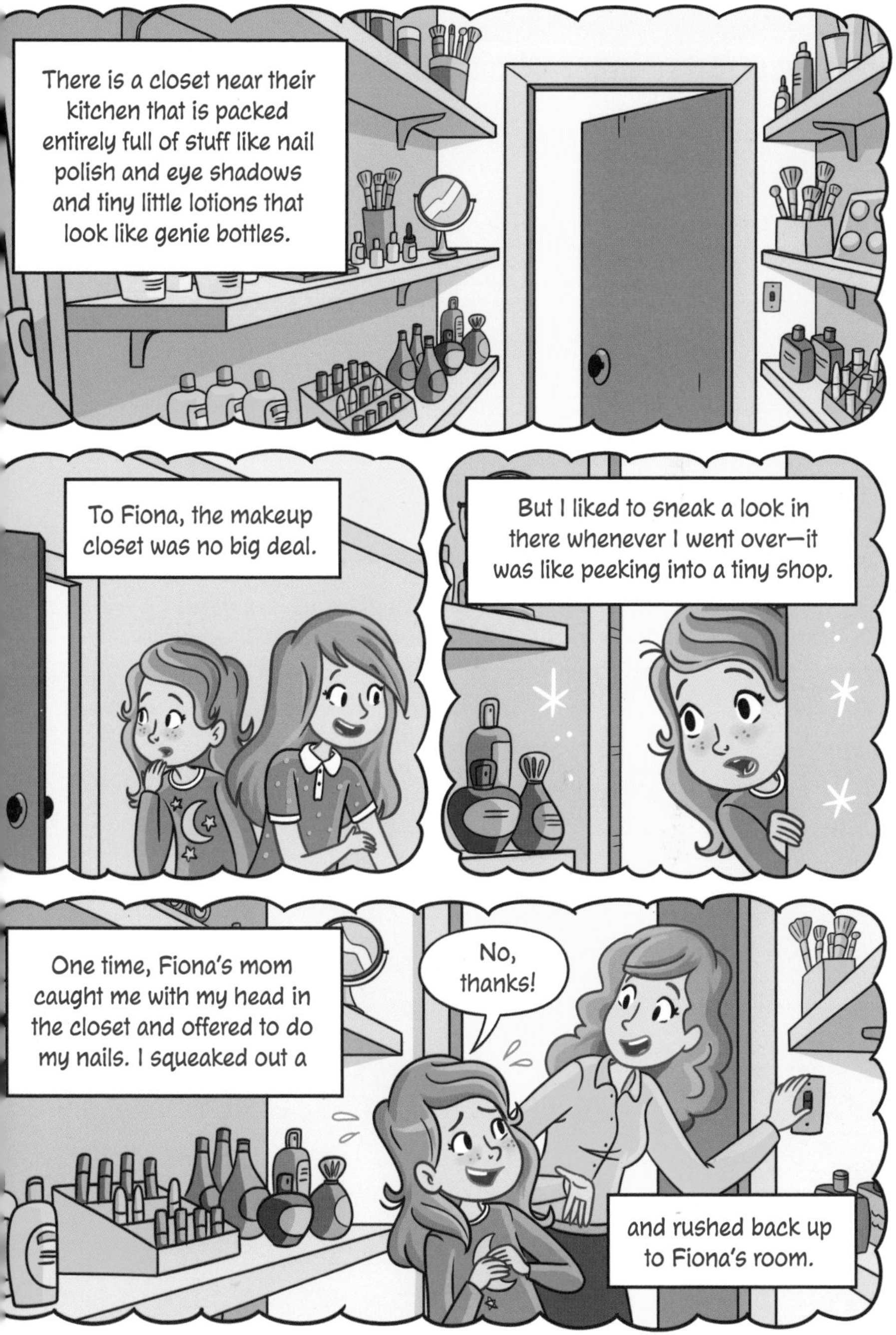
There is a closet near their kitchen that is packed entirely full of stuff like nail polish and eye shadows and tiny little lotions that look like genie bottles.
To Fiona, the makeup closet was no big deal.
But I liked to sneak a look in there whenever I went over—it was like peeking into a tiny shop.
One time, Fiona's mom caught me with my head in the closet and offered to do my nails. I squeaked out a
No, thanks!
and rushed back up to Fiona's room.

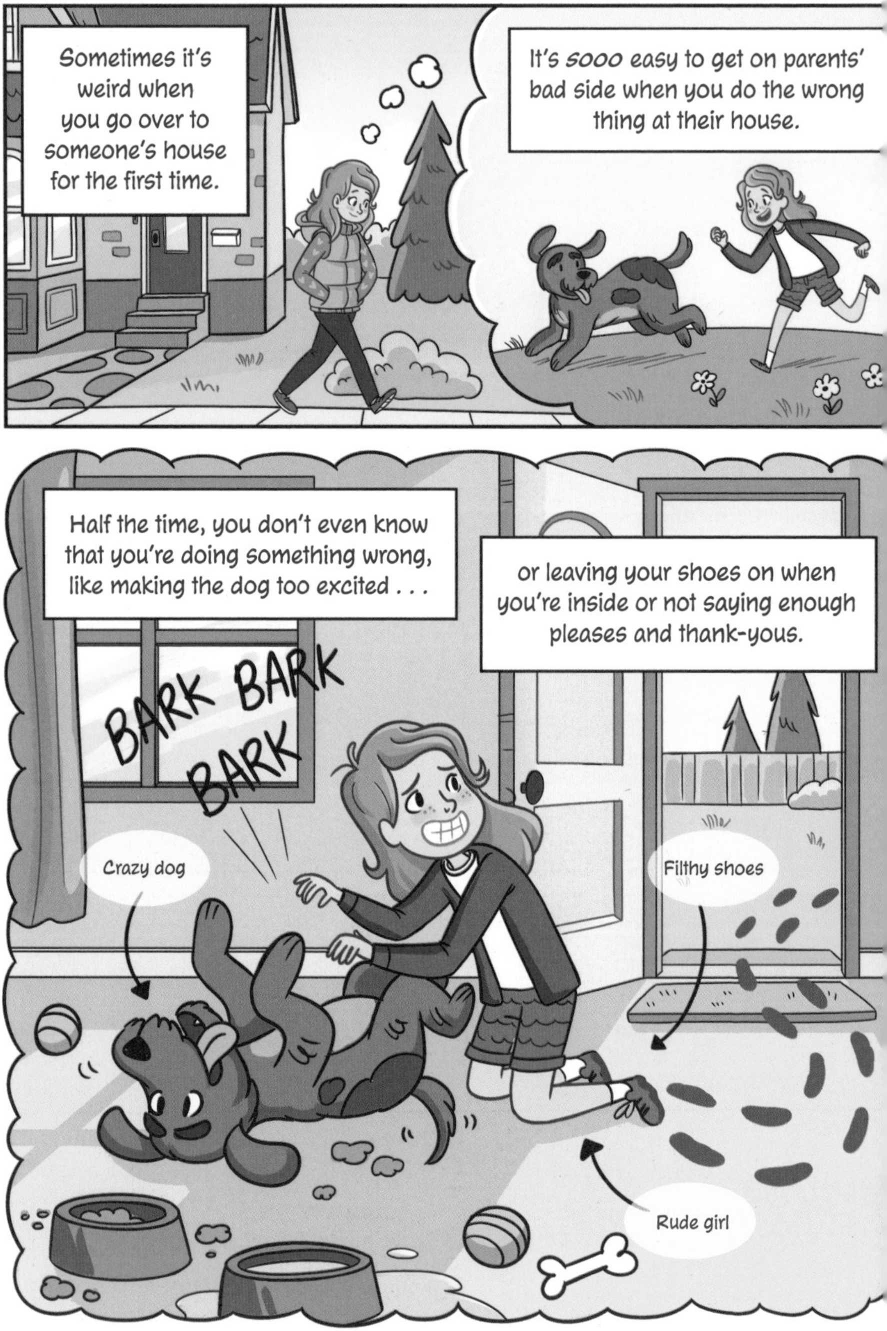
Sometimes it's weird when you go over to someone's house for the first time.
It's *sooo* easy to get on parents' bad side when you do the wrong thing at their house.
Half the time, you don't even know that you're doing something wrong, like making the dog too excited . . .
or leaving your shoes on when you're inside or not saying enough pleases and thank-yous.
BARK BARK BARK
Crazy dog
Filthy shoes
Rude girl

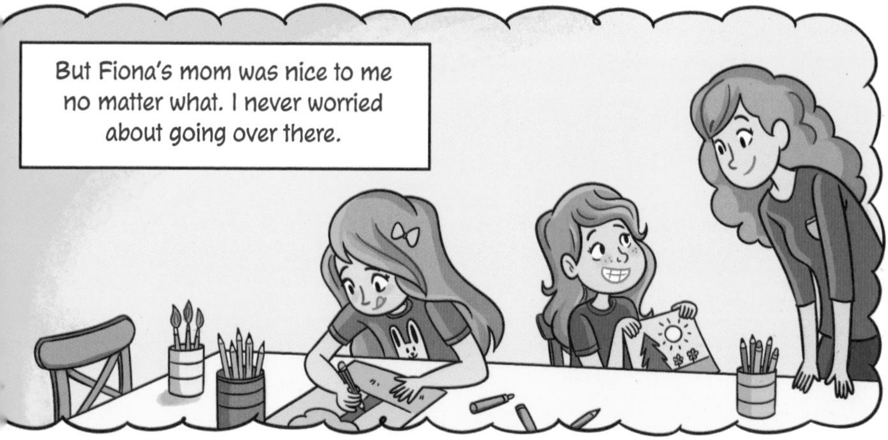
But Fiona's mom was nice to me no matter what. I never worried about going over there.

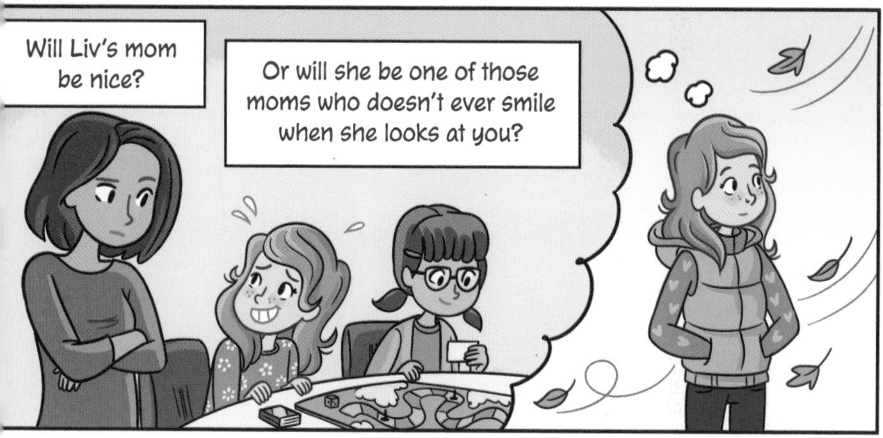
Will Liv's mom be nice?
Or will she be one of those moms who doesn't ever smile when she looks at you?

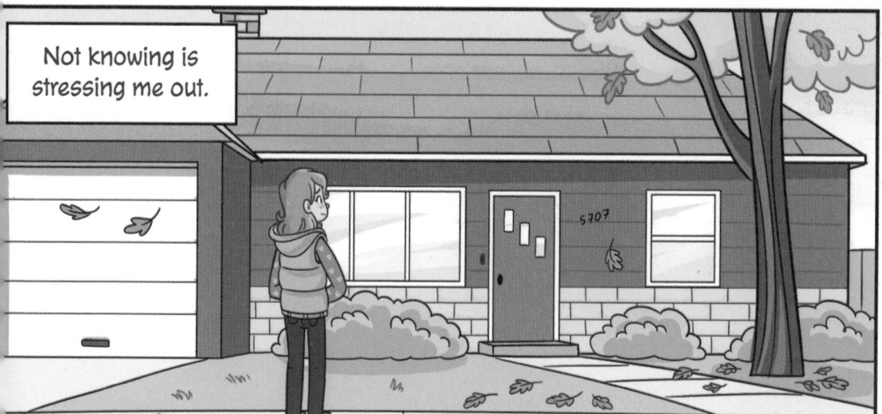
Not knowing is stressing me out.
5707

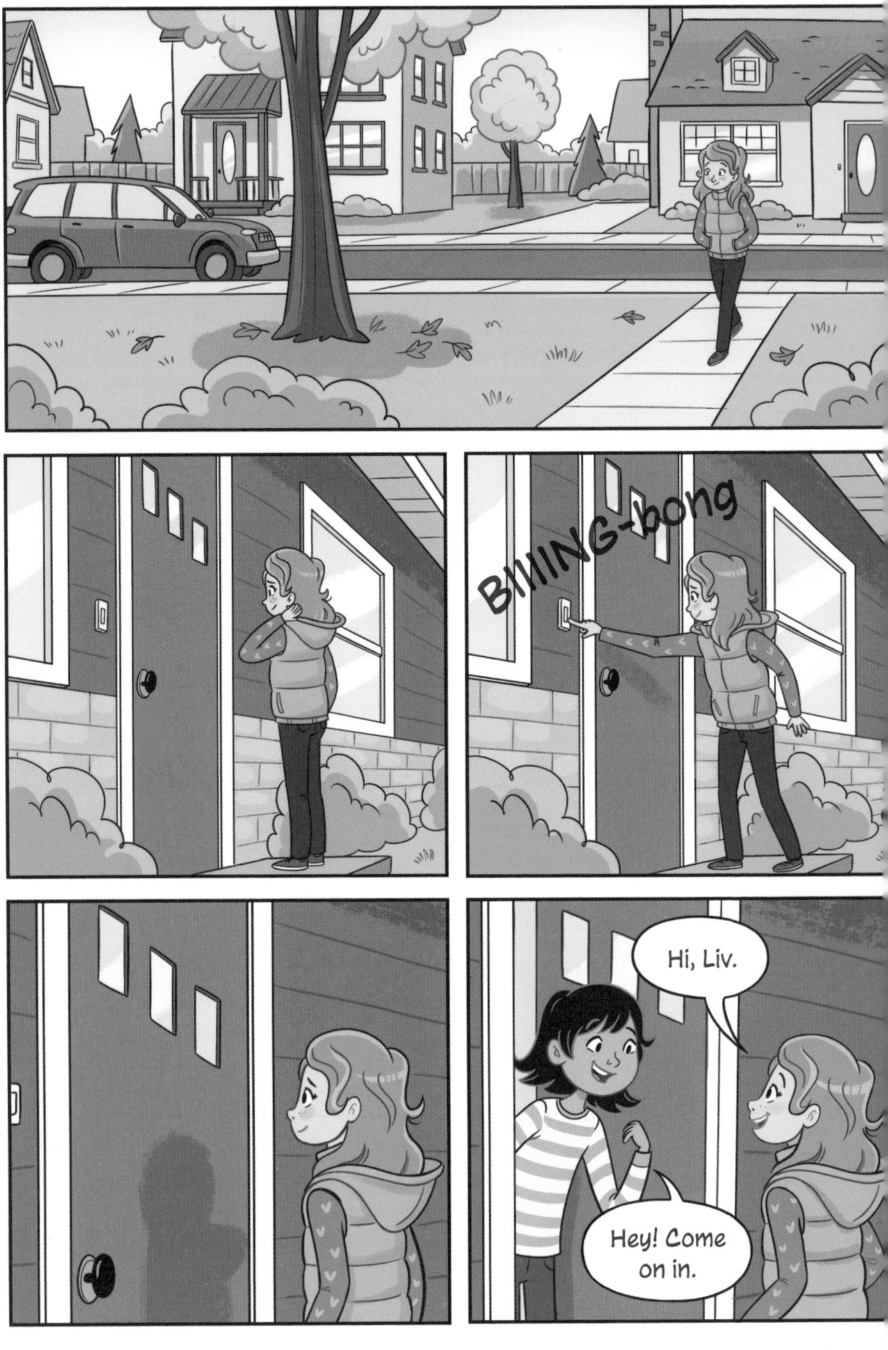
BIIIING-bong
Hi, Liv.
Hey! Come on in.

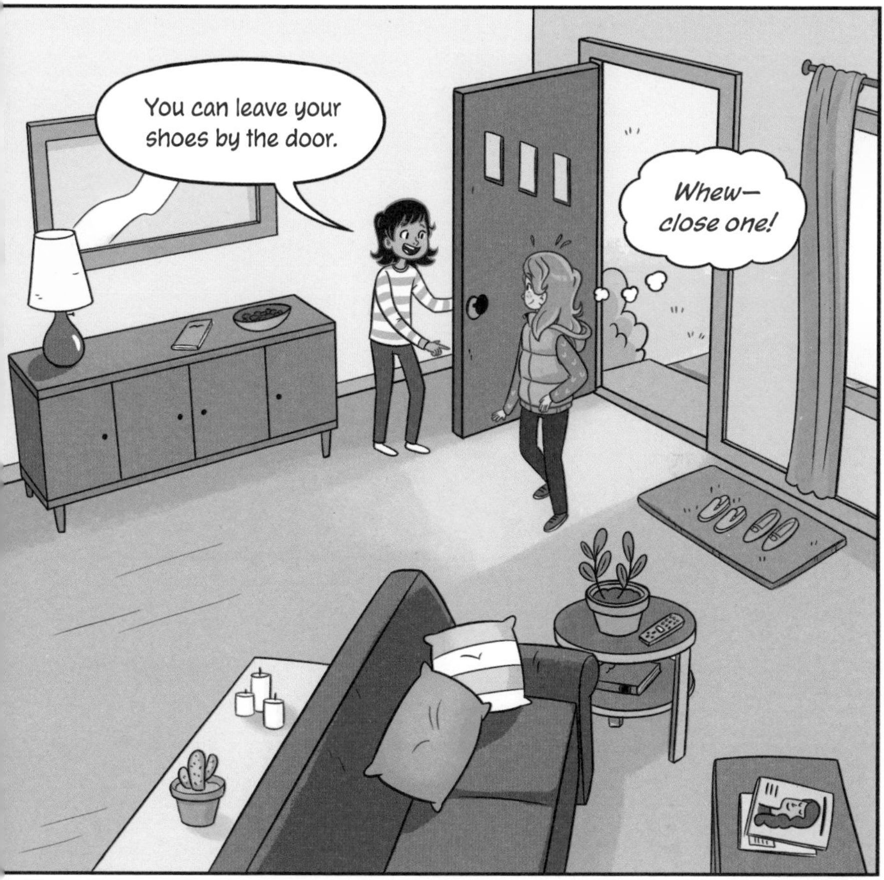
You can leave your shoes by the door.
Whew—close one!

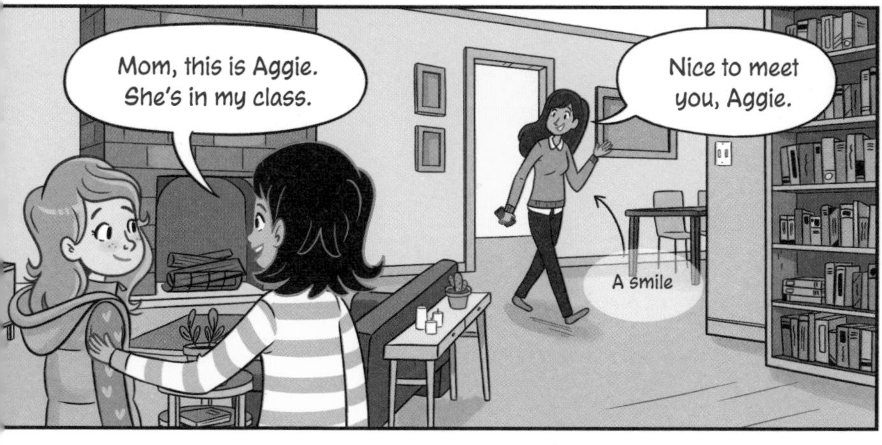
Mom, this is Aggie. She's in my class.
Nice to meet you, Aggie.
A smile

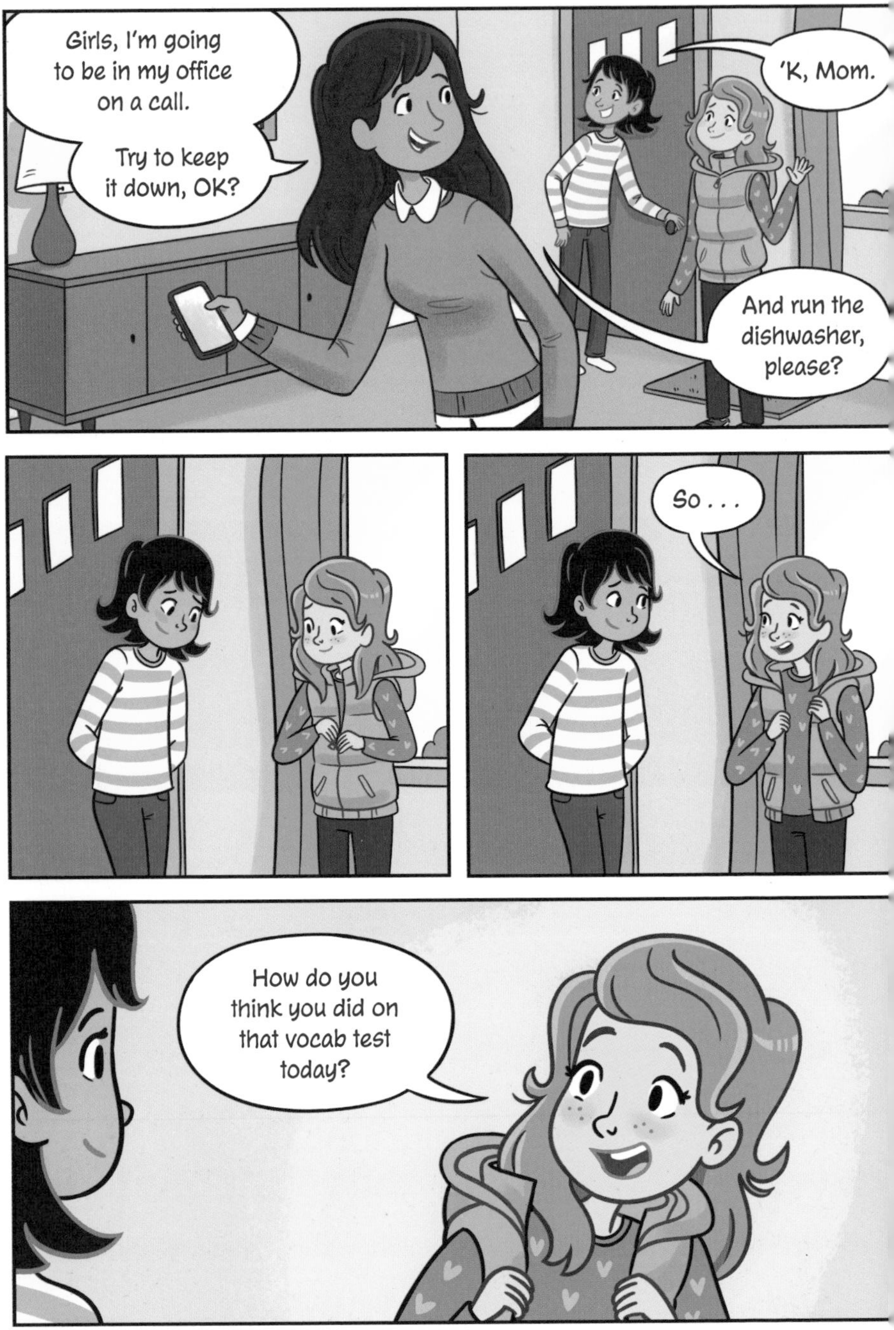
Girls, I'm going to be in my office on a call.
Try to keep it down, OK?
'K, Mom.
And run the dishwasher, please?
So . . .
How do you think you did on that vocab test today?

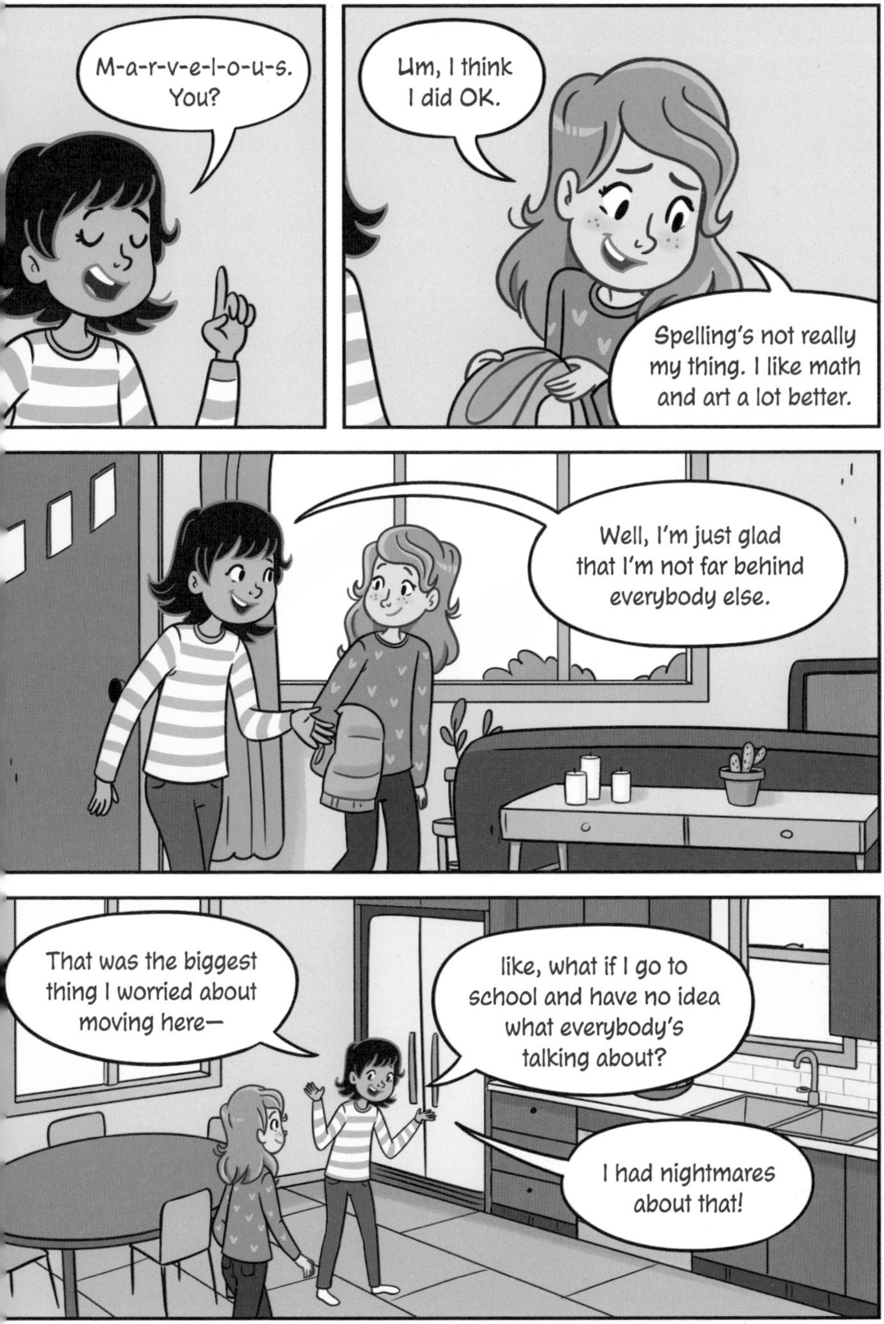

M-a-r-v-e-l-o-u-s. You?
Um, I think I did OK.
Spelling's not really my thing. I like math and art a lot better.
Well, I'm just glad that I'm not far behind everybody else.
That was the biggest thing I worried about moving here—
like, what if I go to school and have no idea what everybody's talking about?
I had nightmares about that!

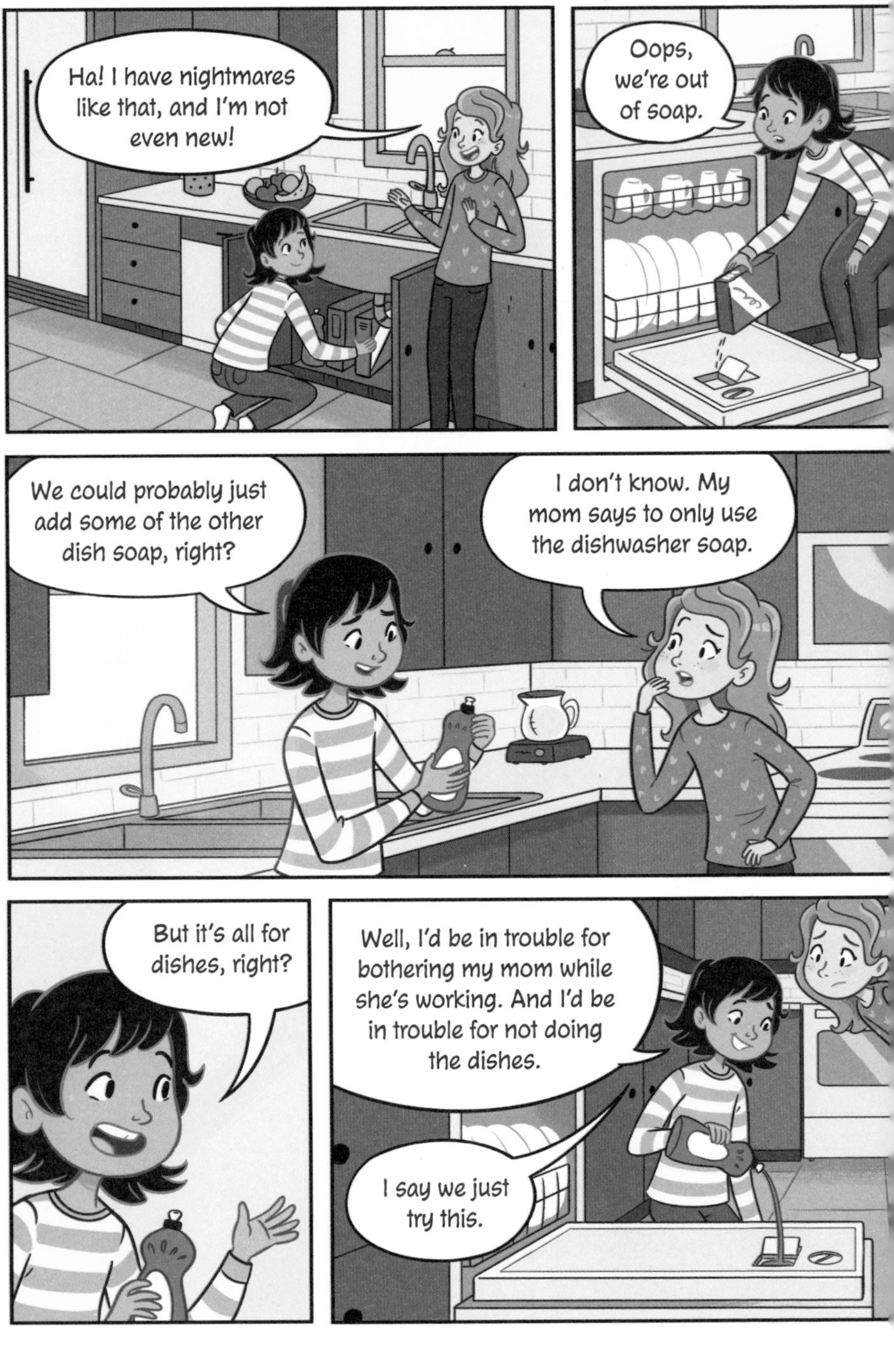
Ha! I have nightmares like that, and I'm not even new!
Oops, we're out of soap.
We could probably just add some of the other dish soap, right?
I don't know. My mom says to only use the dishwasher soap.
But it's all for dishes, right?
Well, I'd be in trouble for bothering my mom while she's working. And I'd be in trouble for not doing the dishes.
I say we just try this.

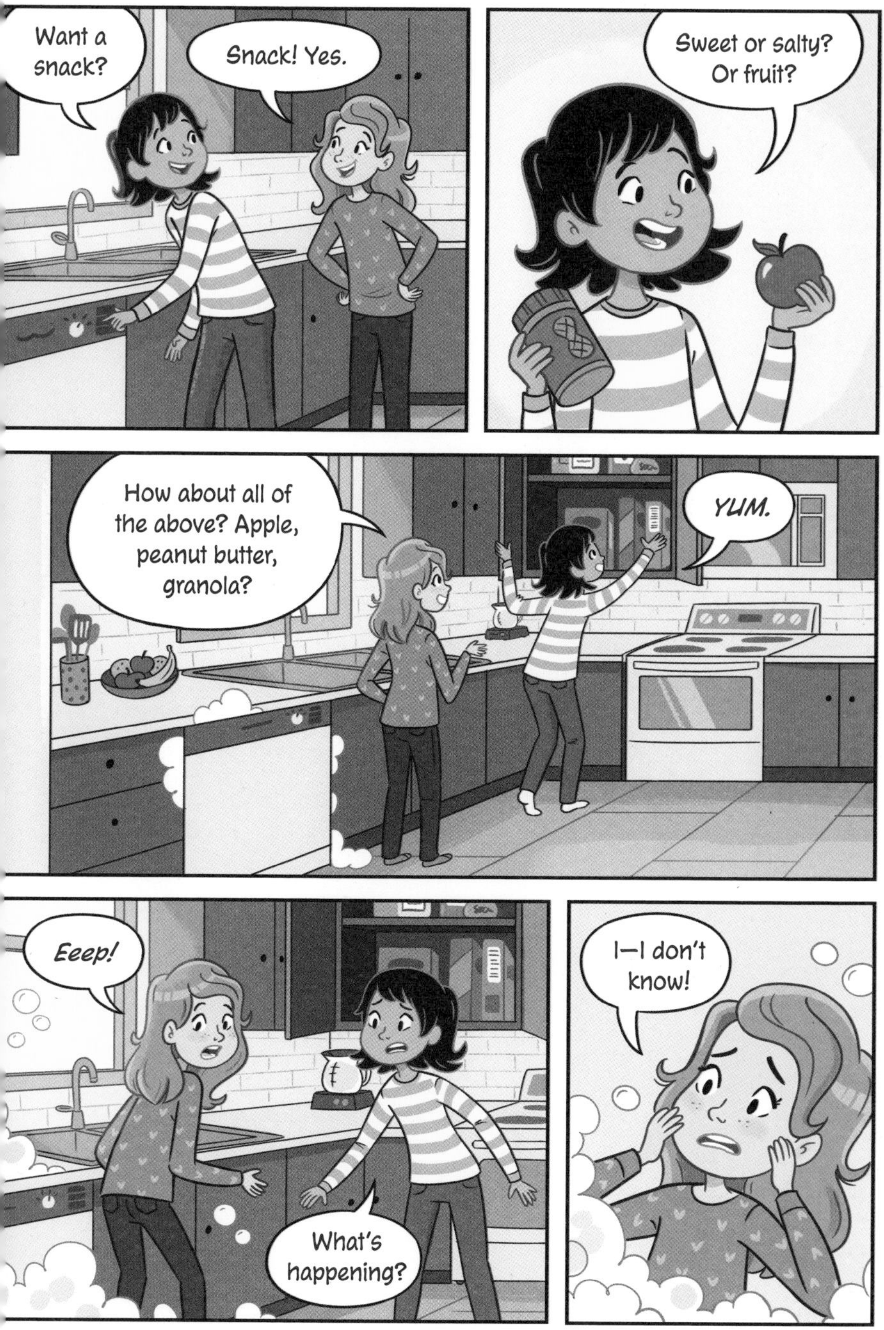
Want a snack?
Snack! Yes.
Sweet or salty? Or fruit?
How about all of the above? Apple, peanut butter, granola?
YUM.
Eeep!
What's happening?
I—I don't know!

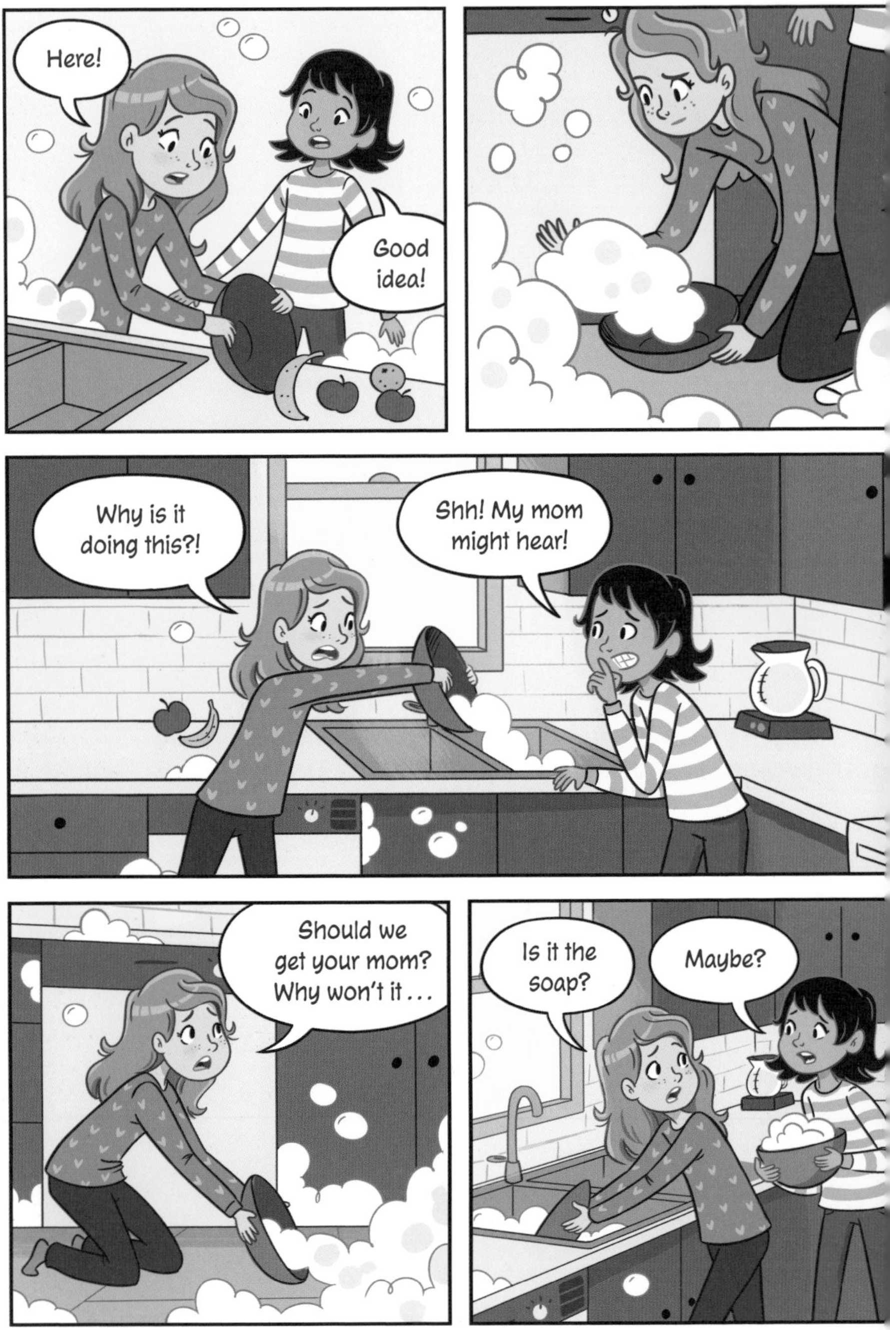
Here!
Good idea!
Why is it doing this?!
Shh! My mom might hear!
Should we get your mom? Why won't it . . .
Is it the soap?
Maybe?

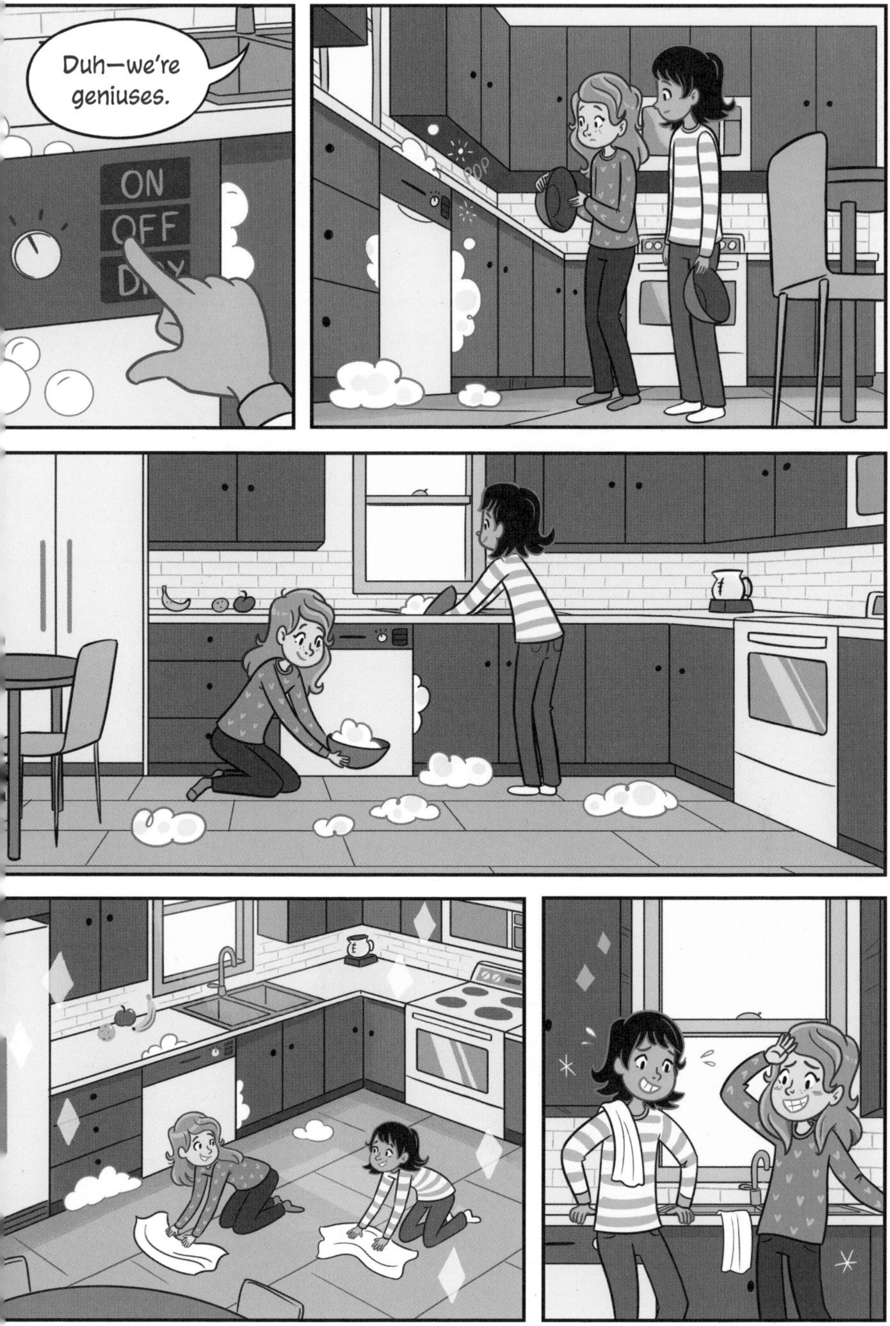
Duh—we're geniuses.
ON
OFF
POP

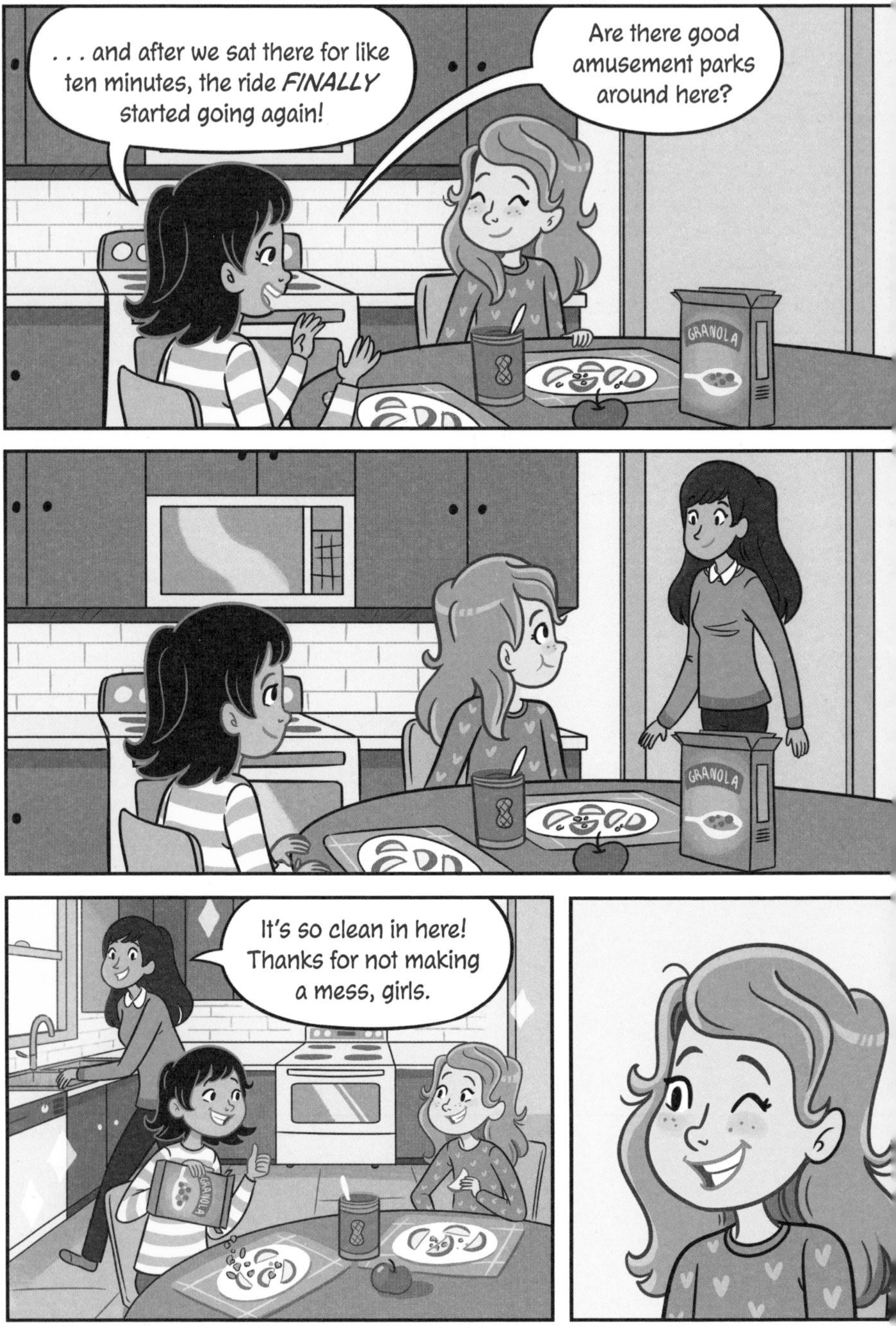
. . . and after we sat there for like ten minutes, the ride *FINALLY* started going again!
Are there good amusement parks around here?
GRANOLA
GRANOLA
It's so clean in here! Thanks for not making a mess, girls.
GRANOLA

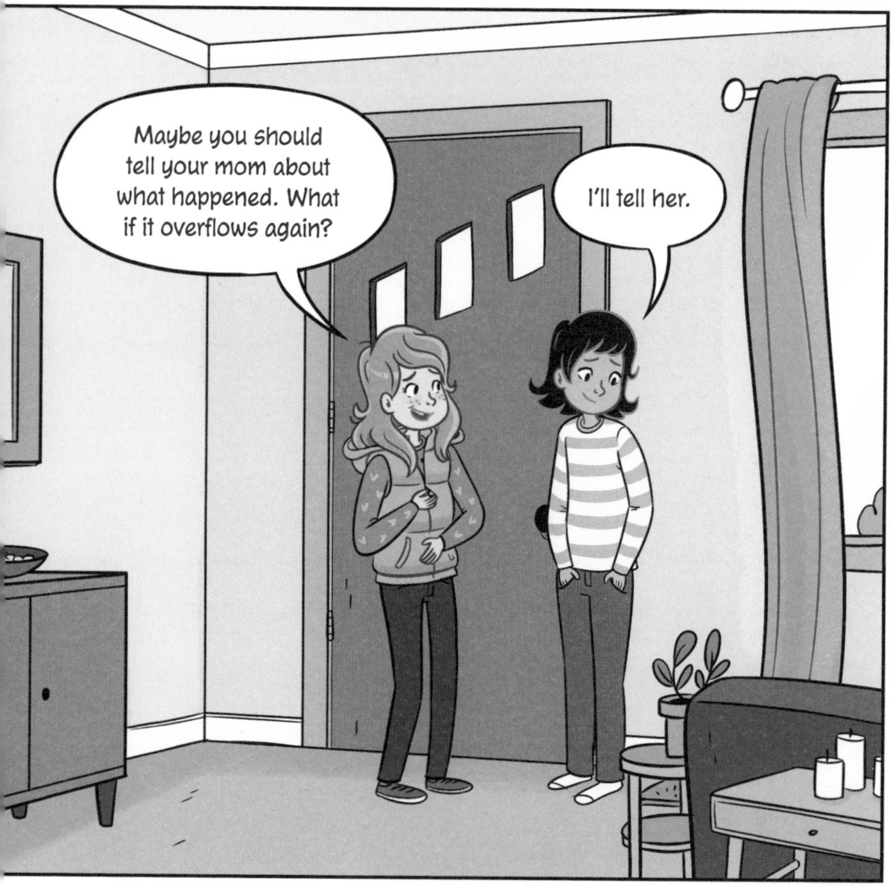
Maybe you should tell your mom about what happened. What if it overflows again?
I'll tell her.

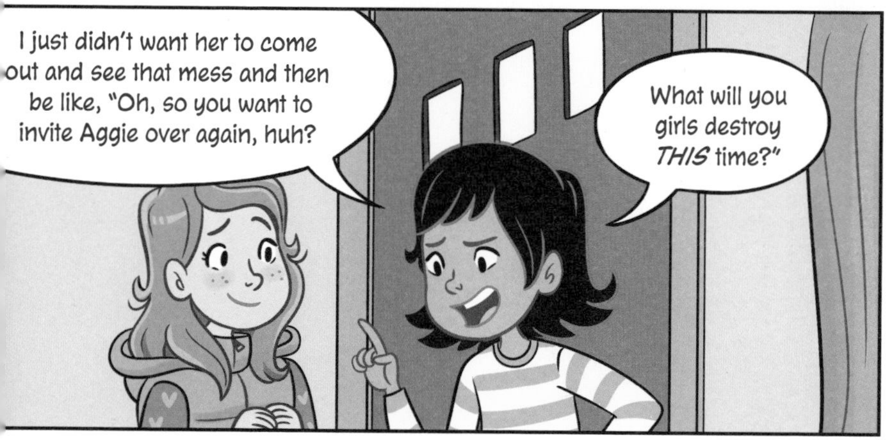
I just didn't want her to come out and see that mess and then be like, "Oh, so you want to invite Aggie over again, huh?
What will you girls destroy *THIS* time?"

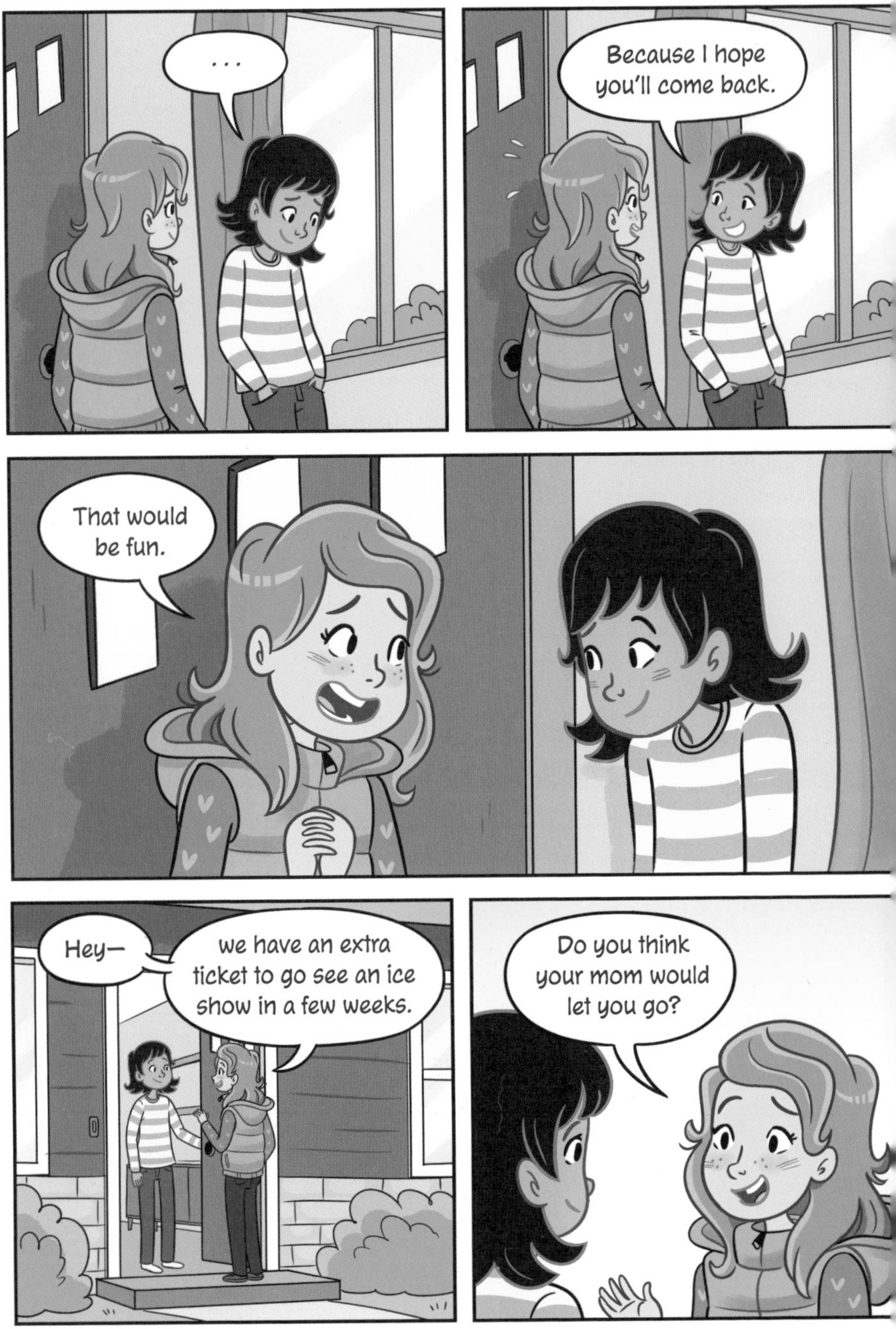
. . .
Because I hope you'll come back.
That would be fun.
Hey—
we have an extra ticket to go see an ice show in a few weeks.
Do you think your mom would let you go?

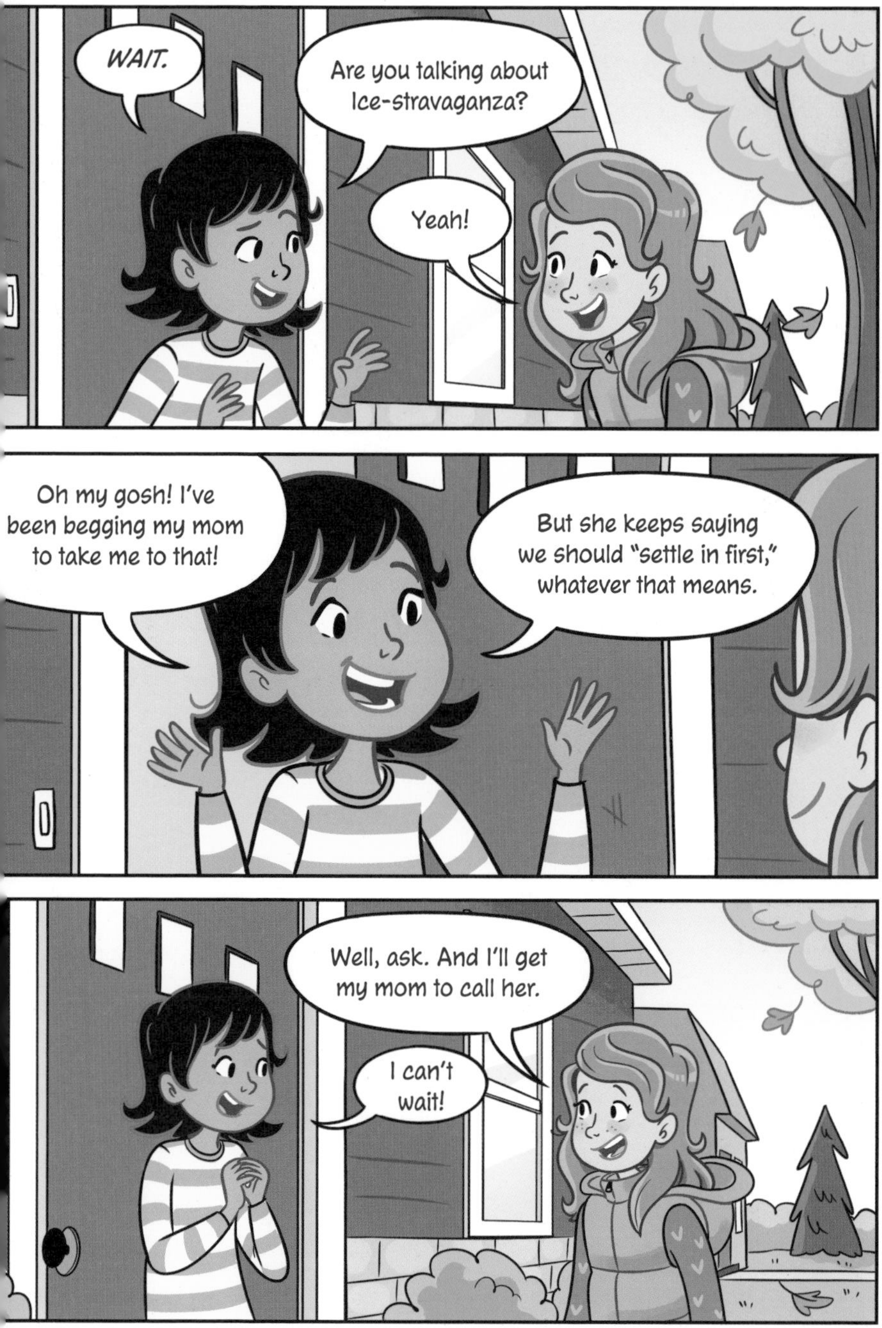
WAIT.
Are you talking about Ice-stravaganza?
Yeah!
Oh my gosh! I've been begging my mom to take me to that!
But she keeps saying we should "settle in first," whatever that means.
Well, ask. And I'll get my mom to call her.
I can't wait!

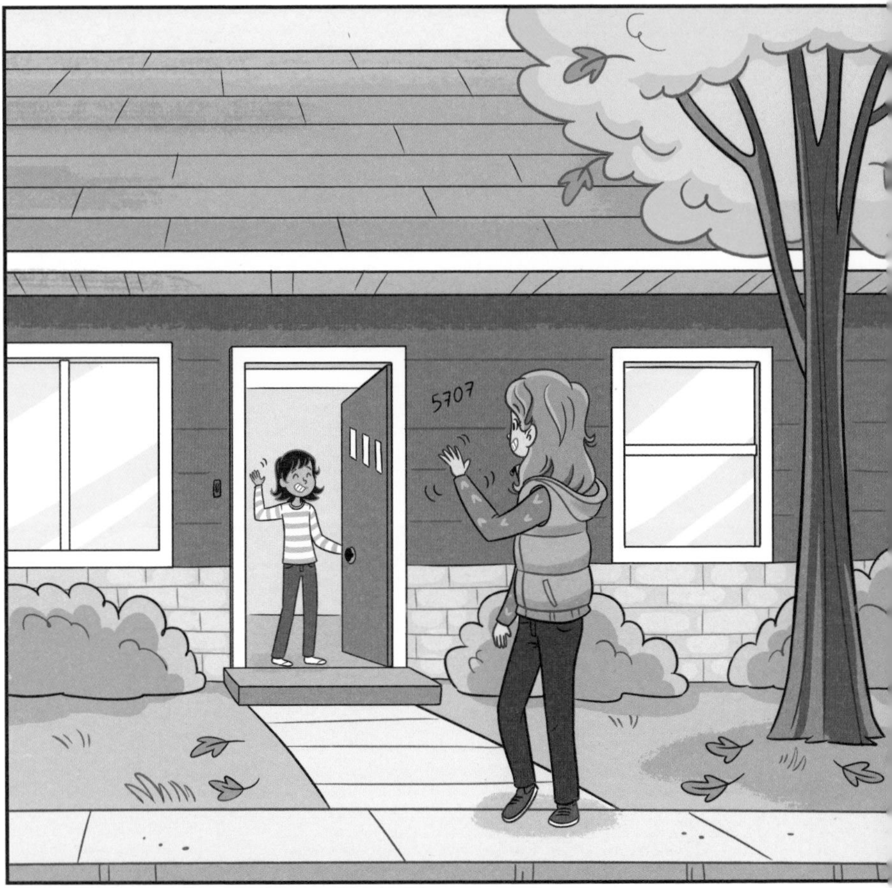
5707

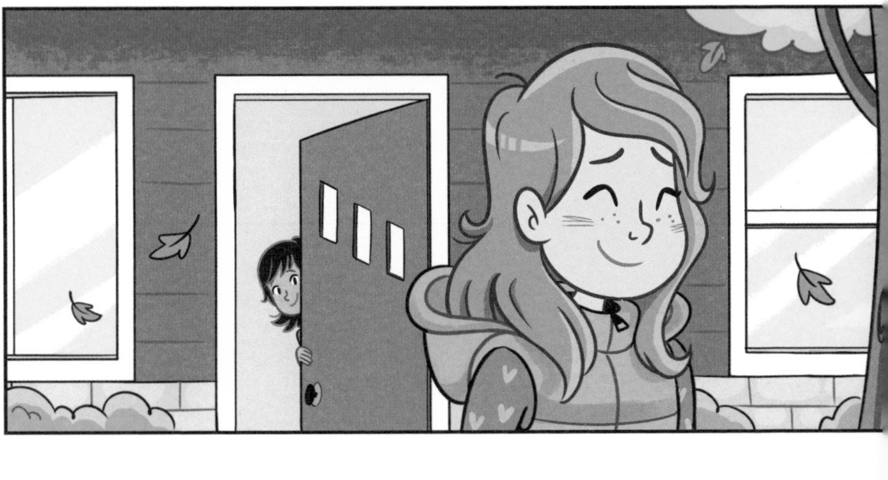

Friendships are funny.
Sometimes two people say "hi" and are friends just like that.

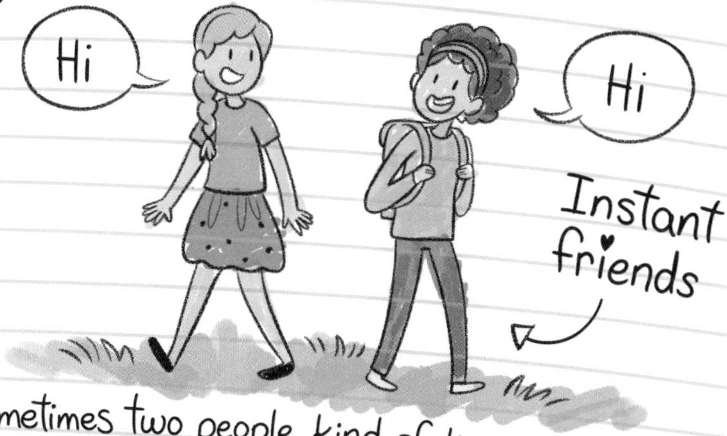
Hi
Hi
Instant friends

Sometimes two people kind of know each other, and then one day they realize that they became friends without even trying.

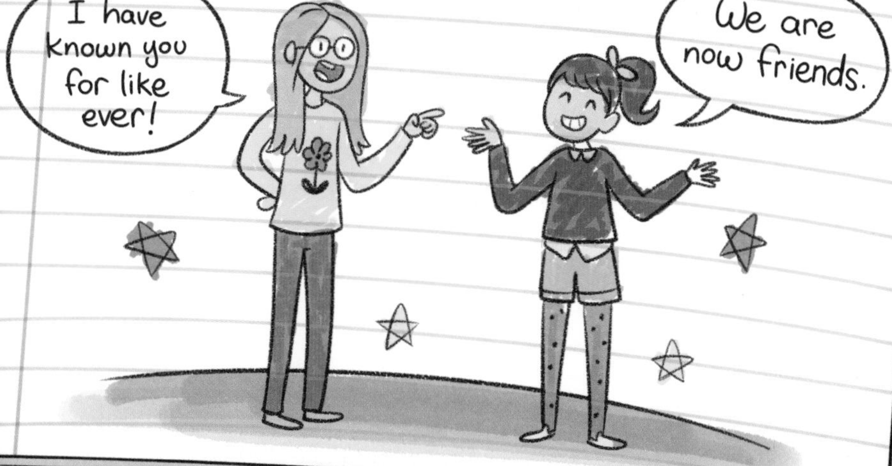
I have known you for like ever!
We are now friends.

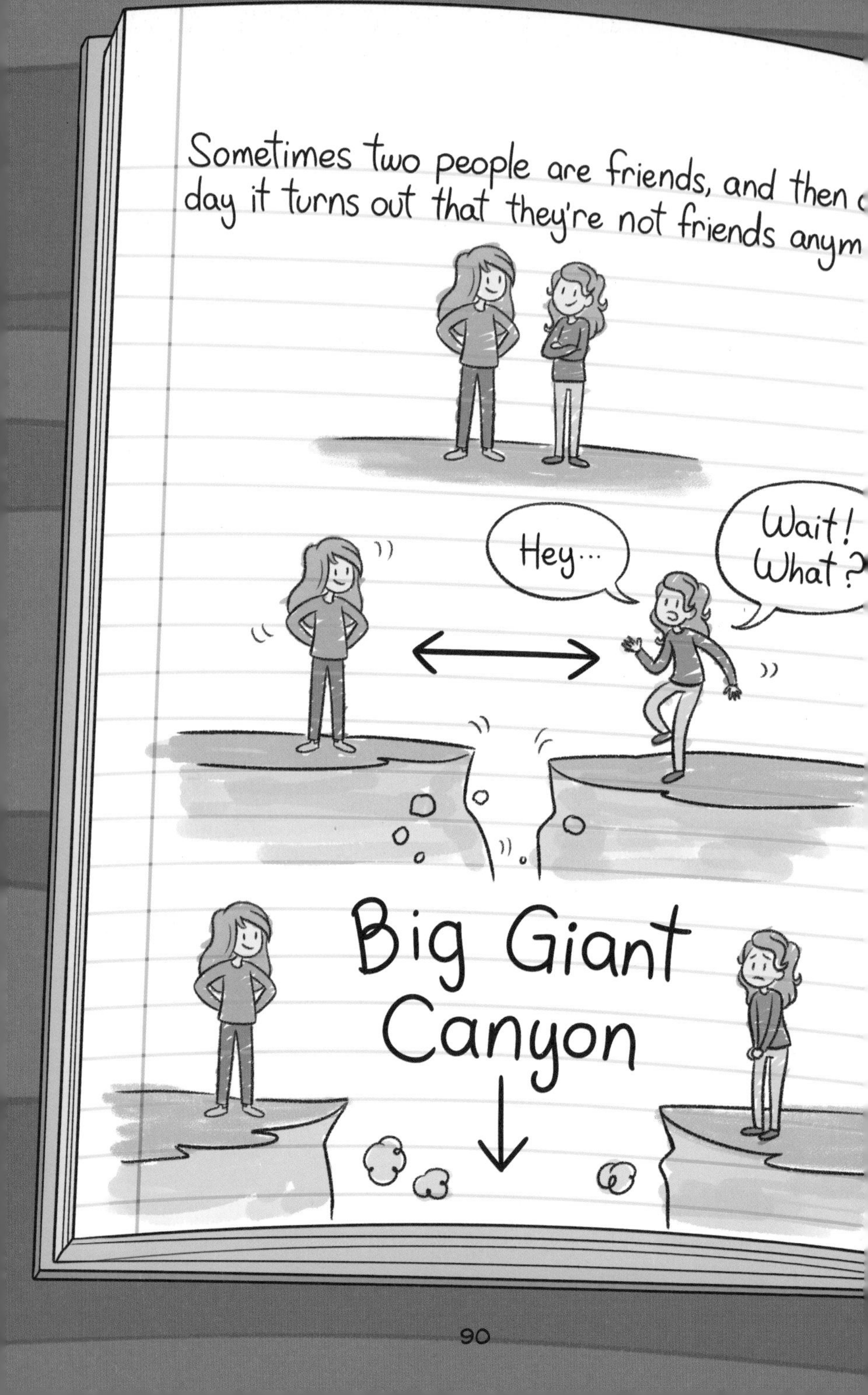
Sometimes two people are friends, and then
day it turns out that they're not friends
Hey...
Wait! What?
Big Giant Canyon

And sometimes something crazy happens, and you get through it together, and then you can't help but be friends afterward.

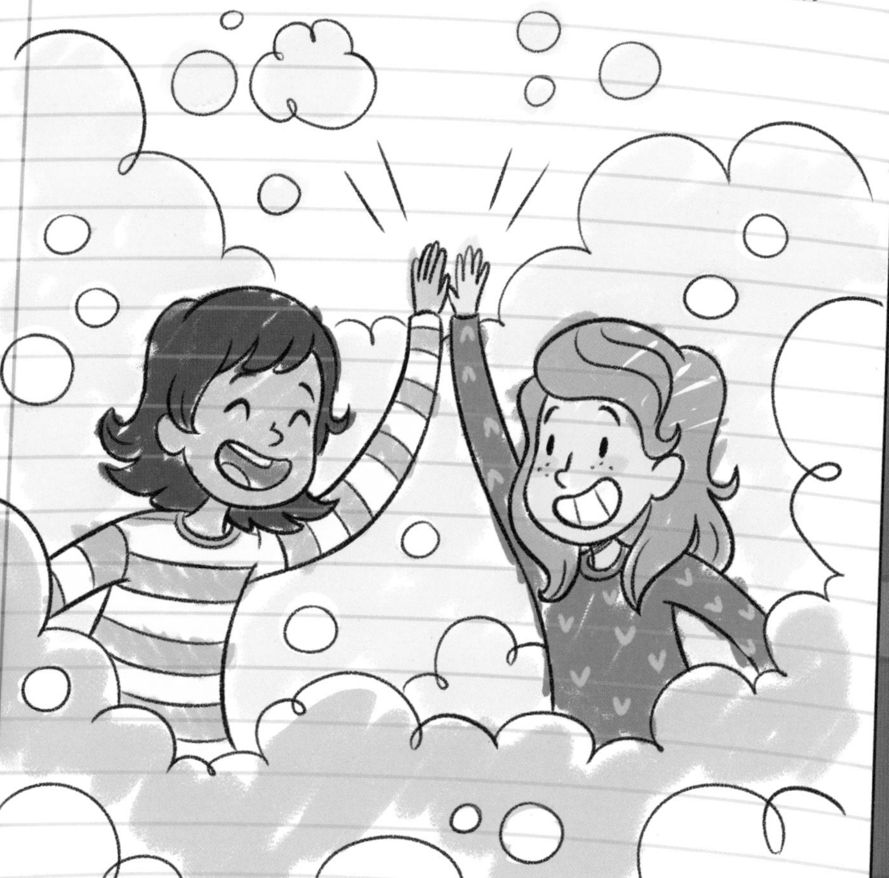

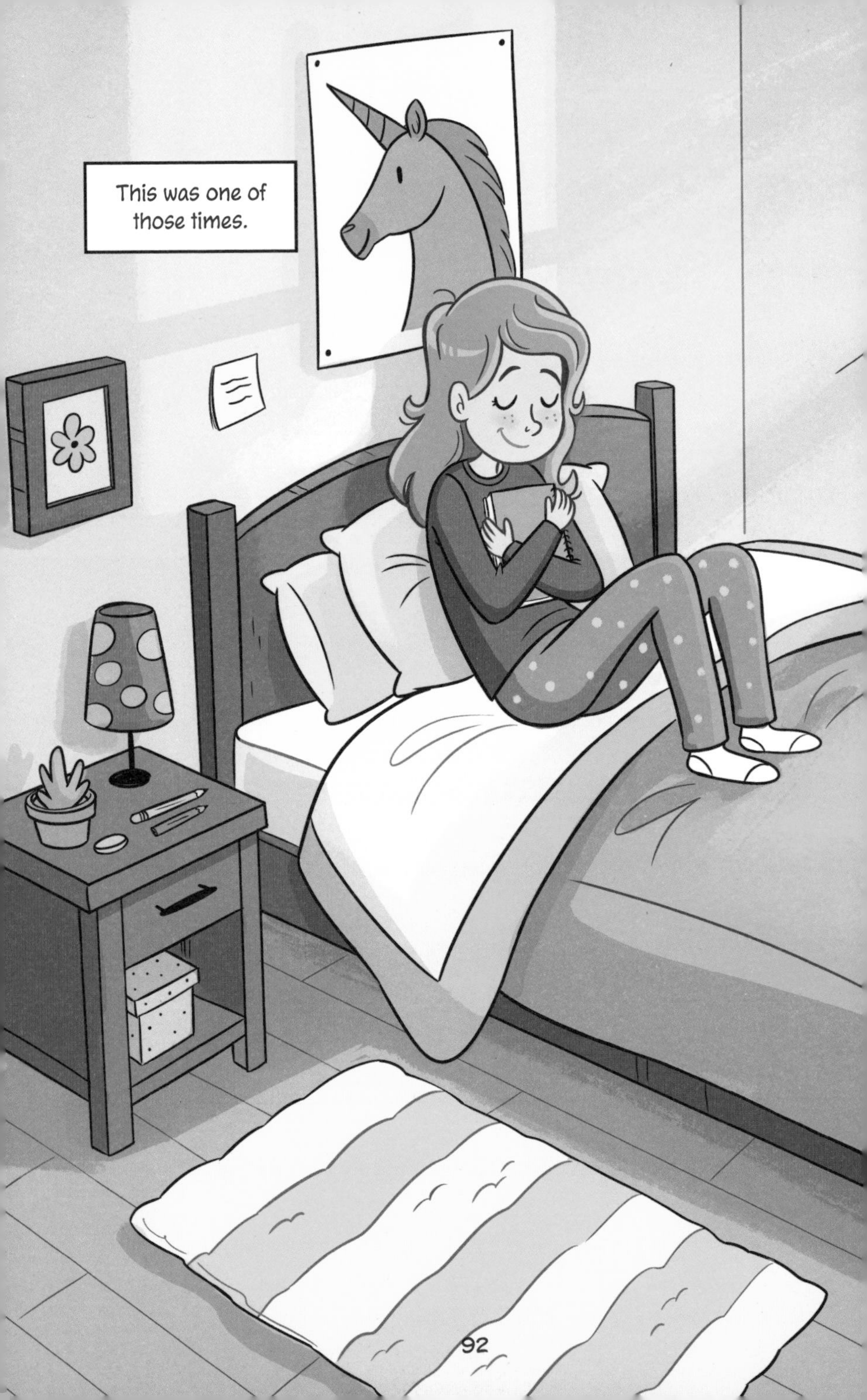
This was one of those times.

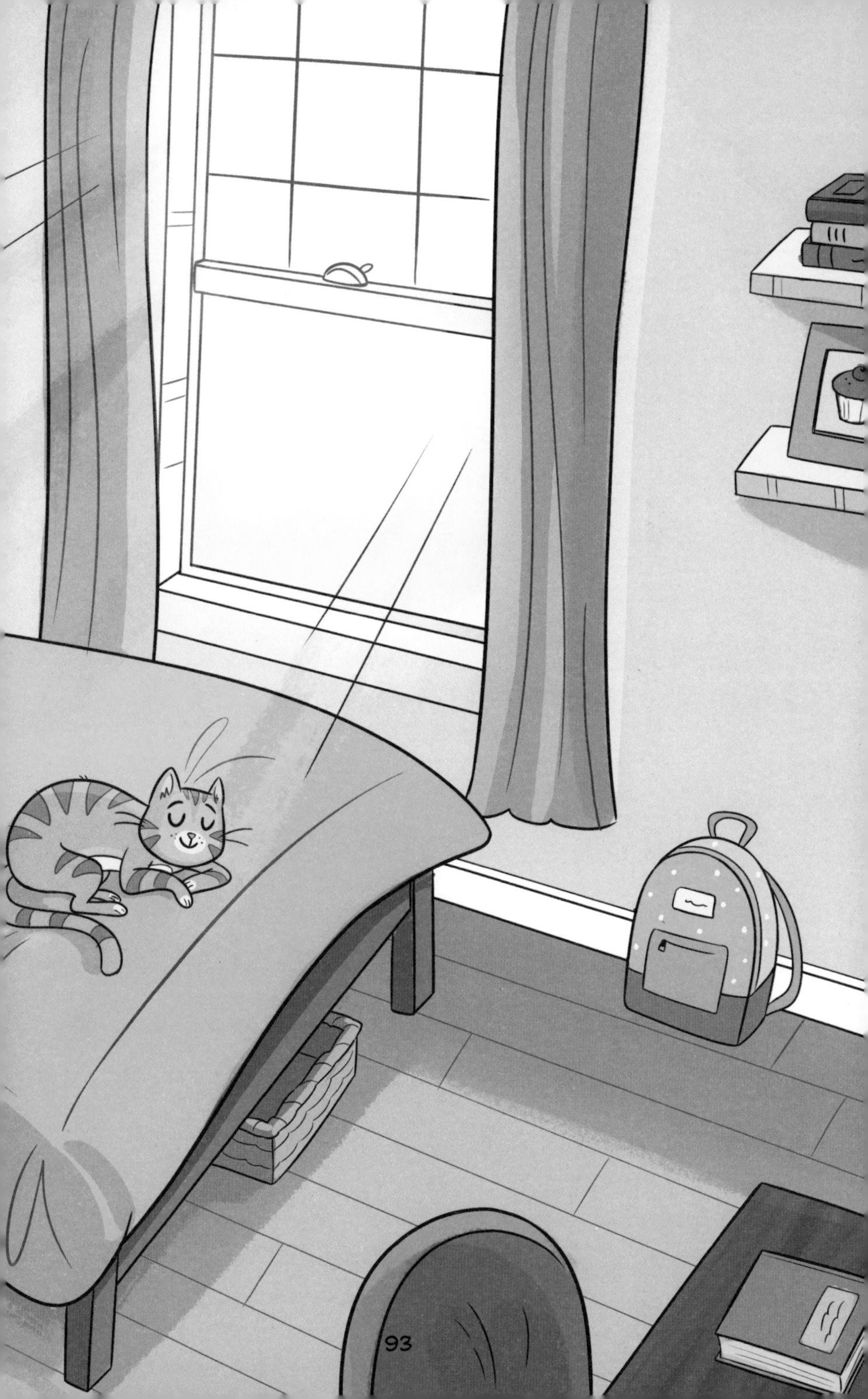

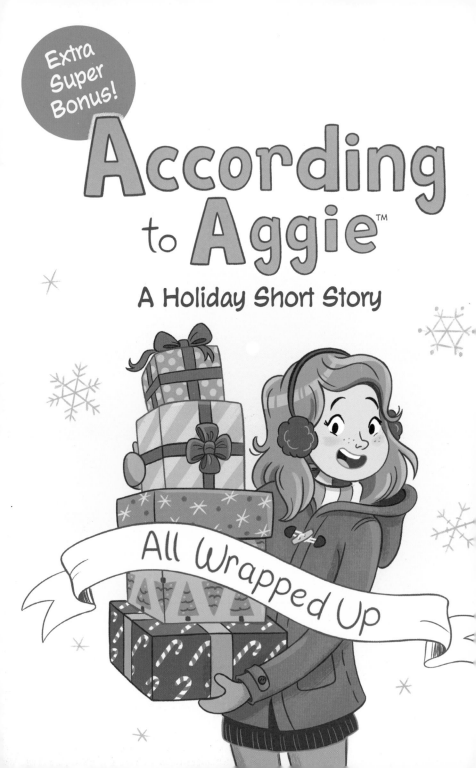

Extra Super Bonus!

According to Aggie™

A Holiday Short Story

All Wrapped Up

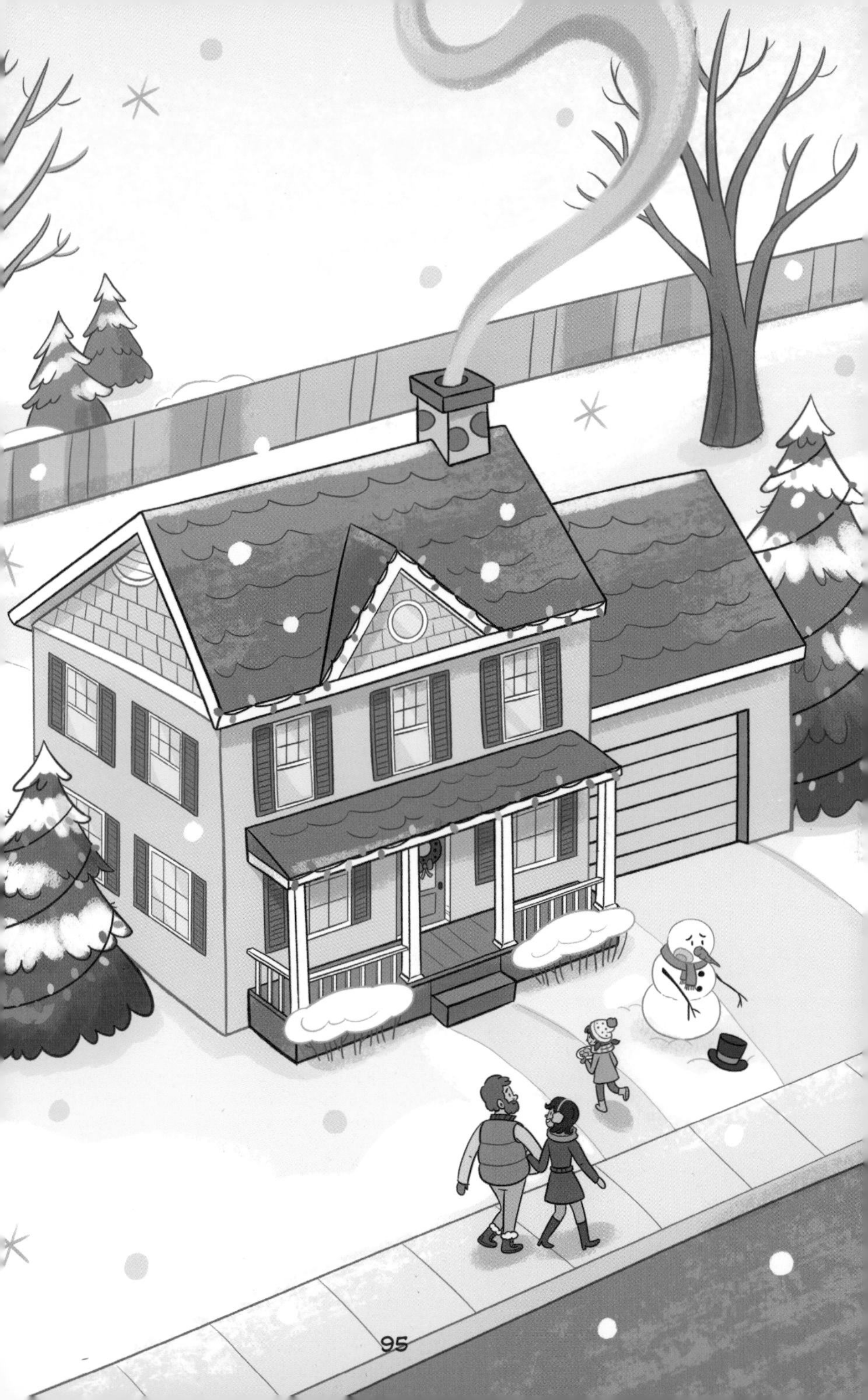

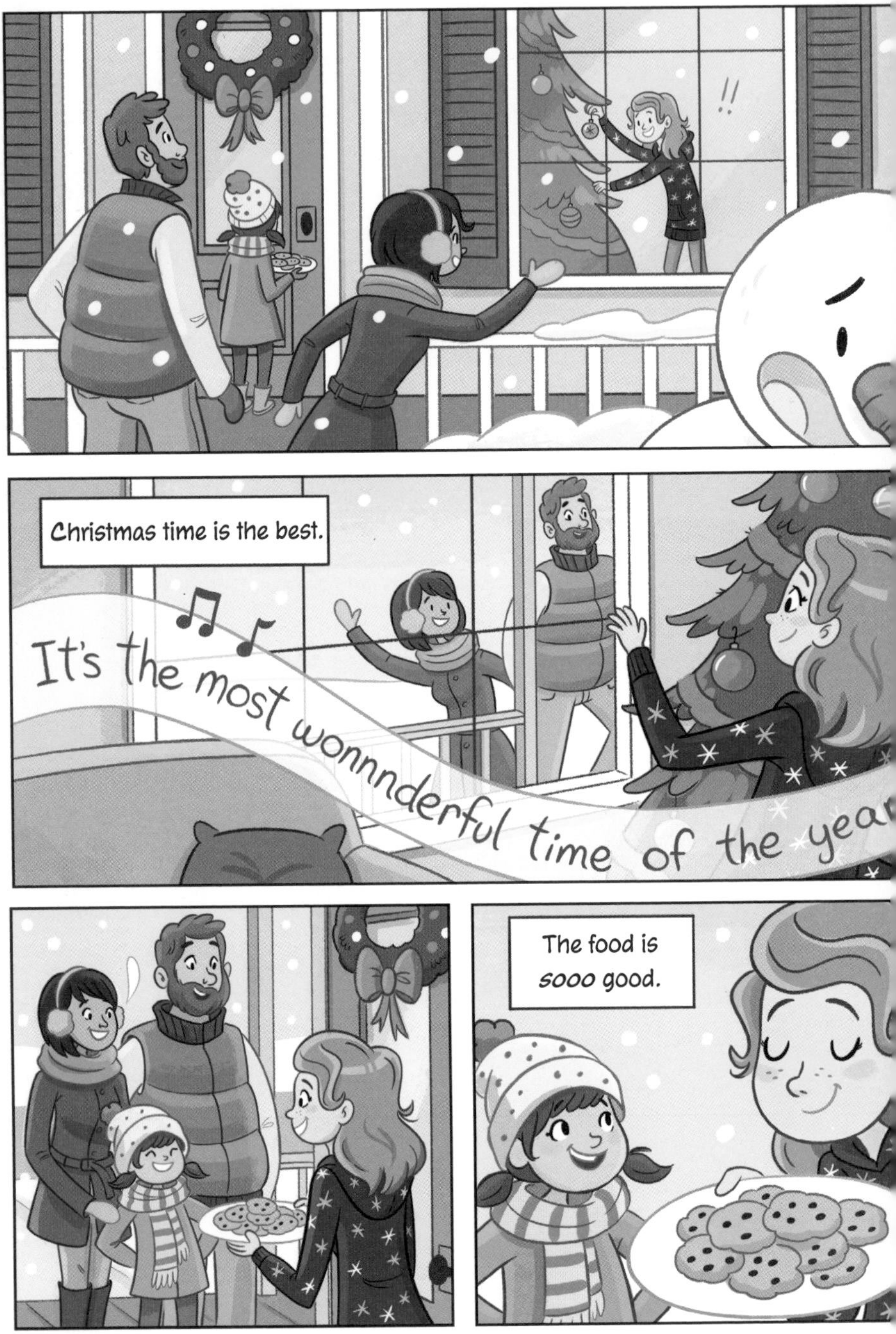
!!
Christmas time is the best.
It's the most wonnnderful time of the yea
The food is sooo good.

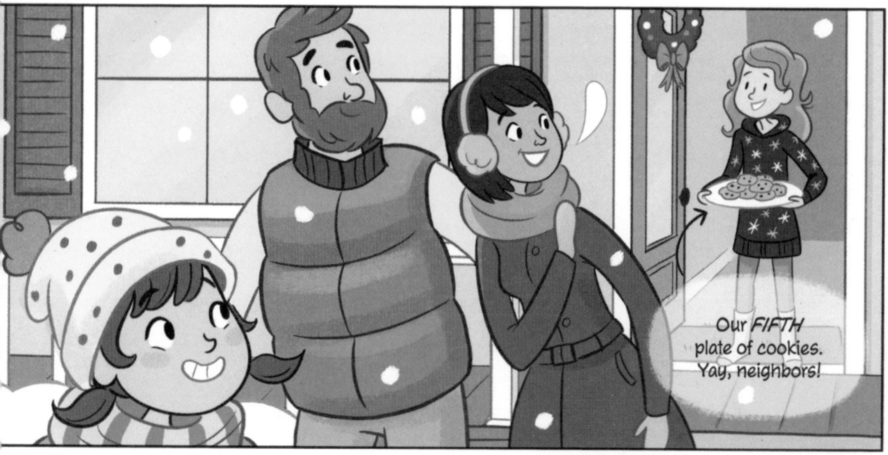
Our FIFTH
plate of cookies.
Yay, neighbors!

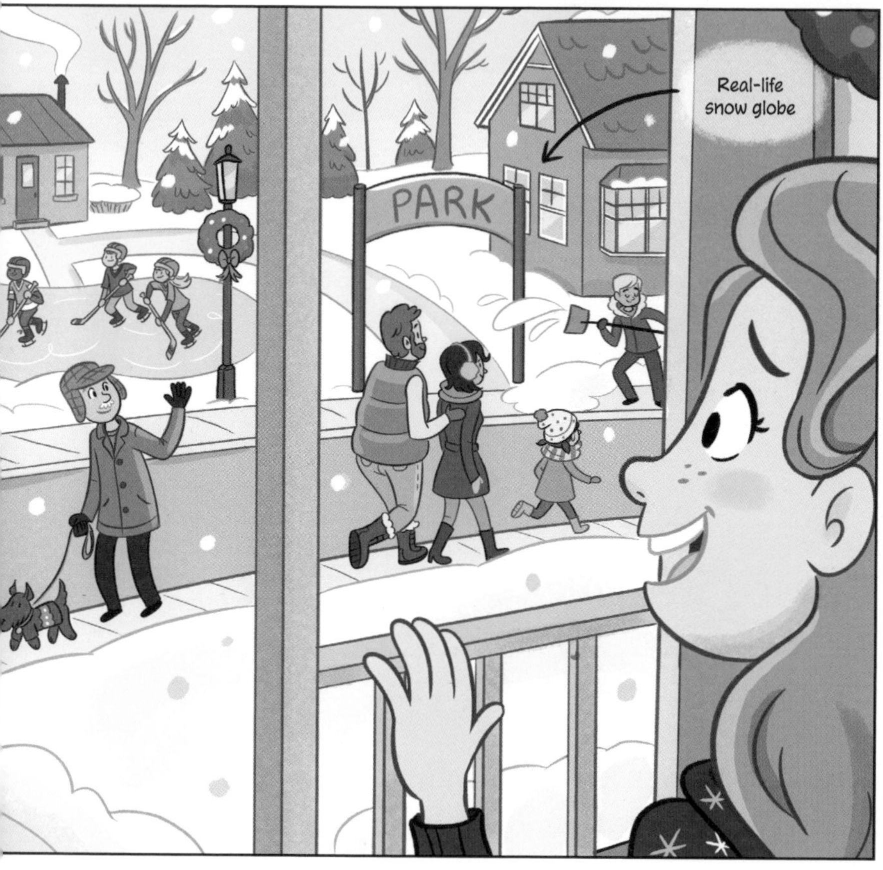
Real-life
snow globe
PARK

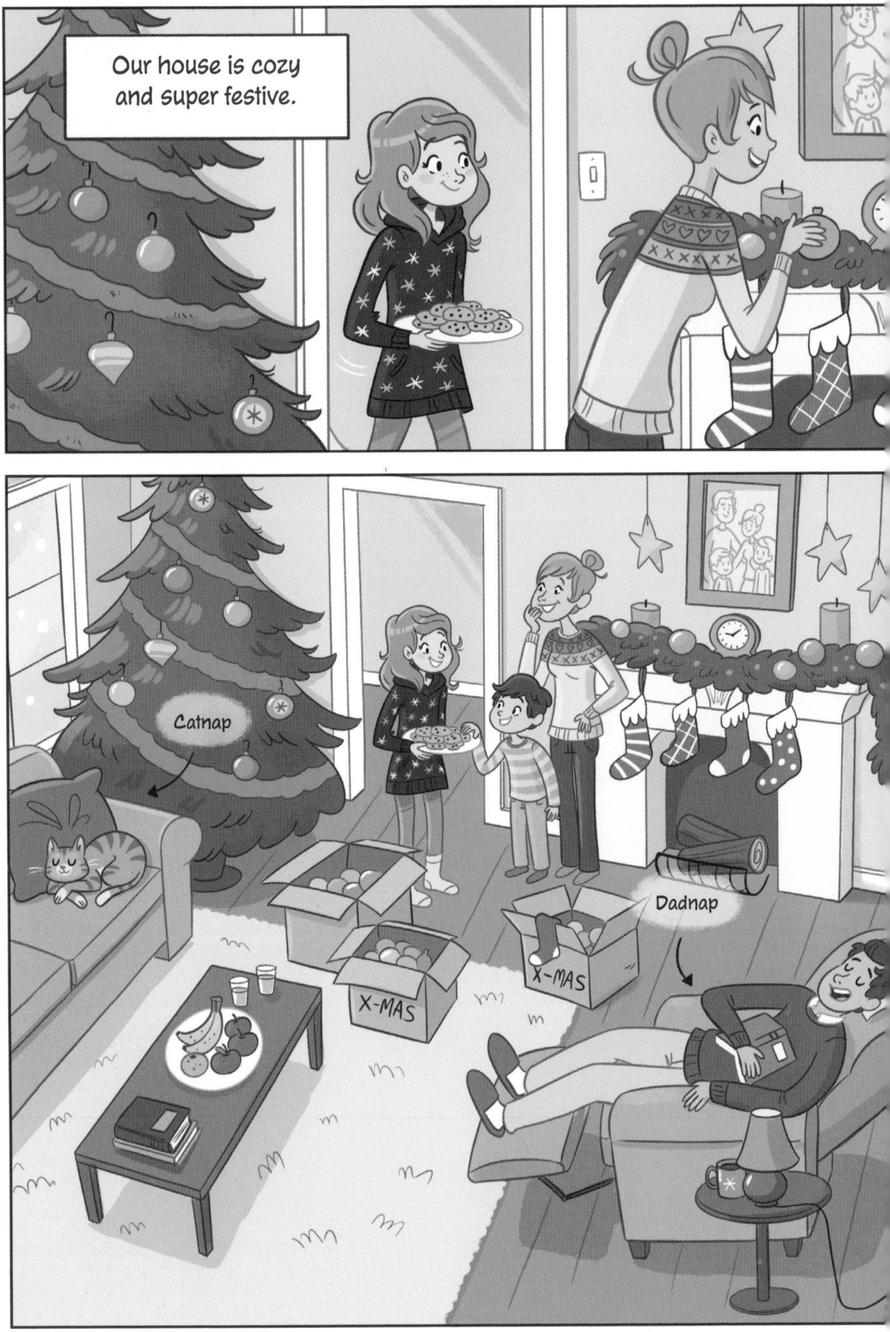
Our house is cozy and super festive.
Catnap
X-MAS
X-MAS
Dadnap

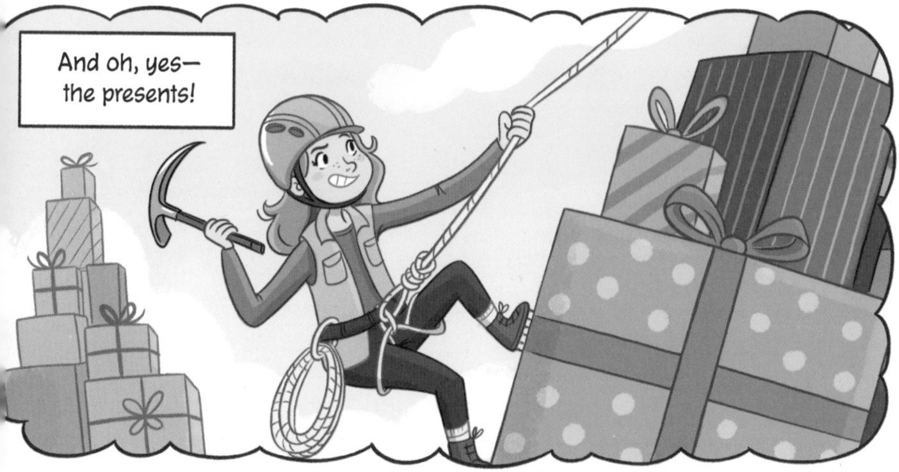
And oh, yes—
the presents!

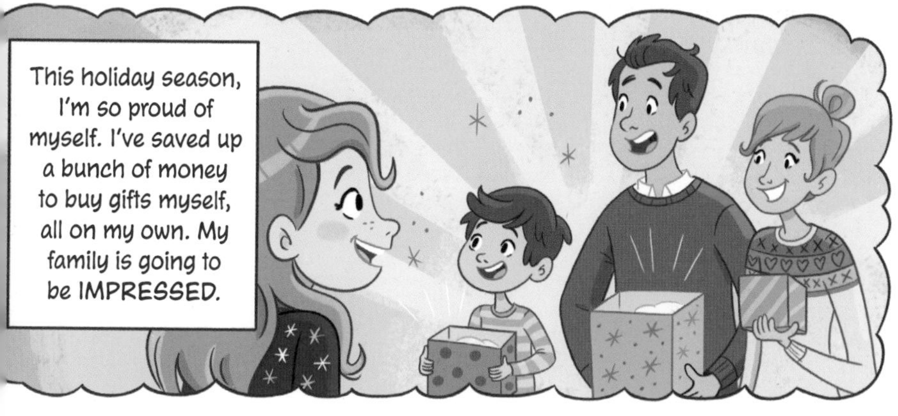
This holiday season, I'm so proud of myself. I've saved up a bunch of money to buy gifts myself, all on my own. My family is going to be IMPRESSED.

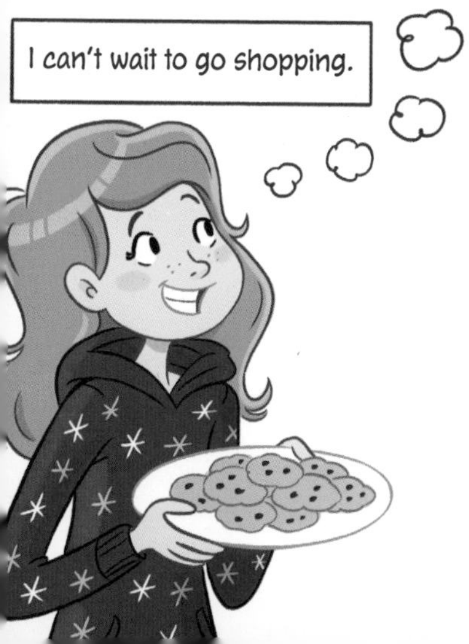
I can't wait to go shopping.

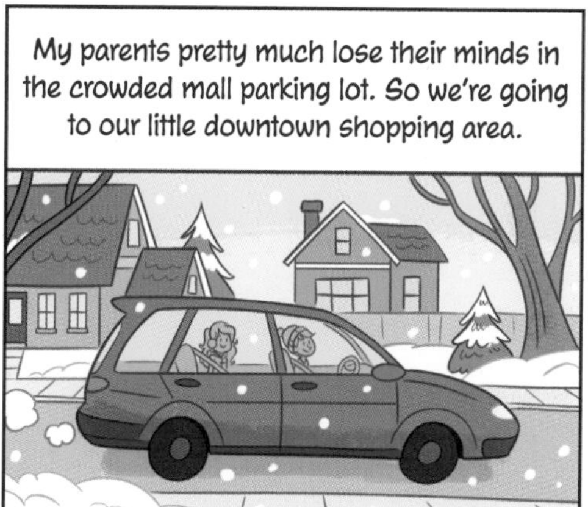
My parents pretty much lose their minds in the crowded mall parking lot. So we're going to our little downtown shopping area.

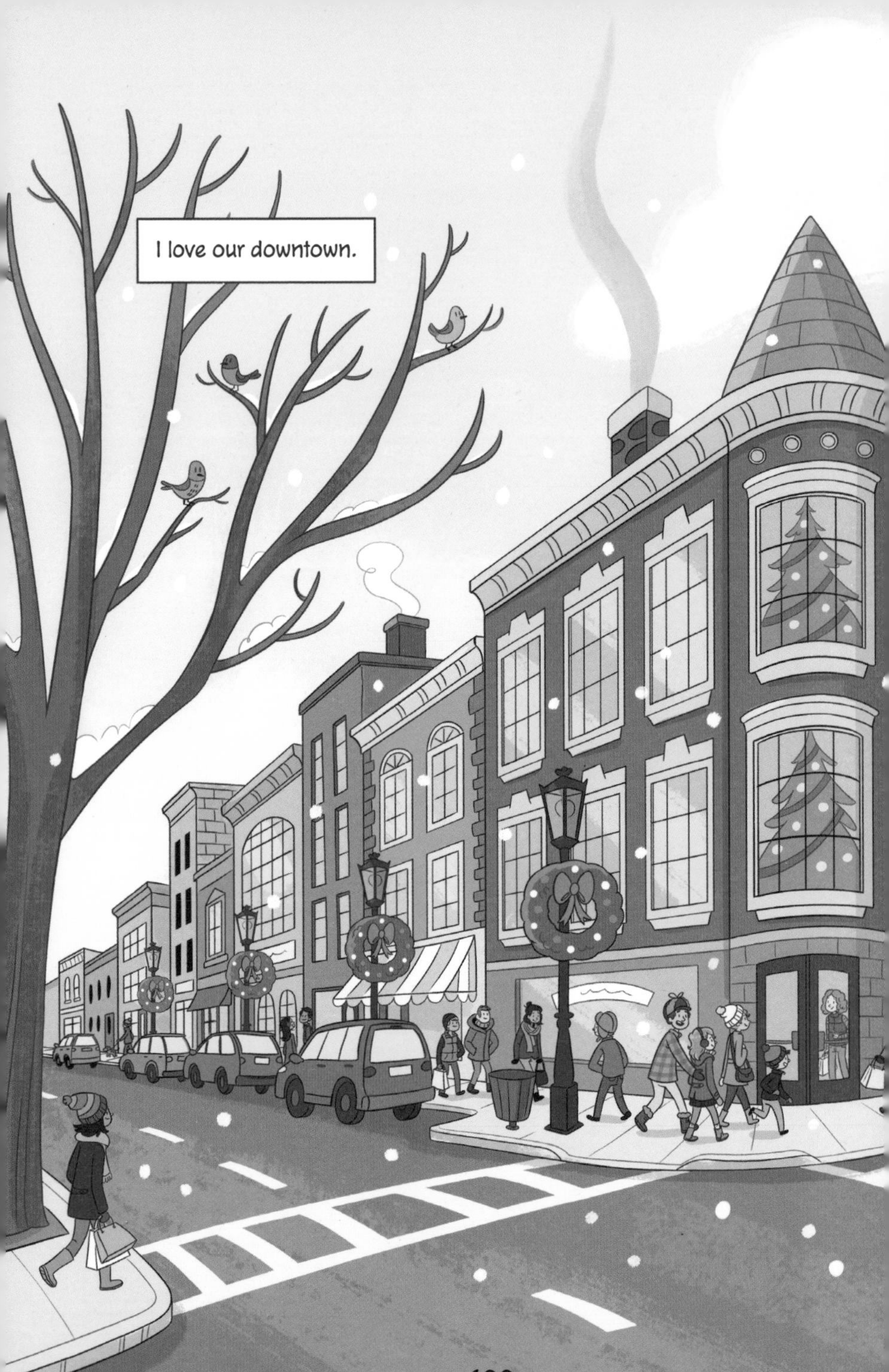
I love our downtown.

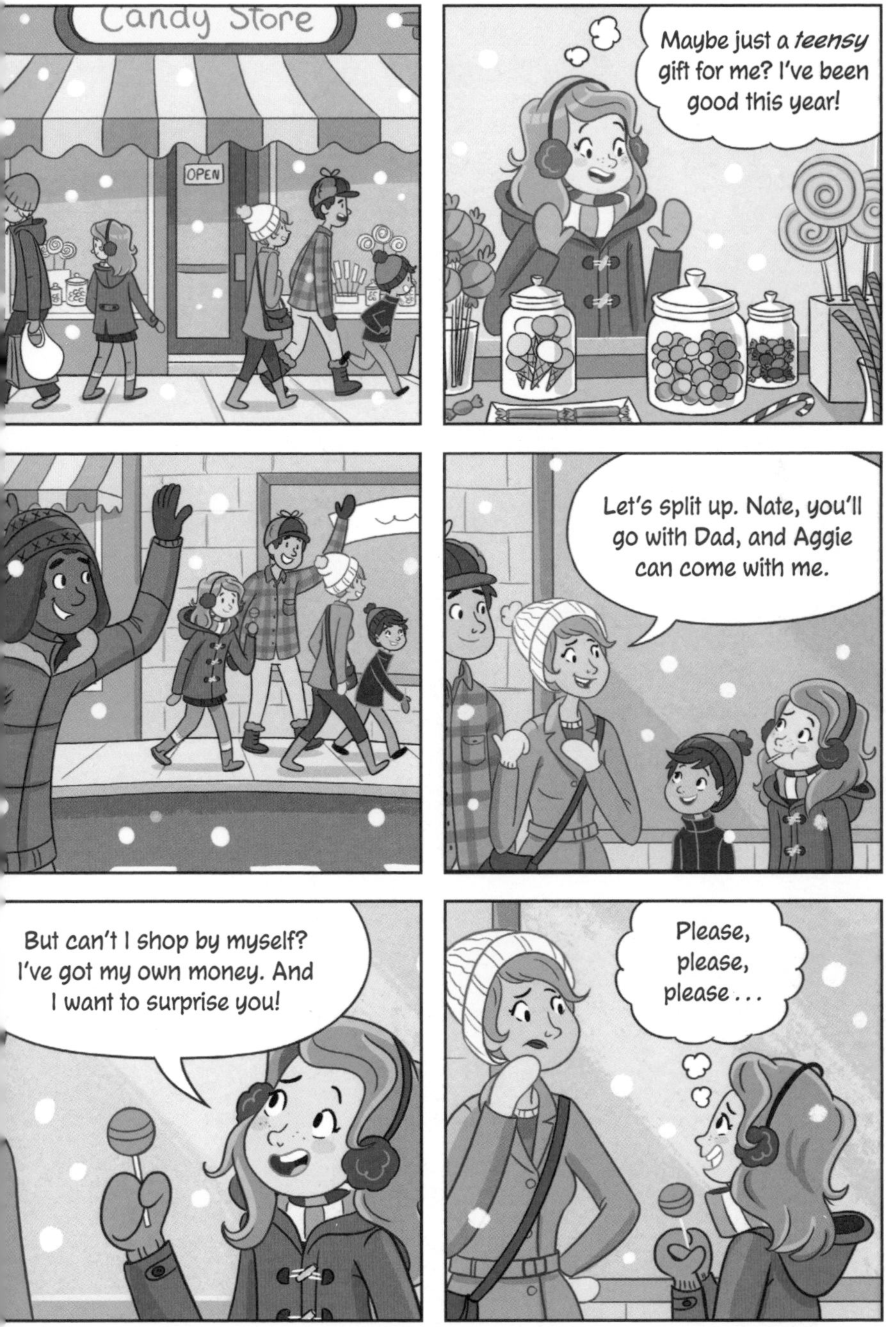
Candy Store
OPEN
Maybe just a *teensy* gift for me? I've been good this year!
Let's split up. Nate, you'll go with Dad, and Aggie can come with me.
But can't I shop by myself? I've got my own money. And I want to surprise you!
Please, please, please . . .

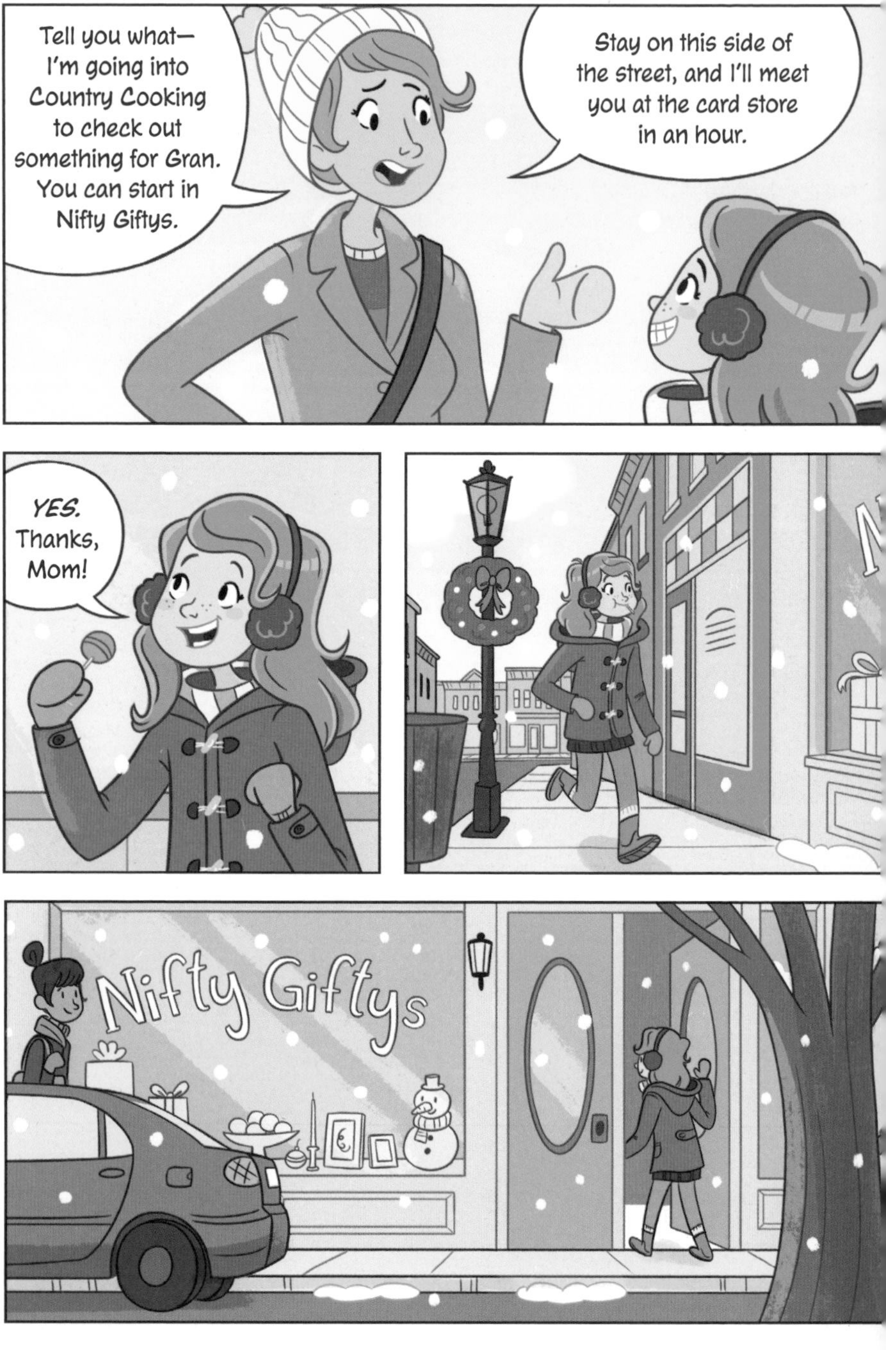
Tell you what—
I'm going into Country Cooking to check out something for Gran. You can start in Nifty Giftys.
Stay on this side of the street, and I'll meet you at the card store in an hour.
YES. Thanks, Mom!
Nifty Giftys

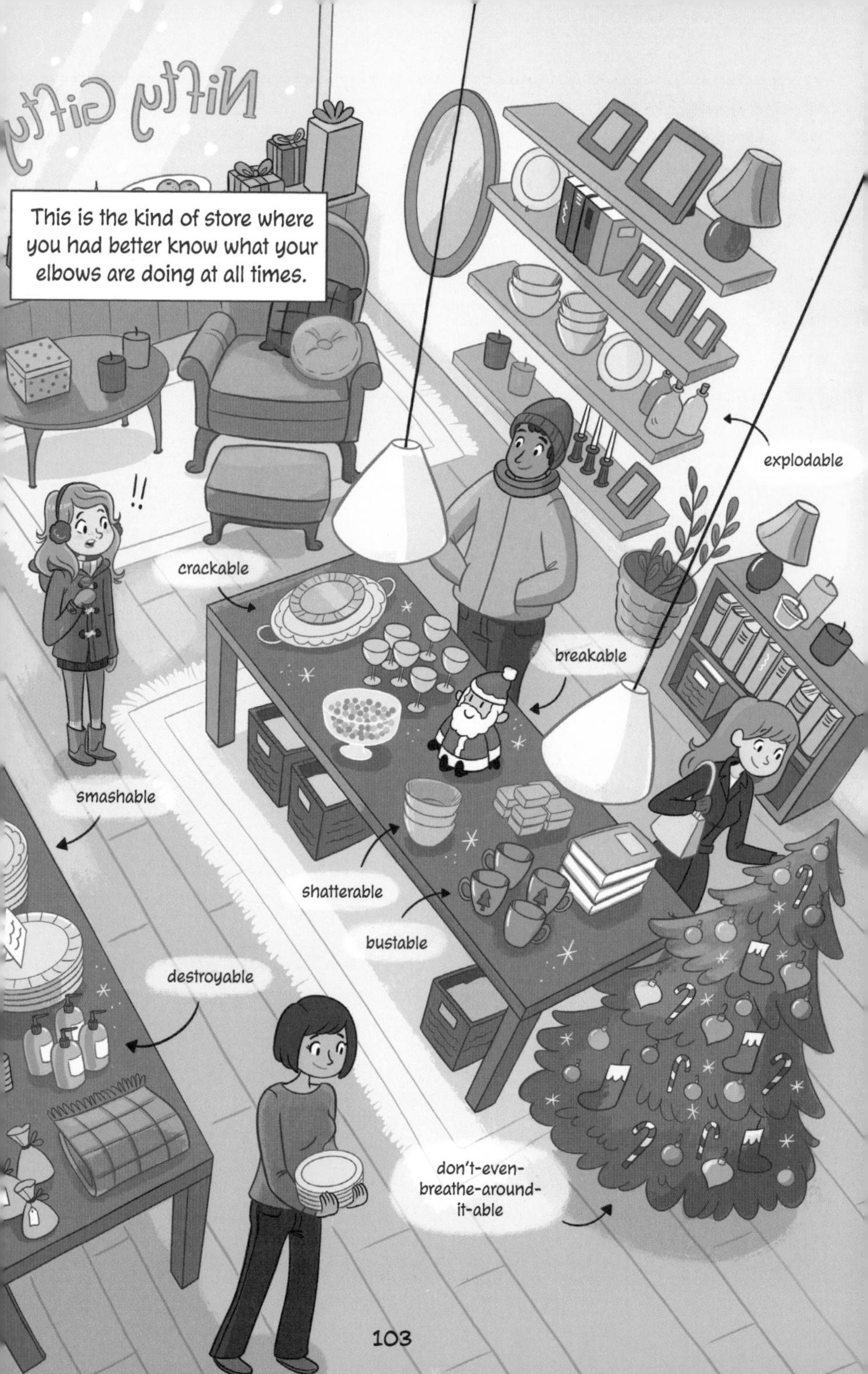

Nifty Gifty
This is the kind of store where you had better know what your elbows are doing at all times.
!!
crackable
explodable
breakable
smashable
shatterable
bustable
destroyable
don't-even-breathe-around-it-able

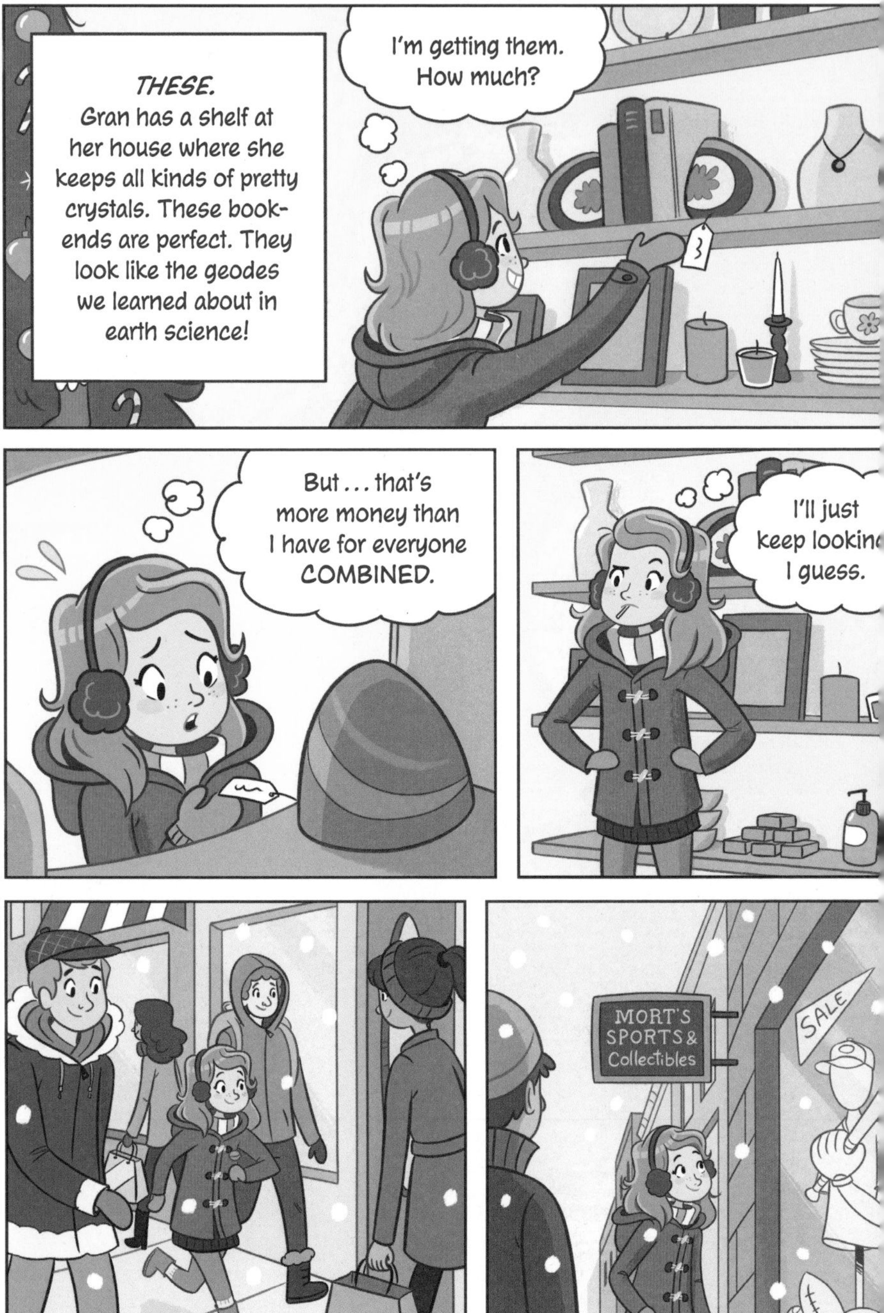
THESE.
Gran has a shelf at her house where she keeps all kinds of pretty crystals. These book-ends are perfect. They look like the geodes we learned about in earth science!
I'm getting them. How much?
But . . . that's more money than I have for everyone COMBINED.
I'll just keep lookin
I guess.
MORT'S SPORTS & Collectibles
SALE

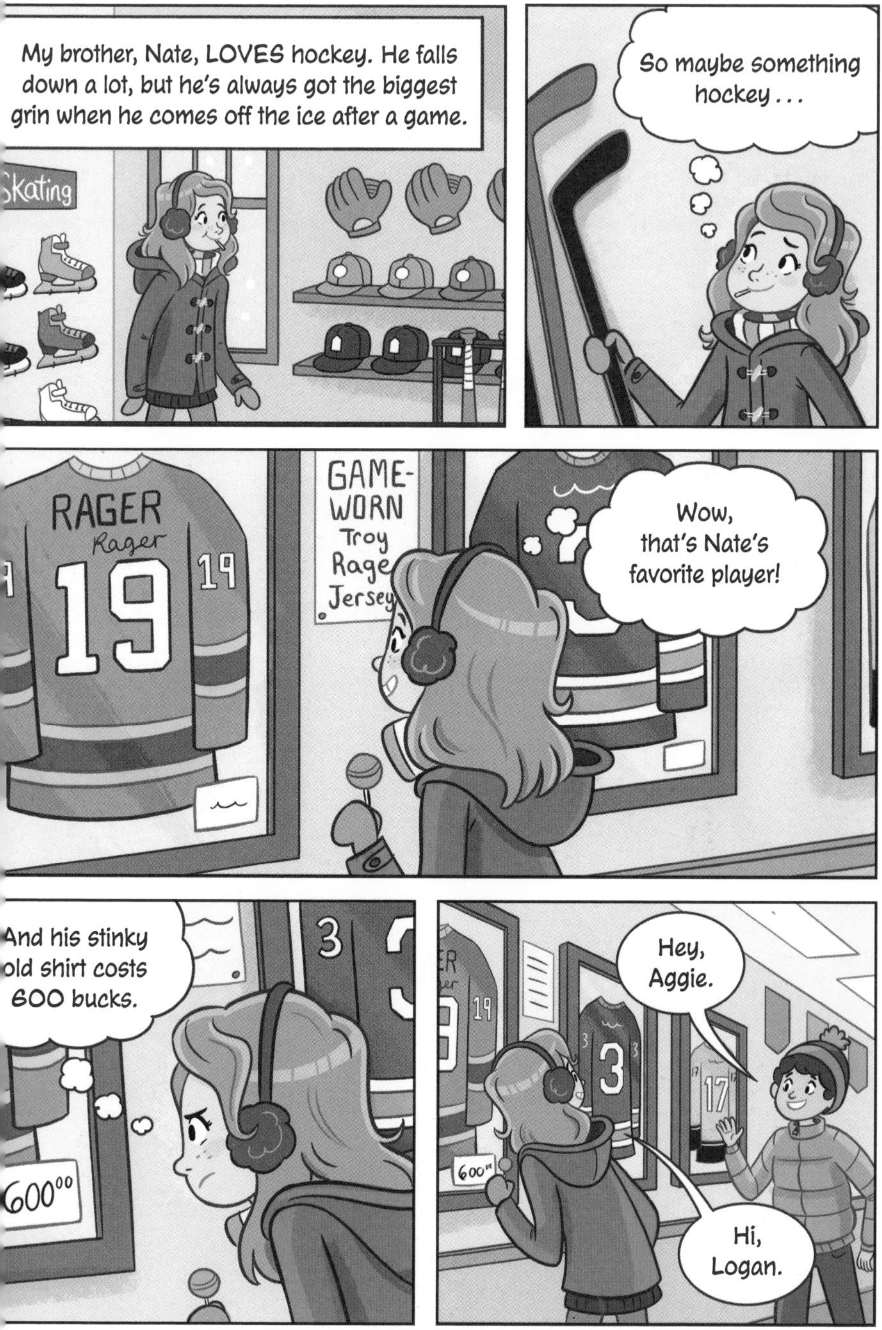

My brother, Nate, LOVES hockey. He falls down a lot, but he's always got the biggest grin when he comes off the ice after a game.
Skating
So maybe something hockey . . .
RAGER
Rager
19
GAME-WORN Troy Rage Jersey
Wow, that's Nate's favorite player!
And his stinky old shirt costs 600 bucks.
600⁰⁰
Hey, Aggie.
Hi, Logan.

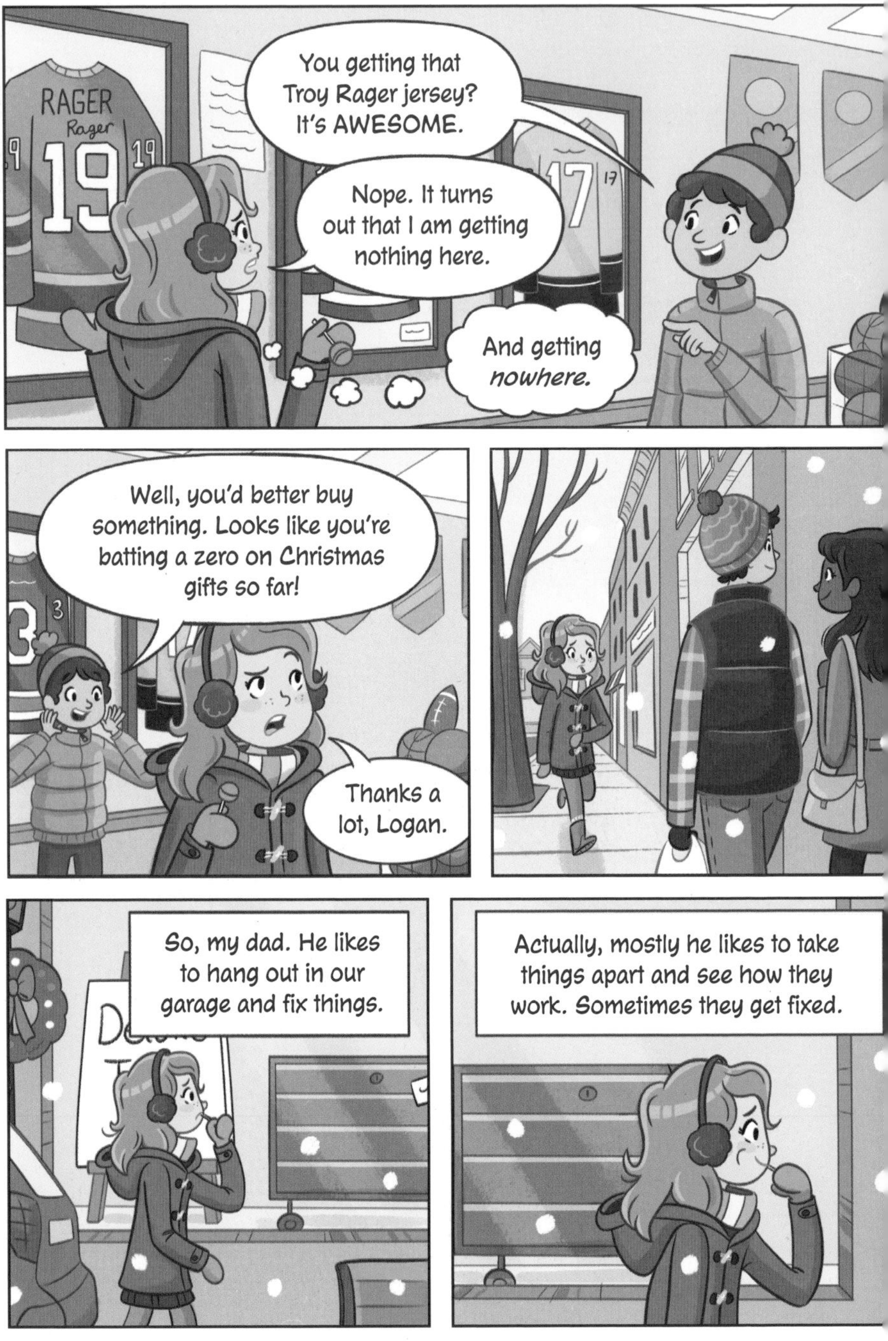

RAGER
Rager
19
17
You getting that Troy Rager jersey? It's AWESOME.
Nope. It turns out that I am getting nothing here.
And getting *nowhere.*
Well, you'd better buy something. Looks like you're batting a zero on Christmas gifts so far!
Thanks a lot, Logan.
So, my dad. He likes to hang out in our garage and fix things.
Actually, mostly he likes to take things apart and see how they work. Sometimes they get fixed.

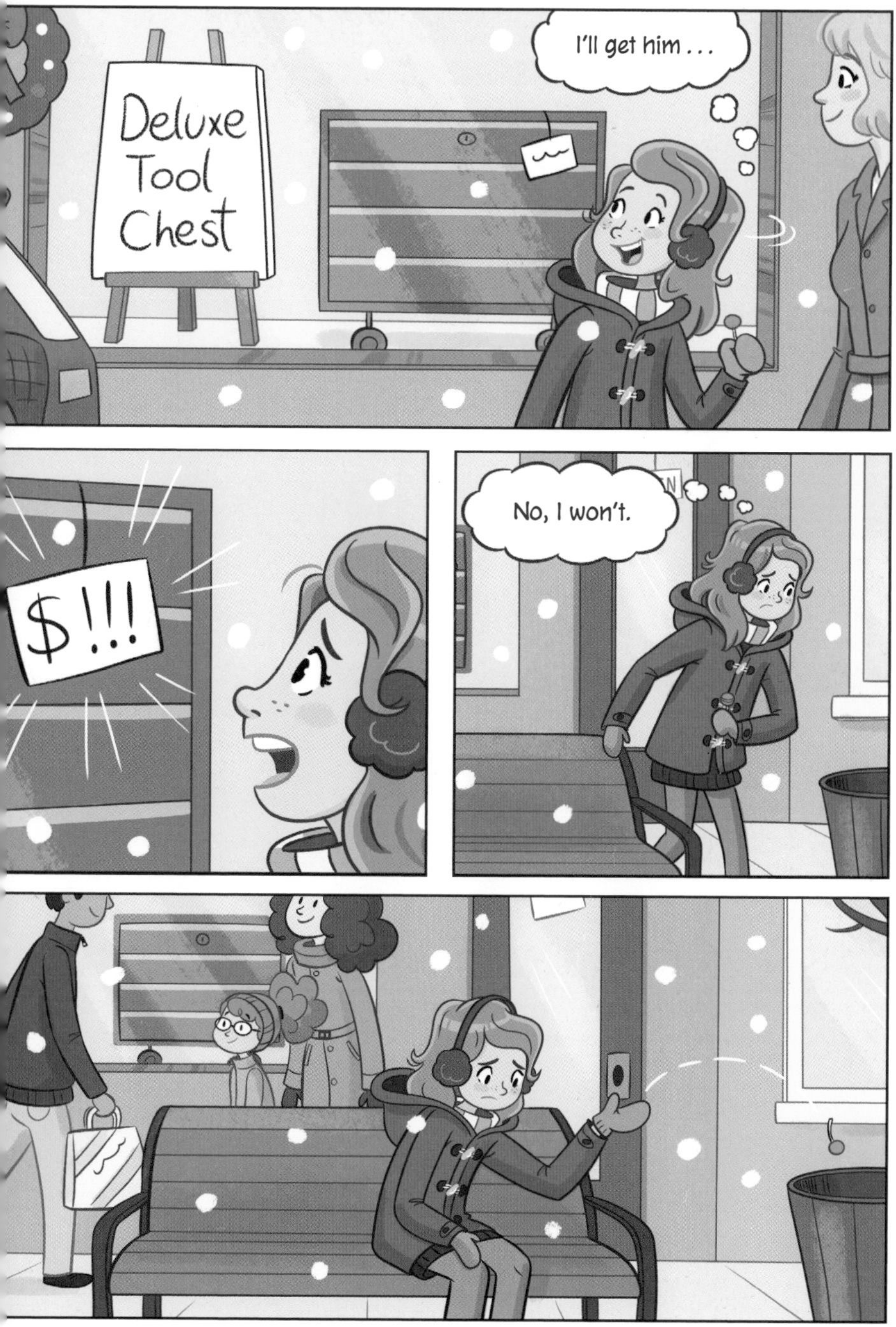
Deluxe Tool Chest
I'll get him . . .
$!!!
No, I won't.

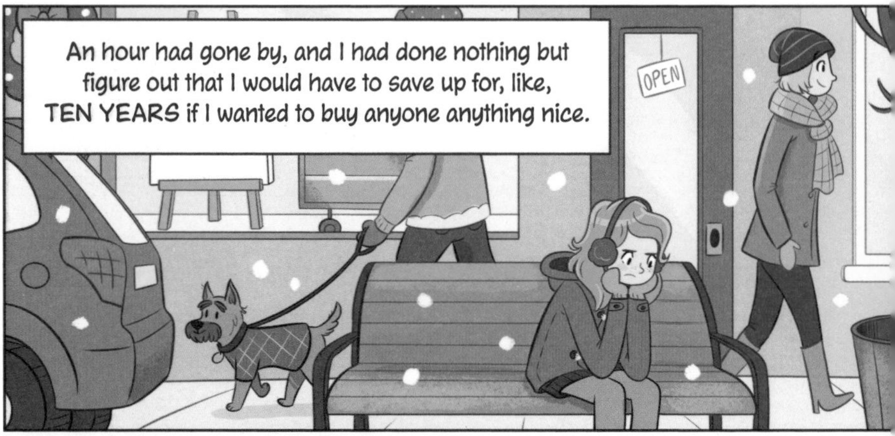
An hour had gone by, and I had done nothing but figure out that I would have to save up for, like, TEN YEARS if I wanted to buy anyone anything nice.
OPEN

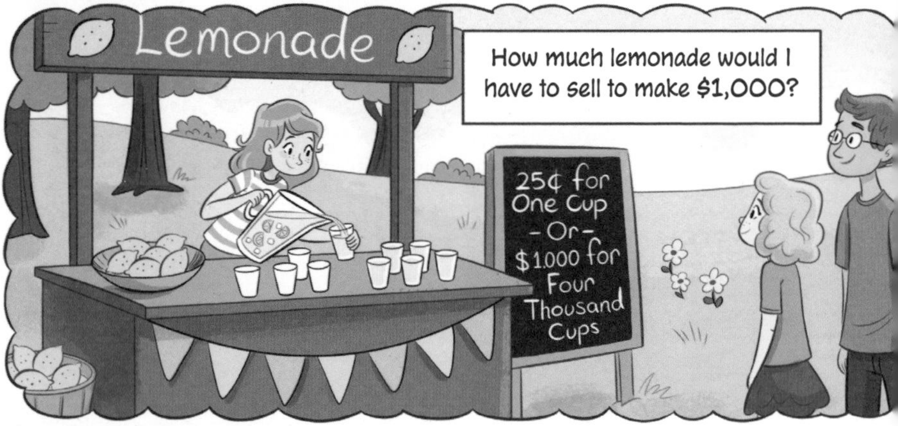
Lemonade
How much lemonade would I have to sell to make $1,000?
25¢ for One Cup -Or- $1.000 for Four Thousand Cups

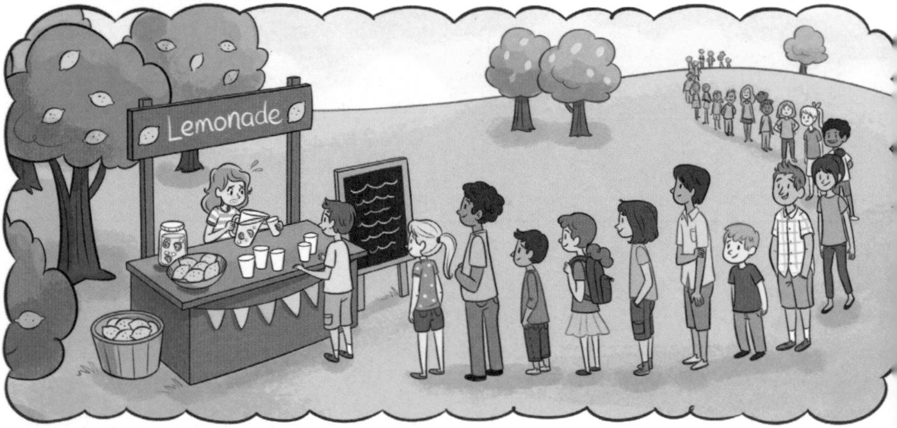
Lemonade

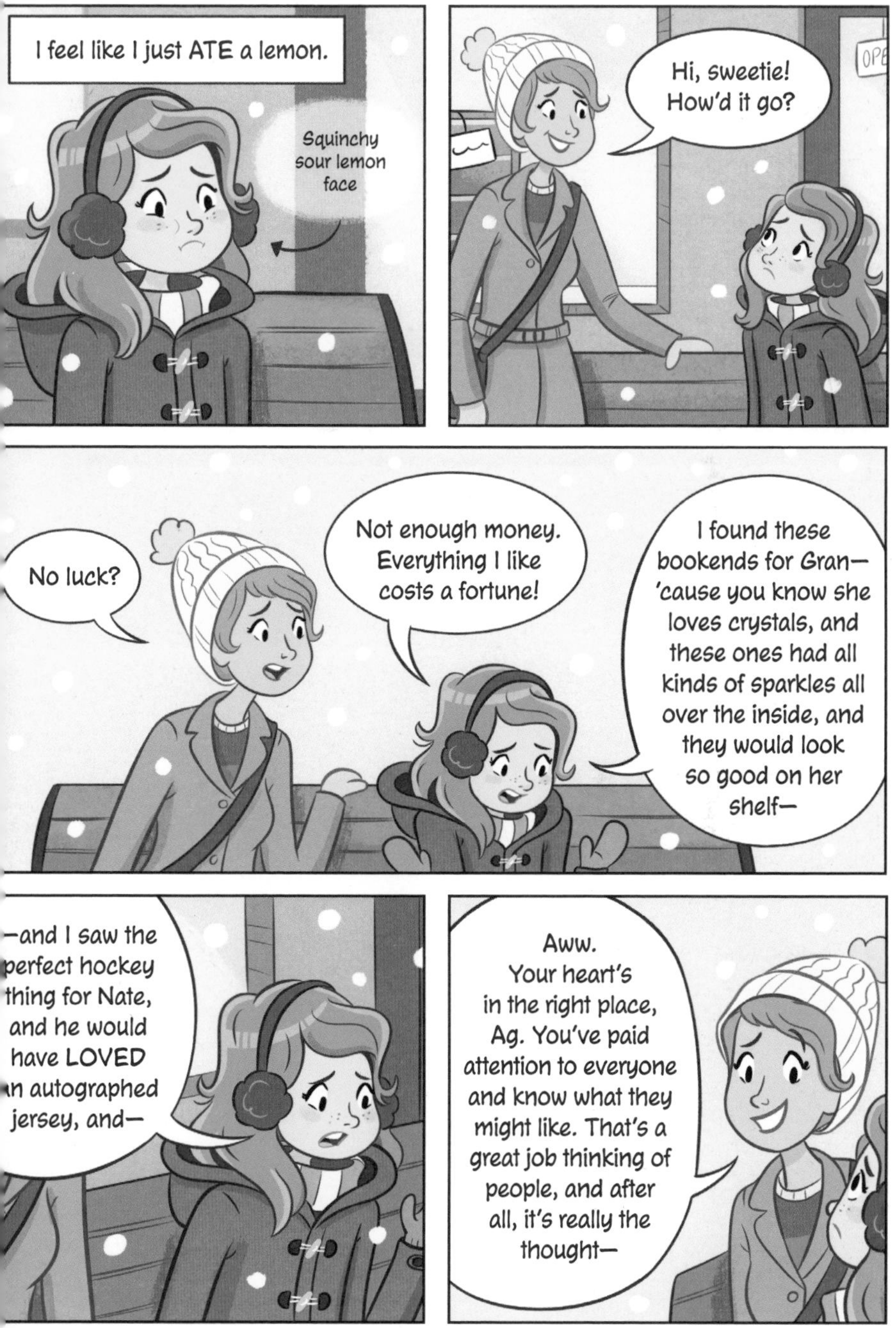
I feel like I just ATE a lemon.
Squinchy sour lemon face
Hi, sweetie! How'd it go?
OPE
No luck?
Not enough money. Everything I like costs a fortune!
I found these bookends for Gran—'cause you know she loves crystals, and these ones had all kinds of sparkles all over the inside, and they would look so good on her shelf—
—and I saw the perfect hockey thing for Nate, and he would have LOVED an autographed jersey, and—
Aww. Your heart's in the right place, Ag. You've paid attention to everyone and know what they might like. That's a great job thinking of people, and after all, it's really the thought—

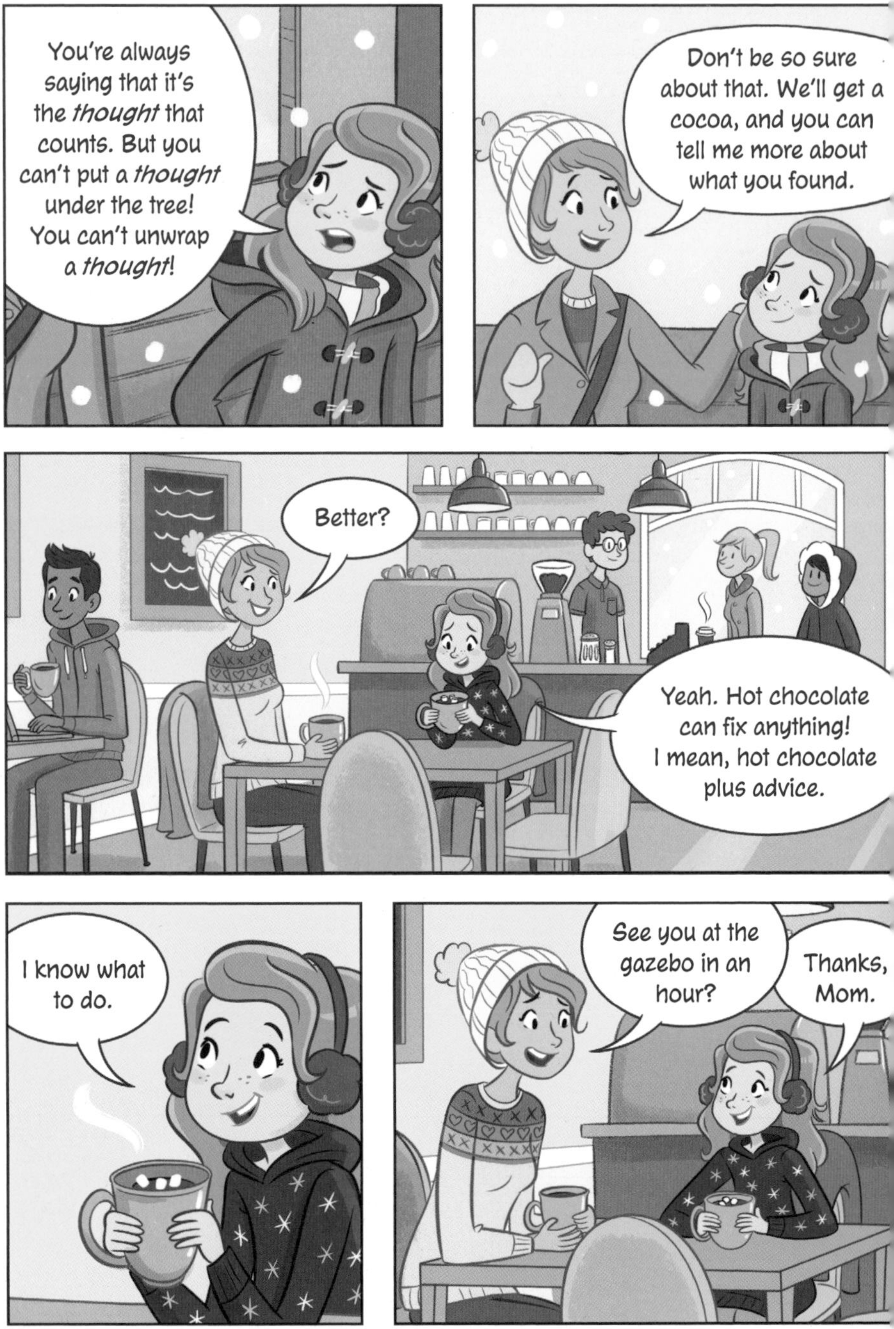
You're always saying that it's the *thought* that counts. But you can't put a *thought* under the tree! You can't unwrap a *thought*!
Don't be so sure about that. We'll get a cocoa, and you can tell me more about what you found.
Better?
Yeah. Hot chocolate can fix anything! I mean, hot chocolate plus advice.
I know what to do.
See you at the gazebo in an hour?
Thanks, Mom.

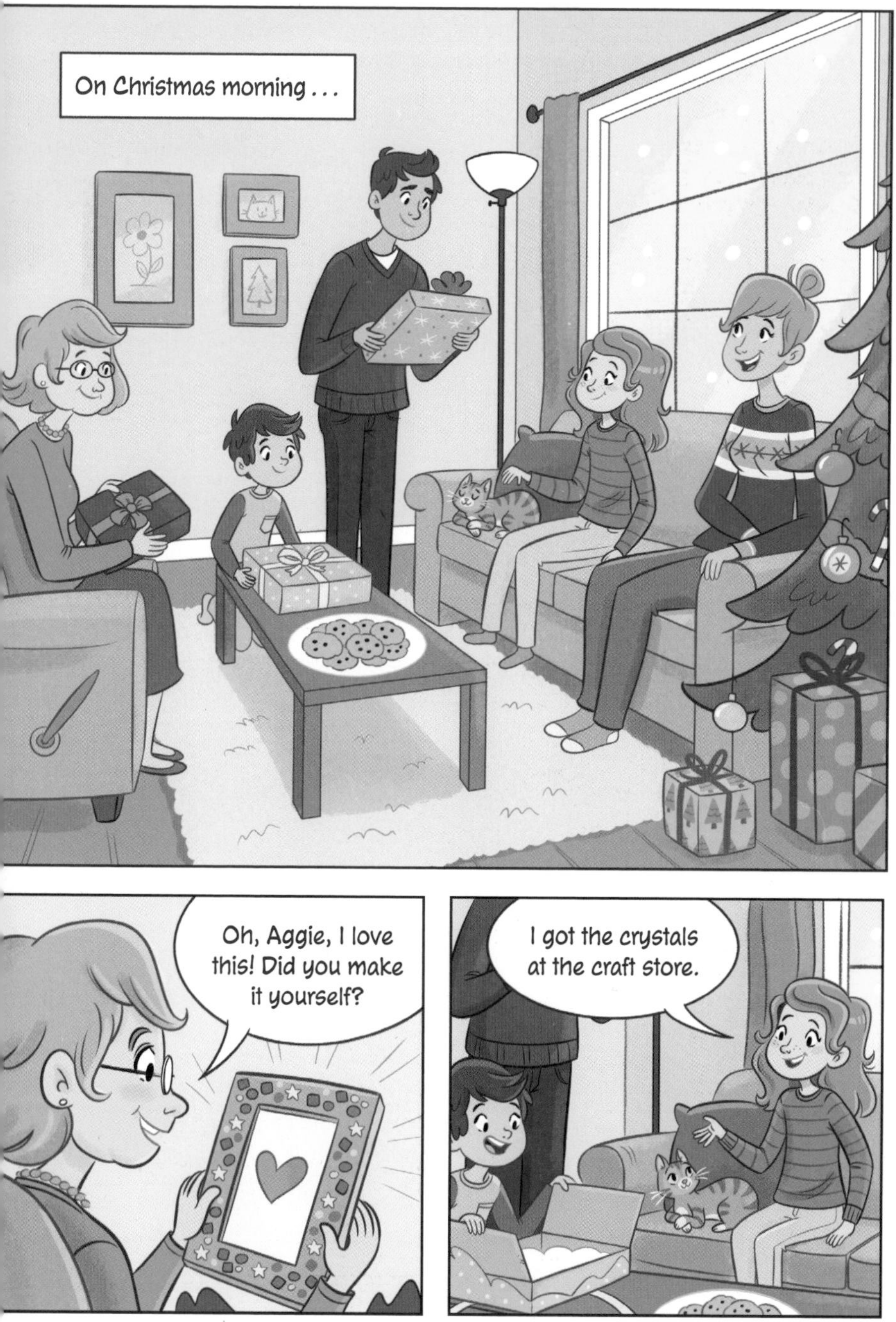
On Christmas morning . . .
Oh, Aggie, I love this! Did you make it yourself?
I got the crystals at the craft store.

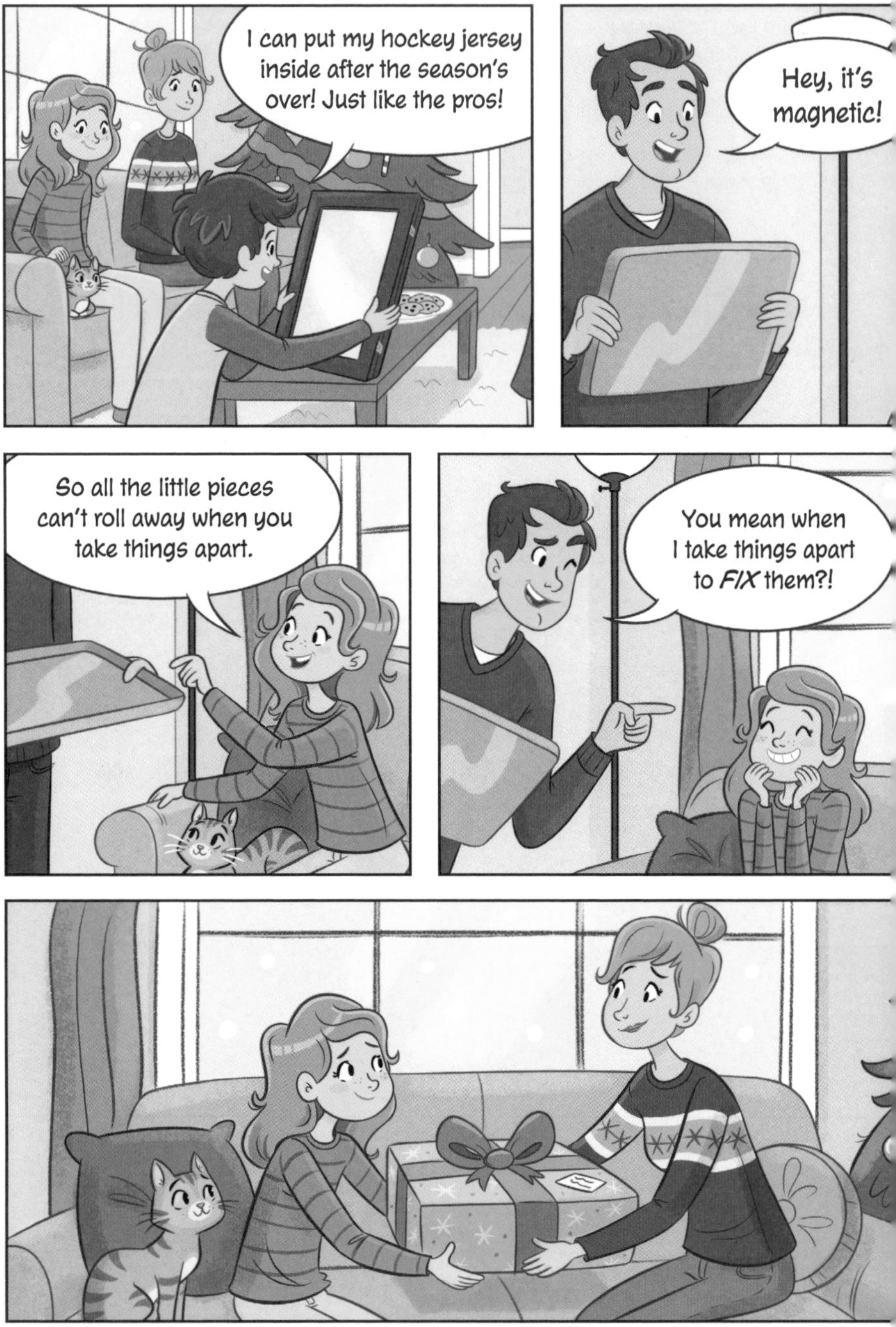
I can put my hockey jersey inside after the season's over! Just like the pros!
Hey, it's magnetic!
So all the little pieces can't roll away when you take things apart.
You mean when I take things apart to *FIX* them?!

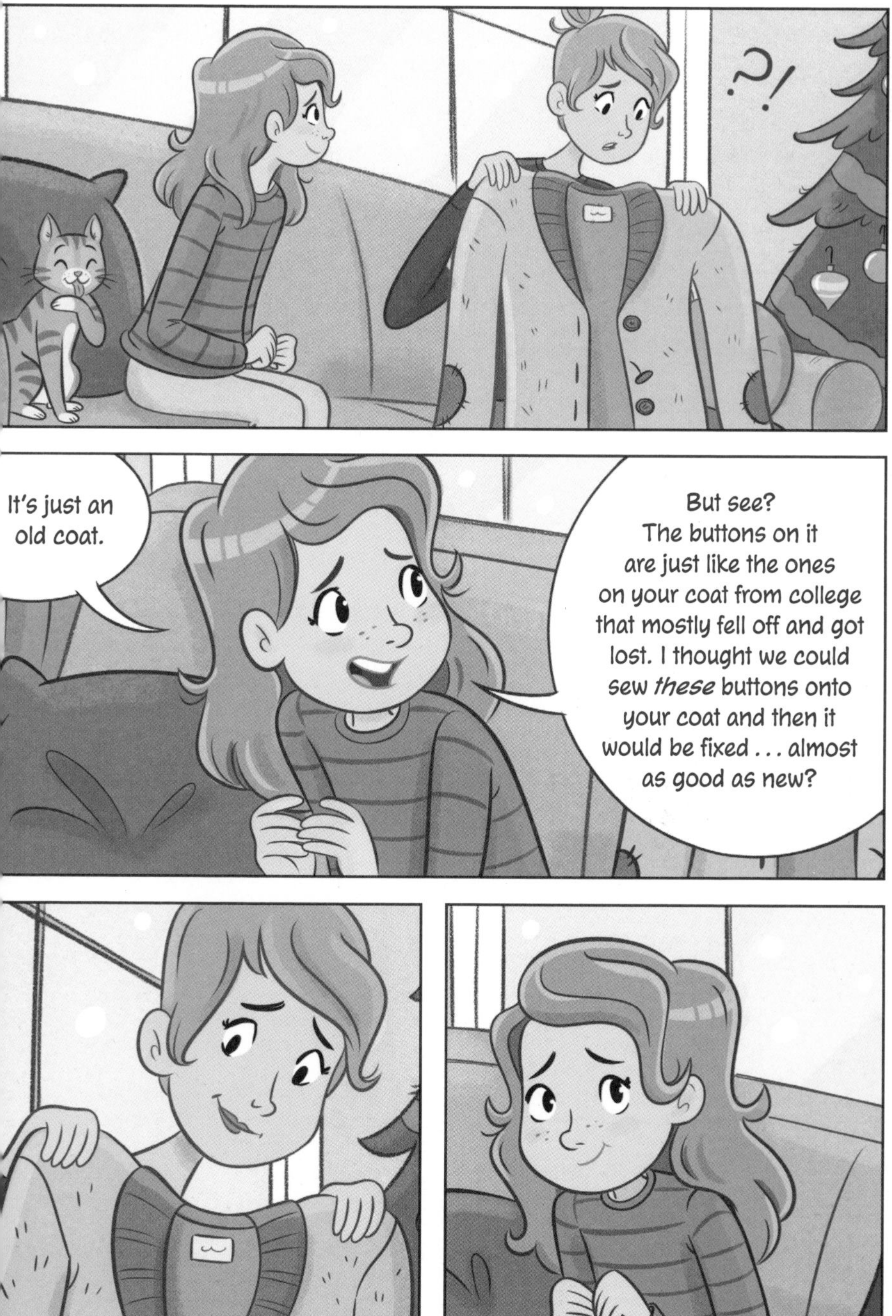
?!
It's just an old coat.
But see? The buttons on it are just like the ones on your coat from college that mostly fell off and got lost. I thought we could sew *these* buttons onto your coat and then it would be fixed . . . almost as good as new?

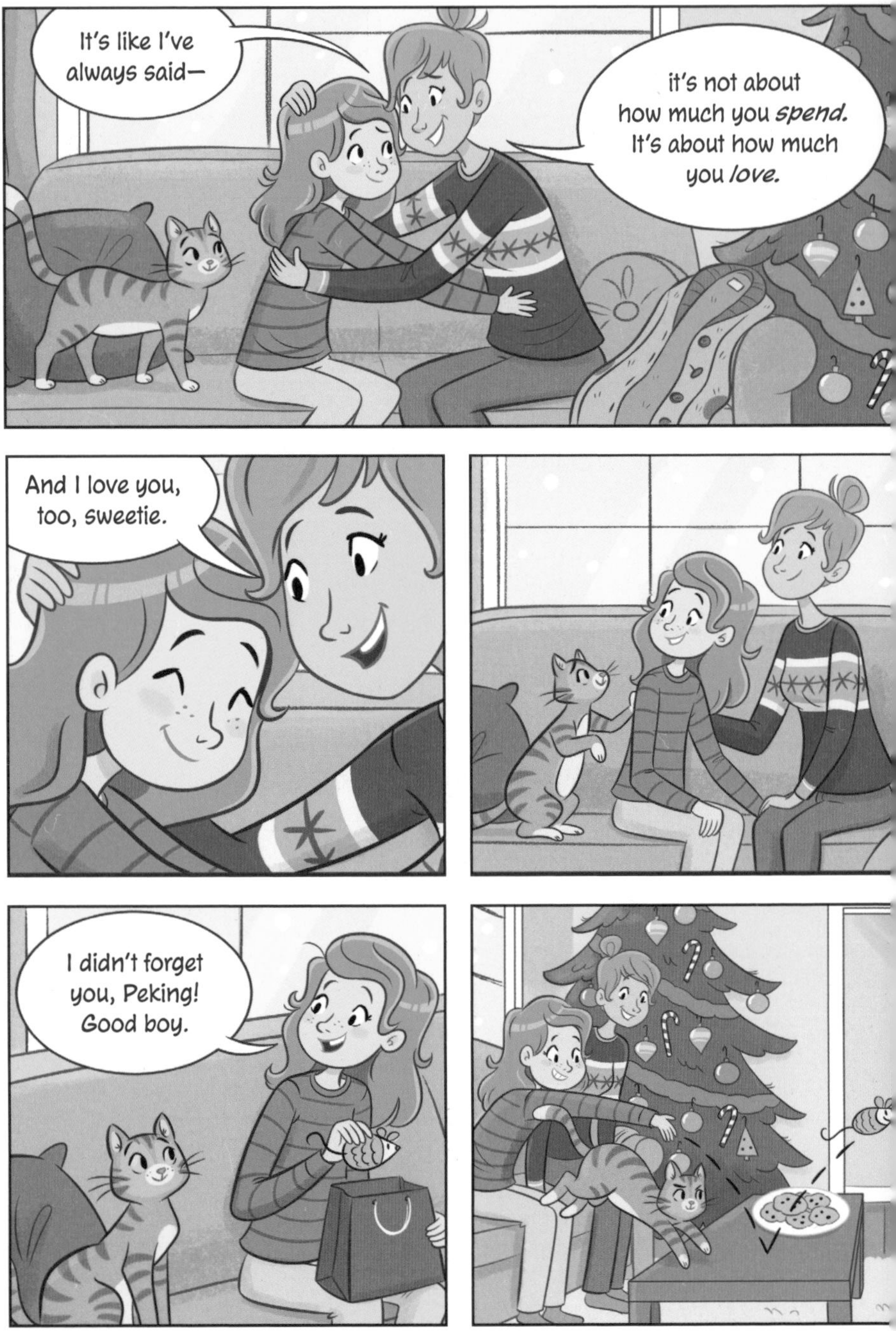
It's like I've always said—
it's not about how much you *spend.* It's about how much you *love.*
And I love you, too, sweetie.
I didn't forget you, Peking! Good boy.

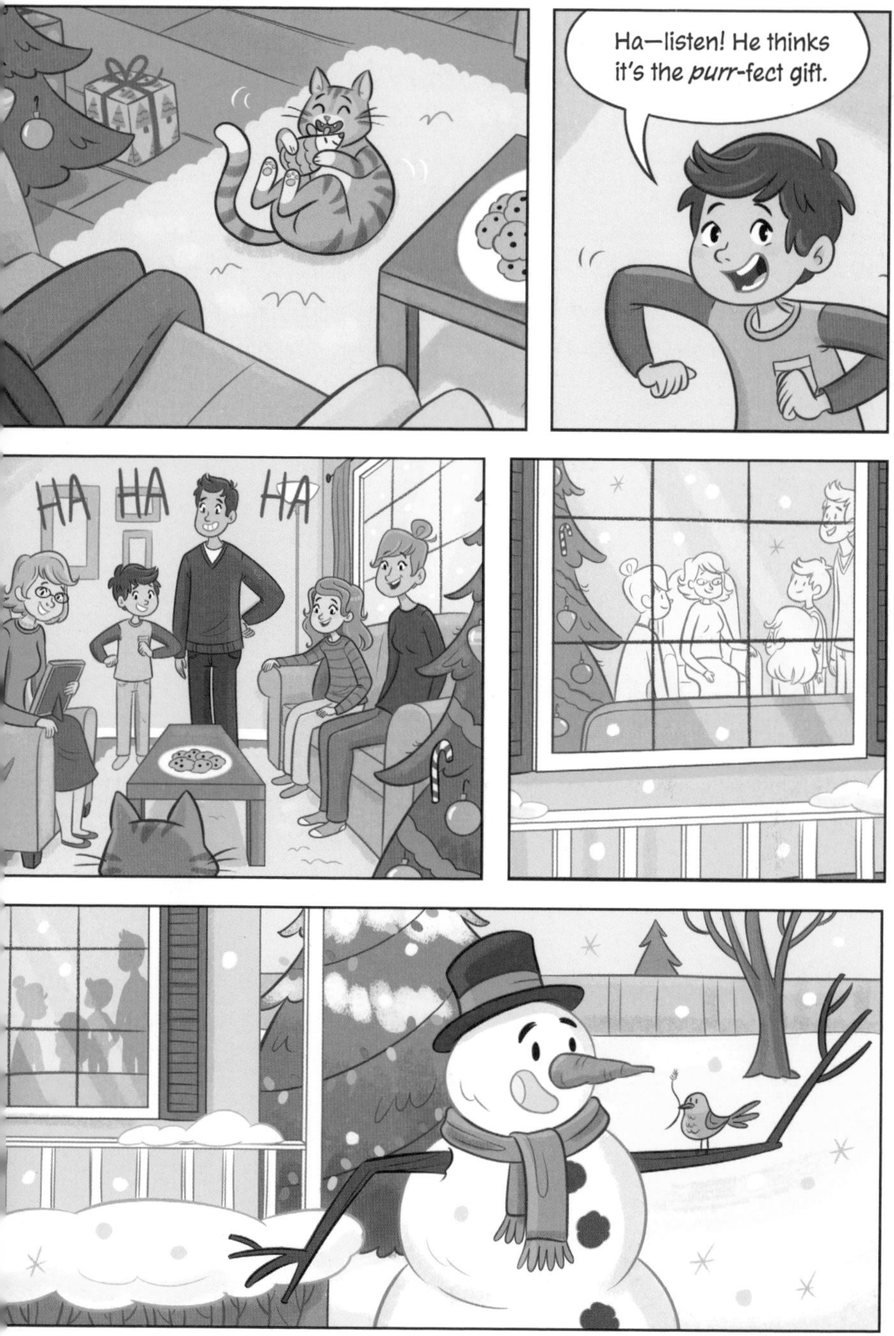
Ha—listen! He thinks it's the *purr*-fect gift.
HA HA HA

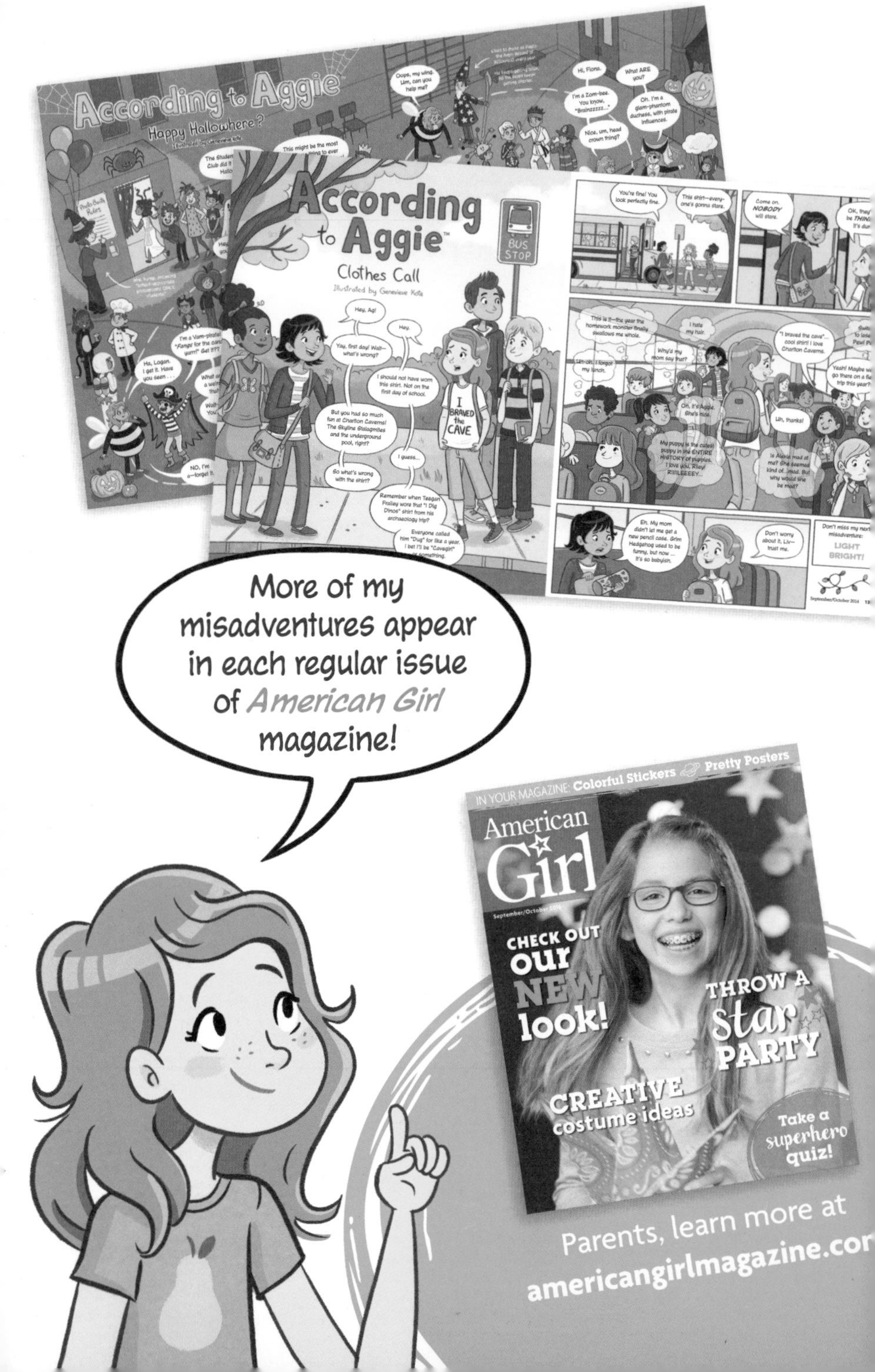
According to Aggie
Happy Hallowhere?
According to Aggie
Clothes Call
Illustrated by Genevieve Kote
BUS STOP
More of my misadventures appear in each regular issue of American Girl magazine!
IN YOUR MAGAZINE: Colorful Stickers Pretty Posters
American Girl
September/October 2016
CHECK OUT our NEW look!
THROW A Star PARTY
CREATIVE costume ideas
Take a superhero quiz!
Parents, learn more at
americangirlmagazine.com